# The Green Man's Heir

# The Green Man's Heir

## Juliet E. McKenna

WIZARD'S TOWER

Wizard's Tower Press

Trowbridge, England

## The Green Man's Heir

First edition, published in the UK March 2018
by Wizard's Tower Press

© 2016 by Juliet E. McKenna

Paperback ISBN: 978-1-908039-69-9

Cover illustration and design by Ben Baldwin
Editing by Toby Selwyn
Design by Cheryl Morgan

Printed by LightningSource

http://wizardstowerpress.com/
http://www.julietemckenna.com/

# Contents

| | |
|---|---|
| Chapter One | 7 |
| Chapter Two | 18 |
| Chapter Three | 32 |
| Chapter Four | 41 |
| Chapter Five | 51 |
| Chapter Six | 60 |
| Chapter Seven | 70 |
| Chapter Eight | 86 |
| Chapter Nine | 93 |
| Chapter Ten | 103 |
| Chapter Eleven | 113 |
| Chapter Twelve | 121 |
| Chapter Thirteen | 130 |
| Chapter Fourteen | 139 |
| Chapter Fifteen | 147 |
| Chapter Sixteen | 155 |
| Chapter Seventeen | 165 |
| Chapter Eighteen | 173 |
| Chapter Nineteen | 190 |
| Chapter Twenty | 199 |
| Chapter Twenty-One | 209 |
| Chapter Twenty-Two | 216 |
| Chapter Twenty-Three | 223 |
| Chapter Twenty-Four | 233 |
| Chapter Twenty-Five | 243 |
| Chapter Twenty-Six | 252 |
| Chapter Twenty-Seven | 257 |
| Chapter Twenty-Eight | 264 |

Chapter Twenty-Nine                          274
Chapter Thirty                               284
Chapter Thirty-One                           297
Chapter Thirty-Two                           307
Chapter Thirty-Three                         320
Chapter Thirty-Four                          335
Chapter Thirty-Five                          344
Chapter Thirty-Six                           356
Acknowledgements                             366

# Chapter One

I wasn't expecting to get caught up in a murder investigation. It had been a long and tiring day and I was looking forward to a long, cool shower. Carpentry up on the top of scaffolding is a hot and sweaty job with the summer sun beating down. Sawdust sticks worse than wet sand on a beach and gets into equally uncomfortable places.

A cold shower and a cold beer. Some food and a DVD on my laptop. Liam Neeson being a badass in some European capital or other. That's all I was thinking about as I drove the Land Rover along the back road heading for the farm where I was currently lodging.

That's how my evening would have gone if I hadn't pulled up in the lay-by to get some fresh air. I didn't exactly have a headache, but I could still feel the pressure of my hard hat across my forehead. Fat lot of use that thing would be if I ever fell head first off some scaffolding. It would hit the ground before I did, but Health and Safety rules every building site now.

Anyway, this looked like an interesting stretch of woodland, tucked away in a narrow valley too steep-sided and rocky for farming. Likewise, the river was too shallow and erratic for a mill. These trees had been left undisturbed for decades; I'd noted that whenever I'd driven home this way over the past few months.

Why stop on this particular day? Because I was uncomfortably aware just how little money I had in my wallet and in my bank account. Okay, there was more work to be done on the barn conversion, but when the project was finished? Downturn, recession, whatever you call the mess the economy's in, the days are long gone when I could get a job by strolling up to a site where a developer was throwing up identikit cul-de-sacs and proving I knew one end of a chisel from the other.

Fortunately I also sell wood carvings at craft fairs and living history days. Ornaments and little boxes and spoons and other everyday things people didn't think twice about before everything ended up made of plastic. So I stopped to walk through that woodland and look for fallen timber I could take away. If I was lucky I'd see a hidden shape in a twisted branch, an animal or a bird, maybe some mythical beast. Today was Thursday, so once I was done with work on Friday, I planned to spend the weekend carving if I could find some decent materials.

Who knew when another vehicle had last stopped in the lay-by; there were no ruts in the thick leaf mould. Getting out of the Landy, I breathed in the scent of the greenery. This smelled like some remnant of ancient wildwood. I could feel it in my bones.

I followed a narrow path up the slope. The ground was steeper on this side of the road. The oaks were gathered in clusters divided by grey boulders of lichen-spotted limestone. A couple of the trees were truly ancient hulks, their crowns of sturdy branches long since shed in favour of twiggy sprays to sustain them in their twilight years. Fungus and beetles had eaten away their heartwood. Anyone who didn't know trees might think they were dead or dying. Not so. It's the sapwood that a tree needs to live, and that's just below the bark.

If a storm struck, old stalwarts like these would survive while younger trees fell. Thanks to their hollow centres, they could flex instead of snapping. I gave the closest old oak a slap on its gnarled grey bark. The year's second flush of leaves was budding on its twigs. Lammas leaves, according to old tradition, not uncommon around the end of July.

I saw lime trees too, the rarer, large-leaved kind that can live for a thousand years if they're tended right. Someone had done that here sometime; these trees had been coppiced and cropped for wood and bark, maybe a century ago. I glanced at the ash trees higher up the slope. No one had touched them since they'd found a foothold where they could claim the light.

I paused, noting hazel, rowan and holly. I know about

8

coppicing in theory. Well-tended woodland can produce no end of things. Birch brooms, different sorts of fencing, stuff for gardeners from hazel hurdles to rustic trellises, bean poles and pea sticks. Then there's specialist stuff like wood for furniture veneers and artists' charcoal.

But coppicing is a long-term business; different types and thicknesses of wood are harvested after five years' growth, or seven, or ten. That would mean putting down more permanent roots than I was used to. For the past half-dozen years, I'd been moving to new places every six months. I'd spent the last few winters working on reforestation projects up in Scotland and found construction jobs each summer, until there'd been no work to be had and I'd come south again.

I went on, scanning the ground for fallen boughs. Trees in their prime will let useful wood fall, especially after a long dry spell, and according to the Met Office on the radio, rainfall since Whitsun this year had been well below average.

I wanted branches that had weathered but not started to rot. I found myself thinking, if I did stop somewhere year round, I could store green wood while it seasoned, ready to use when I wanted it.

But how could I find out who owned this valley? Not to buy the land but to purchase the rights to the standing wood. Though it would probably be a waste of time. The owner had already made their own choices about these woods. I guessed these trees had thrived untouched so the valley could be a haven for wild life.

Though not for deer, it would seem. That was odd, given their numbers are increasing year on year, no matter how many end up as road kill. There was little sign of them being their usual nuisance, browsing on seedlings or gnawing around the bark to kill saplings dead.

'Hey, you!'

I looked around for the unexpected voice.

'Stay there!'

Now I could see a copper, black-trousered and white-shirted under his stab vest. He'd crested the ridge above me.

'Stand still!'

Why was he so agitated? I hadn't moved. I waited while he slipped and stumbled down the slope.

'I'm parked down there.' I gestured down towards the lay-by. The Landy's cream-coloured roof was clear enough through the thick summer leaves. 'I didn't mean to trespass.'

I didn't think I was, but I wasn't about to argue with some local copper. So I'd play nice and say 'Yes, constable, no, constable, sorry, constable' and go on my way.

'You stand there!' He jabbed a shaking finger at me as he reached level ground, going for the radio clipped to his shoulder with his other hand. 'Sarge, I've got someone!'

I couldn't make out the crackling reply, but I didn't like the sound of this. 'I've only just walked up from the lay-by.'

Whatever had gone on in this wood had happened well away from the road, assuming this search had fanned out from the scene of... of what? Of not my problem, whatever it was.

'You wait there.' The constable scowled.

I folded my arms and challenged him with a stare. 'Or what? You're going to arrest me?'

Good luck to him trying that. He was at least six inches shorter than me and looked like he'd just left school. I'm six feet four, take XXL in most clothes and have the muscles to shift anything from whole sheets of fibreboard to Acrow props across a building site.

Still, he wasn't entirely stupid. He wasn't coming within arm's reach of me. His arm or my longer one.

His radio crackled again. Someone asked exactly where he was. 'I'm heading down to that lay-by on the Matlock road.'

I was starting to think there was something very wrong in this wood. The young copper was sweating, and not just because of the summer heat. He had the pasty, wide-eyed look of someone who'd had a nasty shock, and I saw what looked like splashes of puke on his shiny black boots.

I couldn't see a Taser on his Batman utility belt but I decided walking away wasn't the smartest move. This lad was jittery enough to do something stupid, and without witnesses it would be his word against mine.

'Yes, we're happy to wait,' he assured whoever was on the other end of the radio.

Speak for yourself, sunshine, I thought. 'Who are we waiting for?'

'CID.' He swallowed and went even paler.

I held up my hands. 'Look, I only stopped to stretch my legs and get some air.'

I might as well have saved my breath. He wasn't listening, his eyes focused inward on whatever had gone so badly wrong with his day.

CID turned up pretty quickly. A plain-clothes copper maybe a couple of years older than me, on the other side of thirty. He came over the ridge and cautiously down the slope in unsuitable shoes, a couple of uniformed bodies behind him.

'Good afternoon, sir.' He checked his watch as he joined the lad with the puked-on boots. 'Well, I suppose it's good evening now.'

I just shrugged.

'Can I ask what you're doing here, sir?' CID's tone was mild enough, but I saw him looking at me closely. He was a city boy, sharp-eyed, Manchester or somewhere thereabouts. The uniformed lad's accent was as solidly Derbyshire as these Dales.

I made sure to answer calmly. I've come across too many coppers who automatically assume someone of my height and build with a number-one haircut must mean trouble. It never occurs to them that a carpenter doesn't want long hair matted with sawdust and sweat.

'I parked down there because I fancied a walk. I've been up on a roof all day and it's been hot work.'

'Whereabouts would that be, sir?' CID's gaze flickered across to the uniformed lad, who hastily remembered his notebook. Finding a blank page, he clicked his pen eagerly.

'Lambton Farm. They're converting some barns.'

I was about to give him directions, but CID glanced over his shoulder to one of the older uniforms, who nodded confirmation.

'I wanted to cool off a bit before heading home.'

'Where would home be, sir?' CID's smile was as meaninglessly polite as the way he kept calling me 'sir'. 'And sorry, I didn't catch your name?'

'Daniel Mackmain, and I'm living at Kympton Grange Farm. I've been renting there since March.'

CID nodded. 'Do you have any ID, sir? Just to speed things along?'

Tempted to ask when carrying identification became compulsory in this country, I kept my arms folded for a moment, just to make the point. Then I reached into my combats for my wallet. 'Driving licence good enough?' I flipped it open to show him the transparent pocket.

He leaned forward slightly to study the photo. 'And before that?'

'Sorry, what?' I dragged my eyes back to him.

'Where were you living before that, sir?' he asked with emphasis.

'Lanarkshire.' I rubbed a hand round the back of my neck. 'Like it says on my licence.'

'You should get that updated, sir.' He smiled that meaningless smile again. 'Lanarkshire's Scotland, isn't it?' His raised eyebrows invited me to explain further.

I shrugged, unable to stop myself looking over his shoulder, past the uniform cops standing further up the slope. There was a dryad on the ridge line, looking down at me with frank curiosity. That's what had so comprehensively distracted me.

When I say I feel an ancient wildwood in my bones and in

my blood, that's not just New Age fantasy. I'm a dryad's son. No, I don't tell people, not ever. They'll think I'm a nutter, someone to cross the street to avoid or to coax into visiting some mental health professional. Or they might decide my poor parents need to know about their troubled son.

If some busybody ever did try that, my parents would be easy enough to find. At least, my dad would be. I didn't grow up running wild like some second-rate Mowgli, freezing through English winters. After taking redundancy from the engineering firm where he'd worked since leaving school, my dad became the full-time warden of a small local nature reserve on the Oxfordshire-Warwickshire border. He'd been volunteering there over weekends and holidays for more than twenty years before that. That's how he'd met my mother, the last of her sisters still tending the oak trees there.

This dryad looked nothing like my mother. That's to say, I could see her ethereal form in the same way that I could see my mum's, as a shifting, womanly shape of green gossamer and shadow, even though she stood in full sunlight. A beautiful face with emerald-green eyes fixed on me and sparkling with curiosity. She could see that I could see her, and that was a real surprise.

My mother always appeared in her ethereal form decently cloaked with flowing draperies, the sort of thing you see on old Greek vases or in Renaissance paintings of classical nymphs and goddesses. I reckon I can always tell if an artist had ever really seen a dryad. You'd be surprised how many must have, some time or another.

Not this dryad. She stood there unabashed in her naked loveliness. Not some stick-thin fashion-model idea of Photoshopped beauty, but slim-waisted, full-breasted and with a seductive curve to her hip. And as I say, entirely naked. One good look at her and, as the expression goes, I had wood. Hardly ideal when I was being questioned by the police.

'I said, Mr Mackmain, can anyone vouch for your whereabouts an hour or so ago?' CID repeated himself with a crease of annoyance between his narrow, dark brows.

'Sorry.' Now I was the one offering a meaningless smile of

apology. 'About half a dozen blokes on the Lambton Farm job. Phil Caister, he's the foreman, he'll have the time sheet I signed.'

I thanked my lucky stars that I'd gone to find Phil today instead of just scrawling some guess at the time on the clipboard left by the barn door.

The lad with the puked-on boots scribbled all that down. He was still scowling at me. I answered him with an unblinking stare until he looked away.

'What's this all about?' I could see more people moving through the woods on the ridge line. Somewhere well beyond, a dog barked.

The dryad was now circling the grey-haired copper. I kept my attention firmly on CID; otherwise I would have been transfixed by the sight of her gorgeously rounded backside.

'There's been a serious incident.' CID pursed thin lips as he considered what to tell me. 'May I see what's in your pockets, sir?' he asked unexpectedly. 'The quicker we can move things along, the sooner you can be on your way.'

That sounded good to me. I wanted to leave here as soon as I could. I reached into my trouser pockets and showed him my wallet, chewing gum, keys, a grubby hanky, a handful of change and my Swiss Army penknife. I'd left my phone in the Land Rover.

He reached for the knife. 'May I?'

'If you must. It's a legal length,' I said as he opened the big blade with some difficulty. He should stop chewing his fingernails.

'You know all about that?' He looked up from making a very close examination of the hinge end.

'I'm a carpenter. I carry a lot of tools. I like to know where I stand.' I kept my eyes fixed on him.

Seeing me emptying my pockets had piqued the dryad's curiosity. Shifting through the air as easily and swiftly as a breeze, she stood beside me, peering inquisitively at the things I held in my outstretched palms.

14

I could see she was increasingly keen to get some reaction out of me. Her shimmering fingers reached for the handkerchief, the only thing she could touch without burning herself on metal. Well, apart from the gum. Did dryads chew gum? My mother never had, but then she was the only dryad I'd ever met until now.

'A carpenter?' CID looked at me with unwelcome, renewed interest. 'Where are your tools?'

'In my Land Rover.' I jerked my head back down towards the road.

'May we have a quick look, sir?' He reached for my keys.

I closed my hands and shoved everything back in my pockets. 'I'll show you, if you must.'

We walked back down the hill. My work boots gave me a solid footing on the uneven ground, but CID kept slipping on the leaf mould. Whatever had brought him here so unexpectedly, he hadn't had time to change his black lace-ups for a pair of wellies.

Two uniformed coppers prowled the lay-by. The woman was searching the ground for who knows what while the man peered through my Land Rover's passenger window.

'Sir.' He stepped back smartly as CID arrived.

The woman continued her search, utterly focused as she walked along the edge of the tarmac towards the patrol car parked further up the road. To my relief, the dryad went to see what she was up to.

I unlocked the driver's door and held it open so CID could get a good look inside. He took his time before nodding.

'And the back?'

We walked round and I opened up to show him my tools and all the other fixings and bits and pieces I carry. You never know what you'll need on a job only to find no one else has thought of bringing it.

'Thanks very much, sir.' CID stepped back. 'Did you see any other vehicle as you pulled up? Did anyone pass you on your way here, after you'd made the turn?'

I shook my head. 'Sorry, no.'

'Did you see anyone walking in the woods? Maybe down by the river?' He gestured in the direction of the water meadows, where a curving line of black poplars marked the river's course. Those trees had once been carefully pollarded but now grew ragged and wild.

'Not that I recall.'

'And what brings you to Derbyshire?' He looked at me intently.

'A tourist brochure.' I shrugged. 'It looked like a nice place.'

I wasn't about to tell him I was visiting parts of the country where I hoped some overlooked, ancient woodland might still be home to a dryad. I absolutely wasn't going to mention the dreams that had prompted me to turn off the M1 when I saw the signposts for Hardwick Hall.

'I see.' He didn't sound convinced. 'Well, if you do remember anything later, please give me a ring.' He reached inside his suit jacket and produced a business card. 'Even if you don't think it's important, let us decide that. Something that seems trivial might be significant.'

The card told me I was talking to Detective Sergeant Jason Tunstead. 'What's this all about?'

I kept half an eye on the dryad, who was coming to hear what he had to say. Even the way she walked was seductive, her legs long and bare, her elegant feet heedless of sharp stones where the road had been resurfaced.

'A girl was attacked in the woods,' the detective said grimly.

That got him my full attention. 'This afternoon? I was nowhere near here, and you can check that out.'

'We will, sir,' he assured me. 'The sooner we can eliminate you from our enquiries, the sooner we can catch the c—' He caught himself on the edge of an obscenity. 'The culprit.'

I could see that he meant it.

16

'Good.' I meant that as well.

I was also breathing a lot more easily. I had a solid alibi, and there wasn't a spot of blood on me or in the Land Rover or on any of my tools. DS Tunstead's interest in my penknife made it pretty obvious some blade was involved.

How badly was the girl hurt? I remembered the puke on the lad's boots. Better not to ask.

'Can I go?' I shut the back door of the Land Rover.

He nodded. 'We know where to find you if we need anything more.'

'We've got your number plate,' the uniformed lad chipped in, 'and a full description of your vehicle.'

'Thank you, constable,' DS Tunstead said sharply.

I gave the lad a hard stare before getting into my vehicle and turning the key in the ignition. As I drove away, an ambulance passed me. Not in any hurry, no blues and twos indicating some brutally beaten or knifed girl inside with paramedics fighting to save her life.

Further on, I saw patrol cars making a roadblock to question motorists. I slowed, ready to stop, but one of the traffic cops waved me on, talking into her radio. I guessed she'd had a message to let me through.

Once the roadblock disappeared from my rear-view mirror, I switched the radio on, but the local station was only offering traffic reports on the motorways through the county, along with ideas for family fun days out.

I endured the presenter's middle-of-the-road drivel and pap-pop until the headlines came round. There was still no mention of any girl attacked in some woods. Whatever had happened, the police weren't letting the news break just yet.

# Chapter Two

Kympton Grange Farm is tucked below the White Peak and would have supported a large family as well as workers from the village in years gone by. Now the Monkswells are as hard pressed as every other small farmer, so they've converted their outbuildings for holiday lets, including a single-bedroom-and-kitchen-sitting-room flat above the open-sided stone barn where they park their cars. I suppose they thought that would appeal to solo hikers.

I reckon they'd guessed wrong. Cars had come and gone regularly from the family-sized accommodation on the other side of the road ever since I'd got here, but when I'd first viewed the small flat just before Easter, it had the cold feel of somewhere long uninhabited. Sam Monkswell had instantly agreed to me taking it for a full six months. Other places I'd looked at had only been available until the start of the high tourist season in July.

As I parked in the space Sam kept cleared for me below the flat, I looked at the dark bay at the far end, stone-walled on three sides and too inconvenient for any vehicle.

We'd had an idle conversation about that space, one evening as we shared a couple of beers on the barn steps. I'd been explaining how coppicing worked and the things I could branch out into making, if he knew of any local woodland for rent.

We'd agreed there was enough room to set up a little workshop. If I had a workshop, I could have a lathe. If I had a lathe, I could turn out wooden cups, bowls and plates. Those were real money spinners, according to other woodworkers at craft shows.

Of course, even second-hand, any lathe worth having would cost a good few hundred quid. I'd need to pay Sam Monkswell more rent, for use of the space and for electricity. Speculate to accumulate? Not with my bank balance at the moment.

As I left the shadows, I kept an eye out for Chrissie, Sam's wife. As long as there were families in the holiday cottages she had more than enough work to keep her occupied, rushed off her feet on weekend changeover days. When she wasn't so busy, she was always keen to chat about people I didn't know and celebrity news I didn't care about. Today though, I saw her across the road where the converted stables made three sides of a square around the cobbled yard where the visitors parked.

I hurried up the barn's outside stone steps into what had once been a hayloft. Now the door opened into a living room with a kitchenette at one end. That was where the old hatch for pitching out hay bales had been turned into a wide window looking across the lane to the wooded hill beyond. Opposite, a door in a partition wall led to the bedroom, with the small bathroom beyond that.

I unlaced my steel-toed work boots and kicked them into a corner. As I stripped off my sweaty socks, I relished the cool oak floorboards under my tired feet. Steels on a hot summer day are evil, but not wearing them's not worth the risk. I once saw a bloke in trainers have a steel universal beam fall on his foot.

My laptop was on the dining table, which separated the kitchen area from the two-seater sofa and the coffee table where I'd stacked charity shop paperbacks and DVDs waiting to go back now I'd finished with them.

I clicked onto the local newspaper's website. I'd found the Buxton Argus very reliable for the latest traffic updates, and that's important in a rural area where a tractor getting it wrong on a narrow bridge can force everyone into a twenty-mile detour.

Their news reporter was as quick off the mark as their traffic guy. A short paragraph headed 'Young Woman Found Dead' was illustrated with a photo of a copper standing beside blue-and-white tape strung between two trees. A crag I didn't recognise loomed above the grim-faced policeman.

There wasn't much beyond that. The victim's exact age and identity were as yet unknown, though according to the police statement she was five foot five with shoulder-length dark hair, wearing jeans and a scarlet vest top. Details of her injuries were not being released at this time.

The police didn't know how she'd got to the wood and were appealing for any witnesses who might have seen the girl in the area to get in touch, or people could ring Crimestoppers anonymously. That hinted at desperation. Though I've never had anything to do with a murder enquiry, so what do I know?

I leaned back in the upright chair, looking at the screen. No camera would have seen the dryad, not in her ethereal form. I wondered if she'd been there all the same, drawn to unaccustomed activity in her quiet wood. She could well have seen who had killed the girl. If so, what good was that? A dryad was one witness the police could never take a statement from.

What if I talked to her? I fished DS Tunstead's card out of my pocket and tapped it thoughtfully on the table. If the dryad could give a description of the murderer, maybe I could say I'd remembered seeing someone behaving suspiciously?

That would only work as long as the dryad was accurate about what had happened, where and when. If the police could prove I was wrong, they would wonder why I'd been lying. Worse, I'd probably help whoever had done this get away with it.

What about Crimestoppers? I clicked through to their website and read the assurances that calls wouldn't be traced or recorded and no questions would be asked about who was supplying information. That was all well and good, but I could still only help if I could offer accurate information. False leads for the police would surely be worse than no leads at all.

I tossed Tunstead's card onto the table. Who was I trying to kid? I wasn't interested in justice, or rather I was, but catching that poor girl's killer wasn't my job. I wanted to talk to the dryad simply because she was a dryad. Because there was such a lot I didn't know about my heritage, things my mother never seemed willing to tell me.

If I wanted to talk to this dryad though, what were my chances of finding her without tripping over police giving the wood a fingertip search? If I turned up in the middle of his murder hunt a second time, DS Tunstead would give me a much closer look.

I stripped off and shoved my clothes into the washing machine, then headed for the shower to wash off the day's sweat and grime. I couldn't wash away the thought of that dryad though.

There were some wizened mushrooms in the fridge and half a packet of bacon which still smelled okay. I chopped everything up with an onion and slung it in a frying pan before adding a jar of pasta sauce. That went nicely on top of spaghetti as the dusk deepened to twilight. Once the washer had finished with my clothes, I hung them on a drying rack.

As the sky through the end window darkened to star-flecked blue over the black bulk of the hill, I concentrated on a carving I'd begun the weekend before. A loping fox, long and low, was emerging from the straight-grained ash of a broken spade handle. I'd asked Sam Monkswell if I could have it, seeing he was about to chuck it away.

There's something crucial about woodwork that you learn through trial and error. Mostly error. When to quit before you ruin what you're working on. I realised I'd reached that point as my narrowest chisel hovered over the fox's brush.

I set the wickedly sharp blade down. It had originally belonged to my father's grandfather, and now my initials joined all the others burned into the age-darkened handle. Old or new, all of my woodcarving tools were more than long and lethal enough to interest DS Tunstead. I was glad I hadn't had them with me earlier.

I tidied up and glanced at my watch. Nearly midnight. Would there still be any coppers in the wood? Probably, and being caught out there so late would make me look even more suspicious.

I went to bed. I slept like a log. I usually do, pun intended.

Early morning sun through the sloping skylight's thin blind woke me. Rolling over, I reached for my phone to check the time. Five o'clock, near enough. I could drag a fold of duvet over my face and get another hour's sleep before heading for Lambton.

Or I could get up now and drive through that wooded valley. If there was no sign of police, maybe I could pull up in that lay-by, just for a moment. Maybe I'd see the dryad. There had to be some reason why my dreams had brought me to the Peak District, surely?

I was already out of bed and heading for the bathroom. I was dressed by the time the kettle had boiled for a cup of coffee for now and a flask for later. Dividing half a jar of peanut butter between a couple of slices of toast and some sandwiches for my lunch, I ate breakfast on the way down the outside steps.

I didn't see another vehicle between Kympton and the turn to the wooded back road. Mist drifted through the trees on either side of the steep-sided valley while the leaf-fringed strip of sky overhead was a brilliant, cloudless blue.

There was no sign of any coppers. Maybe they'd be coming along later, to talk to people who used this route around the time the girl had been killed. Maybe they were set up further down the lane. If so, I was okay, just on my way to work. This was one of my regular routes to Lambton. Nothing out of the usual here, officer.

The lay-by appeared ahead. I pulled in and picked up my phone. If some copper turned up, I'd say I'd dropped it in the woods yesterday and only missed it this morning. No one had tried to ring me or text me, so no one could prove any different.

I got out of the Land Rover. The air was still cool, with birds singing all around as they challenged rivals, sought mates and warned each other of my arrival. A robin perched on a nearby twig, red breast puffed out belligerently. I whistled his boast back at him, just to give him something to think about.

'Who are you?' The dryad appeared at my side.

22

This morning she chose to show herself to me far more solidly. Close to, she was intoxicating. Her bare skin was the pale golden brown of the scales on oak leaf buds. Her hair was as richly glossy as a newly shelled chestnut. It flowed down past her shoulders, just long enough to brush her nipples—

'Can you please put some clothes on?'

My problem this morning wasn't lust. Looking at her made me think of my mother. Made me think of how my mother might have appeared to my father before I was even dreamed of. I don't care who your parents are, there's no bigger turn-off than thinking about them having sex.

The dryad shrugged, and in the blink of an eye she looked as human as anyone on a city street. So this was her corporeal form, though I'd have settled for her staying ethereal but covered up.

Now she looked like a girl maybe seventeen years old and barely as tall as my shoulder. She was wearing those ballet slipper shoes, a denim mini-skirt and a sleeveless, V-necked yellow T-shirt. Far too close to the description of the murder victim for comfort.

Maybe we should move away from the road. Sure, that would be fine until the police stopped to check on a parked vehicle and found me leading a young girl into the woods. A girl with no ID, and I didn't want to think about the complications when the police asked her who she was and where she was from.

'Who are you?' She looked into my face, her expression all curiosity, no hint of seduction.

'What's your name?' I asked her.

'Tila. What's yours?'

'Daniel.'

'Who are you, Daniel?' She gazed into my eyes, hazel like her own. 'How can you see me when no one else can?'

Every time she blinked though, just for an instant, I glimpsed her true gaze. Her eyes were wholly leaf-green, without white, iris or pupil.

'My mother—' I froze as I heard a vehicle, but some silver-grey saloon hurried past without slowing. 'She was one of your kind.'

'She chose to bear a son rather than a daughter?' Tila laughed, somewhere between incredulity and delight. 'What a wonderful thing!'

It was rare, I knew that much from my mother. Unlike her ethereal daughters, a dryad's sons will be mortal men. Mortal, tall, strong and long-lived by human standards, rarely sick and able to see the supernatural. Wildwood blood inevitably thins in subsequent generations, but if you've met someone with a convincing claim to a sixth sense, the chances are there's a dryad's son or something similar in their family tree.

I looked up the slope into the oak wood. 'Do you have any sisters here?'

My mother occasionally mentions sisters who went away a long time ago. She talks of her mother and aunts, and even a grandmother who died and was buried beneath her favourite tree when Mum was young. As far as my dad and I can work out, that happened sometime around the Reformation. It's hard to be sure. My mother's inclined to reminisce about Roundheads and Cavaliers battling over Edge Hill in much the same way that she talks about scouts camping beside the nature reserve last summer. Dryads have no real concept of human time.

Tila scowled. 'I came here to be on my own.'

'Why?' I was surprised. My mum still talks wistfully of her sisters and aunts, regretting the way they were scattered as the forests were cut back, reducing their beloved oak groves to remnants hemmed in by farmland.

'Because my family are fools.' Green fire glinted in Tila's eyes.

Too late, I also recalled my mother hinting at rivalries and hatreds vicious enough to see an unruly dryad driven out by her kin. I hastily asked a different question. 'Where did you live before?'

'In a wooded valley,' Tila offered with a vague shrug.

Geography's not a strong point with dryads, not in the sense of knowing where human towns and cities might be. Though they can tell you what's beneath their feet, through the soil right down to the bedrock. Either that, or she was being deliberately vague. Dryads are very good at not answering questions they don't like.

I wasn't about to give up all hope of finding some other dryads. 'When did you come here? Were there still men tending these trees?'

'There were.' She seemed pleasantly surprised by the recollection.

Okay. My mother had explained how dryads soon came to see the benefits for their beloved trees when men in the long-distant past began to crop the wildwood. Left to its own devices, a hazel seedling will grow, age and die within forty years. A hazel cut back to the ground every seven years can renew itself for centuries.

I guessed this wood had been coppiced until a hundred years ago, give or take a decade. So Tila had lived somewhere with other dryads around the turn of the twentieth century. That was more recently than my mother had seen any of her sisters.

If I could work out where Tila had come from, perhaps there would still be dryads there. Perhaps one had chosen to bear a son for a human lover within living memory. If so, maybe I could find someone who could tell me how he had kept his secret in this modern age of free-flowing information.

I tried to think how to get something useful out of Tila, a clue about where she'd come from.

She stepped closer, and for one uneasy moment I thought she was having second thoughts about a quickie in the undergrowth. Instead she surprised me with an unexpected request.

'Will you meet me in town this evening?'

'In Lambton?'

She nodded. 'In The Griffin?'

I reminded myself what I was dealing with. She might look about seventeen, but a dryad can shape her corporeal form to suit her current purposes. My mother successfully masqueraded as a human woman all the way from my infancy until after I left school, adding touches of grey to her hair, drawing crow's feet around her eyes and thickening her waist.

Tila must be at least a couple of centuries old and would have been dealing with humans on her own terms all that time. Dryads find mortals who stray into their woods entertaining in many ways, especially when they're looking for partners in the sensuality that goes with being elemental creatures of growth, renewal and fertility. Dryads enjoy sex, and over the course of their long lives they'll take a good many lovers until they choose a man to be their soulmate, as my mother had chosen my father.

But why did Tila want to meet me in that notoriously sleazy pub?

'Why do you want to go there?' I asked.

Tila shrugged. 'There'll be men looking for company.'

Yes indeed, especially on payday. Dean, one of the electricians, had hinted the little park behind The Griffin was the place to find recreational drugs and no-strings sex, as long as I was prepared to pay the going rate.

I don't do drugs; they do nothing for me. I've never had to pay for sex either. Dryads' sons may not have the intense allure of our mothers, but we have more than our fair share compared to most men. Though that's not the advantage you might imagine. There's nothing like a bored girlfriend admiring a stranger to provoke some idiot into starting a fight.

'You want me to come along while you find someone to fuck?' It was ridiculous, but I felt as if I'd discovered my teenage sister was screwing around.

She looked sideways at me and I saw the green veil linger in her eyes. 'The other girls won't make such a fuss if they think I have a man looking after me.'

'You want them to think I'm your pimp? Some big, strong stranger? So they don't threaten to beat you up for taking their trade?'

Whatever I'd thought I might discover by talking to her, it sure as hell hadn't been supernatural prostitution. So much for dryads enjoying innocent encounters with men getting close to nature and getting a lot more than they expected.

Tila tossed her head, unconcerned. 'They say we all need to be careful after what happened yesterday. To tell the tricks our boyfriends expect us back inside an hour. That the other girls remember the cars we go in and we have the GPS switched on in our phones.' Her cheeks dimpled winsomely. 'Whatever that means.'

My hot anger turned to a cold shiver. 'After what happened yesterday? Did you know that dead girl from The Griffin? Did you see who killed her?'

'I wish he'd stay out of my woods.' As Tila scowled, her eyes suddenly burned like sunlit emeralds. It was startling and unnerving. I'd never seen my mum look like that.

'I don't like him bringing his carrion here again.'

'Again?' My blood turned to ice. 'He's done this before?'

If there'd been more than one dead girl in these woods, no wonder CID had come out mob-handed. Did that mean I would still be under suspicion, even though I had an alibi for yesterday?

'They never found the first one.'

Then I was off the hook. After an instant of relief, I was ashamed. Two girls were dead. Their families would be devastated.

'He was unlucky yesterday. A hiker found her body before he could dump it out of sight.'

Tila's tone was casual rather than callous. That convinced me more than anything else that she hadn't ever found a lover whose soul spoke to her own. My mother had once said she hadn't truly understood humanity until she met my father.

27

'I'll show you.' Before I could pull away, she took my hand. I was swept along by her will, as helpless as a leaf on the breeze.

Dryads can take a human with them when they travel unseen and unsuspected, as swift and insubstantial as the wind. They can do a lot more than that, heedless of the impact on mortal men. My father warned me about a week he'd lost, when I'd asked him about those folk tales where a man encounters the supernatural and then comes home to find he's been given up for dead for decades.

Dryads aren't bound to the passage of time in the same way as ordinary mortals. If they want to see a tree grow from a seedling to its first blossoming and the following crop of fruit, they simply adjust their perceptions and see all of that happen in what to them seems like the course of an hour. Never mind how many calendar months and years will have passed by for the rest of the world.

My feet landed with a thump and I felt the strengthening sun on my face. We were standing on much higher ground. Glancing down, I saw Tila had brought me to the edge of a stony cleft fringed with hart's-tongue ferns. Water chattered unseen in the depths, and I remembered reading about the sinkholes and gullies which riddle these hills. The White Peak is limestone country; the soft rock is inexorably carved by the rain to let streams flow unseen underground.

'Where are we?' I fought an urge to ask when. If Tila wanted to meet up in town that evening, I could only hope this was still the same day.

'Where he threw the first one.' Tila walked to the edge of the slick, jagged rocks and peered down into the shadows.

Even when they look fully corporeal, dryads can still walk from treetop to treetop, with sprigs that wouldn't support a squirrel barely bending beneath their feet. I followed a lot more cautiously.

'There.' Tila pointed.

Kneeling down, I could just make out a pale shape. It took me a moment to realise this wasn't a recently dumped body.

A skull looked blankly up at me, empty eye sockets half obscured by matted hair. Stained and faded clothes hid the rest of the bones.

'How did she die?' I sat back on my heels and looked at Tila.

'He cut her and let her run away so he could chase her. When he caught her, he cut her again. He did the same with the one yesterday.' Her nose wrinkled with distaste. 'I don't know why he does it. I don't know why he's come back.'

'Do you know who he is?' I demanded. 'What does he look like?'

'I stay well out of his way.' For an instant Tila flickered into her ethereal form. 'He sometimes drinks in The Griffin. Taller than me. Shorter than you. Brown hair.'

'He's one of the tricks?' That was the word she'd used, however stupid I felt saying it. I looked down into the dank crevice. 'Was she one of... the girls who drink there? When did this happen?'

She shrugged. 'I don't remember.'

'I wonder what her name was.' I was speaking more to myself than to Tila.

'Let's see.' Tila walked as easily down the rock face as a human walks down a staircase. She stooped, then straightened up, waving a discoloured handbag at me.

'Don't bring that up here!'

Too late. She was already running lithely back up the jagged stones, pulling the bag open to dump the contents on the ground.

I saw a chunky black mobile phone complete with stubby antennae and actual buttons to press. A leprous looking purse, hairbrush, lipstick, condoms, a couple of pens and scraps of paper sodden to oblivion.

Tila reached for a warped and wrinkled address book, pathetic flowers still bright on its cover.

'Don't! Please, just put everything back. Put it all back down there.'

Did dryads have fingerprints? I realised I had absolutely no idea. Regardless, they wouldn't be in any database and Tila was sharp enough to disappear, quite literally, if she was picked up by the police.

She huffed with irritation as she scooped everything back into the bag and tossed it down into the gully.

'I thought you wanted to know who she was.' She looked at me, affronted, hooking her thumbs into her waistband. 'Anyway, I've done this much for you, so you should do something for me.'

Remember those old folktale warnings about never owing the fair folk a debt? Keep in mind the ones about supernatural creatures punishing someone who's offended them. More than one dog walker could have avoided a plague of bad luck if he'd only heeded my mum's requests to keep his pet on a lead when the nature reserve's ground-nesting birds were brooding. She never explained how she did it though.

'All right,' I said hastily. 'I'll see you in Lambton this evening, in the market square. Around six?' By then I might have thought of a way to get some useful information out of her.

She looked at me blankly. Dryads don't see any point in clocks.

I calculated quickly. Sunset would be around half past nine. 'With a third of the daylight left between noon and nightfall.'

She understood that. 'Good.' She vanished.

I stood there for a long moment, looking at the pitiful remnants of that nameless victim's life. How long had she been lying dead? I couldn't recall seeing a mobile phone like that one inside the last ten years.

Belatedly, I reached into my pocket for my own phone. What time was it? Nearly 6 a.m. Time I was on my way to Lambton. As long as I could find my way back to the sodding road and my Land Rover.

Heading further up the hill, I was relieved to see the dark line of the road threading through the trees below. I made my way cautiously down the slope, alert for anyone else in the wood or a vehicle whose driver might glimpse me and describe me to the police.

I didn't see anyone. More worryingly, I didn't see anything that I recognised. Where the hell had Tila brought me? By the time I reached the tarmac, my mouth was dry and my heart was pounding. I looked up and down the road. Which way should I head? Was this even the road I had parked on?

# Chapter Three

After a moment of stomach-churning uncertainty, I recognised the dead snag of an oak tree. That meant I was on the right road, looking back towards Kympton with Lambton behind me.

More importantly, I was a lot further down the road than the lay-by and further still from the area the police were so interested in yesterday. If I could get back to my vehicle without being seen, I could be well away before anyone had reason to think I'd been back here.

I began running up the road. Not that anyone would mistake a bloke in combats, T-shirt and work boots for a jogger; I just wanted to be on my way.

Except, all I could think about was that dead girl in the gully. About that phone. Wondering who had been ringing it and ringing it until the battery went dead. Someone must still be waiting and hoping that long-lost girl would turn up on their doorstep even after all this time.

What would her family still be telling themselves, to keep hope alive? Never mind what she'd done in the meantime, they'd say to each other. As long as she came home, nothing else would matter. But that was never going to happen.

My heavy boots were loud on the gravelly road. Breathing faster, I rounded a bend and saw the Land Rover in the lay-by. I was pulling away inside a minute, leaving the woods with their gruesome secret behind.

The valley widened into water meadows on either side of the poplar-fringed river to my right. Crossing a humpbacked bridge, I turned on the radio. The BBC's morning mix of political infighting, economic gloom and speculation seemed even more irrelevant than usual. Then the honey-voiced announcer's words had me gripping the steering wheel.

'Derbyshire police have found a young woman's body...'

All I learned was that the BBC didn't know anything more than the local paper. At least the news was out there nationally. But what use was that if the police didn't even have a description of the guilty man?

I reached the junction, taking the turn towards Lambton. As I drove through the marketplace, I caught sight of one of the few surviving public phone boxes.

Pulling up, I grabbed my mobile. Dad answered quickly enough to reassure me that I hadn't woken him. I hadn't been too worried. He's always been an early riser.

'Dan? Everything all right?' He sounded more surprised than concerned to be hearing from me so early.

'Yes, I'm fine. Well, I'm okay. I could do with some advice.'

'Fire away.'

I heard shuffling as Dad settled in a chair. I explained everything that had happened yesterday and this morning.

'I was thinking,' I concluded, 'I could ring in an anonymous tip to Crimestoppers, about the second body. The first one, I mean.'

'I know what you mean.' There was a pause at the other end of the line. I guessed that clunk was Dad putting down his mug of tea.

'I think that's the right thing to do,' he said slowly. 'As you say, the poor girl must have some family.'

'If the police know this killer's struck before, they might find extra evidence to help catch him.'

'True enough, and they can't pin anything on you if she died when you were up in Glasgow,' Dad said, echoing my own earlier thoughts.

Ten years before, I'd been in my first year at uni, discovering that my abiding interest in the countryside, its wildlife and its history didn't mean I was in the least suited to studying for an Earth Sciences degree.

'Right.' I nodded.

'You say you're seeing Tila this evening?'

I could tell Dad was as intrigued as I was.

'Can you ask Mum what sort of things I should ask her? To find out where she came from?'

'I can try.' He sounded doubtful, as well he might. Dryads aren't much interested in the past, living in the here and now and only looking forward as far as the next cycle of the seasons.

'What do you think knowing that could tell you?' he asked.

'Maybe there are still other dryads there. Maybe there's one who gave a lover a son.'

'Maybe, maybe not.'

'I won't get my hopes up,' I promised.

It wasn't something we discussed much, but he knew I longed to meet someone who shared my heritage.

I suppose I'd first understood how different I was to my classmates at primary school. Not that realising I was different had been at all traumatic. Growing up, I accepted the world as I found it just like any other small child. I loved and trusted my parents as they showed me the wonders of the natural world as well as warning me of its perils, what not to eat or touch, what animals to avoid disturbing. So I accepted them telling me we didn't tell strangers about those aspects of my mother's nature which I'd known about since infancy. Because outsiders simply wouldn't understand.

That made sense. I'd already discovered that other children in the playground couldn't see a boggart scavenging in the rubbish spilled out of a dustbin by an adventurous fox. I was the only one who could see rainbow-winged sprites dancing with the butterflies. When I pointed ethereal creatures out to my nursery school teacher, she smiled and congratulated my mother on her son's wonderful imagination.

My mother had smiled and agreed, and on our walk home together she'd explained to me that folk outside our family would never be able to see what she and I could. So there was nothing to be gained by sharing such marvels. People would only think we were making up stories.

As I grew up, I soon saw the sense of leaving ordinary

people's assumptions unchallenged for the sake of peace and quiet. On the other hand, the older I got, the more I felt I would like to swap notes with someone who truly understood my life.

The phone crackled as my dad spoke again.

'So you're going to call in a tip to the police?'

'I am. I'll do it now.'

'Good. I'll give you a ring later, if your mum suggests something for you to ask this dryad. Let me know how you get on.'

'I'll do that. Give my love to Mum.'

'I will. Bye then.'

The phone went blank in my hand, and I went online to find the Crimestoppers number. I walked over to the phone box and dialled.

'It's about that dead girl in Derbyshire. There's another one.'

I answered the call handler's questions as briefly as possible while giving as much accurate information as I could. When the woman started asking me to repeat myself, I interrupted.

'Sorry, love, I've got to get a wriggle on.'

I don't usually talk like that, but on the off chance that DS Tunstead heard this call, he'd go looking for someone with a Deptford accent like a brickie I'd once worked with. It's not just songbirds I can mimic.

'Have you made a note of your code?' the reassuring woman asked.

'Yes, ta, love,' I lied before hanging up.

I had no interest in collecting any reward. I'd see my bank account down to pennies before I'd put such blood money in it.

All the more reason to earn a full pay packet this week. Checking the time, I realised I really had better get a move on. Phil Caister would let me make up time at the end of the day, but I didn't want to be late meeting Tila.

I headed for Lambton Farm and put in a solid morning's work renewing a substantial stretch of roof timbers ravaged by rain and frost getting in through wind-loosened tiles. I'd reached a good place to stop when I heard Phil shouting down below.

'Come on, you lot, I reckon it's lunchtime.'

I made my way carefully down the ladders, fetched my flask and lunch from the Landy and joined the men sitting on salvaged chairs under an ancient ash tree. Life on any building site goes easier if you make an effort to be sociable, and that's easier given men rarely ask personal questions.

'Ham and lettuce again. I know she wants me to live forever, but would a spoonful of pickle kill me?' Mick was examining the sandwiches his wife had made. 'See the match last night, Dan?'

Phil was pouring himself a cup of tea the colour of London brick. 'That was never a penalty in the second half.'

I ate my sandwiches while the two of them argued the rights and wrongs of the refereeing. Football really doesn't interest me. At school someone my size never got the benefit of any doubt when an A* drama student collapsed in the penalty area, insisting I'd fouled him.

So I'd played rugger instead, in the middle of the scrum. Looking big and mean enough to rip off an opponent's arm and club him to death with it was a positive advantage. But it's easy enough to take a casual interest in football by listening to sports news and glancing at newspaper back pages.

Mick turned back to me. 'You should have got yourself down to The Osprey. They've got the full sports package on satellite, big screen, the lot.'

'Yeah.' I grimaced, apparently regretful. 'Only I'd had a beer when I got in. I didn't fancy risking being caught over the limit. Cops were stopping cars on the Kympton road.'

The other men nodded. Losing your driving licence because you've failed a breathalyser is a catastrophe in our line of work.

'They weren't after boozers.' Lewis, the youngest lad on

the site, looked up from his phone. 'Didn't you hear about that girl? The one they found in the woods?'

'What girl?' Tony turned off the mortar-spattered transistor radio he kept permanently tuned to a soft-rock station.

It turned out only half the circle had caught the local or national news this morning.

'Any idea who the poor little bitch is?' Mick's unthinking coarseness was habit, not lack of sympathy.

'Maybe there'll be something in today's paper.' That was all Phil could offer.

'Never been anything like this round here.' Lewis's dad, Geoff, scowled.

'My Lauren isn't going out on her own until they've got the bastard,' Nigel, one of the older stone masons, declared.

I didn't say that Lauren should be safe if she stayed away from The Griffin. Besides, I didn't know if that was true, I realised. Tila hadn't said the first victim had been one of the wretched girls haunting the park behind the pub. Just that she'd seen the killer drinking there. I should press Tila harder about that this evening, I decided, to see if I could jog her memory and learn something more to pass on to Crimestoppers.

In the meantime, conversation turned to the prospects for the upcoming Premiership season, until Phil snapped the lid back on his plastic sandwich box. I headed back up the scaffolding while the rest of the crew continued with their own tasks.

We knocked off at half five that afternoon. I pulled up in Lambton to buy a bottle of lemonade from the small supermarket, and drank it sitting in the Land Rover and looking at The Griffin.

It wasn't a pub with rich historical ambience to attract the tourists. Sometime before planning controls and conservation areas happened, someone threw up a charmless brick building with frosted glass windows on either side of a central door opening onto the street. A long wing stretched out behind it, flanking a car park in dire need of resurfacing. The walls were stained where blocked gutters had overflowed.

Regardless, the dump was already busy with people keen to start their weekend. I studied the unappealing mix of sullen men and hard-faced women, out to relieve the tedium and desperation of hand-to-mouth lives with cheap booze and illicit pleasures bought and sold behind the plane trees fringing the car park.

Too many townsfolk come to the country and only see the expensive four-wheel-drives, the lovingly renovated old houses, the gastropubs, boutique galleries and workshops. They don't see rural poverty blighting the deep-rooted families who worked on the farms for generations before agriculture was mechanised, or in local factories now demolished in favour of housing developments.

Too many people end up trapped in dead-end, low-paying jobs. There used to be routes to a life with broader horizons, where talents not recognised at school could see a bright girl or boy rise from apprentice to management. My dad had told me often enough how those options had vanished, insisting I stay on at school for A levels and then do a degree. He'd been furious when I turned my back on university after a year. We'd had a rough six months before we came to terms with our difference of opinion.

I contemplated The Griffin's open front door, paint peeling like sunburnt skin. Was the killer already in there, mingling with other drinkers? Was Tila forgetting that I'd told her to meet me outside?

Would Tila be able to point the murderer out? What would I do if she could? I'd need to find out something to pass on beyond suspicion and a description so vague it fitted half the men shambling into the pub.

I waited a bit longer, then crossed the cobbles. One drink would give me an excuse to look inside for Tila.

I took a stool by the sticky bar until the bloke handing out alcopops and bottles of designer lager finally glanced my way. 'Pint of John Smith's, please.'

I should have gone for one of those lagers instead. Whoever kept this dump's cellar didn't know what they were doing. As I took a taste, it was an effort not to grimace at the beer's sour undertones.

The crowd in the bar looked as unpromising as the bitter. Tila was nowhere to be seen, and the regulars giving me the once-over didn't look overly friendly. Apart from one who was much too welcoming.

'Looking for some company?' A skinny blonde with red-veined eyes ringed with smoky makeup hitched herself onto the next barstool. Her sequinned black minidress rode high up her bare thighs and was cut low enough to show anyone who cared that she wasn't wearing a bra.

'No,' I said bluntly.

'Fuck you then.' She clacked away on transparent plastic high heels.

I watched her head for the pool table, where a handful of biker types in dirty jeans and leather jackets were knocking the balls about. One sank a shot more by luck than judgement. He scowled in my direction as the skinny blonde draped herself over his shoulder and whispered in his ear.

For a moment I was tempted to sit there and wait for him to make something of whatever insult she was claiming. He looked just the type. They're easy to spot. I've had enough encounters with some tosser out to impress his idiot mates by taking down the big bloke who's sat in the wrong seat.

I've got used to leaving before they get up the nerve. Besides, I had more important things to do tonight. At least, I did if Tila ever showed up. So I left the vile beer on the bar and went back outside to sit in the Land Rover and wait for her.

But there was no sign of the dryad, not then and not for the next hour. I gave her until eight o'clock and then turned the key in the ignition. The radio was halfway through the headlines.

'... found murdered in Derbyshire. She was originally from Nottingham and police are appealing for anyone with information about her recent movements to contact them.'

I waited for something more, but the newscaster moved on to the latest row over hospital reforms.

I still didn't understand why Tila hadn't turned up. Maybe she'd misunderstood me. Perhaps she'd been waiting in the lay-by. I took the wooded valley road back to Kympton.

As soon as I crossed the stone bridge by the water meadows, I realised the woods were crawling with people. A white square tent shone bright in the dusk among the trees at the top of the hill. So they'd found the long-dead girl. That must have been the news headline.

I didn't want to draw attention to myself by slowing down to stare. Thankfully the driver of a red Audi in front of me had decided thirty miles per hour was the safest way to get past the police without adding to whatever points were already on his licence. So I got a good look at the lay-by.

Tila wasn't there, in her teenage girl guise or her ethereal form. I guessed she must have been so engrossed in watching the police struggling to recover the skeletal remains that she'd lost what little track she had of the time.

We reached the Kympton turn and I headed for the farm while the red Audi sped away to wherever. I pulled into the yard and, deep in thought, switched off the ignition. A knock on the passenger door window startled me into dropping my keys.

For a second, I hoped it was Tila. Then I saw it was Chrissie Monkswell. Great. Just what I didn't need. I reached down for the keys.

# Chapter Four

I got out of the Land Rover and locked the door. 'Is Sam around?'

'He's with the cows.' Chrissie gestured towards the fields with a grimace. She'd told me more than once that she'd never realised how hard farmers worked until she married Sam. They'd met at university in Sheffield, where she'd grown up, a city girl.

I noticed the keys in her hand. The big bunch with all the holiday lets' doors and windows tagged with different colours, and mine along with them. 'Is there some problem up in the flat?'

'What? Oh, no, nothing.' She tried to cover her guilty surprise with a smile. 'I was just over the lane checking everything's okay for the morning. We've got three couples coming in.'

I glanced over the road to see a blonde woman waiting by the closest cottage's front door. I didn't recognise her, but she was wearing yellow rubber gloves. 'You finally got a reply to your adverts for a summer season cleaner?'

'At last.'

'Good.' Now Chrissie would have someone who wasn't me to share local and international gossip with. 'Let's hope your guests get some decent weather.'

I headed towards the outside steps leading up to the flat's front door. Uninvited, Chrissie walked with me.

'You were up bright and early this morning.'

I shrugged. 'I was awake. Might as well get on.'

'I couldn't sleep either.' Chrissie sighed. 'Thinking about that poor girl on the news. Have you heard the latest? Lin told me they've found another body in the woods.' She gestured vaguely towards the cottages, so I guessed she meant the new cleaner. It was hardly surprising that the news was the only topic of local conversation.

'It's awful.' I stood on the bottom step, waiting for Chrissie to go so she couldn't follow me up the stone stairs.

She tossed the keys in her hand, irresolute. 'Everything's going all right at the barn job, is it?'

'Everything's fine,' I assured her. 'I still owe Sam that drink for giving me Phil Caister's number.'

'Maybe we should go out.' She smiled.

'The three of us? Maybe,' I said, non-committal.

Chrissie wasn't really flirting. She was unwittingly drawn by my mother's blood, I knew that, but I didn't want her even wondering idly about a roll in the hay with me. For one thing, Sam wasn't stupid. He'd notice any tension between us, and since he adored his wife I would get the blame. I didn't want to have to move on from here. Not when I might be the only person who could get the murderer caught.

But Chrissie raised her eyebrows at me. 'I meant the four of us. You said Victoria was coming down this weekend. I'd like a chance to catch up with her.'

Crap. I'd totally forgotten, with murdered girls and meeting Tila filling my thoughts. So much for worrying that Chrissie was suddenly finding me irresistible. I should have remembered that she and Victoria always stopped to chat if they passed each other in the yard. 'That's not a problem, is it?'

'Just make sure she parks clear of the gates.' Chrissie rattled the keys again before silencing them in a clenched fist. 'Right, I'd better be getting on.'

'See you.' I headed up to the flat and took a look around. It wasn't too untidy, but I'd better do a bit of cleaning up.

I'd got chatting to Victoria – never Vicki – at a couple of the Borders' craft shows that were big enough to make the trip south from Lanarkshire worthwhile for me. A jewellery designer and silversmith, she was based in Newcastle. Originally a Worcester girl, she'd gone there to university and stayed.

The third time our paths crossed at a living history day in Northumbria, I'd asked if she'd like to go to dinner. Over coffee she asked if I wanted to stay the night at her place before I headed back to Scotland. I wasn't sure if she was offering me the sofa or something more, but I said yes regardless. I didn't sleep on the sofa. I didn't get much sleep either.

Since I'd come to Derbyshire we'd spent a handful of weekends together, here or in Newcastle, or sharing a double room in a bed and breakfast when we were both at a craft show.

Ordinarily I'd be looking forward to seeing her. Just at the moment, I wondered if I should give her a ring and put her off. Then I'd be free over the weekend to try and find Tila. But I couldn't think of a good reason. Saying there'd been a murder in the area and I was afraid that Victoria might be next would sound ridiculous.

Besides, she wasn't coming till tomorrow, and she'd said last weekend that she wouldn't arrive until lunchtime. She wanted to head north early on Sunday afternoon too, to avoid any evening traffic.

So if I cleaned the flat this evening, I'd have tomorrow morning and Sunday evening to find Tila and ask why she hadn't shown up at The Griffin. I'd better get busy. I wondered if I had enough detergent to do my laundry as well as wash my sheets. I knew I was running low, and normally I'd be doing my week's shopping this evening. Since meeting Tila though, going to the supermarket had completely slipped my mind.

When I dropped my wallet on the table, it hit the computer mouse and my laptop screen glowed as it woke. I frowned when I saw the current window. I hadn't been checking my browser history. So who the hell had? Chrissie Monkswell?

I was instantly furious. I'd lived in two other places where the landlord reckoned having a key gave him some right to come in snooping. When I'd realised what was going on, I'd packed up and left, just for the satisfaction of seeing the nosy bastard's face when I told him I knew what he'd done. That had been worth losing a couple of security deposits, back when there was plenty of well-paid work for the taking, wherever I'd happened to arrive by the time my temper cooled.

I couldn't afford to do that at the moment, and not just on account of the money. Nothing would draw police attention like me leaving the area. Then Chrissie could tell DS Tunstead how I'd been looking at online reports about the dead girl and the Crimestoppers website. He'd think I knew something I hadn't told him. He'd know someone had told Crimestoppers where to find the first dead girl. Then every copper would be looking for my Land Rover.

I deleted the browser history and reset the laptop to do that automatically every time it was shut down. Then I updated the security settings I'd never bothered with before. Chrissie could try snooping again, but she had no chance of guessing my password. Not unless she knew the pet names dryads give their favourite trees.

That small satisfaction wasn't nearly enough to cool my irritation, so I did the washing-up and cleaned the kitchenette. I swept the floor and dusted anything that looked like it needed it before heading for the bedroom. I decided to use the last of the detergent to wash the clothes I gathered up off the floor. As long as I got to the supermarket and back in good time tomorrow, I could wash the sheets before Victoria arrived.

I had a shower and cleaned the bathroom. After that, I didn't have anything left to distract me from wondering why Tila hadn't shown up. I racked my brains for a way to go and search her wood without DS Tunstead's underlings catching me.

My stomach growled with hunger and I realised I didn't have anything left in the fridge. I'd planned on picking up a takeaway in Lambton after seeing what I could learn from Tila.

Well, I could do something about that. I got dressed and headed out to Kympton, along the road winding beside the river. I soon saw the ruined tower of St Werburgh's rising above the tree tops. Apparently a medieval village had once flourished in the rumpled turf beyond the abandoned church. Local lore said the people had crossed the Kyme to build new houses in hopes of leaving the Black Death behind. If that was true, their plan had worked. Kympton had flourished through the subsequent centuries.

The Osprey was up at the top of the sloping High Street, where the grey limestone houses opened out into a broad marketplace. Once a coaching inn, it dominated the square. Tables and chairs outside were already filled with people enjoying the fine summer evening, and doubtless the big screens inside were offering noisy entertainment.

I headed for The Grey Goose, on this edge of the town and overlooking the river. Its sign showed St Werburgh surrounded by the pious birds who'd obeyed her appeals to stop eating the villagers' corn, or so the story went. About half The Osprey's size, the pub offered well-cooked local food and beer brewed at the back of the premises by the landlord, Jim. As I pulled up, I smelled the sweet pungency of yeast and hops at work.

On the far side of the five-barred gate separating the brewery yard and the car park, Teddy, the pub's Rottweiler, emerged from his kennel. A handsome dog, young enough to have escaped the barbarity of docking, he wagged his up-curved tail as he recognised me.

I went inside, past the notice board where locals advertised everything from holistic massage to help wanted with gardening. The sizeable bar had tables and chairs under the windows and tall stools in front of the counter. An arch beside the fireplace led to a dining room where customers could linger over several courses.

Jim's wife, Donna, was chalking the day's specials onto a blackboard. 'What can I get you?'

'A pint of IPA, and steak pie and chips. Whenever you're ready.' There was a copy of the local paper on the bar with a photo of a thin-faced, dark-haired girl on the front page. I pulled it towards me.

Donna set my brimful glass down beside it. 'How are the barns coming along?'

The first time I'd come in, she'd recognised me as the new carpenter on the Lambton project. It didn't bother me. Growing up in a rural area, I was well used to everyone knowing everyone else's business. Or thinking they did, anyway. Dad taught me how to let the locals know just enough to convince them that an honest man had no secrets.

'It's all going very well,' I assured her.

'Good to know.' She shook her head as I reached for my wallet. 'Settle up when you've eaten.'

'Thanks.' I took the paper and my drink to a corner table as Donna went through the kitchen door to pass on my order.

I studied the front page. It told me the dead girl was called Shevaun Thomson, summing up her life in short, crisp sentences with a depressingly familiar ring.

She'd been known to Social Services for most of her short life. Her heroin-addicted mother died of an overdose when she was ten. Her father was unknown. Shevaun left residential care on her sixteenth birthday, last summer.

Just before Easter this year she'd failed to show up for her shift at the pizza restaurant where she'd been working since leaving school. Other girls in the house where she'd rented a room reported seeing her going out earlier with a backpack. She'd taken her personal belongings and there was no indication that she'd been forced to leave against her will.

According to a statement from Social Services, her personal advisor had made every effort to encourage Shevaun to follow her agreed Pathway Plan. Sadly there had been no way to compel her to cooperate when she proved unwilling.

It didn't take much reading between the lines to hear an over-worked, under-paid social worker determined to make sure their department didn't end up as the scapegoat for this latest tragedy.

I drank my beer thoughtfully. Moving around the way I do, I come across runaways from time to time. Most are aggressively suspicious of anyone in authority, after too many encounters with indifference or incompetence. I soon realised that half an hour's chat with a stranger won't overcome whatever neglect and abuse wrecked their lives. So I settle for suggesting charities like Shelter and Crisis. If the weather's particularly foul, I can sometimes manage to persuade a sodden and chilled teenager to take a burger and chips, but that's as far as I'll push it. Even so, I've had to convince more than one that no, I'm not looking for sex or a blow job in return.

Perhaps Shevaun had turned to prostitution, using drugs or cheap booze to blot out her miseries. She looked painfully thin in the unflattering photo, presumably lifted from some official file. Easy prey for the sadistic bastard who had murdered her. Poor kid.

I washed away the sour taste in my mouth. At least I'd done what I could to put the police on to her killer. After a few more swallows, the tension in my neck and shoulders began to lessen. By the time my pie and chips arrived, I'd emptied the glass and was feeling more at ease with the world.

'Do you want another of those?' Donna enquired as she set down the plate.

'Please.' I handed her the glass.

She brought it back refilled, along with cutlery, napkin, mustard and sauces. The door from the car park opened and two women and a man joined the handful of customers who'd come in while I'd been reading the paper. The first woman raised a hesitant hand. 'Excuse me, do you serve anything suitable for vegans?'

I was surprised to see Donna frown. She generally had the patience of a saint as people asked for every detail and possible variation on the menu. Then I realised she was looking past the newcomers. Outside in the yard, Teddy was barking so loudly he could probably be heard in The Osprey.

Donna smiled, apologetic. 'Sorry, I don't know what's got into the dog. Yes, we have several vegetarian options, and one of those is vegan. Do you want to eat in the bar or go through to the dining room?'

Pleased, the vegan woman looked at her friends. 'The

dining room?'

'This way.' As Donna led the new arrivals through, Jim appeared behind the bar to serve three lads coming in through the front door.

I turned the paper's front page and stared unseeing at the stories inside. There was a lot still missing from the main story. No information on how Shevaun had died or any mention of the second dead body, which the police had found today. Well, identifying a skeletal body would take time, even with the contents of that handbag to help. Then I guessed the police would have to track down any relatives before they released any details to the press.

There must be a pretty long gap between the deaths. Would there be anything to tie the two murders together? Could a skeleton even show the same injuries as Shevaun's freshly discovered body? I had Tila's word that the same man had killed them, but the police might be forced to conclude this was some macabre coincidence.

Didn't serial killers strike more often? I couldn't be sure. I'm not a fan of those true-crime programmes, and half-remembered wisdom from films and paperback thrillers probably wasn't reliable.

I wondered uneasily if there were other bones hidden in that valley. Tila had said he'd done this before, but she hadn't said whether there were others. I should have remembered it's important to ask dryads exactly the right questions. You can't assume they'll tell you what you need to know. They have different priorities and concerns.

Whoever this bastard was, he was good at covering his tracks. More victims could mean more clues. I needed Tila to tell me everything she knew, everything she'd seen. I drummed frustrated fingers on the table. How soon could I go back to the woods and find her without tripping over CSI Buxton?

The long gap between the murders still bothered me. I vaguely recalled some story in the news a few years back, about a soldier who'd escaped suspicion because he'd been posted abroad, only to kill again when he came home.

Why had I remembered that? I realised I was looking at an advert in the paper offering me a career in the Armed Forces. High-quality training in a range of skills, competitive wages and a chance to see the world were all on offer, apparently. The odds of being shot at or blown up weren't mentioned.

The Army and the Navy have always been popular with men like me, according to my mum, on one of the rare occasions when she talked about other dryads' sons. More than the ships in Nelson's navy had hearts of oak. Though like every other route to a life beyond the greenwood, enlisting had become steadily more complicated as proof of identity was required more and more often.

Closing the paper, I leaned back, thankful as always that my dad had registered my birth properly. Somehow he'd dealt with health visitors and things like vaccinations without anyone asking awkward questions. Me never needing to see a doctor beyond routine checks must have helped.

'Bad business, that.' Jim nodded at the headlines as he came over to collect my empty plate and glass.

'Awful,' I agreed. 'Not a local girl though.'

He looked at me, unfavourably surprised. 'Does that make a difference?'

'Of course not.' I floundered. 'I just meant...'

I didn't know what I meant. I did know I was choked with frustration at the thought of this killer getting away because the police lacked some vital information which only Tila could give them. But how could I pass on anything she told me without drawing unwelcome attention to myself, or even suspicion?

The opening door distracted Jim, or rather, the dog's angry barking did. I saw Donna glance at him, exasperated but unable to do anything while she was so busy taking orders. All the tables and chairs were full by now, here in the bar and in the restaurant.

'Excuse me.' Jim headed for the rear door, putting my plate and glass down by the beer pumps as he passed the bar.

I saw a couple with drinks in their hands were looking for a table so I stood up. Donna had my bill ready as I returned the paper. Taking my change, I realised it would pay for another pint. Why not? Better that than yielding to the temptation to go back to Tila's valley and risking an awkward encounter with DS Tunstead and his minions.

'One for the road.' I handed back the coins.

Donna looked at me quizzically. 'You're sure?'

'I'll walk back,' I assured her. 'Pick up the Land Rover in the morning.'

'Right you are.' Satisfied, she pulled my pint.

I drank it standing at the bar. Jim came back after a few moments, shaking his head. 'I don't know what's got into that dog.'

Teddy was barking again. When I walked through to the gents and glanced through the window to the car park, I saw why. A mob of boggarts was tormenting the dog.

# Chapter Five

Boggarts are vermin. They look like gargoyles that fell off a church and landed hard, face down. Squat and sallow-skinned, they have a sparse pelt of matted hair, noses like a pig that's come second in a fight and ears like a fox's, mostly ragged. They constantly squabble among themselves, biting and scratching. They would be about waist high to a tall man if they stood upright, but mostly they scrabble around on all fours, their limbs stunted and twisted. They stink of their own filth and the garbage they eat. That stomach-churning whiff of an unseen blocked drain? You've most likely just passed a boggart, all unsuspecting.

They're as spiteful as they are ugly. At least, they are whenever they can get away with some petty cruelty. Animals can see them, just like any other ethereal creature, but a horse can't tell its rider that it's shying away from a boggart's crusted, pinching claws any more than a cat can explain the menacing snarl that's making it hiss with bristling fur.

Poor Teddy couldn't tell Jim he was defending the brewery yard. Not that the boggarts were trying to get inside the buildings. These days there's so much metal in doors and windows that folk don't have to nail up horseshoes to ward off the little bastards' thieving and wanton destruction. They'd been raiding the bins; I could see the broad plastic lids flipped back. Jim would doubtless blame the wind, just as he'd blame rats for ripping open the bin bags.

I counted seven of them, and that puzzled me. Boggarts are usually solitary creatures. I'd once spotted a pair and guessed that's where little boggarts come from, which was a revolting thought, but I hadn't seen any boggarts at all since I'd come to Derbyshire. I'd never seen a gang like this.

Strength in numbers was making them bold, perched on the five-barred gate. Bellies filled with garbage, they were gleefully tormenting the Rottweiler. I watched one down in front of Teddy, capering and gesturing. As the dog went for the little beast, another sprang down to bite his tail. When Teddy rounded on it, the first one's claws raked his rump.

I headed for the Land Rover, thankful that I hadn't left my keys with Donna. The boggarts ignored me. They had no reason to imagine I could see them.

I opened the back door carefully all the same. If the boggarts had been teasing the dog all evening, they might be getting bored. I didn't want to scare them off before I'd given them a taste of their own medicine. I was in just the mood.

A place for everything and everything in its place. Dad had taught me that. I could put my hand on a box of six-inch nails without any need for the lights in the car park.

Teddy was still barking, incandescent with rage. The boggarts were capering on top of the gate, and one jumped down into the car park to waggle a taunting arm though the wooden bars. Teddy snarled with frustration. A well-trained dog, he knew full well that he wasn't allowed to jump over the gate.

I counted out nails, careful to put the box back down without a betraying chink of metal. Steadying the first one in my right hand as if I were about to play darts in the bar, I stepped out from behind the vehicle's door.

Not one of the little beasts was looking in my direction. I glanced warily around, not wanting anyone to wonder what I was doing. I had nothing remotely like a sensible explanation for any passers-by.

The largest boggart squatted at the hinge end of the gate. I guessed it was the biggest bully, vicious enough to scare the rest into following and cunning enough to find them food to steal.

My first nail struck squarely between its shoulder blades. The thing screeched like a knife blade dragged across slate, for those who could hear it at least. Ethereal or corporeal, iron always hurts supernatural creatures, and the carbon in steel makes no difference at all.

The nail bounced off as the shock turned the boggart momentarily solid and visible. That's the other thing that iron does. Ever caught a glimpse of something shadowy out of the corner of your eye? There are any number of things that could be, flickering into visibility as it's encountered something ferrous.

The fat boggart squealed and tumbled backwards off the gate. It hit the gravel and bounced onto its taloned feet with surprising speed. Even more startling, it spun around and took a step towards me. As it bared snaggle teeth clotted with garbage, it spread clawed hands with unmistakeable menace.

That was unexpected. I'd thought it would flee for the shadows and that the whole craven pack would follow. Instead they all froze on top of the gate, staring at me. The big boggart took another pace and snarled with a noise like someone gargling gravel. Two more jumped down to back it up. I'd never seen boggarts behave like this.

Two more swift nails stopped the boss in its tracks as the others yelped and recoiled from the steel. That scared two of the ones on the gate into running away. Scrambling across the car park, they vanished into the night beyond the dry stone wall holding back the hillside.

A third's nerve broke and it fled, leaving a dithering runt. It lost its balance and fell off the gate into the brewery yard. The Rottweiler sprang, only to find his jaws closing on a scrawny arm as insubstantial as air. The dog's astonishment was comical. The boggart's terror was palpable as it fled after its mates.

That left the three still crouching in the yard. They leaped at me, clawed feet churning up the gravel. I shoved the Land Rover door at them so hard the hinges squealed. The first boggart screeched as dusty green metal smacked it in the face. It fell to the ground, momentarily stunned, before rolling away to cower under the vehicle.

The boss was quicker on the uptake, or more cunning. Either way, it managed to grab the top edge of the door, hanging there one-handed as it swiped at me with filthy talons. I dug the nails I was still holding into its shoulder. It hissed with pain and hatred, breath stinking like an open sewer.

As I reeled backwards, it dropped to the gravel. It came

rushing forward with clawed hands now at the same height as my groin. I kicked it full in the chest, sending it tumbling backwards head over heels. Now it had had enough, fleeing for the sheltering shadows over the wall. The slowest of the three went with it.

'Shit!' Teeth and claws sank into my calf, sharp enough to pierce my thick trousers and the skin beneath. That last lurking boggart had been waiting for its chance. Cursing, I raked its back with my handful of nails. The little bastard screeched and scurried away, following the rest up the hill.

I drew a deep breath, more surprised than anything else. My mother had always said boggarts wouldn't bother me if I didn't bother them. Though she'd never said what might happen if I did. I should have remembered what Dad liked to say about cornered rats.

Except the boggarts hadn't been trapped. They'd been bold enough to torment Teddy and to attack me. I looked into the leafy darkness beyond the car park wall and wondered if they were laired somewhere in the fields and thickets behind the pub. What was up with that?

I went to retrieve the nails I'd thrown, rather than leave them to puzzle Jim. Teddy was quartering the yard, searching for any lingering trace of the boggarts. Satisfied that they were gone, he returned to his kennel, whuffing quietly to himself.

'Good dog,' I said absently.

The pub door opened and Jim looked out anxiously across the car park. After hearing the dog bark all evening, the silence must have worried him. His face cleared when he saw the Rottweiler settled in his kennel.

I gestured towards the bins. 'I saw a couple of rats. That must be what he was fussing about.'

'I'll put down some traps.' Seeing the open bin lids, Jim went over to close them. He halted as he saw me head for the Land Rover. 'I thought you weren't driving?'

'Just getting a torch for the walk.' I faked unlocking the back door with a rattle of my keys, took out an army surplus flashlight and locked up again. 'I'll be back for it tomorrow.'

I crossed the road to the stone stile built into the wall. A weather-worn fingerpost marked the path cutting across the grassy paddock. This was an old packhorse trail leading from Kympton to Grange Farm, and it halved the distance by road.

The track cut past the ruined church to cross the river by way of an ancient clapper bridge built of flagstone slabs resting on limestone pillars rising from the stream. Tourists liked to picnic beside it and children could splash safely in the gravelly shallows. I'd seen two little boys playing at being trolls, roaring at their sisters even though the bridge was too low to hide beneath.

I remembered asking my mother when I'd first heard those stories at primary school. Nonsense, she'd said, there are no trolls in English rivers. It was only later, when I was older, that I realised that wasn't quite the same as telling me trolls don't exist.

So much for trolls. What about boggarts? This evening's encounter still puzzled me, and my bitten leg was painful. I would never have believed boggarts would have the balls to attack a man as big as me, even mob-handed.

I had no idea why they'd banded together. Hopefully they were just passing through. I couldn't believe boggarts would settle permanently so close to houses where humans tended gardens with noisy power tools, cars and motorbikes coming and going.

If they were tempted to linger, lured by The Grey Goose's rubbish, hopefully the memory of stinging iron nails would make them think twice about that. I hoped so, for Teddy's sake.

I followed the path past the ruined church, taking the route used by dedicated walkers with sturdy boots and hiking poles. The track was fringed with scrubby hawthorns stealthily encroaching on the lost village's grassy hillocks. According to the Kympton and Lambton Historical Society's booklet, which I'd bought from Jim in the pub, nettle clumps among the lumps and bumps showed the site of each house's fireplace, from all those centuries before. The land and its vegetation still remembered what had been lost far beyond living memory.

I switched off my torch, able to see where I was going perfectly well. Excellent night vision is another gift of my mother's blood.

The packhorse trail led up the hill dividing Kympton from Grange Farm. Bushes rustled in the night breeze. A hunting owl drifted across the tree tops. It should have been a reassuring scene for someone with my greenwood blood. Instead I halted as a shiver ran down my back. I thought I heard the scrape of something scurrying across the stony path in the darkness behind me.

I walked on more slowly, increasingly wary. Something was moving in the shadows, keeping pace beside me. But the boggarts had gone in the opposite direction, fleeing up the hill behind the pub. Besides, they wouldn't pursue a fully grown man. Not one who'd already proved he could hurt them.

Except, they'd proved they could hurt me. The ache in my bitten calf was definitely getting worse. I found myself wishing I'd kept those nails in my pocket. I had my penknife, but if I threw that at some boggart in the dark, I'd never find it again.

I forced myself to a quicker pace up the hill. Now I was straining my ears for any unexpected sound. The problem was, the countryside at night is full of random noises. That rap could be a branch striking its neighbour, or it could be a careless boggart flinching from a thorny twig.

A boggart or something worse. My throat grew dry with apprehension as unwanted memories besieged me. In secondary school, in an attempt to interest even the most reluctant readers, Mrs Roberts informed my English class that basilisks and grindylows existed long before Harry Potter. For homework she set us the challenge of discovering other legends J. K. Rowling had drawn on.

We'd all enjoyed that assignment, even if I didn't have the same consolation as my classmates, searching out scraps of English folklore in books of county ghost stories and encyclopaedias of mythology from the local library. They could tell themselves the scariest things didn't really go bump in the night. I knew differently. Soon I couldn't sleep for fear of black shucks and demon horses and treacherous will o' the wisps.

When Dad caught me with my bedroom light still on after the third midnight in a row, Mum sat and patiently listened while I told her everything. She didn't tell me not to be silly, but promised, with utter sincerity, that none of these monsters could be found anywhere near our kindly woods. I knew I could trust her and my terrors receded.

Now though, walking through pitch-black woods with a boggart-bitten leg and only armed with a torch, every damned detail came flooding back. At least I couldn't recall any particularly menacing legends from Derbyshire, not beyond the possibility of wallabies. That was, frankly, not much reassurance.

Certain I heard the sharp click of claws on the stony ground behind me, I switched on the torch and swept the beam in a wide circle. The light didn't catch a thing. Beyond its reach though, the night was now twice as dark, even to my eyes. I switched off the torch and cursed myself for doing such a stupid thing. I might not be drunk, but that third pint was definitely dulling my wits.

Something moved in the undergrowth. Whatever it was, it was closer now, low to the ground and stirring up the leaf litter. I could smell the fresh scent of decay. A badger? A full-grown boar can be a metre long and as bulky as a good-sized dog. I'd seen no sign of a sett though, and I'd walked this path often enough.

I hurried onwards, debating whether to switch on the torch again, to try and flush it out. The back of my neck prickled with unease. Whatever was out there was still dogging my footsteps as I crested the hill. I followed the zigzagging track down the steeper slope towards the farm. My bitten leg burned, threatening to give way beneath me and send me sprawling headlong.

I went as fast as I dared regardless, trying to ignore ever

louder noises behind me. My treacherous ears persisted in trying to make sense of what I was hearing. Slithering? Scraping?

The holiday cottages' lights appeared in the hollow below. Far from reassuring me, the sight made my anxiety soar. I was suddenly desperate to get inside a solid building, to have a sturdy door locked behind me. All I wanted was to shut out the terrifying night. Abandoning the path, I ran straight down the rough slope, stumbling on the uneven grass. I scrambled over the stone wall and jumped down into the lane.

'Fuck!' The jolt sent searing pain through my bog-gart-chewed leg. Limping, I crossed the tarmac and stag-gered up the barn's outside stair, digging in my pockets for my keys. Once I was inside the flat, I slammed the door. My hands were shaking so much it took me three tries to get the key in the lock to secure it.

I leaned my forehead against the age-old wood, hands braced on either side of the doorframe. I sucked in deep breaths, desperate for my heart to stop racing. Panic. Un-controllable fear inspired by the ancient god Pan, lord of the wildwood. I remembered reading about that in one of those library books. But I'd always been perfectly at ease in the countryside at night. What had changed?

Taking a step away from the door, I swore as fresh agony shot up my leg. Stripping off my jeans, I twisted awkwardly to study the back of my calf. I could see dark red punctures, burning like hell.

There wasn't any sort of antiseptic in the flat. I normally ignore the scrapes or cuts I pick up at work; they never fester and I heal fast. Tonight though, I hated to think how filthy a boggart's teeth or claws would be. I keep a first aid kit in the Landy, but that was back at The Grey Goose. I was sure Chrissie Monkswell could supply plasters and disinfectant, but that would mean answering her inevitable questions with lies.

I'm not much good at telling outright lies. Mum can al-ways tell if I'm fibbing. I don't mean she's good at suspecting something's up. She knows, absolutely. That seems to be the trade-off for a dryad's own compulsion to tell the truth, even though they're so skilled at hiding what they prefer not to say with evasions and distractions.

Dad's very nearly as good at seeing through someone trying to deceive him. He says a factory foreman hears every bullshit excuse known to man. All told, I gave up telling lies to my parents before I left primary school.

I hobbled through to the bathroom and rinsed my leg in the shower, keeping the water as hot as I could stand it. At least my leg felt scalded now rather than burning with infection. I would still buy some sort of antiseptic first thing, and I would have to think up some story to tell Victoria. Chrissie Monkswell wasn't going to see me without my trousers on, but Victoria certainly would.

That gave me something to look forward to as I washed a couple of painkillers down with a pint of water and went to bed. Even with the persistent pain in my leg, I fell asleep within minutes.

# Chapter Six

The moonlit clearing was reassuringly familiar. I recognised the individual oaks silvered in the cloudless night. Mum had taught me each tree's different characteristics, as unique as the people I met in the village. These trees were my friends, in my own small way, even if I wouldn't ever know them as intimately as my mother did.

Movement on the far side of the grassy glade caught my eye. I glimpsed an indistinct figure. A shaft of moonlight struck his face. Not a human face but a mask of oak leaves, heavy-browed and bearded. His eyes were burning points of emerald in black hollows while his body was a shifting outline of verdant shadow and moonlit green. He turned and disappeared into the darkness.

The Green Man. So I was dreaming, which explained why I was back in the woods at home. The realisation didn't bother me and I had no wish to wake up. I hurried across the clearing to follow the path the dark figure had taken.

Whenever I saw the Green Man, something significant always followed. Sometimes I woke with the answer to a problem I'd been wrestling with, anything from realising a love affair had run its course to seeing the best way to reinforce a worm-ridden beam.

Sometimes his appearance was the precursor to meeting someone important. At the end of that aimless, endless summer after I'd walked away from university, I went home to tell Dad what I'd done. We had a blazing row, and I left before dawn the next day to go hiking in the Grampians.

I dreamed that I'd woken up chilled to the bone. As I unzipped my one-man tent, I found six inches of snow on the ground. Somehow, in that unquestioning way of dreams, I knew it was Midwinter's Day. Everything was sere and lifeless and the sky was leaden grey. The Green Man stood beside an oak tree with every bare twig rimed with crystal hoar frost.

The leaves of his face were more brown than green while

his body and limbs were as rough as bark, indistinct through swathes of mist. I couldn't put off facing up to things forever, his silent gaze told me. Decisions must be made. As soon as I'd realised that, I woke to a late September dawn in the highlands.

The next day I met Stuart, an amiable wood turner working a pole lathe at a Scottish castle. We chatted about making a living from a deft hand with sharp tools and an eye for the uses and beauty of wood.

After I'd helped him pack up at the end of the afternoon, Stuart suggested I spend a week or so fetching and carrying in his workshop, just to see how I got on. Six weeks later, I went home and Dad and I swapped wary apologies. By Christmas I was informally apprenticed to a joiner called Vince just outside Banbury.

Most recently, I'd dreamed of standing beside the Green Man on a hill overlooking a broad valley with a grand Elizabethan mansion silhouetted on the skyline opposite. After three nights of the same dream, I went looking on the Internet, trying to find it. I soon learned it was Hardwick Hall. That's why I was in the Peak District.

So I was content to follow the Green Man through these familiar woods. When I'd roamed these thickets after school and at weekends, I'd often seen him slipping through the trees while I was wide awake. Not that I'd known who he was. He hadn't been the thickset, bearded man who visited my dreams as I grew older. Instead, I saw a slender youth with bare arms and legs as pale as freshly peeled willow wands and hair as mossily green as his leafy tunic. He seemed like one of those bigger boys taking the bus to the secondary school. We younger kids from the village always wanted to keep up with them.

The first time I saw Jack-in-the-Green with the Morris men on May Morning, I recognised him at once. I asked Mum who was hidden inside the leafy lattice of twigs. When she said it was Billy from the paper shop, I shook my head, insisting she was wrong. Even when Billy took off the costume, I refused to accept it, as stubborn as any seven-year-old can be.

On the walk home, I told Mum about the boy in the woods I could never quite catch up with. I told her about the things I found when I followed him, from a dappled fawn sheltering in its grassy hollow to the dead swan, stinking and heaving with maggots, in a tangle of fishing line. I never knew where he would lead me, but that never stopped me going.

He looked after me, though I didn't tell my mother about that. Once I nearly stepped out into the lane on the far side of the nature reserve. The Green Man had appeared in front of me, scowling ferociously and shooing me backwards. A speeding motorbike rounded the blind corner seconds later. If I'd been in the road, I'd likely have been killed.

My mother told me the Green Man was one of the special people the village folk didn't see. Not that she could tell me much more that May Day, or later on. The Green Man has scant dealings with dryads. He comes and goes through their woods like the breeze carrying pollen. My mother and her sisters have deep roots, caring for their trees and the animals and birds they shelter.

As I grew older I looked for more information, but everything I've read has been just as vague. But I know which unknown craftsmen had wildwood blood in their veins when I see a leafy face in carvings in wood or stone.

In my current dream, I halted, confused. It took me a moment to realise the woods had changed. I wasn't at home anymore. I was on the packhorse trail that curled up the hill on the other side of the road. The Green Man was heading back towards Kympton village. Menacing shadows swathed the trees. As the Green Man strode on, the lurking darkness rippled and recoiled only to ooze back towards the path once he'd passed by.

Don't ask me how or why, but I knew retreating wasn't an option. If I drew back, the shadows would get me. I broke into a run, desperate to catch up. The steep slope tired me out with nightmarish swiftness. My boggart-bitten leg throbbed with pain. Thick cloud shrouded the sky above, so no friendly moon could help me find a path.

Stumbling, I reached for a branch to save myself. The tree spitefully whipped its twiggy bough away. As I fell heavily to my knees, the shadows thickened. My bitten calf was swollen, burning and itching.

The Green Man paused on the crest of the hill, glancing back to see if I was following, as he'd done when I was a boy. Gritting my teeth, I staggered to my feet and struggled after him.

By the time I reached the top of the hill, he was nowhere to be seen. I took a moment to catch my breath, wondering where the hell we were now. There was no sign of St Werburgh's church in the dimness below and not a hint of lit windows to indicate The Grey Goose beyond the river Kyme. But there was definitely a stream down there. I could see glinting silver now that the sky was midnight blue spangled with stars. The menacing shadows had vanished.

The Green Man was at the bottom of the slope, picking his way between hazel thickets and limestone boulders. Ahead of him, the stream rushed noisily over its stony bed, cutting across the water meadow. I followed, wincing with every step. My leg was excruciating.

The Green Man stopped when he reached the pollarded trees. He gestured towards higher ground rising on the far side of the water and I suddenly recognised where we were. This was the valley where the dead girls had been found. The Green Man was pointing towards Tila's woods.

I woke up. It was a bright, sunny morning at Kympton Grange Farm and I was safe in bed. To my relief, the hideous pain of the dream had gone. Bracing myself all the same, I carefully flexed my foot. My leg still felt sore. I threw the duvet aside to take a look. The puncture marks were ominously crusted and ringed with bruising. I tested the purplish swelling with a cautious finger and winced.

I got up, stripped off the bedding, walked through the living room to load the washer-dryer and put the kettle on.

Every step came a little easier, and that was a relief. Phil Caister needed the woodwork done on schedule to keep the barn conversion project on track. If I couldn't do it, he'd find someone who could, and that bloke would get the call about work on Phil's next job. That's how the building trade works.

The clock told me it was half past eight. I'd slept later than I'd realised. I made a coffee, drinking it black once I discovered the milk in the fridge was well on its way towards yoghurt. My last couple of slices of bread were spotted with mould so I ate some soft digestive biscuits lurking in the end of a packet. With Victoria due in a few hours, I'd better do some shopping.

I shook my head. Who was I kidding? The Green Man wanted me to go and talk to Tila. I had to find out everything she knew about this killer. The Green Man didn't want a murderer dumping his kills in that ancient wood. So now I knew why he'd brought me to the Peak District.

I had to work out what to do next. For a start, I needed to know if Shevaun Thomson and those long-dead bones were this murderer's only victims. So I had to find Tila to ask her. Perhaps if I pulled up somewhere on the valley road, she'd spot me before one of the coppers still scouring the valley noticed.

How many coppers would be out in the woods today? I didn't suppose the chief constable would be arguing about weekend overtime with a murder hunt making national headlines. I grimaced. I could hardly tell them I was looking for a dryad.

I couldn't think of anything else to do though. With Victoria visiting, I couldn't go and try to find Tila in The Griffin tonight. Perhaps I could head over there on Sunday, after Victoria went back to Newcastle. If the killer was in the pub, Tila could point him out, discreetly. I wondered if I could persuade the dryad to follow him home, safely invisible in her ethereal form. Once we knew where he lived, I could phone in another tip to Crimestoppers.

Checking the clock, I realised I'd better get a move on. The Land Rover was still at The Grey Goose. As I dressed and found my keys and wallet, I wondered how to convince DS Tunstead that whoever Tila identified was a likely suspect. Hopefully the police would find some evidence if they searched his house, but didn't they need a warrant to do that? If they didn't find any reason to suspect him, that could rule him out of their enquiries, even if I knew Tila could swear he was guilty.

Down in the farmyard, Sam Monkswell was hitching the trailer to his tractor. Weekends don't mean much to farmers. Across the lane, a couple here for a week in the holiday lets were unloading their car. Chrissie's Volkswagen estate was nowhere to be seen, which saved me having to decide whether to ask her for a lift to Kympton.

The woods flanking the packhorse trail looked peaceful and inviting as the breeze toyed with sunlit leaves. I hesitated all the same. Taking the flatter route following the road would be easier on my sore leg than the steep shortcut over the hill. Besides, even in broad daylight, memory of those nightmare shadows sent cold shivers down my spine.

Sod that. I'm a dryad's son. I won't be scared out of any woods. I used the stone stile to cross the wall and resolutely followed the path up the hill. Finding my own footprints from the night before, I was unnerved to see the risk I'd taken when I headed straight for the road. If I'd lost my footing on that steep slope, I could easily have broken a leg.

Was that what the thing lurking in the shadows wanted? I looked warily for any dark hollows. The sun shone, birds sang merrily, leaves rustled and Sam Monkswell's cows were lowing in the distance. I walked on quickly all the same, clenching my fist around my keys.

By the time I reached the crest of the hill, I had other things to worry about. The bites on my leg were burning and itching. As soon as I reached Kympton I headed for the chemist's halfway up the hill towards The Osprey. The helpful woman behind the counter recommended antiseptic-antihistamine cream for insect bites. I really hoped it would work, because I couldn't think how I'd explain these injuries to a nurse in A&E.

Down at The Grey Goose, Jim was watering the flower bed around the pub sign. Teddy the Rottweiler pricked his ears and wagged his tail as I approached.

'No more trouble from him?' I nodded towards the dog.

'No, thankfully.' Jim upended the battered watering can, scattering the last drops.

'Can I book a table for two? About eight?'

'Right you are.' Jim didn't ask who'd be joining me. Donna would have, but that sort of curiosity wasn't his style.

Teddy sniffed at my leg. Something raised his hackles, though he didn't growl. I guessed he could still smell the boggarts.

'Good dog,' I offered.

He answered with a sceptical snuffle.

I rattled my keys. 'Best get on.'

Jim nodded. 'See you later.'

As I turned around in the car park, I was just in time to catch the news headlines on the radio. The BBC had a tearful appeal from Shevaun Thomson's grandma, begging anyone with any information to call the police.

Hitting the button to silence her raw, unbearable grief, I took the quickest route to Tila's valley. I found I needn't worry about attracting attention by stopping. The lane was busier than I'd ever seen it, and the long line of cars was slowing as soon as their drivers glimpsed the white police tent high up on the hill.

The lay-by where I'd parked was off limits with blue-and-white tape strung along a line of tall cones. Patrol cars guarded a Mobile Incident Unit, a big white thing like a building site Portakabin. Men and women stood on the other side of the road, irresolute as policemen standing opposite stared them down.

At least the dawdling traffic gave me the chance to look through the gawkers for Tila in her human guise. There was no sign of her, though, by the time I'd left the trees and approached the ancient hump-backed bridge. Transit-type vans with broadcasters' logos were parked on the far side, with satellite dishes and aerials on their roofs. Two dead girls made this TV news.

Huddles of reporters, cameramen and sound techs were spread out across the water meadow, so well-known faces could film their updates with the woods as a backdrop. Hordes of people crowded the river bank where the Green Man had taken me in last night's dream. Cars were parked on both sides of the road, half on the tarmac and half on the grassy verges. That barely left enough room for two vehicles to pass each other.

A Toyota pulled out ahead of me and I turned into the vacant space. My bitten calf was so painful I could hardly think straight. I found the chemist's cream in my pocket and yanked up my trouser leg to rub on a generous smear. It didn't numb the bites entirely but there was some welcome relief.

My driving seat was high enough for me to see over the parked cars into the meadow. Tila could well be among all those onlookers. Even if she was ethereal and invisible, hopefully she'd realise I wanted to talk to her. Or she would want to talk to me. So I got out and crossed the road. Walking across the meadow felt a little eerie. I had such vivid memories of being here in my dream.

People of all ages milled around, mostly in shoes and clothes suitable for shopping in Buxton or Matlock, not a country hike. A stir ran through the crowd and hands pointed towards the trees. Now the reporters were looking and cameras were turning. A couple of lads ran across the water meadow on the far side of the river, heading for the public footpath sign that marked a gap in the trees.

Two uniformed figures emerged from the woods to wave the youngsters back, pointing at more blue-and-white tape. One sheepishly turned tail but his mate was bolder. The boy ran across the meadow, looking to outflank the policeman heading for him.

The copper didn't bother running. Two more police appeared to intercept the lad just as he thought he'd successfully reached the trees. As they marched him back towards the road, the crowd around me cheered. I couldn't tell if they were congratulating the police or mocking the boy's failure. Cameramen were already turning away, seeing nothing dramatic to film.

'What do they think they'll see?' a woman beside me asked.

'Sorry? Are you talking to me?'

I realised that was a stupid thing to say. The next closest person was ten feet away, a middle-aged man videoing a whole lot of nothing much on a mobile phone.

The woman looked askance at me. 'Who else?'

She was tall, with light brown hair flowing down her back and the square-shouldered, muscular build of a dedicated swimmer. Stonewashed blue jeans and a plain green T-shirt looked good on her. Very good indeed.

'Sorry.' I offered her a friendly grin. 'Have the police found anything else? Any clues?'

She gave me another sideways glance, up and down from head to toe. 'How should I know?'

I raised an apologetic hand. 'Fair enough.'

I looked around the crowd again but I still couldn't see any sign of Tila, and it was clear my chances of searching the woods for her were somewhere between zero and none. I did see DS Tunstead, in jeans and a polo shirt. I wondered if he was looking for the killer returning to the scene of his crime. If that really happened outside TV and movie plots.

Crap. As the fat man he was talking to moved off Tunstead glanced around. I saw him recognise me and he immediately walked in my direction. I could probably get back to the road before he reached me, but with the traffic clogging the lane I'd have no chance of driving away. Then he'd wonder why I was avoiding him.

'Good morning.' He barely bothered with a smile. 'May I ask what brings you here?'

I shrugged. 'I was going shopping in Lambton. I generally

go this way on a Saturday. It's changeover day for tourists so the main roads are always busy.'

If he didn't already know that, one of the local cops could explain.

I nodded at the TV vans. 'I saw all that lot and was curious. No law against it, is there?'

'No,' he agreed tersely. 'Not as such.'

I shrugged again and went on my way, strolling back across the meadow to the road. I got into the Land Rover and waited for a break in the traffic. With cars parking and pulling out as well as simply trying to head in opposite directions, it took a few moments. As I sat there, I saw DS Tunstead on the opposite verge. He was looking straight at me, with the lad who'd puked on his shoes beside him. The younger copper was writing something down in his notebook.

Well, there was nothing I could do about that. I checked over my shoulder and drove away, being very careful not to give the police any excuse to pull me over. Once I'd been to the supermarket, I'd head back to the farm along the main road. After that, unless the Green Man had something else to suggest, or cared to tell Tila where she could find me, I would spend the rest of today and tomorrow with Victoria. I wasn't coming back to these woods until the crowds and the coppers cleared off.

# Chapter Seven

Victoria liked smoked salmon and scrambled eggs, so I got those for a brunch on Sunday. Then I wondered if she'd prefer croissants, so I got some of those as well. Just before I reached the supermarket checkout, I remembered to go back for filter coffee. I got back to the flat for twelve, made the bed and had a last tidy round. As it turned out, I needn't have rushed. Victoria didn't arrive until two-thirty.

That left me sitting idle, wondering what DS Tunstead and the constable were thinking, after seeing me in the valley again. Then I wondered if I was just being paranoid.

Either way, turning up there again would be a bad idea, but I still had to make contact with Tila. I couldn't see the Green Man staying out of my dreams until I'd done what he wanted.

How close did I need to get to her wood for the dryad to sense my presence and ride the breeze to join me? I knew my mum's connection with her own trees extended right to the edge of the nature reserve, but I had no idea how far Tila's bond with her woods might reach.

I was about to ring Dad and see what he could tell me when I heard Victoria's Mazda turn into the yard. I hurried down the outside steps. 'Bad traffic?'

'Pretty lousy.' She grimaced as she slammed her door shut. 'And I got away later than I planned.'

Welcoming her with a hug, I stooped to give her a kiss and rubbed her back at the same time. That eased her stiffness while I felt a little of my own. She was wearing a floaty, flowery skirt and a loose cream top draped nicely over her curves. Though I resisted the temptation to cup a hand around one of her breasts; Chrissie and her new friend, the cleaner, were sitting in the farmhouse's front garden drinking tea and watching us.

'I like your hair.'

She'd dyed pale pink streaks through her blonde spikes. Her earrings were plaits of silver chain long enough to brush her shoulders. I knew she'd made them herself. She never wore anyone else's work.

Victoria broke away from our kiss. 'Any chance of a cup of tea?'

'Absolutely. Where's your bag?'

'Back seat.'

I grabbed it, she locked the car and we went up to the flat. I put the kettle on while she used the loo. I was just dropping teabags into the pot when she reappeared.

'You're the only person I know younger than my gran who uses a tea pot,' she observed. 'Family tradition?'

'Use a pot and you get two mugs out of every teabag.' I went to the fridge for the milk.

Victoria sat at the table. 'How's your diary for the next few months? For shows and fairs?'

'Let me check.' I woke up the laptop and typed in my password. That brought up the local newspaper website.

'I heard about that on the news.' Victoria was looking at the screen, shaking her head. 'Horrible, isn't it?'

'Revolting,' I said with feeling.

'Maybe there's an update on the telly. Where's your remote?' Victoria looked around.

'Over there, I think.' I waved vaguely at the small flatscreen standing on a cupboard in the corner. I couldn't remember when I'd last switched it on.

The TV in Victoria's flat was always on, often muted but still permanently tuned to the news unless she wanted to watch some other programme. That baffled me. The same stories just kept coming round on an hourly loop. Even when something newsworthy does happen, and that's a low bar these days, the first few hours will just be reporters speculating in front of not much happening at all. Either that or the same recycled people will be speculating pointlessly in a studio.

'Didn't you want me to check my diary?' I put down her tea and sipped my own as I sat on the other side of the table.

'Right.' Victoria got out her phone.

I told her the dates and places I had booked. 'How many of those are you doing?'

'I'm not sure.' She was still busy swiping at her screen.

Her vagueness surprised me. Before I could ask if everything was okay, she crossed the room to the stack of toolboxes where I keep my carvings. I use those cheap black plastic ones from DIY stores that are no use for real tools.

'Anything new in here?'

'A few things.' I showed her the dog fox and a couple of other pieces.

'Nice,' she said.

'I'll need to get a lot more finished in the next few weeks. I've been wondering if Sam will let me set up a workshop.'

'Go on,' Victoria prompted.

'If I've got a workshop, I can have a lathe.' I explained what I could do with that.

'You'd set that up here?' Victoria tilted her head, her silver earrings trailing down her neck. 'Not closer to home? War-wickshire?'

'I'm here, aren't I?' I shrugged. 'Do you want another cup of tea? Something to eat?'

'I stopped for lunch on the way.' Victoria busied herself with her phone again. 'Have you got anything planned for dinner?'

'I booked a table at The Grey Goose. Eight o'clock.'

'What shall we do till then? I've got some DVDs in my bag. Or...?' She leaned forward with an inviting smile.

I grinned. 'A little "or" sounds good to me.'

I went to lock the door. When I turned around, Victoria was laying her skirt and top neatly over the back of her chair. She was wearing rose-pink silky underwear trimmed with creamy lace.

'Did you dye your hair to match that?' The shade was exactly the same.

'It seemed like a good idea at the time.' She smiled sunnily.

We stood and kissed, then we went through to the bedroom. I ran my hands over her smooth skin and the silky underwear. I kissed her neck, her breasts, and eased creamy lace back with one fingertip to tease her nipple with my tongue.

'Lie down.' She reached up to my shoulders and gently pushed me down to sit on the end of the bed, before pulling my T-shirt over my head. She unbuckled my belt and stripped off my jeans and underpants.

'Ready as always,' she observed.

'What do you expect, dressed like that?' I couldn't decide if I wanted to ease that bra off first or slide a finger inside those panties.

'Let's see how long we can last.' She knelt and took me in her mouth.

She was good, very good. I'd found that out the first time we went to bed. Then the better we got to know each other's bodies, the better the sex became. I gave in to the exquisite sensations until the risk of cutting the ecstasy short became too much to bear.

'Your turn,' I gasped.

Victoria stood and I sat up. I stripped off her panties and laughed. She'd dyed a diagonal pink streak into her blonde pubic hair.

She giggled. 'You know I pay attention to detail.'

I lay back again, my hands holding her hips to draw her with me. She walked up the bed on her hands and knees until she sat on my chest, her knees on the pillows and her thighs flanking my head. After a bit of shifting to get comfortable, I cradled her buttocks in my hands and drew her forward.

Now it was her turn to breathe deep, shifting back-

wards and forward as I tantalised her with lips and tongue.
I thought I'd gone too far when she stiffened and pushed
against the wall to raise herself above me. No, it was okay.
She was still the right side of an orgasm.

She looked down with a wicked grin. 'Fuck me.'

I didn't know if that was an exclamation or an invitation,
and I didn't care.

'Any time you like.'

I got up to get a condom and she lay down on the bed.
I knelt between her thighs and slid into her with a deep
indrawn breath of pleasure. She tightened around me as I
thrust and thrust, and her eyes went distant as she locked her
legs around my hips to draw me in as deep as possible.

Then everything went away except that indescribable
sensation of you and her and the moment that's going to
last forever. It didn't. It never does. Though Victoria and I
gave it a good hard try until we finally slowed, breathless and
sweating.

She moved over and I lay down beside her, wrapping the
condom in a tissue and chucking it on the floor. I'd bin it
properly in a moment.

'Mmmm.' She cuddled up close and I raised my arm so
she could tuck herself against my side.

I lay back, closing my eyes as she draped her arm across
my chest. 'Did you drive all the way in that underwear?'

She giggled. 'Hardly. I got changed when I went to the
loo.'

'I wondered what was taking so long. Ow.' I pretended to
protest as she pretended to punch my chest.

'Do you want to shower first?' She snuggled up closer.

'In a minute.' I wondered vaguely what the time was.

I honestly think I'd have gone to sleep if she hadn't
twined her foot around my leg and accidentally raked those
sodding boggart bites with her toenails.

'Fuck!' I sat bolt upright.

'What is it?' Victoria sprang up, startled.

'Sorry. Never mind.' But those bites hurt like buggery again. I drew my foot up to see if she'd drawn blood.

'What happened?' She came closer to look at the inflamed punctures.

'Barbed wire,' I said through gritted teeth. It was all I could think of.

'Where? When?' She leaned closer. 'That looks like a dog bite to me.'

'Never mind.' I waved her away. I didn't want to start making up some story I'd probably forget and end up contradicting. Crap, my leg really hurt.

Victoria narrowed her eyes at me with abrupt irritation. 'Have you seen a doctor?'

'I got some cream from the chemist.'

Without another word, she grabbed a towel and stalked into the bathroom. I heard the shower start.

What had I done wrong? I looked at my leg and wondered where the antihistamine cream was. Then again, there was no point using that if I was going to shower.

I went out into the living room and put the kettle on. For the first time in a long time, I switched the sodding telly on, just to have a voice break the awkward silence.

The sound of running water stopped, and a minute later I heard Victoria in the bedroom. 'Shower's free.'

She didn't sound cross. She didn't sound much of anything. When I went into the bedroom she was getting clean underwear out of her bag. Plain white cotton.

I showered. At least the burning sensation in my leg was subsiding. After I got out of the shower, dried off and dressed, I found Victoria sitting at the living room table, looking at something on her phone. She had a mug beside her.

'I made a pot of coffee.' She didn't look up. 'Why've you passworded your laptop?'

I poured myself a cup from the cafetière beside the kettle and leaned against the counter top. 'I think Chrissie

75

Monkswell's been coming in here while I've been at work.'

'What's your problem with her, Daniel? She's only trying to be friendly, but you barely give her the time of day.'

'I say hello and goodbye. I'm always polite,' I protested. 'But why do we have to be friends? She's my landlady. I don't need to know her life story and she sure as hell doesn't need to know mine.'

'What about me?' Victoria shot back.

'What do you mean?' I didn't like the way this conversation was going.

'Why don't I need to know how you hurt your leg?'

'I told you, I caught it on some barbed wire. I walked back over the hill from the Goose the other night.' That was close enough to the truth.

'But you didn't say that when I asked, did you?' Victoria wasn't letting up. 'You just said it didn't matter.'

'It doesn't, does it?' Now I was starting to get irritated.

Victoria opened her mouth then changed her mind about whatever she'd been about to say. In the corner a cheery weather forecaster started talking about the prospects for barbecue weather on Sunday. I slammed down my mug and went to turn the TV off.

'It wouldn't matter how you hurt your leg, if that's all there was to it,' Victoria said finally, still looking down at her phone.

I wished I hadn't just silenced the telly. I couldn't think what to say.

'I hate to sound like a bad chick flick,' Victoria said, exasperated, 'but we need to talk, Daniel.'

'Why?' I challenged her. 'Why can't we just enjoy each other's company? I don't ask you endless questions.'

'No, you don't.' Victoria put her phone down. 'But I've told you about my mum and dad anyway and you know I've got a brother and a sister, though I don't suppose you remember their names. Even if you've never shown any interest in meeting them.'

'Okay—' I broke off. I'd been about to say we could do that, if it mattered that much to her. But honestly, I didn't want to, and pretending that I did would mean lying through my teeth. Then I'd have to tell more lies, when the inevitable questions about my family came up.

'You change the subject every single time I ask about your parents, did you know that?' She looked up at me, blinking and going unflatteringly red.

I hoped she wasn't about to cry. She'd be furious if she did. Victoria despised women who used tears to twist a situation to their own favour.

'Sorry. I didn't realise.' But I knew that sounded nothing like a sincere apology.

Victoria glared at me. 'If something happened, if there's some reason...' She shook her head. 'Look, I don't mean to be nosy. But you always shut me out. You shut everyone out.'

'I don't mean to.' That wasn't a lie, but I knew exactly what she meant.

The worst thing was, I'd grown closer to Victoria than any of my previous girlfriends. Once, just once, driving back here after a weekend together in Newcastle, I'd even started wondering if I'd finally found someone to share my life.

All of my life? Was she someone I could take home to meet my parents? Darling, this is my dad, and yes, I know he's old enough to be my grandfather, but that doesn't matter because my mum is an ageless tree spirit. The reason she remembers the Battle of Trafalgar is because that's when the Navy stopped cutting down oak trees to build ships to fight Napoleon.

There wasn't a hope in hell that could work. So I'd told myself we were fine as we were. It looked like I'd been wrong about that. The awkward silence lengthened.

'Is that all you've got to say?' Victoria looked at me, exasperated. 'This strong, silent act isn't as sexy as it looks in the movies. It's just tedious.'

'It isn't an act,' I retorted, stung.

Victoria pursed her lips, tapping her phone screen. 'You

know I said I need to be back home for Monday morning? Well, I'm going to look at a shop.'

'A shop?' That was a surprise.

'The lease on my studio's up for renewal so I thought I'd see what else was available.' She spoke quickly. She'd re-hearsed this in the car on the way. 'The estate agent sent me details with a place where I can have a workroom and a shop. There's a flat above it too.'

'Okay,' I said slowly.

'I could sell my own work as well as sell on stuff for other jewellers and metalworkers. All under one roof, with mail order online.'

I tried to keep up with this abrupt shift in the conversa-tion. 'So that's why you won't be doing so many craft shows.'

Victoria nodded. 'Honestly, with the cost of petrol, I've done too many where I've barely broken even in the last six months. But the thing is,' she continued quickly to stop me speaking, 'setting up a shop and an online business properly is going to take up all my time, so really, I think, you and me, I think we're done.'

'Oh.' What else was I supposed to say?

She cleared her throat. 'I know you won't ask, but I'm going to tell you anyway. There's no one else. If there was, I would say. You know that, right?'

She looked at me for reassurance and I nodded. It didn't take a dryad to see she was telling the truth.

Victoria bit her lip. 'But there might be someone else, some day, and I don't want that complicated by –' she ges-tured as she searched for the words she needed '– by some-thing that's never going to be more than what we've got now.'

She looked at me with appeal in her eyes. There wasn't a hint that she would change her mind though.

'I'm supposed to say I understand?' I demanded, goaded. 'To tell you we can still be friends? When you've come here, fallen into bed for a quick fuck and dumped me. How long since you decided all this? Days? Weeks? Why didn't you just text me and save yourself the petrol money?'

Victoria glared at me. 'Maybe I should just have waited for you to notice that I'd changed my status to single. I could have sent an email and you'd have found out sometime next month.'

She wasn't wrong.

'I didn't know I was going to go through with it until just now.' Now she sounded hurt. 'Yes, I did hope we could stay friends. I thought we'd had a lot of fun. I thought I owed you more than a phone call.'

'Sorry. I didn't mean to sound like a prick,' I said stiffly.

I've been dumped by phone and it was a kick in the balls. On the other hand, one of the two times I've been the one calling things off, I got sucked into a shouting match. Victoria hadn't done that and she deserved better from me.

I glanced at the bedroom. 'At least we went out on a high.'

She managed a weak attempt at a laugh. 'If sex was all that mattered, I'd never let you out of bed. But...'

'Real life's more complicated,' I said wryly. It was one of her favourite sayings, whenever some talking head on the news tried to reduce some complex debate to a sound-bite.

Victoria sighed with a mixture of regret and relief. 'It really is.' Her overnight bag was by her chair. She reached for the strap and stood up.

'You're not going?' That was an unwelcome surprise. Then again, none of this was what I'd expected.

'I think I will. I can get back home before it's too late. I'm sorry, I really am.' She looked at me, clearly not about to change her mind.

I couldn't think what else to say. I shrugged. 'Suit yourself.'

Victoria narrowed her eyes at me and headed for the door. As she turned the key in the lock, she looked back. 'If you do ever want more from a girl than fun in bed, you'll have to let her into your life, Daniel. Honestly, it's not that fucking difficult.'

Now she sounded angry. She headed down the steps, not

looking back.

Right, because it would be so fucking easy to explain just how sodding complicated my life really is. I stood in the middle of the room, my anger slowly building. As I heard the Mazda's engine start and tyres crunching on the gravel, I hurled my empty coffee mug into the sink. It smashed, startlingly loud.

Pointless destruction didn't change anything, of course. Except now I had to pick broken crockery out of the sink. At least that gave me something to do as I snarled inwardly at the unfairness of it all.

Dryads' sons in days gone by had simpler lives, no question. Five hundred years ago, I could have walked a hundred miles to start a new life. Wherever I ended up, chances are no one around would have travelled half so far in their lifetime. As long as I worked hard and kept to the straight and narrow, no one would have any cause to doubt whatever I said about my family or where I was born.

A hundred years ago, a man could travel from Warwickshire to Scotland and then go to Derbyshire and give himself a new name and story each time he moved. No one would be any the wiser, as long as he didn't give some official a reason to start asking questions. Victoria liked those programmes about celebrities tracing their ancestors or those solicitors who hunt out heirs when people die without a will. That sort of story came up time and again.

These days? I suppose I could lie to a girlfriend and say my parents were dead. So what would happen when I was caught sneaking around and telling lies to cover up phone calls to Dad? Cutting off all contact was out of the question.

If I told her the truth? Any ordinary girl would think I was deranged or deluded and that would just cause more trouble. Even if I convinced her to come and see the truth for herself, I couldn't imagine my mother agreeing to meet anyone outside our little family, not in her true guise. Taking human men as lovers was all very well, but she and her sisters had spent centuries avoiding unwelcome mortal attention.

If I could ever persuade my mum to show her true self to

a woman I loved, I'd have to be utterly certain that this girl-friend was always going to love me back. That she wouldn't betray us all if we broke up. I couldn't imagine ever being so certain.

So unless I found a partner willing to settle for what I was able to offer, it seemed my wildwood blood meant me living out my days alone. I tried to tell myself that wouldn't be so bad. I couldn't really believe it with the scent of Victoria's shower gel still hanging in the air.

I looked at the clock over the sink. It was only half past five. So I could sit here and feel sorry for myself until it was time to go to the Goose and eat on my own before coming back to my solitary bed, or...

Sod that. I had no need to wait until tomorrow to try finding Tila anymore. I rang The Grey Goose to cancel the table. Thankfully Jim answered the phone and 'Change of plans' was all the explanation he needed.

'Thanks for letting us know. Cheers.' He rang off.

As I was about to drive out of the yard, Chrissie Monkswell crossed the lane from the holiday cottages. She waved me to a halt, standing in the middle of the gateway so I couldn't drive past her. She made a winding-down-the-window gesture. Gritting my teeth, I did so.

'Is everything okay? What's happened? You said Victoria was staying the weekend but I just saw her leave?'

I'd managed to keep my temper with Victoria. Chrissie Monkswell had no such luck.

'What the fuck's it got to do with you?'

Chrissie took a startled step back. 'I only—'

'Just mind your own sodding business.' I revved the engine to drown out her indignant protests and drove away.

The crowds on the valley road had mostly disappeared, but a whole lot of coppers were still hanging around the mobile incident room parked in the lay-by. No great surprise there.

I kept driving. If there was still no sign of Tila in The Griffin this evening, I'd call home first thing tomorrow and ask if Mum had some advice on letting a dryad know I wanted to talk to her.

I didn't want to ring Dad tonight. He'd hear in my voice that something was wrong and I wasn't ready to talk about Victoria and me breaking up. Hell, I'd barely told him anything about her while we'd been seeing each other.

By the time I reached Lambton, the Saturday evening crowd was arriving at The Griffin. They looked even less appealing than the losers and chancers I'd seen the day before. Unsurprisingly this week's fresh crop of tourists were steering well clear, heading for The George on the far side of the marketplace instead.

I parked over that way. I wasn't going to risk leaving the Land Rover behind The Griffin for some sleaze to try his luck with its locks.

Walking across the cobbles, I tried to look through the pub's filthy windows. If Tila was inside, I'd go in. Then we could find somewhere quiet and she could tell me whatever she knew.

But she wasn't there, not that I could see. I thought about going inside for a better look around. If some prick tried picking a fight with me, I was still in a filthy mood. Landing a few good punches on someone who deserved a lesson in manners would be a lot more satisfying than smashing a coffee mug.

Satisfying but stupid. Coppers called to break up a bar fight never believe it's the shortarse bleeding on the floor who started all the trouble. I wouldn't be able to find Tila if I was spending the night in the cells.

Maybe she was out the back. I walked through The Griffin's car park, its tarmac littered with cigarette butts, to the playground beyond the trees. The air was sweet with pot smoke, and teenagers huddled on the swings and roundabout with cans of lager and cheap cider. They stared at me, wary and suspicious, but not about to get mouthy with someone my size.

I ignored them, looking beyond the benches over by the far wall to the field beyond. There was no sign of anyone, human or ethereal.

Maybe she'd come along later. There's a good Chinese takeaway a few doors up from The George, so I bought a special-fried rice and a couple of cans of Coke. I ate sitting in the Landy, keeping watch on The Griffin. Not what I'd had planned for Saturday night.

I gave some serious consideration to going to the supermarket and buying a bottle of whisky to take back to the farm with me. That would be one way to stop myself brooding. Except I couldn't afford anything halfway drinkable, and waking up with a hangover wasn't going to make tomorrow look any better.

There was still no sign of Tila by the time the church's floodlights switched themselves on. My phone chimed with a text from Victoria.

*Just got home. Thanks for being so understanding. Hugs*

I stared at the screen, trying to find a reply. The more I thought about the way she'd dumped me, the more pissed off I got. We might have had no long-term future, but I'd have been happy with another six months of good fun and better sex.

But it takes two to tango. I'd stayed with the girl who'd ended up screaming insults at me for months after I'd been ready to call it a day, just because she got so upset when I dropped my first hints about going our separate ways.

Finally I settled on three brief words for Victoria.

*Good to know.*

I hit send and then nearly dropped the phone when someone knocked sharply on my driver's door window.

I recognised the young constable who'd puked on his boots out in the woods on Thursday evening. Tonight he was all dressed up in hi-vis gear, ready to keep the peace when pubs started turning out.

I lowered the glass. 'What do you want?' I was in no mood for any more crap today.

'I could ask you the same thing, sir.' His chin jutted, belligerent. 'You've been sitting here for well over an hour.'

'So what?'

'You parked up here yesterday evening too.' He stared at me, clearly expecting me to justify myself.

He was going to be disappointed. I just shrugged.

'What about yesterday morning? You stopped to make a call from the phone box over there, very early.'

'How the—' I barely managed to stop myself swearing at him.

He smirked and gestured towards the bank on the far side of the square. 'CCTV, sir. Very useful. And no, there's no law against using a public call box, but we're on the lookout for anything out of the ordinary at the moment. I'm sure you understand, sir, what with two dead girls in the local woods.'

I took a steadying breath. Punching the sneer off his face would be a very stupid thing to do.

'I came to get a takeaway and I decided to sit here and eat it while it was still hot.' I waved a hand at the empty rice carton and two Coke cans on the passenger seat.

He nodded, smugly satisfied at getting an answer out of me. 'And Friday morning?'

Don't push your luck, sunshine, I thought. 'My mobile was out of battery. I wanted to check something with my dad.'

'That early?' He looked sceptical.

'We're a family of early risers,' I said tersely.

But would he follow up on that? Did I have to ring Dad and ask him to lie for me?

What about Crimestoppers? They said they kept all tip-offs anonymous, but were calls time-stamped when they reached the police? Was someone going to see that as well as the CCTV footage and put two and two together?

I reached for the ignition key. 'If that's all, officer, I'd like to go home now.'

He waited for a long moment before stepping back. 'Drive

safely, sir.'

I didn't bother answering. Resisting the temptation to take the valley route, I followed the main road. Being seen a couple of times on CCTV in Lambton was one thing. Being logged driving past a murder scene twice in one night was another.

Where the hell was Tila? Was she deep in the woods, still fascinated as the police searched for clues? Could she have upped and left, furious at this upheaval ruining the peace of her valley? Maybe she'd gone back to wherever she'd come from. That would be another kick in the teeth if she had. I hadn't had a chance to find out where that dryad grove might be.

But would a dryad abandon her beloved trees because a human died, even if it was a violent death? It would be a fleeting event by the standards of their long lives, and the first murder hadn't driven her away.

I'd ring home first thing in the morning. Mum would have something to say about that. I'd better remember to warn Dad as well, in case that keen little copper did ring up to ask about me phoning him. We'd better agree what the hell we were supposed to have been talking about.

Tense with exasperation by the time I got back to the flat, I fell into bed, only to toss and turn for what felt like hours before finally falling asleep.

# Chapter Eight

Someone shook me awake. Brutal fingers dug into my biceps, lifting me up from the mattress. I opened my eyes and yelled. The Green Man's leafy face was inches from my own, and the rich, earthy scent of the woodland filled the room. His emerald eyes bored into mine.

I went rigid with shock. I blinked and he was gone, letting me fall back onto the bed. I was gasping for breath as though I'd just run a mile, and my bitten leg was burning. As I reached for the cream on my bedside table, my hand shook so much I knocked it onto the floor. Swearing, I reached down to retrieve it.

At least that soothed some of the searing pain. It wasn't just my leg that was hurting though; my upper arms ached viciously. The half-light of the moon through the sloping skylight showed me bruises already darkening on the pale skin above my tanned forearms. The marks of gripping fingers.

This hadn't been a dream. The door to the living room was open and I knew for certain I'd closed it. Just as I knew beyond any possibility of doubt that the Green Man wanted me to go to Tila's wood. Right now. This minute. In the middle of the night.

My hands were still trembling as I reached for my phone. It was just after 3 a.m. Three in the morning or afternoon, I'd bet good money the police would still be guarding the woods. DS Tunstead wouldn't want the ghoulishly curious or some ambitious journalist sneaking around in the dark, destroying evidence or falling into that gully to break their neck.

The old barn's timbers creaked ominously all around me. It made me think of ancient trees battling a rising storm, and I sensed the Green Man's presence.

'All right,' I said aloud. 'Let me think.'

With any luck, the coppers on night duty would be

parked up in the lay-by and guarding the actual crime scenes. Patrolling through the trees by torchlight was asking for one of their own to break an ankle.

I could take a look at least, if I went the long way round, through Lambton and then back up the valley road as far as the hump-backed bridge. That was well short of the lay-by. I'd be able to see any lights in the trees from the water meadow. If there was no sign of any coppers, then I could cross the bridge on foot and cut straight across the grass.

'I'll go as far as the edge of the woods.' I looked around the dark room. Was there some unseen presence in the shadows, or was it just my imagination sending cold shivers down my spine? 'After that, it's up to you. Tell Tila where to find me.'

I'd have to think of some convincing story if I did encounter the police, especially after the run-in I'd had with that constable outside The Griffin. Staying in bed wasn't an option. If I ignored the Green Man, I would get another visitation, no doubt of that.

I threw back the duvet and dragged on my trousers and a sweatshirt. I found my boots without turning on a light and carefully negotiated the outside steps still in my socks. Then I realised trying to be stealthy was pointless. The Land Rover's engine was brutally loud in the night. The best I could do was get out of the yard as fast as I could, barely touching the accelerator to keep the revs low.

I switched on the headlights, taking the main road to Lambton. The marketplace was deserted and even the church floodlights were switched off. Did that mean CCTV cameras wouldn't be able to see me? Well, there was nothing I could do about that.

The narrow road through Tila's valley looked very different in the dead of night. Judging the distance to the bridge proved unexpectedly difficult, and I really didn't want to use my headlights' main beam. Anyone in the woods would know a vehicle was coming. Hell, if it wouldn't be asking for trouble from any police I met, I'd have just been using sidelights.

I slowed and pulled up a good way short of the bridge.

I got out of the vehicle. The night was silent and still. Not peaceful though; this felt like the ominous calm before a storm. I glanced up, expecting to see thickening clouds, but stars twinkled overhead.

The little river chattered in its stony bed, muted after weeks without rain. I looked towards the woodland, alert for any sign of torches. Nothing. Still tense, I crossed the ancient bridge and cut across the tussocky grass. Even with my dryad's blood, finding solid footing was tricky in the half-moon's light.

As I approached the trees, something rustled in the shadows. A fugitive breeze shifted the leaves, and I glimpsed a grimy, hairy flank.

The boggart scurried up the hill. I heard the stifled hiss of another. Until yesterday, I hadn't seen a single boggart in Derbyshire. Now they were everywhere.

I followed the vermin. Don't ask me why, or how, come to that. Smaller and swifter, they should have been able to outpace me. Ethereal, they left no tracks for me to follow. But tree branches kept parting to let the moonlight show them scuttling away. Tangling undergrowth hindered them at every turn and fork in the path. I heard them jabbering with increasing agitation. Was this the Green Man's work or Tila's?

A barren stretch of limestone suddenly offered them a clear escape route. They scrabbled up the stone and vanished over a shallow rise. I skirted the rock and halted, appalled.

Half a dozen boggarts shoved and jostled in the hollow behind the outcrop. They were all ripping into some carrion, cackling with relish. I swallowed sudden nausea. Perhaps it hadn't been slow decay or innocently foraging foxes and badgers that had stripped the flesh from those pathetic bones in the gully. Maybe the killer's fondness for these woods had drawn so many boggarts here.

I shuddered as I watched the gobbling creatures. What were they feasting on? Had this maniac killed again, sending a 'Fuck you' to the coppers by dumping another body right under their noses?

I dropped into a crouch and looked hastily around. There was no way I could talk myself out of handcuffs if the police caught me here in the dead of night, beside another corpse.

My sudden movement startled the boggarts. One looked up and squealed. Its shrieks panicked the rest. Clawing and biting each other, they fled the hollow. Now I could see what they'd been gnawing.

I choked on utter horror. Tila lay sprawled there, as ethereal as she'd been when I first saw her, now repellently defiled. Her glossy hair was tangled and dulled with dust. Gashes marred her pale brown arms and her hands were twisted and broken. She'd fought to save herself but her struggles had been in vain. Deep wounds ripped open her breasts and belly. Ravening bites tore at her thighs.

There's normally no colour by moonlight, even for humans with wildwood blood. Tonight though, the clouds parted to let the cold radiance show me every wound on Tila's ravaged body. Her flesh was the pale green of sapwood beneath freshly scored bark and her wounds glistened with golden ichor.

I knew that was the right word. Ichor. I found it in a library book when I was reading all the Greek myths I could find, after a teacher told us about Zeus pursuing woodland nymphs.

That's when I learned dryads aren't immortal. That was a nasty shock. Still, thanks to my mum's stories about her mother and sisters, I'd calculated a dryad lives for somewhere between a thousand and fifteen hundred years. Knowing my mother would outlive me became a very personal consolation. A reassurance I'd never told anyone about, not even my parents. Especially not my parents.

I can't say when I first realised other kids at school had grandfathers as old as my dad. But I remember when Andy's mum came into class in the middle of the day and took him home. Mrs Ryland said Andy's granny had died and we must all be very kind to him and his sister because they would be very sad. I think that's when I first realised my grey-haired and weather-beaten dad was going to die a lot sooner than anyone else's.

Death was no mystery to me, growing up in a nature reserve. What I feared first of all was losing his love and protection. As I grew older, I dreaded losing his friendship and all the wood lore and craft skills he could teach me. But I held on tight to the secret knowledge that my mother would never leave me. However long I might live, I would die before she did. Even though my mother had told me dryads could fade away if they were ever bereft of their trees, I knew that would never happen to her, in those protected woods.

I sure as hell had never imagined that a dryad could be murdered. Tila had died a violent death; that much was clear. Not killed by boggarts though. Her wounds gaped ragged-edged where the vermin had been scavenging, but a straight, sharp edge had made the fatal blows.

A knife? An axe? How? As soon as she felt the first wound, even caught unawares in her human guise, Tila could have vanished into thin air. Literally.

Any ethereal creature could do that. Once, out for an early morning walk, I'd seen a boggart eating a road-killed hedgehog. A van appeared unexpectedly. Panicked, the little beast ran full tilt into barbed wire. For a moment it hung there, skewered on twisted metal spikes with black blood trickling down its arms and legs.

In the next instant, the boggart disappeared. Once the van had passed by, it materialised in the ditch, looking this way and that. As it scurried back to its feast, I saw that its wounds were already healing. Mum explained how shifting to an ethereal state and back renews a supernatural creature's corporeal body.

So how could Tila be dead? What could possibly have cut her so deeply and so savagely? I looked at her body again. Her leaf-green eyes, half open, were now a withered autumn hue. Resinous amber scabs crusted her wounds where oozing ichor had dried and hardened. She'd been dead long before the scavenging boggarts found her, I slowly realised.

Was that why she hadn't turned up at The Griffin? Or had she died later on Friday night? Was that why the Green Man had visited me in that dream? If I'd come at once, could I have saved her? That thought was truly sickening. But how the fuck could someone kill a dryad? How had Tila died?

I don't know how long I crouched there with these questions chasing each other uselessly around in my head. Then a new thought hit me like a slap in the face.

The Green Man damn well knew. He owed me some answers. Standing up, I scanned every shadowed branch and leafy hollow for some sign of his presence. But no, he wasn't there. The trees which had so readily betrayed the boggarts stood motionless, aloof.

I needed some way to find him. Maybe something my mother knew could help. I needed to ring home first thing in the morning. Right now, I needed to get out of here.

I looked down at Tila's ravaged corpse again. My first instinct was to bury her, to deny her to those filthy scavengers. But the soil was parched and hard, and I only had my bare hands and a penknife. Besides, what would DS Tunstead and his coppers make of a fresh grave, even if they dug it up and found nothing inside?

I rubbed a hand over my stubbled chin. Had the man who killed those two girls murdered Tila as well? Did he know she could identify him? Had he seen her talking to me and butchered her to keep her quiet?

If so, that meant he could see a dryad in her ethereal form. That's how Tila had died, never mind what weapon he'd used. I felt sick. Did that mean the murderer was another dryad's son? Had I finally found someone who shared my heritage, only to discover a killer?

Had being able to see things no one else believed driven him mad? Keeping my own secrets was enough of a burden, forcing me to keep people at a distance, but at least I had Mum and Dad. How would I cope without their support? The thought of such loneliness left me hollow.

Was that why he'd slaughtered one of his mother's own kind? Was that what had enraged the Green Man?

One of the few things my mother told me about dryads'

sons was that they'd customarily banded together in her grandmother's grandmother's time. They called themselves Men of the Oak and often had dealings with the Green Man. She didn't know what had become of them by her own mother's lifetime. Much later on, I worked out these were probably the Celtic druids so ruthlessly exterminated by invading Romans.

I turned my back on Tila's corpse. I hated the thought of leaving her, but there was nothing I could do. If I was going to avenge her murder, I needed answers. I had to get back to the farm and ring Dad, where no one could overhear me.

I made my way back through the woods to the water meadow and cut across the rough grass. No shouting coppers shattered the silence. All I could hear was the reassuring flow of the river.

Reaching the road, I broke into a run. I had my keys in my hand before I was over the bridge. I started the engine and wrenched the wheel around, to drive back to Kympton the long way. I didn't want to go any deeper into Tila's valley tonight.

# Chapter Nine

The eastern horizon was pale with false dawn when I reached the farmyard. I turned off the engine and coasted silently through the gate to come to a halt beneath the barn.

It was still much too early to ring Dad. For the next hour and more I could only pace the flat, checking the time on my phone in the gloom. I didn't dare turn on a light, in case Sam Monkswell saw it on his way to morning milking.

I made a cup of coffee but barely drank half before the bitterness repelled me. Gradually the daylight strengthened. Finally I couldn't resist the urge to ring home any longer.

'Dad?'

'Daniel! Good to hear from you.'

I was surprised. He sounded as if he was expecting my call.

'Have you heard the news this morning?'

Of course. He always turned the radio on first thing.

'No.' My thoughts were so full of Tila, it hadn't occurred to me to switch on the laptop or telly. Her murder wouldn't make a headline. I was the only person who cared she was dead.

'They've identified the second dead girl. Can you see if there's anything more online?' Dad's never bothered solving the complications of getting a broadband connection out at the nature reserve. If he really needs to, he uses the computers at the local library.

'Give me a moment.' Holding the phone to my ear, I opened the laptop and booted it up. 'Okay, here's something. Effects found with the body...'

Thank fuck I'd made Tila put that handbag back. But that made me think of the way I'd seen her then, compared to her murdered corpse. I choked on unexpected grief.

'Dan? Are you okay?'

'Yes. No.' I drew a deep breath. 'Dad, the dryad I told you about—'

It took me several attempts to get the story out. As I fell silent, I could feel Dad's tension as clearly as if he were standing next to me.

'What do you think could have killed her?'

'I don't know.'

'Let me get your mother.'

A few moments later, her voice made me break down again.

'Your father told me what has happened. Oh, my dearest boy, I am so sorry.'

We weren't on a conference call. My mother can't use a phone. Holding anything with that much metal in it would cause her intolerable pain. But Dad has told me often enough how years ago he'd taken an old transistor radio into the woods to listen to some music as he spent a day hedging and ditching. My mother had been fascinated. More than that, she'd somehow sensed the radio waves in the air. She soon worked out how to tune into whatever she liked, mostly classical music but occasionally something more modern. She was very fond of folk songs, unsurprisingly.

This talent helped her to masquerade as a human woman after I was born. Other mums at the school gate might struggle to understand someone who never watched any telly, but the teachers could accept a parent who only listened to Radio 4 and Classic FM. Later on she discovered how to eavesdrop on mobile phones and join conversations with me and Dad.

At the moment grim silence hung in the air between us. I found a handkerchief in my pocket and wiped away tears and snot.

'Are you sure she was a dryad, not a hamadryad?' my mother asked eventually.

'She didn't say.'

'Did you ask?' Mum persisted.

'No.' I considered this possibility. Could Tila's death just be a tragic, ill-timed accident?

'Have you seen any trees felled locally?' Dad asked urgently.

He's read the same myths and legends as me. That's how we both learned a hamadryad is bound to a specific tree in a very different way to the tie that links dryads and their oaks. If a tree under a dryad's care is felled, that causes her pain and sorrow. But if a hamadryad's tree dies, so does she. Mum's never been able to explain it, and since it makes hamadryads even rarer than their dryad cousins, she can't recall encountering one since before her grandmother died.

I racked my brains. 'What are their trees? Oak, walnut, elm, fig...' Not that the last two would be growing around here.

'Vines and mulberry,' my mother reminded me.

'Black poplar and dogwood,' Dad concluded the list.

'There are poplars in the water meadow,' I said slowly. 'But hamadryads are bound to their trees at birth. Tila wasn't born in this valley. She said she'd come from somewhere else, to be on her own.'

'Any idea where from?' Dad asked, intrigued.

'No clue.' I was finding this explanation less and less likely. 'But if it's that simple, that her tree's just been cut down, why is the Green Man so agitated?'

'I don't know,' my mother admitted. 'No dryad can answer for him.'

'You're the only one who might get answers, if he ever lets you close enough,' Dad observed.

He's never had dealings with the Green Man himself, but he's never needed convincing of a mighty power deep within the greenwood. A power best not angered.

'I didn't understand when he tried to warn me. I didn't realise she was in danger.' Guilt got the better of me again, my throat tightening.

My phone beeped its low-battery warning. I was about to swear at it when a yawn cut me short. 'I'm sorry, I'm knackered.'

'You've been up half the night,' Dad pointed out. 'Listen, Dan. You can't blame yourself. You couldn't have got into those woods yesterday without ending up on the wrong side of the police. As for Tila, the chances are you couldn't have done anything to save her. You could well have ended up with a knife in your own guts.' His voice was rough with concern.

'Go to bed.' Mum's voice was warm with affection and unconcerned with might-have-beens. I didn't doubt her distress at Tila's death, but she's never understood humanity's obsession with ifs and buts. Dryads live in the here and now.

'Right.' I barely managed to get the word out before another jaw-cracking yawn overwhelmed me.

'Ring us when you've had some sleep. Who knows, maybe you'll learn something useful, if you see the Green Man in your dreams,' Dad offered.

If I did, I'd be grabbing hold of him myself, to shake some answers loose. 'Okay, I'll call you later.'

'Sleep well.' Dad rang off.

I'd been too wound up to even sit still before I'd spoken to my parents. Now I was barely able to put my phone on charge and strip off before I fell into bed. I didn't dream of the Green Man or Tila or the boggarts or anything else.

Insistent hammering on the flat's door startled me awake. Still half-asleep, I dragged on some underwear and hurried to answer it. There must be some emergency.

I had to shade my eyes with my hand to see DS Tunstead standing there in the bright sunlight. I glanced over my shoulder; the clock showed half eleven in the morning.

'Can I come in, sir?' he asked, expressionless. 'Just a few routine questions.'

'I suppose so.' Much as I wanted to, I couldn't think of any

96

good reason to refuse. Not without looking suspicious. 'I'll just go and get some clothes on.'

He surprised me with a grin. 'Shall I put the kettle on?'

'Okay.' As I headed for the bedroom, I wondered if he was playing good cop, bad cop all by himself. I also thought he should have someone with him to take notes. Otherwise, any dispute about who said what would come down to his word against mine.

What did he want to know? Had that little git of a constable told him about me keeping watch on The Griffin two evenings in a row? Had CCTV seen me driving through Lambton twice in the middle of the night?

I dressed as quickly as I could, had a pee and cleaned my teeth. My mouth tasted so stale that my breath was probably a criminal offence. When I went back into the living room, DS Tunstead had found mugs, coffee and sugar and was sniffing the milk from the fridge with the caution of a long-term single man. The kettle was just coming to the boil.

'How do you want it?' He put the milk down to pick up the coffee jar, spoon in hand.

'White, two sugars. Thanks.'

As he turned back to the counter, I glanced at the laptop. There was no sign that he'd opened it. If he had, he wouldn't have got very far, thanks to Chrissie Monkswell.

DS Tunstead carried the mugs over to the dining table and took a chair. I sat on the other side.

'You said you had some questions?' I prompted.

'Sam was saying you sell wood carvings at local craft fairs?' Tunstead raised his eyebrows enquiringly as he sipped his coffee.

I nodded. 'It's a sideline.'

'Can I see some of your work?'

'Sure.' I couldn't see why not.

I fetched the plastic toolbox from the top of the stack and opened it up to show him the little animals and carved studies of twigs and flowers in the top tray.

He picked out a long, smooth handle with a bulbous, deeply grooved end. 'What's this?'

'A honey dipper.' They always sold well.

He put it back carefully. 'One of my aunts had a wooden paperknife. God knows what it was made of, but she could cut parcel string with it. Do you ever make things like that?'

I shook my head. 'What was the wood? It would have to be something tropical if it was hard enough for any sort of cutting edge.'

'No idea. It was black, but I think it was stained with something.'

I caught a thoughtful glint in his eye. I took my time closing up the case of carvings.

'So,' he said, calculatedly casual. 'Warwickshire, Lanarkshire, quite a few other places. What brings you to the Peak District?'

I shrugged. 'I like to see new places, and I prefer the countryside to towns.' That was the truth, if not the whole truth.

He nodded at my arm. 'How did you get those bruises?'

I looked down involuntarily. The T-shirt I'd grabbed covered my upper arms, but of course, he'd have seen the marks left by the Green Man's grip when I opened the door, bare-chested.

'I stopped in Lambton on Friday night for something to eat and a drink after work. The George was heaving so I thought I'd try The Griffin. That was a mistake. It's a dump, and I was only in there five minutes before some tosser reckoned I was eyeing up his girl.'

So far, so truthful, mostly. Now for the lie.

'I was already leaving, but he wanted to make something of it. He grabbed me but I shook him off. He backed down quickly enough. I decided to go and eat at the Goose in Kympton instead.'

DS Tunstead was welcome to try proving or disproving that. Of course, anyone he asked in The Griffin would tell a different story, but that shouldn't be a problem. I'd bet good money that the regular lowlifes were well known to the police and equally well known to be liars.

He put down his mug. 'You get that sort of trouble a lot, do you?'

'Not if I can avoid it,' I said neutrally.

'You don't always manage to,' he observed. 'Suspended sentence for occasioning actual bodily harm plus a community order.'

I took a steadying breath before answering calmly. 'If you've checked up on me, you know I pleaded guilty even though I had mitigation. I did my community service by the book and I haven't been in trouble since. If you want to hear the full story, ask the Warwickshire police to put you in touch with Sergeant Fulbrook.'

Dave Fulbrook is one copper I do trust and respect. He's a lifelong friend of my dad's and he'd been on the team responding to the 999 call when Dad and I surprised half a dozen bastards digging into a badger sett on the nature reserve. Their dogs had already killed a pregnant sow, ripping her open to spill her guts and unborn cubs across the grass. Badger baiting.

As soon as Dad got on his mobile, most of the scum ran off, but one grabbed his spade and went for my dad. I got between them and took the spade off the prick. With the benefit of hindsight, that's where I should have stopped. Unfortunately I thumped him with it, good and hard. A broken arm put an end to his nonsense, but if I hadn't injured him I'd probably have got off with a caution.

Still, his screaming and swearing had thrown the others into a panic. My mum enlisted her trees, and what with one thing and another they were all still stumbling around in the woods when Dave Fulbrook and his lads arrived and nicked the lot of them.

'You've learned how to keep your temper, or just learned how not to get caught.' DS Tunstead was studying me closely, looking for a reaction. 'Will we find that tosser from The Griffin with two black eyes and a broken nose if we go looking? There are other cautions on file, when you've got into trouble in pubs.'

Trouble I'd never started, but there was no point me saying so. My word against the Police National Computer was no contest.

When I didn't answer, Tunstead leaned forward, his words clipped and cold. 'Mrs Monkswell says you went out in the middle of the night. She heard your vehicle sometime around three.'

'I couldn't sleep. I went for a drive.' I drank half of my coffee. 'I didn't think about the noise. I'll apologise to Sam and Chrissie for disturbing them.'

'Why couldn't you sleep?'

'With everything on the news? With half the county trying to get into that wood yesterday so they can say they've seen a murder scene?' I met his gaze, stare for stare. 'It's not exactly restful, knowing there's some maniac out and about, carving up young girls.'

'Who says they were carved up?' he demanded. 'We haven't released any details of their injuries.'

'Just a figure of speech.' I shook my head to cover my exasperation at being so stupid. I mustn't even hint that I knew what had happened. 'Isn't that what journalists mean when they talk about a frenzied assault?'

I did my best to stay relaxed, but I could feel my neck and shoulders tense. If he asked me why my Land Rover had been parked on the valley road last night, I couldn't think how to explain that.

He leaned back and pursed his lips, non-committal. 'If you ever see something suspicious when you're out and about at night, make sure you give us a ring.'

'Of course. Anything else?'

'Not at the moment.' He drained his mug and stood up. 'Thanks for the coffee. You're not the only one having trouble sleeping.' That sounded like a genuinely unguarded remark.

'I hope you catch the bastard, and quickly,' I said fervently as I followed him to the door.

If this murderer had killed Tila, he wouldn't find any dryads to slaughter locked up in high security for life. But I still wanted to know how he'd murdered her.

I stood at the top of the steps and watched Tunstead cross the farmyard. A police car and an unmarked vehicle were parked just inside the gate. Two more coppers came out of the farmhouse, a woman in a trouser suit and a man in uniform. I recognised the young constable who was so keen on checking CCTV.

Sam and Chrissie Monkswell followed, stopping by their front garden gate. Chrissie slid her arm around Sam's waist as the woman copper hurried over to Tunstead, flipping back the pages in a notebook.

She must have said something. They all looked up at me. No one was smiling. I waved a friendly hand and got no response.

Sam scowled and turned to go back into the farmhouse. Chrissie didn't go with him, heading for the cottages across the lane. I could see her anxious expression as she passed by the barn. I realised belatedly how bad all this could be for their business. Come to Derbyshire – we're on Crimewatch! I couldn't see the local tourist board using that as a slogan.

I closed the flat door. There was nothing I could do about Sam and Chrissie's problems. There wasn't anything else I could do, until I got some clue about the man who'd killed Tila. Once I knew for certain he'd killed those other girls, then I could decide what to do next.

I needed to find a way to contact the Green Man. I fetched the box of offcuts I hadn't found a use for and spent the rest of the day carving the Green Man's face out of lime wood.

I found it surprisingly easy. It was also distinctly eerie, looking into the empty eyeholes of the mask as I finished it. I half expected to see emerald light kindling. If it had, I'd have crapped myself.

I locked it in the plastic toolbox while I ate stale croissants for supper. When I went to bed though, I left it out on the dining table, forcing myself to leave the bedroom door ajar.

It didn't work. He didn't take the challenge. I slept through the night without dreaming, without stirring until the alarm woke me up.

Monday. A work day, and I needed the money. I dragged myself out of bed and headed for the barn conversions.

# Chapter Ten

During another long day up the scaffolding, every moment demanded conscious effort to concentrate on the job in hand. If I let my thoughts wander, I pictured Tila's dead body. Every time, I slowed to a halt as I asked myself yet again how someone like me could murder a dryad.

How could anyone with wildwood blood slaughter a creature so full of life and allure? I couldn't come up with any answers, any more than I could work out how I could possibly have saved her.

When I finally came down the ladder to sign off for the day, Phil Caister was assessing overall progress. Mick and Nigel had finished remortaring the stones around this barn's doors. The rest of the gang had been laying new floors in the other buildings.

'If we get Ryan and Lewis fixing roof battens tomorrow, can you keep an eye on them?'

The two lads were officially apprenticed as bricklayers, but Phil was always ready to use them wherever he needed a pair of hands.

'Fine with me.' I checked my watch and scribbled the time by my name on the clipboard.

Phil nodded, satisfied. 'Right. See you tomorrow.'

Outside, Lewis and Geoff were standing by their Transit's open doors, looking at the local paper.

Geoff glanced over. 'They've found out who that other dead girl is.'

'The second one,' Lewis added. 'The first one, I mean.' He showed me what looked like a school photo on the front page. 'Amber Fenham, confirmed by dental records.'

'Poor little cow,' Geoff said with a sigh. 'Runaway from Darlington. Last seen in 2001.'

Lewis shook his head. 'Leaving all that evidence. On Law

and Order—'

'Bugger that,' Geoff snapped. 'This isn't some bloody silly TV show. There's a family grieving for that girl.'

'At least they know what happened.' I could safely say that much. 'That's got to be better than wondering.'

Geoff grimaced. 'Every parent's nightmare.'

Lewis glanced warily at his dad. 'Wonder how she got here from Darlington.'

'I'm wondering how he knew that would be a good place to dump her,' Geoff said grimly. 'So she wouldn't be found in a hurry.'

'Let's hope the coppers catch the bastard. See you tomorrow.' I put my tools away and left.

As I drove out of the yard, I switched on the radio. The BBC was talking to a woman with a Geordie accent.

'... always said she'd go to London, every time she had a row with her mam. Hitch-hiking, A1 and M1. She had it all planned.' The speaker stifled a sob.

'That was Emma Wellfield, a school friend of the murdered girl, speaking earlier today,' a smooth-voiced Scot explained. 'In a statement, Derbyshire police said it's too soon to know if there's any connection between Amber Fenham's death and the murder of Shevaun Thomson, whose body was discovered in the same area of woodland last week. Detectives have appealed to the public for their help.'

Hearing DS Tunstead's strained voice, I guessed he hadn't got much sleep last night either.

'Whether or not their deaths are connected, we need to find out what happened to both these young girls. Please look carefully at their photographs. If you remember seeing either of them, maybe on a bus or at a railway station or a motorway services, please contact us on—'

I switched off the radio so I could concentrate, casting my mind back to my conversation with Tila as I drove. She hadn't said she'd seen the dead girl in The Griffin, had she? Just the killer. So where had he met Shevaun Thomson?

Picking up runaways made more sense than chatting up local girls in The Griffin. Any number of witnesses there might remember the two of them together. Selling stolen goods, skunk and smack in the dark corners of the car park was one thing, but murder was something else. Someone would point the finger, if only for the money from Crimestoppers.

If the killer only drank in The Griffin, did that mean he was a local? I'd seen for myself how the dump hardly welcomed newcomers. I thought about what Geoff had said. The killer had picked that valley to dump two victims. He knew where to go.

Were there more bodies hidden among those rocks and trees to give DS Tunstead sleepless nights? Was that why the bastard killed Tila? To stop her showing me more corpses holding clues for the coppers? Though that still didn't explain how he'd managed to kill her.

I thumped the steering wheel, frustrated. A moment later, I realised I'd left Lambton so deep in thought that I'd been driving on autopilot. Now I was heading up the lane to the wooded valley. Great. Some helpful copper could tell DS Tunstead my Land Rover had been seen passing through yet again.

A Škoda was so close to my exhaust that I couldn't simply swing around and head back to Lambton to take the main road instead. I scanned the verges for somewhere to pull off so the Škoda could go past.

Instead, I saw the Green Man like I'd never seen him before. Bushes along the roadside shaped themselves into his frowning face. As I looked up at the trees, his dark gaze fixed on me, accusing. I sensed his anger in the quaking branches. Birds arrowed across the road, fleeing the eerie commotion. I barely avoided braking so hard the Škoda rear-ended me.

As soon as we reached the straight stretch of road leading up to the bridge, I slowed down, indicating I was about to pull onto the churned-up verge. No copper could accuse me of driving without due care and attention.

The Škoda driver veered around me and sped away.

There were no other cars parked today. Morbid curiosity was weekend entertainment, but Monday meant other priorities. The TV vans had gone as well, headed to Nottingham or Darlington to set up in front of grieving families' houses as journalists tried to unravel the dead girls' fates.

I sat there, breathing hard. Whatever the Green Man wanted with me, I had questions for him. But when I looked at the trees now, there was no sign of his presence. Just sunlit summer woodland.

Remembering my conversation with Mum and Dad, I opened the glove box and got out the binoculars I kept there. I searched the edge of the woods for any sign of trees recently fallen or felled. If Tila was a hamadryad the Green Man might want something done about the witless woodcutter who'd killed her.

No. This was ancient woodland, untouched for decades. I realised that was another argument for the killer being a local man. He'd know there was no danger of a working forester finding his victims.

I used the binoculars to study the black poplars along the river bank, adjusting the focus for a clearer view of the gnarled trunks bristling with thickly leaved branches. There was no sign that anyone had cut those back recently. Besides, pollarding wouldn't kill a poplar. The whole point of old-style woodland management was keeping the central trunk alive so the shoots and branches would grow back and be harvested year after year.

These poplars had suffered, left to their own devices. Three had been felled by wind and weather, though some broken branches had rerooted themselves in the dark soil. Others hadn't been so lucky. Several trunks were split all the way from the old pollard's crown down to exposed roots clawing at the river bank. Green leaves still crowned them, but black rot was consuming pale, exposed wood from the inside out. That was a shame. Poplar's nice to work with, good for decorative pieces.

Something crossed my field of view, an indistinct blur. I lowered the binoculars and saw a woman standing by the bridge. After a moment's confusion I recognised her. She'd been in the crowd at the water meadow.

I hadn't heard an engine. I looked up and down the road. No sign of another vehicle. As I looked back, she folded her arms and angled her head with unmistakeable expectation. She was wearing the same blue jeans and green T-shirt and they still looked good on her. Would the local knife-wielding nutter agree?

I got out of the Land Rover. 'Do you want a lift?'

'No, thanks.' She looked at me intently.

I glanced up and down the road again. 'Are you waiting for someone?'

She smiled, oddly amused. 'Yes.'

I weighed my keys in my hand. 'Do you want me to wait with you?'

She stuck her hands in her pockets, smiling. 'Why?'

I couldn't see the joke. 'Because some maniac is murdering girls in these woods.'

'I know all about him.' Now she stared at me, unblinking. 'The police won't be able to stop him.'

I clenched my fist so hard the keys bit deep into my fingers. There are some notorious killers you just can't help knowing about. The Moors Murderers. Fred and Rosemary West. Where they say the victims didn't realise they were in danger because a woman approached them first.

The back of my neck crawled and I heard leaves rustle behind me. I turned quickly, in case some accomplice was creeping up on me. I was such a fool; the Green Man was warning me to stay out of the woods. I'm big and I'm strong but if there were two of them—

'I thought you'd want to know that he buried Tila.'

'What?' I spun back around.

'The Green Man. He buried her.' The woman blinked, and even with the distance between us, I saw her eyes momentarily veiled with sparkling turquoise. 'Would you like to know where?'

I could barely catch my breath. 'Do you know who killed her? Did the same man kill those other girls?'

She considered her reply for an agonisingly long moment. 'Yes. He killed them all.'

'Why can't the police stop him?'

'Because he's one of us.'

'What do you mean?' I took a step forward. 'What is he?'

I wondered what she was. Not a dryad, that was certain.

'A wose.' She glowered. 'Now he's got a taste for blood, he won't stop. Not unless you stop him.'

'What the fuck's a wose?' I stared at her, bemused. 'Something out of Winnie the Pooh?'

'How's your leg?' she asked instead. 'Be thankful for your mother's blood. Without that, you'd be in hospital by now. Though of course, that means the boggarts know that you have greenwood kin.'

'What do—?'

The sound of a distant engine interrupted me. I looked down the lane towards Lambton. I really didn't want to be parked here if a cop car was coming.

For the moment, the road was still empty. I turned back. 'Who are you? How—'

She was gone, and the vegetation around me was thrashing wildly again. I didn't need the Green Man to warn me twice. I drove away.

By the time I got back to Kympton, I'd realised I'd met a naiad. The mysterious woman must be a water spirit, linked to the stream cutting through the valley. Though I couldn't remember much about them from my reading. I vaguely recalled asking my mum sometime or other, but she'd simply said there were no naiads where we lived, and that had been the end of that.

Why hadn't Tila mentioned her? Then again, why should Tila say anything about a naiad? She'd been more concerned about the dead girls. But why the hell hadn't Tila told me the killer was an ethereal being? Or had she just assumed I'd see his nature for myself, when she guided me to him? She'd never met a dryad's son before, I reminded myself. There was no saying what she thought I could and couldn't do.

At the moment, I couldn't do much. Though I did remember the thing in Winnie the Pooh was a woozle.

When I reached the farm, I headed straight up to the flat. Chrissie Monkswell and her cleaner were chatting by the farmhouse, but I pretended I hadn't seen her wave. I didn't have time for them at the moment.

I called Dad on my mobile and opened up the laptop. As I waited impatiently for him to pick up, something jogged my memory. Tolkien. He'd used 'wose' as the name for an old secretive race living in Middle Earth's woods.

Ever since I first read The Lord of the Rings, I've been curious about Tolkien and trees, and not just because of the Ents. Was there a dryad's son among his ancestors? Did that inspire the woodlands in his writing, from the safe and serene to the murky and menacing? He had family in Warwickshire, after all.

I typed in the word, looking for a fuller explanation. Wood wose. Wild man. An ominous figure in mythology all across Europe, as far back as the Ancient Greeks. Human in form but bestial and covered in hair.

Derived from travellers' tales of encountering gorillas? I didn't think so, and certainly not in Derbyshire. As usual, finding anything useful among the masses of irrelevant stuff online would be a challenge.

Dad answered my call. 'Dan. How's things?'

'Work's fine.' That was enough normal conversation for today. 'I just met a naiad.'

'Really?' His voice rose with interest.

'I'm sure that's what she was, and she said that a wose is killing those girls. Is Mum around?'

'She'll be somewhere close.'

I heard the background noises change as Dad walked out of the house.

'Daniel?' Mum's voice cut through the birdsong.

'I met a naiad today.' I told them how the Green Man had brought me to a halt by the hump-backed bridge.

'He was warning you to leave,' Mum said sharply. 'Naiads are dangerous. Stay well away.'

'She wanted to tell me the Green Man had buried Tila,' I protested. 'She offered to show me where.'

'To lure you off the road,' Mum retorted. 'To get you closer to her stream. If she can persuade you to touch the water, she'll drown you there and then.'

I didn't know what to make of her unexpected hostility. 'She said that a wose is killing these girls. She said that it killed Tila.'

The stillness as Dad and I waited was broken only by a thrush's carefree trills far away in Warwickshire.

'A wose can be a fearsome thing,' Mum said doubtfully. 'But naiads lie,' she added with swift contempt. 'You cannot trust a word they say.'

I couldn't recall when I'd last heard her so vehemently set against anyone. What had a naiad ever done to her? This wasn't the moment to ask. 'What exactly is a wose?'

Mum was more than happy to change the subject. 'They are strange and solitary creatures. Where we thrive in sunlight and lend our strength to life and growth, they are attuned to the darker depths of old forests. They used to cherish the hunting beasts which lived there, from the martens to the wolf and the bear. As humanity spread through the wildwood, the woses became more ferocious. They were guardians of the thickets and crags where such creatures laired and whelped. As mankind pursued the hunting beasts more savagely, tales spread through the trees of woses driving intruders mad. Senseless with fear and rage, huntsmen would turn their swords and arrows on each other. The trees say a wose once killed a king, the one they called Rufus.'

'William the Conqueror's son.' I remembered visiting the Rufus Stone in the New Forest.

'That caused a bitter rift between my kind and those

dwelling in the dark woods. But that's a far cry from murdering young women,' she said firmly. 'My mother spoke of a wose who guarded our woods when she was young. A ruler of the men who dwelt here said that all the maidens within his domains were his to take out of lust, as of right.'

Her disapproval rang clearly through the miles between us. For dryads, sex is a gift to be given, never demanded, or worse, coerced. Woe betide any over-eager youth who tried to force his way past a girlfriend's protests in my mother's woods.

Mum was still speaking. 'This petty king would rape young girls and discard them, sometimes living, more often dead. He and his men pursued one who fled deep into the forest, so the wose bade the oak trees shed their boughs to block the king's path. My mother said the falling branches killed the king and his men. One of my aunts told a different story. She said that the wose himself fought the king, challenging him to trial by combat. When the mortal was defeated, the wose executed him and his men for their crimes. Either way, the trees remember how that hunting party never left the wildwood, while they showed the girl her way safely home to her family.'

'Are there any woses still lurking here?' Dad didn't like the sound of this and I didn't blame him, even though, like me, he must have worked out that regal rapist must have been a king of Mercia before the Normans landed at Hastings.

'I haven't heard the trees tell of a wose since the battles for and against the king's son,' Mum assured him. 'As the slaughter moved on, the woses followed. None have ever returned.'

No wonder she'd never mentioned woses to my dad if she hadn't seen one since the English Civil War. We both knew which king she meant. Charles II is one of the few human historical figures who interests my mother. She has always insisted that he couldn't have hidden in the Boscobel oak without a dryad's help. He was also six feet tall in an age when the average man was so short that 'two yards high' was the most notable detail on his 'Wanted' posters. I've often wondered about wildwood blood in his family tree.

I frowned as I considered what my mother had said. 'But these girls weren't intruders. He brought them to this valley deliberately. Tila said he tormented them for fun. He let them run and then he chased them, cutting them when he caught them. Then he let them go, to hunt them and hurt them again.'

'Dear God!' Dad was revolted.

'That hasn't been in the news,' I said quickly. 'Don't let on that you know.'

I heard Dad suck his teeth.

'The police still have their eye on you? Perhaps you should come home for a while. Till all this blows over.'

I decided against telling him about DS Tunstead's Sunday morning visit. 'If I leave, how many more girls will this thing kill?' I asked instead. 'How are the police supposed to stop it? They have no idea what they're dealing with.'

'How are you going to stop it?' Dad shot back.

'I don't know.' I was forced to admit it. 'Mum, have you ever heard of a wose being killed?'

'No, never, and do not trust this naiad to help you,' she added with swift venom. 'Stay away from her. Promise me, Daniel.'

'I don't think I can do that,' I protested. 'She's the only one who seems to know—'

I realised I was talking to dead air. Was Mum so angry with me that she'd ended the call? I'd wanted to ask her about the boggarts and see if she had any advice about my leg. I redialled my dad. His phone rang unanswered until it went to voicemail. I didn't leave a message. I couldn't think what to say.

# Chapter Eleven

Before I could make any sort of plan, I needed more information. Unfortunately a whole evening searching Internet backwaters and blind alleys didn't give me anything useful. I needed books. Those slender volumes of local supernatural goings-on, stories about ghosts and apparitions handed down through the generations. It didn't matter how out of date they were. In some ways, the older the better. Victorian folklorists and antiquarians happily repeated the tallest tales and wildest speculation.

I knew I wouldn't find what I wanted in the local charity bookshop. That had paperback popular science books and the occasional thriller to interest me, but not much else. A quick search for local second-hand bookshops looked promising until I saw their prices. I'm sure they were only charging the going rate but that was still way beyond my reach, especially when I didn't know which books would tell me what I needed.

I needed a library. The Net is great when you know what you're looking for. Libraries are where to find what you didn't realise you needed to know. I tried a new search for local public libraries, more in hope than expectation given recent council cuts.

Surprisingly, Lambton still had a branch library. Better still, its late-opening night was Tuesday. I could stop off there after work tomorrow, or rather, later today. Realising it was after midnight, I headed for my bed. To my relief, I slept dreamlessly, though my bitten leg roused me momentarily every time I rolled over.

Another long, hot day working on the barn conversions dragged endlessly. I kept checking my watch. My leg ached vilely and that didn't improve my temper. At least fixing battens to roof trusses wasn't overly demanding. Nail gun in hand, I could do that on automatic pilot as I wondered what

I might find in Lambton Library. It wouldn't be up-to-date scholarship deconstructing the anthropological basis of legends, but that wouldn't be a problem. I wanted local lore.

If Mum wasn't going to help, I wanted something to help me ask the naiad the right questions to find out what she knew. Assuming I could find her again. That was one useful thing about dryads. Once you knew their favourite trees, you could pretty much guarantee finding them close by, even if you had to wait a while before they noticed you. But I had no idea how far a naiad's home waters went.

I realised I couldn't hear any hammers. Lewis and Ryan were nowhere to be seen. Slacking off again, and I hadn't even noticed them go. I looked down the scaffolding, into the dark barn. To my relief, they were climbing back up, boasting about PlayStation exploits.

'Where've you two been?' I demanded.

'Run out of clout nails.' Lewis had a fresh bagful in one hand.

'Get to work. No, not together. Down the end, Lewis, and Ryan, you work over there.' I scowled at Ryan, who was definitely the one leading Lewis astray. Not that Geoff's lad was off the hook.

After spending the rest of the morning forcing the pair to focus on the job, I was in a sour mood by lunchtime. I got my sandwiches and headed for the chairs under the shady tree. Sitting down, I fought an urge to scratch my itching leg.

'You all right, Daniel?' Tony's enquiry surprised me.

'Yes, fine,' I said curtly. 'Why do you ask?'

He shrugged. 'No reason.'

Nigel looked up from his newspaper. 'Got something on your mind?'

I could hardly tell him I was trying to find an ancient malevolent wood spirit abducting and murdering young girls. A mythical tree nymph was going to tell me what she knew about the murders, but unfortunately she's dead too. Now I have absolutely no idea if the river maiden I've just met wants to help me or drown me.

'No,' I said curtly.

'Suit yourself.' Nigel went back to his paper.

I signed out promptly at five-thirty and packed up my tools without stopping to chat. I was out of the barnyard's ramshackle gate before the others had unlocked their vans.

Turning on the radio, I heard the police repeat their appeal for any sightings of the murdered girls at motorway service stations. A woman copper was speaking.

'We've now confirmed reports that Shevaun Thomson was seen at the south-bound Woodall services on the M1 in Yorkshire on the eighth of July. At the moment, this is the last known sighting of her alive. We very much want to know where she went after that, where she spent her last few days.'

'That's Detective Constable Katherine Redmire—'

I turned off the radio as the female presenter with an attractive hint of an Asian accent repeated all the contact details.

Lambton's Market Square was still busy with shoppers and tourists. I circled in hopes of a parking space and saw a woman with three children in tow heading for a people carrier. Pulling up and indicating to stake my claim on her space, I waited as she strapped the kids into their seats.

I contemplated The Griffin. If the naiad was no use, could anyone in there shed some light on the man I was looking for? What would persuade some local low-life to share a likely suspect's name or address? Money, most likely, but I had none to spare.

A few early drinkers had arrived. I frowned and focused more closely on one man standing by his open car door. Markedly shorter than me, and his middling brown hair could do with a trim. He wore a long, dark leather jacket, which was odd given the heat.

He was talking to a young woman, a slender teenage girl in cut-off denim shorts and a skimpy, strappy white top. Dark straight hair brushed her shoulders in the same sort of style I'd seen in Shevaun Thomson's and Amber Fenham's school photos.

I watched the man walk around the clapped-out Ford to open the front passenger door. He was gesturing to the girl. He fitted Tila's description of the killer, for whatever that might be worth.

An impatient horn sounded behind me. The mum driving the people carrier was heading out of the car park. If I didn't take that empty space, I'd lose it. I quickly pulled in and ignored an insulting gesture from a Toyota driver.

The girl in the denim shorts was walking away from The Griffin, heading towards the newsagent. The dented and rusted Ford was still in the car park, though the bloke in the leather jacket was nowhere to be seen.

Was this how it was going to be? Me watching everyone suspiciously, imagining the worst, with no proof and no way to find out if I was right or wrong, until another dead girl hit the headlines? That would just leave me wondering what the hell I'd missed, or what I could have done to save her. The police had no hope of stopping these killings if the murderer really was a wose.

I headed for the library. As I reached the steps, I stopped dead, struck by sudden realisation. That man in The Griffin car park couldn't have been the killer. Not if the naiad was telling the truth. Even if a wose could manifest in a human form, he would still be an ethereal being. There was no way he would get inside a car, voluntarily enclosing himself in steel. He sure as hell couldn't drive a vehicle.

'Excuse me, young man.' A perplexed pensioner waved a hand.

'Sorry.' I got out of his way.

Inside the library, I had to fill in a form, and the librarian looked dubiously at my driving licence when she noted the Scottish address.

'I should get that updated if I were you.'

'I will,' I assured her.

'You'll get your library card by post within seven days.'

'Can't I borrow some books now?'

'Yes, of course.' She glanced at the clock. 'We close at seven.'

That gave me long enough to look through their modest myth and folklore section. I read a few pages here and there and picked out the books likely to be most useful. The library also had a good selection of Ordnance Survey maps, including the sheet covering Tila's valley at 1:25,000 scale. I spread it out on an empty table and studied the river's course upstream and down. Not that there was any helpful symbol for 'Here Be Naiads'.

'Good evening. The library will close in ten minutes.'

The announcement surprised me. I hadn't realised how quickly the time had gone. I gathered up my books and got them issued at the desk.

Back at Kympton Grange Farm, I ate smoked salmon sandwiches, careful not to leave fishy fingerprints as I sat at the table and leafed through my library books.

I closed the last one and leaned back, easing my stiff shoulders. Tales of scary things in dark forests went back long before Roman times. Apparently wood woses were one possible origin of the werewolf myth. That was unnerving, given everything going on around here.

My mug of tea was long since stone cold, but I drank it anyway, wondering about the naiad. Plenty of myths link supernatural women with rivers and lakes. Very few do anything as useful as handing out magic swords to once and future kings. Generally mortal men who encountered naiads or their like came to a very bad end. The stories mostly involved treachery as well as seduction. No wonder my mum had warned me.

What did this naiad have to gain by trying to convince me this killer was a supernatural creature? He couldn't be, if DS Tunstead was right and this killer was hunting for prey among the runaways hitching between motorway services. With any luck, the police would soon find out who'd picked up Shevaun Thomson and make a solid case against him. Assuming Tila was right, and the same bastard had killed both girls, that would be that. The killer would be locked up.

It wouldn't matter if Amber Fenham had died too long ago for the coppers to get him for that murder too.

If DS Tunstead was right. That was the key. If he wasn't, if the naiad was telling the truth, then the police had no hope of catching this killer. And I still couldn't see how an ordinary, mortal psychopathic slasher could have killed Tila. He wouldn't even know she was there, still less that she'd told me he was slaughtering innocent girls.

I drummed my fingers on the table. If the naiad expected me to do something about a murderous wood wose, we needed to talk. That would surely be more important than getting me close enough to her river to drown me, with all due respect for these myths and my mum's mistrust.

Which brought me back to the same problem I'd had with Tila. I had no clue how to contact the naiad. I didn't even know her name. I certainly wasn't going back to the hump-backed bridge, to hang around near two murder scenes for no good reason I could give a copper.

Staring across the room as I racked my brains for an answer, I saw my lime wood carving of the Green Man. That hadn't drawn him into my dreams. Well, perhaps I could make another use of it.

I went online, to check what I thought I remembered from the maps in the library. Yes, there was a curve in the main road before the junction, which drew close to the river upstream from Tila's woodland. There was even a viewpoint where tourists could park and admire the scenery.

I picked up my car keys, my phone and the carving, and checked the time. Half nine. That was okay. If anyone asked, I'd just say I'd gone to the Goose for a quick pint. Actually, that was a good idea.

With the route clear in my mind, it didn't take long to get to the river. A shallow crag overlooked the stony stream. I couldn't tell if the slope below the road had been deliberately cleared or if the soil was too shallow for anything to take root. Either way, I made my way down to the water's edge easily enough.

I flicked my wrist and sent the wooden mask skimming into the river. Now it was up to the naiad to work out what my message meant. Or maybe the Green Man would tell her where to find me, or he could show me where she was, if he was so keen to involve me in this. I'd give it half an hour and then I'd go for a beer.

Five minutes. Ten. Waiting was no hardship, listening to the quiet music of water over stones and the murmur of a breeze in the trees. The night was fragrant with summer and I felt the stresses of the day drift away.

By ten o'clock I'd given the naiad long enough. I climbed back up to the road and headed for The Grey Goose. As I was pulling into the car park, my night took a very different turn. Headlights carved a bright arc through the night. A vehicle shot past the pub sign so recklessly I had to stamp on my brakes to avoid a collision.

Stalling the Land Rover, I was startled to recognise the dented and rusted Ford from The Griffin. Cars like that stand out among all the silver-grey super-minis and hatchbacks. I also saw that the leather-jacketed driver had a passenger.

The dark-haired girl was in the back seat and she was struggling with the door. She wanted to get out, now the driver had been forced to slow. He accelerated and the car swept past. I saw him raise a fist. As the desperate girl tried to grab his arm, he smacked her in the face with a vicious backhand.

Cursing, I restarted the engine and hauled on the steering wheel. Circling the Goose's sign as tightly as I could, I put my foot down. I took the bends along the unlit lane as fast as I dared, and soon saw the Ford's tail lights ahead.

I accelerated, getting close enough to read the Ford's number plate and committing it to memory. DS Tunstead had asked me to report any cause for concern. I could do that, even if I saw this arsehole drop the girl off wherever she lived and drive away. I'd witnessed Leather Jacket as-saulting her. I'd say so on oath or under caution or whatever they wanted. That should be enough to get the police to take a closer look at him. If this was the killer, then everyone's problems would be over.

The Ford turned into the lane running through Tila's valley. After a short distance, Leather Jacket pulled off the tarmac. His red lights bumped along a track so narrow I hadn't even registered it before.

I switched off my headlights and followed. There was just enough moonlight to show me the way. Trees pressed so close on either side that twigs scraped both doors. Thankfully sturdy tyres and Land Rover suspension made light work of the rutted ground.

The Ford stopped in a dank clearing, headlights dimming. The driver got out. As I pulled up, I saw him grin with feral glee as he opened the rear door and dragged the girl bodily out of the vehicle. He twisted a hand in her black skirt, fabric stretching as he yanked it down, revealing her pale knickers.

She fought to pull herself free, fists flailing, screaming defiance. He used her skirt to pull her feet out from under her and she sprawled on the leaf mould, trying to kick him but hampered by her skirt round her ankles. High heels might have done some damage, but she'd already lost one strappy sandal.

He grabbed her bare foot and twisted her leg to turn her face down in the dirt. Now he ripped her skirt right off and grabbed at her underwear. She was fighting to get her hands and knees together, but he still had hold of her foot, forcing his boot between her thighs.

I flicked the Landy's headlights on and was halfway across the clearing before he realised someone was coming for him.

'Hey, fuckwit!'

# Chapter Twelve

Leather Jacket froze like a rabbit in the headlights, letting go of the girl's foot. 'Who the fuck are you?'

Seizing her chance, the girl scrambled away. Leather Jacket rounded on her, slamming her into the Ford with a brutal kick to the stomach. Stunned, she collapsed, loose-limbed and retching.

The bastard tried to run away down the track, deeper into the woods. I went after him, taller, faster, stronger. When I got within a stride of him, I grabbed his collar, hauling him backwards. Thrashing, he managed to slip free of the jacket. That didn't do him much good. Unbalanced, he went sprawling.

I kicked him in the ribs. Let's see how he liked that. If I'd been wearing my work boots, that would have been the end of things. He rolled away from my trainers, cursing me for a cunt. Quicker than I expected, he was back on his feet

Stepping in close, I punched hard and fast. One fist to his gut, the other to his unshaven face. He reeled backwards and I hit him again, ignoring the pain in my hands. This was worth cracking a knuckle.

He swung for me but he didn't have the reach to make contact before I dropped him with a tackle that would get me sent off any rugby pitch. We fell together, landing hard. My weight crushed the breath out of him. All fight gone, he lay limp and wheezing.

What now? Knocking someone unconscious with a punch might look easy in the movies, but I didn't want to try it. I wished I could remember more about the use of reasonable force in defence of self or others.

Screw it. I got to my feet and kicked him in the balls. He'd barely recovered enough breath to squeal as he curled up around his agony. Fine by me. I grabbed a handful of his greasy hair and dragged him back to his car. He reeked, his body and clothes unwashed for who knows how long.

'It's all right. I've got him,' I called out as I hauled the bastard across the clearing.

The girl didn't answer. She was huddled on the ground, hugging her knees, her sobs on the edge of hysterics.

I threw the bastard in the Ford's back seat. He screeched as I slammed the door on his trailing leg. I caught the handle as it bounced, and he managed to drag his foot inside before I shoved the door closed.

I took the keys out of the ignition and locked the car. I guessed he'd engaged the child locks on the rear doors, which was why the girl couldn't get out. Still, between that kick in the nuts and whatever damage the door had just done to his leg, hopefully he wouldn't be climbing into the front seats to get out any time soon. By then the police should be here.

'I'm going to call 999.' I backed off to put some distance between me and the sobbing girl.

I wanted to offer a hand, to get her to her feet, maybe even put a comforting arm around her shoulders, to promise she was safe. But I remembered the rape crisis leaflets my Glasgow tutor had insisted all her students read, male and female alike. The last thing this girl needed just now was someone my size looming over her. I knew I was a good guy, but she had no reason to think that.

I'd been in my last year at secondary school when I first realised that girls who didn't know me would cross to the other side of the road if they saw me on a dark street late at night when there was no one else around. At the time it made me furious. Since then I've seen for myself how creeps won't take no for an answer when a woman has caught their eye. They have a lot in common with the tossers who won't back down from starting a fight. None of them come with 'arsehole' helpfully tattooed across their foreheads.

So I gave the girl some breathing room. She needed trained, professional care. I found my phone, my hand shaking as the adrenaline drained away. No signal.

'Fuck,' I spat, infuriated.

The girl flinched, her face still buried in her arms.

'Sorry.' I shoved my phone back in my pocket. 'There's no mobile reception.'

I looked into the Ford. The would-be rapist was still curled up, eyes closed, both hands cradling his aching balls.

I didn't think he was faking. I wasn't about to leave him here with the girl though, while I went in search of a phone signal. I tried to think of viable options. I could offer to drive her to the police, or at least as far as we needed to go to call 999. That would be asking a hell of a lot though, after what had just happened, expecting her to get into a stranger's car.

Then I remembered the mobile incident room, parked in the lay-by further down the road. If there weren't any police on duty in the middle of the night, there'd be a phone signal and the coppers would know exactly where to find us when I told them what had happened.

As long as I had his keys, Fuckwit couldn't drive away. If he did recover enough to head off through the woods before the police arrived, DS Tunstead could call up dogs to track him. They could get a scent off his stinking jacket.

When I went to fetch it, I felt the solid square of a wallet in a pocket. Good. Even if he did run off, the coppers would know who he was. DS Tunstead could send his minions to grab the bastard the instant he turned up at home. If he was stupid enough to go home.

First things first. I had to persuade the girl to come with me, assuming she could walk that far in her night-out sandals. She was still sitting hunched up on the ground, her shoulders shaking as she wept.

'There's a police van further down the road. It's a bit of a walk, but hopefully there'll be someone there.' I tried to sound reassuring. 'Or I can drive you. Whatever you want, really. We don't have to do anything until you're ready. Here's your skirt.' I threw it carefully to land just in front of her.

She didn't look up. I couldn't see any sign that she'd even heard me through her crying. Okay, I'd just have to wait, however long it took.

I glanced at the Ford. Fuckwit was still motionless on the back seat. For want of anything better to do, I decided to take a look in his wallet. Getting it out of an inside pocket released a gust of stale body odour, and I dropped the stinking jacket to the ground.

He had a few creased receipts and a couple of credit and debit cards. Apparently he was J. Raynott. I was about to see if a different card gave his first name when I took a second look at the one in my hand. The expiry date was 2008. Puzzled, I checked the rest. A couple were valid till 2009 and one was 2010, but none were any later than that. I couldn't make out any detail on the faded receipts, so I went to get a better look in the Land Rover headlights. The few dates I could see were all from 2008 as well.

Why the hell was he still carrying them around? It barely takes a month before I'm sick of the wad of receipts in my wallet; then I sort out the ones I send to Dad for the accountant who does my taxes and bin the rest. Not my problem. I closed the wallet and shoved it in my pocket. Though I'd wait to pick up that rancid jacket until the girl was ready to go to the police.

I looked across the clearing for some sign that she was getting over the worst of her shock. She glanced up. For a moment, I thought that was progress. 'My name's Daniel—'

But she didn't look at me. She was staring into the night, her eyes white-rimmed. Pressing grimy hands to her tear-stained face, she whimpered with fear.

I realised the shadows under the trees were moving. Impenetrable darkness oozed into the clearing, defying the moonlight. My skin crawled as I remembered the encroaching menace on the path from Kympton.

The Ford's headlights yellowed and went out. The night breeze suddenly felt unnaturally cold, carrying a strengthening scent of damp and decay. Looking up, I saw the moon growing hazy, as though veiled by smoke. The inky shadows advanced.

Now I could hear stealthy movement in the trees. Something too big to be a boggart. It snickered with evil anticipation. The bites in my leg started throbbing. I'd forgotten them until now.

Terror paralysed me. Cold sweat slid down my forehead, stinging my eyes. I couldn't even raise a hand to wipe it away. Blinking to clear my blurred vision took an insane effort. I couldn't draw a breath—

The girl screamed and sprang to her feet. She ran away down the track, not caring about her missing sandal. She wasn't heading for the road but deeper into the woods, further away from help with each uneven step.

I tried to follow but my foot barely moved. My bitten leg had sunk ankle deep into the rotted leaves. Except when I looked down, I saw that it hadn't. Somehow that realisation freed me. I took one long stride, then another, breaking into a run as I chased after the girl.

Thick shadows slid across the ground, dense as oil. Any moment and the blackness would meet to bar my route. Breathy muttering beneath the trees hemmed me in on all sides. I barely got out of the clearing before the slithering shadows merged. A frantic glance over my shoulder, and I saw the darkness pursuing me.

I ran as fast as I could. Not just to catch the girl; I had to get away from the evil presence in this wood. It wouldn't be easy. Where the track had looked clear before, now it was choked with undergrowth. Hawthorns clawed at my arms while brambles tried to snare my ankles. A vehicle must have got down here sometime though. I stumbled on tyre ruts, risking a sprained ankle every time the ridged earth crumbled beneath my trainers.

A spray of leaves and thorns raked my forehead. Blood blinded me. I raised an arm to wipe it away and tried not to think how close that had come to my eyes.

Somewhere up ahead, the girl screamed. I tried to run faster but the track was even more overgrown. I could hear her ragged, breathless sobbing, but I couldn't even find whatever path she'd trampled.

She shrieked with fresh terror. I ripped at the tangling vegetation, swearing as it cut into my hands. I didn't stop though, remembering the creeping darkness pursuing me.

Finally, I forced my way through the brambles to find another clearing. The girl stood in the moonlight. She was reeling from side to side and she wasn't alone. The attacker slashed at her face with one hand. As she raised her arms to protect herself, he ripped at her belly with the other. Her white shirt was already a bloody mess. She doubled over and he ripped a handful of hair from her head, tossing it aside to flutter away on the breeze.

Her screams tore through the night. His gleeful laughter echoed back from the trees. Inhuman laughter. It wasn't a man attacking the girl. It was a nightmare scarecrow woven from fallen branches lashed together with ivy stripped from strangled trees. The swirling darkness swept past, no longer concerned with me. Those shadows were all part of this evil. It could only be the wose.

Crowing with triumph, it threw back its head. For a moment the shifting surface of its face looked like crumbling bark. In the next instant, I saw withered leaves. Bare twigs rose from its head like spines, rattling loudly. As it lifted sinewy arms to defy the moonlit night, the darkness swirled around it.

The girl stumbled backwards, blinded by her long hair sticking to the tears, muck and bloody scratches on her face. The thing followed, step by stealthy step. It mocked her with crooning noises before lashing at her with more brutal blows.

I forced myself to stand still. The wose hadn't seen me. Either that or it didn't think I could hurt it. The creature must be taking a corporeal form to wound the girl, but it could turn ethereal in an instant. It had no reason to imagine I could see it once it did. I fervently hoped so anyway.

As stealthily as I could, I searched my pockets for my penknife. As soon as I had it, I tucked my hands behind my back, fumbling to open the biggest blade. Then I gripped it and charged at the wose. It whirled around to face me.

'How did you kill Tila?' I had no idea if the wose could

understand me. I just wanted to hold its attention until I got close enough to—

The girl shrieked and stumbled backwards, still blinded by swathes of hair. She turned and staggered towards the gap where this new clearing narrowed into the track leading still deeper into the woods. There was nothing I could do to stop her.

The wose leaped. Not trying to escape, but straight at me. It jumped faster and further than I could have imagined. Now it was on me, forcing me backwards. It was far heavier than it had any right to be, made of fucking twigs, and hellishly strong. I fell backwards and landed with a rib-cracking thud.

The wose had me pinned, clawing with talons sharper than the worst thorns. My shirt ripped and I felt blood welling from a gouge across my breastbone. Twisting and kicking, I tried to throw it off. That only gave the bastard thing a chance to wind its wiry legs around my knees. I yelled with pain. Whatever it was made of bit viciously deep into my thigh muscles. Its many-fingered hands seized my shoulders.

I'd dropped the sodding penknife. I tried to take hold of the wose's wrists to break its grip on that side. Instantly my arm stung as if I'd been thrashed with nettles. Terrifyingly close to my face, I could see the wose was covered with tiny rootlets, fine as hairs. They twisted towards my eyes like questing tendrils searching for water before they withered and died.

The wose's talons pierced my shirt and then my shoulders, slowly, sadistically. It had no need for the swift violence it had used on the girl. It had me at its mercy. I was paralysed with terror. Its grip was going to tighten, little by little, until its claws scythed through my flesh and bone. Then it would tear bloody lumps right off me. The only question was would I bleed to death or would those rootlets suck the life out of me first.

The wose leaned forward. Its face was a shifting mask of shadows and autumnal colours, impossible to focus on. The deep hollows which passed for its eye sockets were lit by pinpoints of reddish light like burning marsh gas. It didn't speak. It didn't need to. Its contempt for my pitiful defiance, for my puny mortal body, filled my thoughts. As its fungus stink suffocated me, my chest heaved, desperate for fresh air. Blood pounded in my temples, every heartbeat like a hammer blow. My legs were going numb while my shoulders were burning with pain.

How dare I trespass in this mighty creature's domain? The wose was lord of this forest and it would punish me with the suffering I deserved. My kind had no place here, no rights over the greenwood. I had no hope of escape now I'd stumbled into its clutches and I had only myself to blame.

Some bloody-minded part of me resisted. That girl hadn't been trespassing, so that was bullshit for a start. She'd been brought to these woods by a stinking rapist and this vicious thing had been waiting for them. All of a sudden, I was sure of that.

I let go of its wrists, clawing at the ground on either side instead. My flailing hand found the penknife. With the last of my strength, I drove the blade deep into the wose's side. If it had been human, I could have hit a kidney. As it was, the thing sprang off me with an ear-splitting howl.

I struggled to my feet, legs aching savagely as the blood flowed to my feet again. The wose stood with its arms outstretched, quivering like an aspen. It was keening, a sound so low I could barely hear it but so penetrating that my bones ached with its agony.

It was solid now; I could see its twitching shadow on the moonlit ground. Much good that did me. It might look like something cobbled together from dead sticks, but I'd felt its inhuman strength. I wasn't going to tear it apart with my bare hands.

Its noise changed. Now it hissed defiance, eye sockets blazing with eerie crimson light. It began plucking at the penknife sticking out of its side. Every time its many-fingered hands touched it, the thing snarled, savage and feral. Even with the knife's red plastic casing, it still couldn't touch that much metal without searing pain.

That didn't mean it wouldn't touch it. Its gaze fixed on me, the wose grasped the penknife's handle. It wrenched the reluctant blade free with a snarl of savage triumph. I dodged as it hurled the knife straight at my face. Too quick for thought, I caught the blade and took a step forward. I don't know if I was hoping to defend myself or attack the wose again.

It didn't matter. With a last snarl, it turned translucent then vanished completely.

# Chapter Thirteen

The unearthly shadows had gone, taking that eerie cold with them. I still stood there shivering despite the balmy night. My chest burned where the wose had clawed at me and so did the gash on my forehead from the thorn branch earlier. My thighs and shoulders felt as if I'd been beaten with a scaffolding pole. On the plus side, the boggart bites and the bruises from the Green Man's grip barely registered now.

I should head back to the Landy and its first aid kit. But the girl was still lost in the woods. If the wose had gone after her, I didn't know if I could lure it away a second time. I wasn't even sure I'd have the guts to try. I felt physically sick at the thought of being at its mercy again.

Fuck that. First things first. I had to find the girl. I walked cautiously down the track. 'Hello! Are you there? Are you all right!' Since I didn't know her name, I could only hope she'd recognise my voice and head towards me.

I halted for a moment. The only sound was the soft rustle of the leaves. At least there was no sign of that ominous, unnatural darkness. All I saw were normal night-time shadows. But there was no sign of the girl.

The land began to slope more steeply. The track petered out. It didn't look as if anyone had come this way. I couldn't see broken twigs or scuffs in the leaf mould. I stopped, wondering what to do.

Light caught my eye. Headlights down in the valley bottom showed the line of the road. I wondered if the girl had seen a passing vehicle. Maybe she'd remembered what I'd said about the police mobile unit further down the road. That's where I should go, regardless. I could search these woods all night and still not find her. The sooner the police took charge, the better. The sooner that rapist would be in handcuffs.

As I headed down the hill towards the road, I reached for

my phone, hoping for a signal. No phone in any of my pockets. Fuck. I must have lost it fighting the wose. Thankfully I still had my keys and the rapist's wallet for the police.

Okay. I'd go and see if there were any coppers in the lay-by. With any luck, that's where the girl had gone. If I was shit out of luck and there was no one there, I'd follow the road back to the turn-off, find the Land Rover and drive to a call box. If the rapist was still there, I'd leave him alone. He'd be sure to fight back, and after tangling with the wose I didn't think I could get the better of a six-year-old.

I tried to recall if I'd seen a phone box any closer than Lambton. Kympton Grange was closer but there was no landline in the flat. Maybe it would be quicker and simpler to drive straight to Lambton police station. I recalled seeing it on the same street as the library. I could hand over the rapist's wallet and tell them what had happened, and they could start a search for the girl lost in the woods. I tried not to imagine her cowering in some hollow, scared witless, bleeding and bruised.

I reached the road, and as I started walking towards the lay-by I saw lights almost immediately, flashing blues above bright halogen headlamps. A police van, one of those customised Transits. I raised my hands to wave it down, heaving a sigh of relief. The girl must have got to the lay-by and found help.

The coppers halted well short of me. I was painfully dazzled by the headlights. The passenger door opened and a figure carefully got out. He stayed behind the open door, a bulky shadow. I heard another car stop, its doors opening, and a second shadow slid along the white side of the van.

'Armed police!' somebody yelled. 'On your knees! Do it! Now!'

After an instant of complete disbelief, I did exactly as I was told.

'Hands on your head!' the voice ordered. 'Lace your fingers together!'

The idea of guns made me very nervous. A shotgun to

keep down rabbits or woodpigeons is one thing, I'm used to those, but these police would be carrying something else entirely.

'My colleague is going to come and cuff you,' the armed officer shouted. 'Try anything stupid and you will regret it.'

I didn't doubt that for a second. Another copper was already on his way, walking towards me on the opposite side of the road so as not to block the gunman's shot. Meantime, kneeling in the full glare of the van's headlights, I was the easiest imaginable target.

I wished the one with the cuffs would hurry up. I ached from head to toe and the effort of holding my hands on my head was unbearable. The last thing I wanted to do was let my arms fall and prompt a bullet. I really didn't want to add 'carpenter' to the tally of innocent tradesmen the cops had killed by mistake.

'Right, you be sensible and this will all go a lot easier.' The copper with the cuffs was approaching from the side.

I began to turn my head. 'It's not—'

'Eyes front!'

'Don't move!'

Whoever was doing the shouting barked his order at the same time as the officer beside me.

'Sorry'. I caught a glimpse of metal as the copper seized my wrist. Drawing one hand down my back and then grabbing the other, he clicked the rigid restraints closed.

'Right, up you get.' He shoved a hand under my elbow, urging me to my feet.

'Shit.' I couldn't help swearing. My shoulders were agony thanks to the cuffs forcing my arms behind my back. Blood trickled down my chest as the wounds from the wose's claws were wrenched open.

'Let's not have any nonsense,' the copper behind me warned.

I noticed they weren't calling me 'sir' tonight.

'I was looking for a girl. I saw her being attacked.' I wasn't going to fight back, but I wasn't going to keep quiet. 'She ran off into the woods. Did she find her way down to the road?'

The copper continued as though I hadn't spoken.

'You're not under arrest, but we are going to take you to Lambton police station. I am going to caution you now. You do not have to say anything but it may harm your defence if you do not mention when questioned something which you later rely on in court. Anything you do say may be given in evidence. Do you understand?' He tightened his grip on my arm, in case I wasn't paying attention.

'Yes, I understand.' I also understood they weren't going to tell me a sodding thing.

I was very tempted to keep my mouth shut. I hadn't done anything wrong. But by the time they worked that out and let me go, I didn't want to come back and find my Land Rover stripped to the chassis, or worse, not there at all. I tried again.

'My car keys are in my right-hand pocket. My Land Rover's parked up a track just after the turn from the Kympton road. I don't know if the sod who attacked the girl is still there, but his car should be. I locked him in it. I've got his keys too. Can you please make sure that's reported and both vehicles are kept safe. I don't want to lose my tools. They're my livelihood.'

The copper still didn't answer, but once he'd delivered me to his colleague at the back of the van he walked off to stand behind the patrol car pulled up a little way back down the road. As he talked into the radio clipped to his shoulder, I didn't catch everything he said but he did at least mention 'two vehicles'.

'In you get. Mind your head.' The copper opening the van door raised his hand to shield my scalp.

I had to stoop to get up the steps without braining myself on the roof. There was a metal cage inside the van. I didn't need telling to get inside and sit on the hard bench. The copper closed the cage, slammed the door with a solid clunk and got into one of the front seats. A small window with thick glass nearly opaque with metal mesh meant he could keep an eye on me.

The armed response vehicle's lights shone through the small windows in the rear doors as the van pulled away. I had to brace my feet on the floor to wedge myself into a corner. That saved me from sliding off the bench, but sitting with my hands trapped behind my back was excruciating. I closed my eyes and tried to think of something, anything else.

That was a bad idea. As soon as I shut my eyes, I saw the wose's shifting, shadowy face. I felt his burning hatred. He would know me again. Worse, he knew me for his enemy.

I needed to talk to the naiad. She needed to tell me absolutely everything about the sodding wose. There was no fucking way that man accidentally turned up with a victim for the monster to torment after he'd raped her. And I was in no mood for the usual guessing games, trying to work out the precise questions I needed to ask to get useful answers.

Though I would answer some questions first, to satisfy the police that I had nothing to do with these attacks. At least it was a short ride into Lambton. The van pulled into an underground garage. A copper opened up the back and I got out, nice and quiet. Three police officers escorted me to the custody suite.

The grey-haired sergeant in charge looked as though he'd seen it all. 'Good evening, sir. Name and address?'

I gave him my information and he noted it down unhurriedly.

'Please empty your pockets.'

I looked over my shoulder and the policeman who'd put me in the van uncuffed me. It was an effort not to stretch my arms over my head to ease my shoulders, but I didn't want anyone thinking I was about to throw a punch. Trying to ignore the discomfort, I began filling the plastic tray on the counter top.

'Not your first night in a cell,' one of the coppers observed pointedly.

I retorted despite myself. 'I don't make a habit of it.'

The custody sergeant ignored us both, using his pen to

gesture at my torn and bloodstained shirt. 'What happened there?'

'I got caught up on some thorns in the woods.'

'We'll get the duty doctor to have a look at you.' The sergeant made a note.

'The Land Rover is mine. This Ford belongs to the bloke who attacked the girl I was trying to find.' I set the rapist's keys down on the counter, not in the tray with my own stuff. 'They're both parked in the woods, up a track just after the Kympton turn. Please, I'm a carpenter and my tools—'

The officer who'd cuffed me spoke up. 'It's being taken care of, sarge.'

'This is my wallet.' I laid it down in the tray. 'This one belongs to the shit who was attacking the girl, the man who drove the Ford. Can you please tell Detective Sergeant Tunstead about it as soon as possible.' I put that down on the counter beside the Ford keys.

Inscrutable, the sergeant made another note. 'Is there anyone you want notified that you're here?'

'No thanks.' I wasn't going to have them ringing Dad in the middle of the night, and no one closer needed to know.

'You're entitled to legal representation. Do you have a solicitor you would like us to contact, or would you like us to provide you with one?' The sergeant looked at me, pen poised.

'Not at the moment,' I said cautiously.

'Then that's all we need to be going on with.' The sergeant nodded at the coppers flanking me and lifted up a hinged flap so they could usher me through the counter. He unlocked a heavy steel door to the rear and led the way. 'Number six.'

The floor was tiled with black vinyl. The walls and cell doors were all painted white. With the slides to their peepholes shut, I couldn't see if any were occupied. The sergeant was unlocking the door at the end of the row. I halted a handful of paces short. He looked at me, exasperated. 'Come on now.'

I meekly went into the cell. As the door slammed shut behind me, I breathed a sigh of relief. I'd recognised that stink in the corridor. The rapist was behind one of these doors. I still wanted to know for certain that the girl was safe though.

Exhausted, I sat down on the concrete bench fixed from wall to wall at the far end of the cell. A thin slab of plastic-covered foam barely softened it. There was no point in trying to sleep though, if a police doctor was going to turn up.

I stripped off my ruined shirt. Dried blood and woodland grime crusted the gouge across my chest. It was viciously sore, but I told myself it would be more painful, and probably still bleeding, if there was any serious damage. I could only hope so. I did my best to look at my shoulders. Those bruises were going to be something special. I leaned back against the wall. Despite my best efforts, I was asleep within seconds.

Rattling keys woke me as the sergeant escorted a young bloke in a short-sleeved grey shirt and chinos into the cell. He was carrying a tray wrapped up in blue paper.

'Duty doctor.'

'Right. Thanks.' I noted the sergeant was holding the door ajar, and at least one other indistinct figure was on hand outside. They really needn't have worried.

'What happened to you then?' The doctor pulled on purple sterile gloves.

I stuck as close to the truth as I could. 'I got lost in the woods in the dark and got caught up in something covered in thorns.'

'Let's get you cleaned up.' He set the tray down on the bench and unfolded the paper to reveal wipes, dressings and tape.

I had to bite my lip as he cleaned the blood off my forehead. Leaning closer, he frowned. 'Hold still.'

I sat motionless as he used blue plastic tweezers to pick the broken spines out of my face and closed the wound with steri-strips. 'This might leave a small scar.'

'Right.' I tried to smile with gritted teeth.

I saw him taking in the marks on my shoulders, as well as the older bruises on my upper arms. He didn't say anything though, turning his attention to the gouge on my chest. I was relieved to see his face clear as he got the blood and muck off.

'This isn't nearly as bad as it looks. What concerns me is how deep the dirt has gone. I'm not going to close it up and risk trapping infection. You need to get plenty of dressings like these and magnesium sulphate paste. Any chemist will have them. That'll draw out the rest of the muck, and then you must let it heal naturally. Don't cover it with plasters or anything like that.' He taped gauze pads over the torn flesh. 'Do you know when you last had a tetanus booster?'

'Six years ago.'

The doctor looked up. 'Most people can't remember.'

'I'm a carpenter. I work on building sites. A nail went through my boot. That's not something you forget.' I tried to ignore the stinging from the disinfectant wipes.

'Fit to be interviewed?' The sergeant looked me over thoughtfully.

'I'd say so, once he's had some sleep.' The doctor wrapped up the tray piled with soiled wipes and other rubbish in the blue paper. He looked at me. 'Do you want some painkillers? Any allergies?'

'No allergies, and yes, please.' Maybe he'd tell me what the coppers wouldn't. 'I was trying to find a girl in the woods. Is she okay? I didn't hurt her—'

The doctor nodded. 'She—'

'He doesn't need to know about that.' The sergeant called out to the shadow in the corridor. 'Fetch us some water in here, Tom.'

Abashed, the doctor pressed two pills from a foil strip and dropped them into my outstretched hand. I washed them down with a paper cup of water brought in by a copper I hadn't seen before. The sergeant ushered the doctor out and locked the door.

I lay down and went straight to sleep. The look in the doctor's eyes had been enough. He'd seen the girl and he'd nodded. That was the worst of my fears relieved. Everything else could wait until morning.

# Chapter Fourteen

I'd been lying awake for a while when the sergeant peered through the door flap.

'Morning.' He walked off, returning a few minutes later to unlock the cell door and offer me a plastic mug of tea.

'Thanks.' I drank it down in one.

He grunted, non-committal. 'Want another? Hungry?'

'Yes, please.'

He brought the refilled mug back along with a freshly cooked bacon roll. If I'd been free to go, that would have been a good start to the day. As it was, I was already late for work. So how long would they be keeping me here?

'Good morning, sir.' The female detective who'd come to the farm with Tunstead appeared as I was finishing the tea. She offered me a faded red sweatshirt. 'You should have been given this last night,' she said stiffly. 'Our apologies.'

'Not a problem.' The sweatshirt was actually big enough to fit me, fresh from a washing machine.

'This way, please.'

She led the way and I followed with the sergeant bringing up the rear. We left the cells through a different security-locked door and went down a carpet-tiled corridor to an interview room with a table and four chairs, two on either side. DS Tunstead sat opposite a man in a suit much more expensive than his own.

'Good morning, Mr Mackmain.' DS Tunstead gestured to the empty chair beside the man in the suit. 'You're not under arrest, but I have asked Mr Willersley to join us in case you need any advice. He's the duty solicitor.'

'Okay,' I said slowly. The lawyer was maybe ten years older than me and looked like a long-distance runner, wiry and long-limbed. I wondered if he was on my side or the police's.

The female detective was unwrapping two old-fashioned

cassette tapes. She put them in a black twin-deck recorder and pressed a few buttons. A red light came on as the reels started turning.

'Interview commencing at 9.30 am. I'm Detective Sergeant Jason Tunstead. Please introduce yourself for the benefit of the tape.'

I gave my name. Apparently the solicitor was Andrew Willersley of Willersley, Rose and Slater, and the woman was Detective Constable Katherine Redmire.

'I know you were cautioned last night, but for the benefit of the tape I'm going to do so again.' Tunstead repeated the formalities. 'Do you understand?'

'Yes.' I was getting impatient. 'Did you find the girl? Is she okay? How badly was she hurt?'

The solicitor had been getting a writing pad and an expensive pen out of his briefcase. He looked up, pen poised to record the policeman's answer.

Tunstead considered his reply. 'Yes, we found her. She's in hospital with minor injuries and abrasions as well as severe shock. What can you tell us about what happened?'

I'd been thinking about what I should say ever since I woke up. Better stick as close to the truth as I could, like before.

'I was going to The Grey Goose for a pint. Just the one, since I was driving,' I added. 'I was turning into the car park when I saw a Ford pulling out in a hurry. I had to brake to avoid hitting it. I saw a girl in the back seat. She looked as if she was trying to get out. Then I saw the driver hit her in the face.'

Tunstead looked levelly at me. 'Why didn't you ring 999?'

'I didn't want to make a fool of myself if they were just a couple having a row. So I decided to follow the car. That way, if everything turned out okay, I wouldn't be wasting your time. But I followed them into those woods and I saw him drag the girl out of the car.'

I made no attempt to hide my distaste as I told them what followed. Tunstead stopped me several times to make me explain something more fully. I couldn't tell if that was to help me remember or if he was trying to catch me out. The woman, DC Redmire, took continuous notes.

When I finally stopped talking, the solicitor cleared his throat. 'Do you have any reason to doubt that Mr Mackmain was attempting to save the young woman from a serious assault, Detective?'

Tunstead was still looking at me intently. 'Do you know the girl?'

I shook my head. 'Not as far as I'm aware. We might have said hello in the Goose sometime, but I don't think so.'

'What about the man who allegedly assaulted her?'

'Never met him,' I said firmly. Seeing him in The Griffin car park wasn't meeting him. 'I'd remember anyone who stinks like that.'

From DC Redmire's involuntary grimace, I guessed she'd been in an interview room with the bastard.

'Was he sleeping rough?' I asked. 'Living in his car?'

DS Tunstead didn't answer that. 'What happened after you locked the alleged attacker inside his own vehicle?'

Now I had to choose my words very carefully.

'The girl panicked and ran off into the woods. I followed her, but it was dark and I didn't have a torch. When I realised I couldn't find her, I made my way down to the road. I was going to go and get help. Your van found me first.'

'Did you see anyone else in the woods?' Tunstead looked at me, unblinking.

Had the girl said anything about the wose? Anything that the police could take seriously? But she hadn't seen me fighting it. She'd run off before the creature and I had come to grips.

I shook my head. 'There may have been someone else out there, or I could just have been imagining it.'

Tunstead's expression was still unreadable. 'Would you be willing to give us a DNA sample, sir? And your fingerprints. So we can rule you out of our enquiries?'

'Me?' For a moment, I was horrified by the idea. I had absolutely no idea what might show up in my DNA.

'Mr Mackmain's not under arrest, Detective,' the solicitor said quickly. 'He's free to decline.'

'That's true.' DS Tunstead's face hardened. 'As long as he's not under arrest.'

Right, and I was pretty sure he could find something to charge me with, if he really wanted to. Slamming a car door on a rapist's leg after I'd already kicked him in the balls would probably do.

I told myself not to panic. They'd find no trace of me on the girl, first and foremost. I'd touched the doors on the Ford but that would just back up my story, and there was no danger of them finding my prints inside. If my dryad heritage meant something about my DNA puzzled Forensics, there still wouldn't be any match to the murders.

'It's okay,' I said slowly. 'I can tell you now, it'll rule me out of whatever's going on around here.'

The solicitor chipped in with a pointed smile. 'When that's established, Detective, we will want confirmation that Mr Mackmain's samples are being destroyed in accordance with current legislation.'

'Of course.' DS Tunstead checked his watch. 'Now, Mr Mackmain, where exactly were you going when the armed officers found you?'

'I lost my phone in the woods. I hoped there might be a patrol car where you've got that incident centre in the lay-by. If not, I was going to have to find a call box.'

That was the truth, after all, though I saw that glint in Tunstead's eyes again.

'Are you absolutely certain that you didn't see anyone else in the woods?'

'I didn't see anyone, but I can't be certain there wasn't someone out there.' I was starting to think the girl must have said there had been a second attacker. I realised something else. I had absolutely no idea what the rapist might have said. Had he told the police I was involved, just to drop me in the shit? My mouth went dry.

'Very well, Mr Mackmain, that's everything we need for the moment. Thank you. Interview ending at 10.23 a.m.' Tunstead's face gave nothing away as he switched off the tape recorder.

'I'm free to go?' I was caught between relief and surprise.

Tunstead nodded. 'Though we'd be grateful if you didn't leave the area. We may need to speak to you again – as a witness.'

'Okay.' I tried to sound co-operative. 'So who was the man in the Ford?'

Tunstead shook his head. 'I can't discuss that with you in case he's brought to trial.'

'If he's found fit to plead,' DC Redmire muttered.

Tunstead shot her a quelling glare. 'Do you want your copy of the tape, or shall we send it to Mr Willersley?'

'I'll have it, thanks.' I had no clue what sort of legal bill I was already liable for.

The solicitor didn't seem offended. He was putting his notepad away in his briefcase. 'I'll see you through the DNA testing, Mr Mackmain, and then we can both get off home.'

'I'll need my Land Rover to get back to Kympton. Have you got it here?' I looked from Tunstead to DC Redmire, who was busy taking the tape cassettes out of the machine.

'We have.' Tunstead stood up. 'You're free to take it.'

So I guessed it had been thoroughly searched without the coppers finding anything to incriminate me. 'Thanks.'

'Just a moment, please.' DC Redmire was still busy with the tapes. As Tunstead left the interview room, she handed me a printed form and a pen. 'Please sign this to confirm that I've sealed the master tape in your presence.'

As soon as I'd done that, she handed me another piece of paper. 'This explains how we will use the second tape as our working copy and what will happen in the event of any charges being made.'

'Okay.' I sincerely hoped I wouldn't need to worry about

that.

She put all the tapes and paperwork into a folder. 'Now we'll take your fingerprints and DNA, and then you can be on your way.'

That was a lot less bother than I'd expected. Filling in the forms took more time than having a cotton bud wiped around the inside of my cheek, and they had a special scanner for my hands. Then I signed another set of forms to confirm I was getting all of my belongings back from the custody sergeant.

'Thanks.' I put everything back in my pockets. 'Can you tell me where to collect my vehicle, please?'

'It's in the yard.'

'I'll walk Mr Mackmain out, sergeant,' the solicitor offered.

'Thank you, sir.'

I wasn't sure who the sergeant was talking to. It really didn't matter. I followed Mr Willersley through the station garage and into a high-walled yard full of vehicles, my own among them.

'I think it's reasonable to assume there's no undue cause for concern.' The solicitor spoke slowly, choosing his words carefully. 'In the absence of any compelling evidence that you were somehow directly and deliberately involved, you'll only be wanted as a witness, and only if this comes to court.'

'If this comes to court.' I remembered what DC Redmire had let slip. 'Because he's not fit to plead?'

'That remains to be seen,' Willersley said judiciously. He offered me his card. 'With any luck, we won't need to see each other again. Still, you may as well have my number.'

'Thanks anyway.' I shook his hand.

He headed for his BMW and I went over to my battered Land Rover. Nothing seemed to be missing, though a good few things had been moved. When I got into the driver's seat, I saw white powder on the dash and the doors, on the driver's side and the passenger's. Well, they wouldn't find any prints from the girl or from the rapist.

144

I saw a copper opening up the yard gate to let the solicitor out. I quickly turned the ignition key and followed. As the copper waved me through, I checked the dashboard clock. Half the morning was already gone and I was in dire need of a shower, not to mention a new phone. Phil Caister would be wondering where the hell I was and why I wasn't answering his calls.

Checking my mirrors, I got a look at my face. I looked like an extra from some zombie apocalypse movie, unshaven, bloodstained, my eyes hollow with exhaustion. I really should go home and clean up before I did anything else.

As I pulled away from the gate, I saw the solicitor's BMW bombarded with camera flashes. He accelerated and the pack of reporters surged towards me. The lights left me squinting as I tried to drive off without one of the idiots ending up under my wheels.

When I reached the market square, I saw the TV news vans were back from wherever they'd been. Now their reporters could say how little they knew with the police station behind them. I didn't rate my chances of parking to buy a new phone without being pestered with questions, not looking the way I did.

I drove back to Kympton Grange Farm. My heart sank as I pulled into the yard and saw Chrissie Monkswell unloading groceries from her Volkswagen. I parked under the barn and tried to hurry up to the flat.

'Daniel!' Chrissie rushed over, alarmed. 'What on earth happened? Your face—'

'It's none of your business.' That came out a lot harsher than I'd intended.

Chrissie halted, as shocked as if I'd slapped her.

'Sorry.' I tried to apologise through gritted teeth. 'I just meant... There's nothing for you to worry about.'

'I won't then,' she said acidly. 'By the way, someone came looking for you yesterday evening. A woman, tall, long brown hair. I did try to call but you weren't answering your phone. Does Victoria know about her? If she was some casual pick-up, I'd prefer you didn't give this address to strangers.'

She turned her back on me and stalked away.

'I'm sorry—'

Chrissie slammed the farmhouse door behind her and I swore under my breath. A tall woman with long brown hair could only be the naiad, and I'd missed my chance to speak to her. I couldn't possibly go back to the woods today, not now the police had a whole new crime scene to search.

I wished something could go right, just for a little while. Up in the flat, I dumped my clothes by the washing machine and headed for the shower. Before I turned it on, I studied my injuries as best I could in the mirror. The gash across my forehead was already scabbing over and none of the other scrapes and grazes on my face looked to be festering. So far, so good.

It was a different story from the chin down. The bruises on my shoulders left by the wose's talons added to the marks of the Green Man's grip on my arms. I looked as if I'd been beaten with a stick. Purpling bruises ringed my legs just above each knee where the wose had pinned me down. I gave one a cautious prod and swore as the pain set my boggart bites throbbing.

I tried to peel the dressing off my chest but the gauze was thoroughly stuck to drying scabs. I'd have to soak that off. So I got in the shower and did my best to wash away the last twenty-four hours. I didn't bother towelling off, not with all these bruises. Now I wanted coffee. Careful not to slip on the oak boards, I walked out of the bedroom and stopped dead. 'How the fuck did you get in?'

The naiad looked me up and down and gave an appreciative nod. 'Your mother's kind breeds handsome sons.'

'Wait there.' I went back into the bedroom to find some underpants and trousers. This wasn't a conversation to have bollock naked.

# Chapter Fifteen

When I came back out of the bedroom, the naiad was looking idly around the living room.

'How did you get in?'

She nodded towards the window over the sink looking towards Kympton Hill. It was open a crack. 'Through there.'

'Did Chrissie see you? The woman you spoke to yesterday?'

The naiad shook her head. 'No one saw me come and none will see me go.'

'How did you know where I live? How did you get here from the valley?'

She smiled with secret satisfaction. 'Haven't you visited the tourist caverns? My kind have been carving our own routes through these hills since long before your father's kind returned as the ice retreated.'

I was too tired for this. 'What do you want?'

She looked momentarily irritated, her eyes flashing turquoise. 'We need to stop the wose. He is hunting again.'

'I found him last night.' Still shirtless, I gestured sourly to my bruises. 'You couldn't have done something to help?'

She ignored that. 'Have the police captured the man he had under his influence?'

'The man he's been persuading to kidnap girls?' If she was going to answer questions with more questions, so could I. 'Why didn't you tell me he was keeping someone human outside the usual flow of time?'

I'd been thinking long and hard about the stinking rapist as I lay staring at that police cell ceiling. Several of the library books said the wood wose legend was the origin of the were-wolf myth. One ancient Greek legend caught my eye. Apparently a man could choose to become a werewolf by hanging his clothes on an ash tree and swimming across a secret lake somewhere in Arcadia. Nine years later he could come back, return to his human form, even put on the clothes he'd been wearing, and those lost nine years would be added to the length of his life.

I had another theory about that particular story. What if that so-called werewolf had fallen under a wose's influence, unleashing all his violent, murderous impulses? Could such a man be an evil counterpart to a dryad's human lover who lost all track of time? That would explain how a man could disappear and turn up in the same clothes nine years later. That would explain why the rapist had those long-expired credit cards in his wallet and why his attacks were apparently years apart. As far as he was concerned, he was on a spree, with one rape following close after another, but the police wouldn't see it like that.

If the man I'd caught last night confessed to attacking Amber Fenham just a few days ago, that would explain why the police thought he was a nutter. Maybe he hadn't confessed, but was just insisting it was 2008. I wondered who he was. One of the thousands of adults who go missing every year, never to be seen again, according to some documentary I'd watched with Victoria. There might be a file on him somewhere in Lambton station. If he was local, that would explain how the bastard knew so much about those woods.

For the moment, getting him locked up was what mattered. There could be no doubt of his guilt, with forensics to back the girl's testimony and my own.

'The police have caught him?' The naiad fixed her turquoise gaze on me.

I nodded. 'Where did the wose find him? How did it persuade him to do its hunting? Where did they get that car?' There was no way the Ford had been parked in a wood for years and still started.

'He shows his puppet where to find a vehicle and how to steal the keys.' The naiad looked amused, before she turned sternly serious. 'Now you cannot leave the job half done. The wose will soon find another puppet. His will is strong and your kind are easily swayed.' She corrected herself. 'Your father's kind, anyway. Your strength to fight the evil miasma that surrounds such creatures of darkness is rooted in your mother's stock.' She gestured towards my bitten leg. 'A wholly mortal man would be dying by now, his flesh rotting.'

I remembered the dark despair the wose had breathed into me. I recalled the uncanny fear creeping like evil mist along the packhorse trail from Kympton. I knew how close I'd come to succumbing.

I shook my head stubbornly. 'He won't find a new accomplice so easily. There aren't that many psychopaths around.'

'One will be drawn here, and sooner rather than later,' she said with absolute certainty. 'It's not only dryads who give mortal children wildwood blood.'

'You're saying that woses...?' What a revolting thought.

The naiad shrugged. 'There have always been mortal women attracted to darkness and violence. Some rebel against a father or husband by taking a wildwood lover. Some can be beguiled for the sake of having their miseries blunted, just for a little while.'

She waved that away. 'Like calls to like, and the wose will find another human man to do his bidding. More girls will die, this year, next year, sometime, whenever. Can you live with that on your conscience?'

'See these bruises?' I spread my arms wide. 'How can I fight a creature like that?'

'You attacked it without thinking,' she countered. 'You won't make that mistake again.'

'How do you know?' I protested. 'I'm a dryad's son, but the only dryad I've ever met is my mother. Apart from Tila, and I barely spoke to her before the wose murdered her. I don't even know how it killed her!' My voice was rising and I didn't care. It was good to have a target for my anger.

The naiad contemplated me for a long moment, her gaze impenetrable, shimmering turquoise. She blinked and her eyes passed for human again.

'He killed Tila just as a mortal man kills a mortal woman, with greater strength and merciless violence. He brutalised

149

and wounded her until her life drained away.'

'But she died in her ethereal form.' I desperately wanted to deny that Tila's fate could be so simple. That my mother could be so vulnerable.

'The wose attacked her in his ethereal body.' The naiad was growing impatient. 'Like can always attack like.'

'I can't do that,' I pointed out. 'As soon as it's ripped me to pieces and shifts to its ethereal state, I haven't got a hope of hurting it.'

She shook her head. 'I never met a dryad's son who was a coward.'

'Really?' I sneered. 'How many have you met?'

She replied with unexpected seriousness. 'Over the centuries? Perhaps a dozen.'

That startled me, but before I could ask her more, she continued.

'Then you must bind him to his solid form. Once that is done, you can destroy his trees and he will be totally undone. Did your mother teach you nothing?' She looked at me with glittering irritation again. 'Woses are akin to hamadryads.'

'What trees?' I wondered how much trouble I'd be in if the police caught me using a chainsaw in Tila's valley. It was a fair bet there were preservation orders on the most ancient and rare trees.

'He is bound to the black poplars in the meadow below Tila's woods.' For the first time, the naiad hesitated. 'Though I don't know exactly where the heart of his power lies among them.'

'Because that would be much too easy,' I said sarcastically.

This complicated things. Poplars send out suckers and their broken branches readily root themselves in soft, wet ground. A long-established thicket can consist of dozens of trees which are actually offshoots of the same parent.

I had other concerns which I doubted the naiad shared. Not many black poplars survived after the Victorian uses for their timber declined. I couldn't remember if it was currently the British Isles' most endangered native tree. Regardless, it was high up on that list. I knew it was a criminal offence to damage or destroy a protected tree, though I couldn't recall if the fine was theoretically unlimited or merely a hundred thousand pounds.

The naiad was still talking.

'You must destroy all his trees, root and branch. While the wose lives, they will draw on his strength and regrow. Likewise, even if you destroy the wose's body, as long as a single shoot survives where his power is rooted, he will endure as an ethereal creature. In time, as the trees recover, he will manifest as a corporeal being again. So you must destroy them both, the wose and his trees, at one and the same time.'

'How?' I demanded.

'With fire.' The naiad was wholly serious. 'That's why you must be the one to do it. My touch quenches flame.'

So she wanted me to commit arson, probably in a site of special scientific interest. I had no idea what the penalties for that might be. Prison and throw away the key, probably.

I shook my head. 'What about poisoning the trees?'

I've used industrial herbicides to clear undergrowth off building sites. Use something slow-acting and I could be well away before anyone noticed the trees were dying. Much better than being caught red-handed with a box of matches.

The naiad's eyes flashed lightning-bright with anger. 'Poison the trees and you poison my waters.'

I raised defensive hands. 'I was just thinking aloud.'

'So you agree it has to be done.' She traced a cool finger down my bare chest.

I felt the gentle pressure of her breasts against my upper arm. A breath of wind through the open window brushed her hair against my shoulder. She wasn't wearing a bra under her T-shirt, and I realised how thin the cotton was. If she took it off, her long hair would reach down to cover her breasts. I could picture the tantalising glimpses of her nipples that would come and go as she moved above me, her hips riding mine. She smelled fresh and enticing. Her mouth was moist and kissable.

I blinked and took a step backwards. This wasn't right. The blink of an eye ago, the naiad had been standing on the other side of the living room. Now she was close enough to touch my chest and I hadn't even seen her move.

I gripped her wrist. 'I don't go to bed with women when I don't know their name. What should I call you? Jenny Greenteeth? Melusine?'

Those were just two of the dangerous water women in those library books.

'So you're not such a dumb woodcutter's son.' She rippled into her ethereal form, her wrist melting through my fingers as she stepped away.

She was gloriously and wholly naked, outlined in glistening silver and shadowed with dusky blue. I was overwhelmed with the desire to kiss and caress her. I longed to feel her hands sliding over my skin as I spread those thighs and sank into her moist warmth, thrusting ever deeper. Blood pounded in my ears and I felt light-headed, my erection pressed painfully hard against my trousers.

I shook my head, furiously rejecting that fantasy. Reality was Victoria, adorable in her pretty underwear. Real sex is sticky and sweaty. It's condoms and tissues and creaky beds putting you off your stroke or making you both laugh. It's taking turns in the shower while one of you makes some coffee. And great sex isn't enough, if that's all a relationship is. Victoria and I had proved that.

'I am not some sweaty-palmed teenager who'll run any stupid risk for the chance of fucking you,' I said hoarsely.

'You see. If you can resist me, you are strong enough to resist the wose.' She was back on the far side of the dining table. She was still attractive in jeans and T-shirt, no question of that, but no more likely to excite uncontrollable lust than any other woman walking down a street.

The naiad blew me a mocking kiss. 'You can call me Kalei.'

'Kali?' Wasn't that the Hindu goddess of death?

'Kalei.' She drew the last syllable out, almost splitting it into two, to finally rhyme with 'day'. 'If I can't reward you with pleasures of the flesh, at least let me wash your wounds clean.'

She gestured before I could say anything, and I gasped as every sense told me I'd just been plunged into deep, cold water. In the next breath I realised that all my cuts and scrapes and gouges weren't hurting nearly so badly. I couldn't even feel the boggart bites.

The naiad smiled with smug satisfaction. 'So, tell me, what is your price for putting an end to this wose and his killing?'

'Nothing,' I said curtly. 'You have nothing I want.'

'I doubt that very much.' She unknotted the white scarf she wore like a belt round her jeans. Pulling it loose, she held it out towards me. 'Wet this and I will feel it. Use it when you wish to talk to me again, when you have decided on your price.'

I wondered what the gauzy cloth really was. Her jeans hadn't been belted with anything when she'd been trying to seduce me. I was certain of that because I'd been wondering how quickly I could undo that button, pull down the zip and ease stonewashed denim and any panties down over the swell of her hips—

'Don't take too long.' Her eyes flashed turquoise again. 'No one else can do this, because no one hereabouts can see the wose to kill him. As soon as he finds a new partner, their victims' blood will be on your hands. Worse will surely follow. As the wose grows stronger and bolder, all manner of unclean things will be drawn to such a dark miasma.'

I frowned. 'Is that what's drawing so many boggarts here? What's making them so aggressive?'

'Among other things.' Turquoise momentarily veiled her gaze. 'I will leave you with something else to bear in mind, dryad's son. You don't want to make me your enemy. That would be as dangerous as being my friend could be pleasurable.'

The room filled with cold white mist, prompting goose-flesh on my bare skin. An irresistible, orgasmic rush left me gasping as the mist swirled around before spiralling away through the open window.

I didn't dare move in case my knees gave way. I could only stand there, fists clenched as the dizzying ecstasy faded and stickiness spread through my underwear. Angry and humiliated, I went to take another shower. This was one encounter with the naiad I wouldn't be telling my parents about.

Not that it made any difference. Never mind whatever switch the naiad thought she could flip in my brain or my balls, I wasn't going up against the wose again unless I could come up with a plan I was sure would defeat him. Getting myself killed wouldn't save the girls he preyed on.

# Chapter Sixteen

When I got out of the shower, I remembered I'd wanted a coffee. I examined my various injuries while I waited for the kettle to boil. A second soaking meant the gauze pad on my chest was peeling off of its own accord. The raw gouge still looked pretty grisly but it wasn't bleeding anymore. A lot of muck came away with the dressing and I guessed I had Kalei to thank for that, but the deepest tear still looked fairly dirty. I remembered what the police doctor had said about infection

I dug out an old black T-shirt which wouldn't show any blood if the uncovered wound started oozing, and headed out. There was no sign of Chrissie Monkswell. That was a shame, because I owed her an apology. On the other hand, I was relieved because I had no idea how to explain the naiad away.

At least I knew her name. Kalei. I'd also had an unforgettable lesson in one of the ways she could bring a mortal man to his knees. Well, forewarned was forearmed, if she tried that on me again. Though if an instant and incredible orgasm was the carrot she had to offer, I wondered what she was capable of by way of a stick.

I didn't really want to find out, any more than I wanted to hear that more girls had been murdered around here. It didn't matter if that was next month, next year or in ten years' time. I'd know what had happened, and yes, fuck it, that blood would be on my hands.

I drove to Lambton as quickly as I could, watching every other vehicle to make sure I didn't have to brake suddenly. Even so, by the time I got there the seatbelt felt like it was cutting me in half. With a minor stroke of good luck, I pulled straight into an empty parking space in front of the pharmacy. Better yet, it was on the other side of the market square from the TV vans. Still, I wanted to be in and out of the town as quickly as possible.

Inside the pharmacy I picked up some packets of gauze dressings and some tape. At the counter I asked for the strongest painkillers they could sell me and magnesium sulphate paste.

'You use it like it says on the label.' The amiable woman behind the counter showed me the instructions on the plain white pot. She looked sympathetically at my forehead. 'That'll draw out any bits of thorn still in that scratch. Do you want a bag?'

'Thanks.' I paid and took the plastic carrier.

'Hi there!' Outside, a bright-eyed lad greeted me, phone in hand. 'Callum Nailor, Northern News Bureau. Didn't I see you coming out of the police station a while back? You were driving that Land Rover?'

There wasn't any point denying it. That didn't mean I had to answer him. I headed for the phone shop.

'We'd really appreciate your help understanding what happened last night.' About a foot shorter than me, the journalist had to half-run to keep up with my long stride. 'If there's something you think the public should know, to keep local women safe—'

'I'm sure the police will cover that.' I stopped on the phone shop's step. 'So, no comment, okay?'

I leaned towards him, scowling. Most of the time, I do my best not to loom over people. It unnerves them. Sometimes, though, it comes in useful.

Not this time. He offered me a business card, still smiling cheerfully. 'Give me a ring when you're ready to talk.'

I ignored the card and went into the shop. The little bastard followed me in.

'Can I help you?' The lass behind the counter looked from me to him and back again.

I took a step backwards and gestured to the reporter. 'Go ahead.'

'Oh, no, I'm fine. Just browsing.' He grinned and started reading the little cards explaining the handsets on a display rack.

I took a deep breath and forced myself not to scowl. The girl was already looking nervously at me.

'I've lost my phone,' I said as calmly as I could. 'I need a replacement.'

'Okay.' She looked relieved. This was something she could cope with. 'Can you give me your number?'

With a journalist standing ten feet away, listening eagerly? Not a chance.

'Let me write it down for you.' I reached for her pad and pen.

'Okay.' Bemused, she typed it into her computer. 'Daniel Mackmain? Kympton Grange—'

'Yes.' I reached for the monitor, turning it so I could see the screen, turning it back before the journalist could get a look at it. 'All those details are correct.'

'Thank you.' The girl was looking nervous again. 'Did you know you're due an upgrade? There are three handsets on your current plan—'

'I'll take the simplest one.'

She looked at the screen again, puzzled. 'You don't use it a lot, do you?'

'No,' I said curtly.

She showed me the phones and I picked one quickly enough, but she still had to print out forms for me to sign. The journalist was reading every page of a home broadband brochure, seemingly fascinated.

Finally the assistant put the sim card into the new phone. 'Have you backed up your contacts to cloud storage? Would you like me to sync it for you?'

I reached for the phone. 'That's fine. I'll get everything from my laptop.'

'Okay then.' She smiled. 'When your number's activated, you'll get a text message. Just switch the phone off and on again and everything will be ready to go. It'll be some time in the next twenty-four hours.'

'Thanks.' I gave the reporter a hard look as I walked towards the door, but there was nothing I could do to stop him chatting up the phone girl to see what she could tell him about me.

Outside, a handful of journalists were standing around my Land Rover. Several of them tried the same sort of matey greeting.

'Hi there!'

'I wonder—'

'Could you tell us—'

I ignored them all, even when I was dazzled by a camera flash. At least they all backed off when I started the engine. My relief was short-lived though. Two cars followed me out of the marketplace, making no attempt to hide it. I guessed they were planning to follow me home and knock on my door for the rest of the day, until I told them whatever I knew.

Sod that. I drove to The Grey Goose and went straight into the gents. They could hardly follow me into a stall. I took my time sticking a fresh dressing on my chest and read the back of the packet of painkillers. I hate swallowing tablets dry, so I decided to buy a drink to wash them down. Actually, I might as well stop for some lunch.

The bar was surprisingly crowded, given it was midweek. I expected Donna to look a lot happier about having a houseful, but she was shaking her head at some bloke eagerly leaning forward at the other end of the bar.

'Daniel, what can I get you?' Jim appeared from the kitchen.

'Tuna mayo sandwich, please, brown bread, and a pint of Coke.' I handed over a tenner.

'Ice and lemon?' As he gave me my change, his eyes went to the gash on my forehead. 'What happened there?'

'Went for a walk in the woods and forgot to duck,' I said, offhand.

He set my Coke down on the bar and leaned forward,

low-voiced. 'It was you I saw last night? You went after them? I saw him grab the girl, when I went out to see what the dog was barking at, but I didn't have a chance to stop him. All I could do was ring 999. Did you catch up with them?'

'Yes, and the girl got away, only she got lost in the woods.' I swallowed a couple of painkillers with a mouthful of Coke. 'I'm not sure I should be talking about it. Have you spoken to the police?'

Jim nodded. 'A copper called me this morning. She said they'll be coming to take my statement later.'

I nodded. That was good news. Jim's version of events should help convince Tunstead I was one of the good guys.

'So you were here last night? You saw what happened?'

Neither of us had noticed an amiable young woman sidle up to eavesdrop on our quiet conversation.

'Do you know the girl who was abducted? Does she live around here?'

I'd had enough of this. 'What the fuck's it got to do with you?'

'Just curious.' The questioner hastily retreated, though she couldn't get very far with the pub so crowded.

I drank the rest of my Coke and put the glass on the bar. 'Do me a favour,' I said quietly to Jim. 'Don't tell anyone else I had anything to do with this. I don't want to spend the rest of the week saying "No comment."'

'No problem,' he assured me. 'Bloody ghouls.'

'Make them pay double for drinks and food,' I suggested. 'They'll be gone soon enough.'

'Probably won't notice, if they're used to London prices.' He managed half a smile.

A waitress arrived with my sandwich. Business must be good if Jim had taken on casual staff. I picked up the plate. 'I'll take this outside.'

All the beer garden tables were occupied, but that didn't bother me. I went over to lean on the brewery yard gate and looked at Teddy as I ate. The dog was lying down in his kennel, watchful but comfortable, and too well trained to come and beg for food.

I wished I could ask what he'd seen last night. My mum is always confident that she knows what animals are thinking. Maybe the naiad could communicate with the dog. Though asking her to do me that favour would mean that I'd owe her. That's something else folklore gets right. Ethereal creatures keep a very precise tally of favours granted and what they've decided they're owed.

Turning around, I looked over the road towards the river, to the packhorse bridge and the ruined church. The day was warm and sunny, but cold shadows hung around the weathered arches, and the roofless walls were as jagged and off-putting as broken teeth.

The idea of heading home by the path through the woods made my skin scrawl. Was that my imagination or the wose's doing? Or just the after-effects of being beaten up and barely getting four hours' sleep last night? But that's why I'd come to the Goose – to leave the Landy in the car park and give whoever had followed me here the slip.

If I was going to do that, I'd better make a move. A news van had just pulled into the car park with a crunch of tyres on gravel. I was over the road and walking away across the meadow before anyone could recognise me.

I hurried along the packhorse trail. There were no ominous shadows under the trees, no hints of movement in the undergrowth to suggest lurking boggarts. I sensed a brooding watchfulness among the trees regardless. I couldn't hear any birdsong, and even the rustling leaves sounded subdued. This wood wasn't a happy place today, despite the bright sunshine. I walked back to the farm as quickly as I could, trying to ignore the sting of sweat in my cuts and grazes.

Sam Monkswell was in the yard, checking his tractor's tyre pressures. He stood up and called out. 'Daniel? Can I have a word?' He didn't sound his usual amiable self.

'I'm sorry, honestly, very sorry. I know I owe Chrissie an apology.' I really hoped he could see I meant it. 'I snapped at her and she didn't deserve it. I've had a crap few days but

I know, that's no excuse. What can I do to make it up to her? Flowers? A bottle of wine?'

Sam wasn't to be placated. 'You've been damn rude, twice now, and no, she doesn't bloody deserve it. Anyway, it's more than that. I don't know what's going on with you, but you've been in and out at all hours lately. Lin says people in the cottages are complaining. They come here for some peace and quiet, you know.'

I bit back an urge to argue. I'd had precisely one early start this week, and when I went out last night the pubs had still been open.

'I am sorry.' I did my best to sound contrite. 'It won't happen again.'

'Chrissie says some woman called here yesterday. Said she was a friend of yours, but you obviously weren't expecting her and she didn't have your mobile number.' Sam's unspoken question hung in the air.

'We've only just met.' I couldn't think how else to explain the naiad. 'Victoria and I split up at the weekend.'

That wasn't a lie, though telling Sam something so personal stuck in my throat. On the plus side, hearing about my love life seemed to embarrass him just as much.

'Okay, well, that's none of my business.' He tossed his tyre pressure gauge from hand to hand. 'But you've got to see it from our point of view. Your friend wouldn't leave her name or any message. Chrissie nearly rang FarmWatch to report a suspicious intruder.'

'It won't happen again,' I assured him.

Though I wondered how I was going to make sure of that. I wasn't ready for another conversation with the naiad just yet. For one thing, I still didn't feel she'd told me the whole story.

As I went up the stairs to the flat, exhaustion hit me like a sandbag. I opened up the laptop to plug my new phone in and update it with all my contacts. I left it charging while I tried to work out what to do for the best.

I guessed Kalei wanted the wose gone for much the same

reasons as Tila. Dead mortals drew unwanted attention to the valley and most likely polluted the naiad's river as well. I remembered the flowing water deep in the gully where Amber Fenham had been thrown.

So much for ethereal concerns. This trouble was spilling into the everyday world. I thought about the uneasy atmosphere in the woods on Kympton Hill and how grim the ruined church had looked. Jim and Donna might be making money out of the journalists at the moment, but that wouldn't help them for long if tourists started shunning the Goose for the bright lights and friendlier atmosphere up the hill at The Osprey.

Then there was Sam and Chrissie's business. I guessed bookings would soon drop if holidaymakers in the cottages overlooked by those trees found themselves moody and out of sorts, their dogs snappish and unpredictable.

Meantime, the wose would be looking for another depraved partner. That might not take very long at all. There were plenty of lowlifes in The Griffin. Given how easily the naiad had got inside my head, I guessed the wose would find it easy enough to lure another bastard already inclined to rape and murder.

Which was all very well, but I had no idea how the fuck to kill a sodding wose and burn down a meadow full of poplar trees, just to make sure the bastard thing stayed dead. If last night was anything to go by, I'd be the one who ended up dead.

I jumped as my new phone beeped with a text message. It was the network notification, telling me to turn the handset on and off again. I did that, and when it powered back up, the phone went berserk.

There were a dozen or more missed calls and text messages from unknown numbers. I ignored those, more concerned to see three voicemails and two texts from Phil Caister. More baffling, there were two missed calls from Victoria. First things first. I rang Phil.

'Daniel? Where the hell are you?'

'Home. I... I had a really bad night, throwing up, and I've had the shits. I'm sorry, I should have rung—'

'Will you be in tomorrow?' Phil cut me off, his tone harsh.

'Yes, absolutely. Must have been something I ate.'

'Right then.' He rang off.

I stared at my phone, not sure what to make of his abruptness.

The mobile rang and I answered it, expecting to hear Phil again.

'Daniel?' It was Victoria. 'What the hell is going on?'

'What do you mean?'

'Have you seen the TV today?' Her voice rose, exasperated. 'Go on, turn it on. Quick, so you catch the headlines.'

'Okay.' I got up and found the remote.

'Twitter's going mental about you.' Victoria sounded really upset.

'I don't use bloody Twitter,' I protested.

'You think that matters? They're saying all sorts of horrible things.'

'Who are? Hang on.' My stomach hollowed as I watched the news summary. According to the BBC, a man was helping police with their enquiries into the Derbyshire murders. Another man had been interviewed and released. A statement from some superintendent or other said their investigation was ongoing.

The newsreader said all this over a repeating loop of video clips. One showed me driving out of the Lambton police station. I was clearly visible through the windscreen, my face menacing, bruised and filthy. I looked appalling. No one watching would be able to tell I was only screwing up my eyes because I was half-blinded by camera flashes.

'I haven't done anything, I swear,' I said to Victoria. 'Well, I have, but listen, I was the one who stopped some prick abducting a girl—'

'Then say so,' she urged me. 'Get online—'

'Not a chance. The police will go nuts.' I was sure of that.

'You need to tell your side of the story,' she insisted.

'I will, when I'm a witness in court.'

'You are so bloody naive!'

Before I could answer, she rang off. I was about to call her back when I realised something. Phil Caister must have seen the news. That's why he'd sounded so odd. He knew I was lying to him. I would have some explaining to do in the morning. Fuck.

I dialled Dad's number. I desperately needed to talk to someone about what had really happened, someone who would understand. Maybe Mum could tell me something more about the wose, now that I'd actually tangled with it.

No such luck. The number I was calling wasn't currently available. I should try again later.

I left a brief message. 'Hi, it's me. If you've seen the news, don't worry. I'm okay. Well, pretty much okay. Give me a ring when you get this.'

Then I gave up and went to bed. It was the middle of the afternoon but I was absolutely knackered. I half hoped the Green Man might show me some answers, but there was no sign of him in my dreams. Just glimpses of the wose's menacing face as I tossed and turned through the night.

# Chapter Seventeen

When my alarm shocked me awake, I felt as though I'd barely slept. As I switched on the radio and the newsreader calmly announced the day, the date and the time, I could hardly believe it was only Thursday morning.

A week ago I'd never met another dryad besides my mum. I'd never imagined meeting a naiad. No one had any idea there were two dead girls in that little valley, one who'd lain there for over a decade. Now no one but me knew the true killer.

I got up and dressed. The magnesium sulphate paste had done its job getting the last of the muck out of the gouge in my chest. I put on a fresh dressing and found my loosest T-shirt in hopes of hiding that as well as the scabs and bruises on my shoulders and arms.

The bathroom mirror still showed me a face most people would cross the road to avoid. The thorn scrape across my forehead might be healing, but this past week of not nearly enough sleep had left ominous shadows under my eyes.

I ate breakfast, made sandwiches for lunch, filled my flask with strong, sugary coffee. At least there was no sign of any reporters as I took the main road to Lambton and headed to the barn conversions. As far as I could tell, no one was following me.

I was the first one to arrive, apart from Phil Caister signing a lorry driver's docket for a delivery of sand. As I got out of the Landy, I spoke quickly, before he did.

'I'm sorry I didn't tell you the full story yesterday. I didn't realise my face would be all over the news.'

'So what happened?' He looked at me, unsmiling.

This was no time to lie, but I'd have to be very careful about exactly what truth I told.

'A girl was snatched from the Goose's car park on Tuesday night. I saw it happen as I was pulling up, so I went after the car. Jim at the Goose can tell you about it, he dialled 999. I caught up with the prick on the back road near where those dead girls were found, and I beat the shit out of him. Only the girl ran off into the woods and I caught my face on a low branch when I was trying to find her. I was going for help when the coppers caught up with me and it all took a bit of sorting out.'

'Is it all sorted?' Phil demanded.

'I think so.' I fervently hoped so.

'Then why the fuck did you lie to me yesterday?' Phil glowered.

'I'm really sorry. It was a stupid thing to do, but I wasn't sure how much I could say.' I did my best to sound contrite. 'They've arrested the bloke who grabbed the girl and I'll be a witness when it comes to court. Doesn't that make everything sub judice, or whatever they call it?'

I didn't actually know, and it was a fair bet that Phil wouldn't either.

He had other concerns. 'Is the girl okay?'

I nodded. 'As far as I know. The cops wouldn't tell me a lot.'

To my relief, Geoff's Transit turned into the yard, ending the conversation.

'Right. Best get on.' Phil still wasn't looking too friendly. 'But Daniel, the next time I catch you bullshitting me, you're out on your arse, understand?'

He walked away before I could answer.

'Hiya.' Lewis was getting out of the van, his face alight with curiosity.

I gave him a warning look that made him take a step backwards.

'Right,' I said, satisfied. 'Now you can show me what you and Ryan got done yesterday, unless the two of you were just pissing about up there.'

'We did our best,' Lewis said, defensively enough to convince me that they had indeed been as idle as they could get away with.

I spent the morning on the supporting timbers for the windows going into the roof, while the two lads finished nailing up the tile battens. They were down the ladders like squirrels in a drainpipe when Phil called a halt for lunch. I took my time before following. That meant I overheard Nigel and Geoff as they stood on the far side of the barn door, each smoking a cigarette where the breeze blew the smoke away from the blokes still eating.

'The news is saying there was a second man involved.'

'If the coppers really thought it was him, they'd never have let him go.' Geoff sounded doubtful all the same.

'They have to, if they haven't got enough evidence. PACE and all that,' Nigel said vaguely.

'He doesn't look the type.''

'What type is that?' Nigel countered. 'What do we know about him anyway?'

I silently climbed a few rungs back up the lowest ladder, then banged the hammer hanging from my tool belt against it as I came down a second time. When I walked out of the barn, Nigel and Geoff were heading back to the chairs under the tree.

As I fetched my sandwiches, I saw Lewis and Ryan sitting in the open door of Geoff's Transit, avidly reading a couple of newspapers.

'WHAT DOES HE KNOW?' one tabloid demanded, beside a photo of me which must have been taken in Lambton when I went to the phone shop. At least I was cleaned up, but I still looked ready to rip the photographer's head off.

'PEAK KILLER CAUGHT?' the other paper wondered, alongside another grim picture of me, giving exactly the wrong impression, whatever the tiny writing underneath the snapshot might say.

My first impulse was to sit in my driver's seat to eat my lunch. But that would look really suspicious, so I joined everyone else and ate in silence. No one asked me how I'd got the scrape on my forehead or the bruises on my hands.

No one mentioned the dead girls or anything that had happened on Tuesday night. No one said much of anything apart from Lewis and Ryan bickering over the merits of rival computer games both called something like Call to War.

When everyone started packing up their lunch boxes and flasks, I walked over to Phil. 'Everything's ready for those windows. What do you want me on this afternoon?'

'Get number three and number four ready for tiling. We're not going to be lucky with this weather for much longer.' He gestured at the cloudless sky. 'Ryan and Lewis can help Nigel lay the floor screed in number one.'

That left me working on my own, which suited me fine. I could think through my current predicament and consider what I might do next. The temptation to pack all my stuff and take off for Cornwall or Caithness was considerable. But that wasn't really an option. If I vanished, the first place DS Tunstead would look was my parents' home. I wasn't going to drag Mum and Dad into this.

I dug my phone out of my pocket and tried Dad's number again. Still no reply. I sent a quick text.

*Give me a ring when you get a chance.*

I ground my teeth as I fired nails through battens. I guessed the nature reserve must be besieged by another mob of reporters and TV vans. At least one reporter knew my name, and it wasn't as if I was called John Smith. How many Mackmains would some journalist have to check before a clue led them to my old address? If they couldn't find out where I lived, pestering my mum and dad would be the next best thing. I guessed he must have turned off his phone to avoid their calls.

I fired the last nail in the gun through a batten. As I re-loaded it, I tried not to think of some nosy hack discovering there was no official record of my mother before I'd been born. There was no point imagining all the worst possible consequences of this current mess. I had to work out the best way to get through it, and fast.

By the time Phil called a halt to the day I'd worked out a

few things. I'd also realised I needed answers to some very specific questions. I drove back to the farm by the main road. There was no sign of any reporters, thankfully. As I walked up the steps to the flat, I wondered if I was about to do something monumentally stupid.

I took the naiad's white scarf out of the kitchen drawer and looked at it for a moment. Then I turned on the tap and held it in the running water.

With a rattle like hail on the glass, the window above the sink turned opaque with fog. I pushed it open and the mist swirled inside to coalesce into Kalei.

She looked completely different, with wavy blonde hair brushing her shoulders. Only her eyes remained the same, with that flash of turquoise whenever she blinked.

I was astonished. Whether a dryad's masquerading as a human or appearing in their ethereal form, they're still recognisably the same person. 'You can completely change how you look?'

'You said you didn't want your landlady to see me here again.' She shrugged. 'I'm water. I can be whatever I want to be. So what do you want?' She ran the tip of her tongue along her lips suggestively.

'Forget it,' I said curtly. Now I knew how easily she could tap my lustful instincts, it was easier to stay unbeguiled.

Kalei grinned and was all business. 'Why the summons?'

I dropped the gauzy white fabric on the table, reminding myself that ethereal creatures will find whatever meaning in a mortal's words which best suits their own purposes.

She spoke first. 'I found this downstream. I thought you might want it back.' She laid the mask I'd carved beside the scarf. The Green Man looked none the worse for wear, however far the piece had tumbled and floated down her river.

'What does he feel about the wose attacking these girls and involving a mortal man in these murders?'

'I've no idea.' Kalei sounded sincere. 'He's of the air and I'm of the water.'

I gazed at the mask. 'I have a proposal for you.'

'Go on,' she prompted.

'I want to find another dryad's son. Your help with that is my price for tackling the wose.'

She took a moment to think about it. 'I can tell you where to find a dryad's grove.'

I considered that very carefully. 'A grove where a dryad still lives?'

'Yes.' She smiled. 'It's the wood where Tila was born, before she came to my valley.'

My mouth was dry. I'd been searching for dryads without success for nearly a year now. This could be just what I was looking for. If she was willing to do me this favour, Kalei must really want to be rid of the wose and she must need me to do it for her. If the bastard thing had already killed Tila, presumably it could kill a naiad.

Okay then. I just had to do this without the bastard thing killing me.

She took my silence for agreement. 'I will help you take him by surprise. If I beguile a girl into the woods, he won't be able to resist—'

'No,' I said sharply. 'We're not putting anyone else at risk. Lure it yourself. Pretend to be a pretty girl.' I gestured at her new appearance.

She looked at me, exasperated. 'The wose will know my true nature whatever outward form I'm wearing.'

'Then lure it as yourself.' I wasn't giving up. 'He killed Tila because she was telling me his secrets. Make him think you're going to do the same.'

Kalei shook her head in absolute refusal. 'No.'

'Okay then.' I threw up my hands. 'Good luck dealing with it on your own.'

For a moment, her outline blurred and I saw wisps of mist curling through her hair. Then she became fully corporeal once again. 'Perhaps I can find a way to draw him out. What will you do then?'

'That depends on what you can tell me about it. If I'm going to try to do this, I'll do it my way and in my own time. If I don't think I've got a decent chance of succeeding, and of getting away without the police locking me up for arson, I'm not even going to try. Our deal will be off.'

Kalei sat on one of the chairs. 'What do you want to know?'

I took a deep breath and asked the questions central to the plan I'd been devising while I nailed those battens down. A treacherous part of me hoped she'd say no to something vital, meaning it couldn't be done. She never did.

Finally, I ran out of questions. 'One last thing. It's been a dry summer and there's no telling how far a fire could spread. I don't want to set the whole meadow alight.'

Kalei nodded. 'I can make certain of that.'

'Then I'll see you on Saturday night.'

'Thank you.' She smiled with satisfaction that bordered on smugness.

That unnerved me, but before I could ask her anything else, she disappeared through the open window.

I sat at the table, gazing at the evening sky as the dusk deepened. I remembered what Mum had said about naiads being manipulative and deceptive. Was I being taken for a fool here, tricked into doing exactly what Kalei wanted while I imagined this was all my idea?

Except I wasn't doing this for the naiad. Two girls were dead, and a third had come close to being the wose's next victim. Tila had been murdered. I was doing this for them, or trying to, at least.

If there wasn't something vital Kalei hadn't said, the answer to a question I hadn't known I needed to ask. I couldn't shake the feeling that there was still a lot the naiad wasn't telling me.

On the other hand, the Green Man had brought me here. He had to have some reason for doing that. Maybe he was killing two birds with one stone. If I could do this, the valley would be free of the wose and I'd be on my way to learning

171

more about my mother's kind from some unknown dryad. Everyone wins.

I still wasn't convinced. I still had a faint, uneasy suspicion that there was more going on here than I realised.

When it got dark, I gave up and went to bed. As I drifted off to sleep, I wondered where I'd be on Monday morning, or if I'd be in any fit state to care.

# Chapter Eighteen

A news van and a hatchback were parked outside the Kympton Grange gate on Friday morning. I turned on the TV to catch the review of the day's papers while I ate my toast.

A smartly dressed newsreader on a red sofa was summarising the pages open in front of her.

'... he went to university but dropped out after a year. He seems to move around a lot, never stays in one place for more than six months or so, a loner...'

Great, they were making me sound like every nutter who ever went on a rampage with a gun. Then it got worse.

'He has one conviction for assault, and apparently there have been other incidents—'

'The police have stressed that he's only been interviewed as a witness,' the bearded co-presenter quickly added.

I turned off the TV and checked my phone, in case I'd missed a call while I was in the shower. No such luck. Dad still hadn't rung, and I was starting to get seriously concerned.

I looked at the text messages I'd ignored so far this morning. One was from Willersley, Rose and Slater.

*Current news coverage just the safe side of actionable. Will be happy to advise should that change. Ring to discuss if you wish.*

I couldn't decide if that was good news or not. Even if the papers and TV weren't saying outright that I was a killer, people reading half-truths and old gossip would be telling themselves there was no smoke without fire. There were still people convinced that the parents had done away with that little girl who'd gone missing in Portugal, no matter what anyone said. There was that murder case where the papers went after a school teacher who turned out to have nothing to do with it. He'd got a sizeable payout, but only after no end of grief. I'd prefer to come out of this with no money and no more aggravation.

I went out, making very sure to lock the door behind me. Unfortunately Sam had bolted the yard gate, so I couldn't just drive through and be on my way. I had to go and open up to get the Land Rover out.

'Hi, Daniel.' It was the cheery lad who'd been eavesdropping on me in the phone shop, with a photographer a few steps behind him. 'Sorry to hear you split up with your girlfriend.'

I concentrated on working the bolt and opening the gate, telling myself if I looked up, a flash would go off and that photo would be in all the weekend papers. It took all the self-control I could summon not to grab the little shit by the throat and shake him until he told me what the fuck he knew about Victoria. Who the hell had he been talking to? Chrissie Monkswell or her friend, Lin?

I managed to drive the Land Rover out, park and close the gate again behind me without flattening the journalist or his photographer. That was one achievement to start the day.

Checking my mirror, I saw them getting into their car. They didn't follow me though, still sitting there when the turn of the lane hid them from view. That wasn't much of a relief. Chrissie Monkswell or her nosy new friend could still offer them coffee and an exclusive. That would pay me back for being so aggressive when we'd last spoken. I thumped the steering wheel as I drove, frustrated as well as angry with myself.

I really didn't need this, on so many levels. If more reporters were waiting for me at the Lambton barns, that would really piss off Phil Caister and I couldn't afford to lose this job. I also had a hell of a lot of things to get done before I met Kalei in The Griffin on Saturday night. Things that would prompt endless questions if anyone was following me. Tension knotted my shoulders.

I breathed a little more easily, seeing no sign of any reporters when I arrived at the barns. Not that I had a particularly pleasant day. No one wanted to talk to me. At lunch, Mick and Geoff were determined to discuss the new season's prospects for Chelsea and Man United while everyone else listened, or at least pretended to. Lewis was bent over his phone, his fingers busy, occasionally nudging Ryan to show him something. They both kept looking furtively at me and I was sure I caught Lewis snatching a photo. When we all got up to get back to work, I had to stop myself grabbing the phone and hurling it into the cement mixer.

I stayed on till just before six to finish the last frame for the roof windows in the remaining barns. Even though Geoff and Lewis had already scribbled their going-home time down as quarter to, I still only signed out for half past five.

Phil grunted as he took a pen from behind his ear to amend my time. 'Let's not have Sue in the office thinking we've got some sort of time warp here.'

I hoped that attempt at a joke meant I was forgiven for Wednesday. 'Cheers.'

I tried a grin but he didn't smile back.

'See you Monday,' he said briefly.

At least he hadn't told me not to bother showing up next week, I told myself as I drove off. Now I just had to hope I'd be able to go to work, not stuck in a police cell, a hospital bed or worse.

For that to happen, I had to concentrate on the job in hand. Checking my mirrors for any sign of a following car, I drove away from Lambton, taking the main road towards the motorway. I turned on the radio to catch the news and learned that a man had appeared before Derbyshire magistrates charged with kidnapping and assault. James Raynott had been remanded in custody and psychiatric reports had been called for. Apparently the police hadn't ruled out the possibility of further charges.

So that was the rapist's full name. Then I wondered about all the things the newsreader hadn't said. There was no hint of where Raynott was originally from, or his age. Well, if he'd spent years in thrall to the wose, DS Tunstead had a real puzzle on his hands and no clue about the pieces he was missing. With any luck, that would keep him busy enough to stop him

175

looking in my direction. Hopefully this new information would send all the reporters off trying to find out who James Raynott was as well.

As I headed north, the Friday night rush hour traffic was vile, especially around the junction of the M1 and M18. It took me almost three hours to reach the safely anonymous retail parks in the middle of the urban sprawl between Huddersfield and Leeds. What seemed like the entire population of West Yorkshire was doing their weekly shop. At least that meant I could lose myself among the crowds. No one took any notice of me buying a couple of cartons of egg whites and a bag of granulated sugar in three different supermarkets. A DIY store supplied me with a big box of empty glass jars for home pickling enthusiasts and a couple of other essentials.

Buying the petrol I needed made me a bit more nervous. CCTV might be there to catch people driving off without paying, but if I did get collared on Saturday night, running the Land Rover through number plate recognition would soon show DS Tunstead which two filling stations I'd visited. He'd see me filling up a five-litre can at each of them, and he was bound to wonder why I was buying petrol for a vehicle with a diesel engine.

Well, there was nothing I could do about that. I grabbed a service station pasty and chips and drove back to Kympton. Thanks to the slackening traffic I arrived back at Grange Farm just before eleven-thirty. Hopefully that would avoid annoying the Monkswells any more than I already had. And thankfully there was no sign of any journalists.

As I rounded the corner of the barn, though, my heart sank. Sam was waiting, sitting on the steps up to the flat.

'Hello,' I said cautiously. 'Do you—'

'We're giving you notice to quit.' He stood up and handed me an envelope.

I felt like I'd been slapped in the face. 'Look, I'm really, really sorry. Truly. I'll apologise to Chrissie, do whatever I need to make things right—'

'It's not just that.' Sam shook his head, resolute. 'The farm's been all over the telly. We've had a family due in tomorrow ring up and cancel. The people in the end cottage want a refund to make up for all these reporters ruining their holiday. No one's been able to set foot outside without getting a microphone shoved in their face—'

'It's only been one day and it's not my fault.' I kept tight hold of my temper. 'All I did was—'

'I don't want to know what you did! I just want you out of here.'

I realised Sam was shaking with more than outrage over what I'd said to his wife or from the chill of the night. He was scared, and not just of the damage this was doing to their business. Sam was scared of me.

I looked down at the envelope. 'How long are you giving me to find somewhere else?'

'Two weeks, legally,' he said curtly. 'We'd like you out sooner. You'll get your deposit back.'

So they were playing fair by me and the tenancy agreement we'd signed. That made it worse, somehow. I cleared my throat. 'I'll see what I can do.'

I didn't hold out a lot of hope. My bruised and cut face would be enough to put any prospective landlord off, even if they hadn't seen me all over the papers and the telly, with reporters hinting I was mixed up in a murder. Well, I'd slept in the Land Rover before, and at least the summer nights were mild.

'Right then.' Sam headed for the farmhouse, his pace quickening with every stride.

I went upstairs and looked around the flat. Packing up my stuff would be easy enough. I was used to doing that. Where to go was much more of a challenge. I shook my head and headed for bed. I'd decide what to do once Saturday night was over. By then I'd know if there was any point in making plans for the future.

I set my alarm for an early start. Hoping to leave without

177

pissing off the holidaymakers in the cottages any further, I kept the engine revs as low as I could as I pulled out of the yard.

The main routes were already filling up with Saturday's changeover day tourists. Each time I got stuck in traffic, I checked my phone. Still no text or voicemail from Dad. I barely resisted the temptation to try calling him yet again, but I reminded myself the last thing I needed today was some traffic cop pulling me over for using a mobile phone while driving.

Once again, there was no sign of reporters following me, and that was a relief. Not that they'd have been able to follow me very far. I went off-road when I reached the bleak moors up around the High Peak. A rutted track led me to a secluded gully where I carefully turned the petrol I'd bought into jellied fuel.

It's surprising what you pick up by way of useful knowledge. I worked with a bloke on a Scottish forestry restoration project who'd grown up in a bit of Manchester where the pit-bulls go around in pairs to watch each other's backs. We'd been watching some mediocre action-thriller on DVD one evening, where the implausibly lucky hero improvised Molotov cocktails from bottles of booze and cloth ripped from the heroine's blouse, helpfully exposing most of her equally implausible tits.

Halfway through a six-pack of lager, Alec was loud in his scorn. He'd been a lot more entertaining than the movie, as he explained how a bottle of spirits would shatter in one quick burst of flame, giving the unspecified, brown-skinned bad guys little more than flash burns.

Apparently the experienced rioter adds a measure of washing-up liquid and a judicious quantity of sugar to make the best Molotov. Given a bit more time, Alec continued with a wave of a freshly opened beer can, making some jellied fuel would be even better. Come the zombie apocalypse, he'd be ready with plenty of that.

I wasn't interested in survivalist fantasies, but I remembered the proportions of egg white to petrol to sugar he'd quoted. I'd done this a few times before. Solid fuel can be useful stuff. So I got the job done quickly and easily and drove back to Lambton obeying every single speed limit, road sign and traffic light. Even with the pickling jars sealed as tightly as possible, a strong smell of petrol still filled the Landy.

Any copper who had reason to stop me couldn't fail to notice that. Once the police had searched the vehicle I'd have a lot of explaining to do. After I'd tried and failed to convince them I was a law-abiding citizen, the only question would be whether they charged me with intent to commit arson or with some more drastic terrorist plot.

I didn't go back to the farm. Following a single track road I'd scouted out online, I drove in a wide circle around the valley and headed for the far side of the low, scrub-covered hills overlooking the water meadow. Kalei had described a particular limestone outcrop in precise detail. If I couldn't find that, our whole plan was in trouble before we'd even got started.

Thankfully the crag was hard to miss. I parked as far behind the jagged grey stone as I could force the Land Rover through the bushes, and got the cheap black plastic toolbox full of jars out of the back. At least the smell of petrol wasn't too strong out in the open air. I carried the toolbox further away from the road and soon found the storm-felled beech tree Kalei had told me about.

I set the jars down and went back to fetch the second toolbox from the Land Rover. Once I'd stowed everything deep in the crater behind the beech tree's torn-up roots, I cut tangles of bramble and chucked them over the boxes to hide everything from any passing dog walker.

Shoving secateurs and work gloves into a pocket, I looked around yet again to make certain no one was watching me. No one mortal anyway. I took the lime wood carving of the Green Man out of another pocket and tucked it among the thorny sprays.

'If you want this done, you need to make sure that no one finds any of this. Especially not the wose.'

I'd bought most of the things I needed brand new, ready to discard them once the job was done, but there were some things I simply couldn't afford to buy, never mind sacrifice. That meant using some of my own tools. Tools I'd registered to make sure I could claim on their warranty if I needed to, so they would be quickly traced back to me if this all went horribly wrong.

The trees all around the hollow were still and silent. I searched the leafy branches for some indication that the Green Man had heard me, that he was going to take care of this cache. Nothing. I waited a while longer, but no sign of his presence appeared.

Better make sure this looked like any other ordinary Saturday, if any copper had some reason to come asking on Monday. So I went to the supermarket and was staring blankly at the ready meals on offer when my phone rang. When I saw it was Dad, my hands shook so much I nearly dropped the damn thing before I could answer the call.

'Are you okay?' I asked urgently.

'I'm fine. Your mum's fine. I'm really sorry I didn't ring you back sooner,' Dad said. 'Dave Fulbrook gave me the nod on Thursday, said that the newspapers had been calling him to ask about you.'

My heart sank. 'Have you had a lot of hassle?'

'No, not at all,' he assured me. 'I locked the gate at the far end of the track, to stop anyone coming up to the door. Your mum's been making sure any strangers on the public footpaths come straight out on the other side of the reserve without realising they should have been able to see the house.'

'Right, okay.' That was a relief.

'The thing is though, your mum decided to cut off their phones and radio reception. She said if they couldn't contact whoever sent them here, they'd simply have to leave.'

'That makes sense.' I guessed she'd started listening to the news on the BBC, if she'd been working out how to frustrate them.

'Yes, but that's not the whole story. You know how your

mum is.' Now he sounded exasperated. 'I told her that meant I couldn't talk to you and she kept coming up with excuses. It's taken me ages to get some straight answers.'

'How do you mean?' I was at a loss.

'If we couldn't talk to each other, then you couldn't ask her questions she really doesn't want to answer.'

'About what?' I realised the answer at once. 'About woses and naiads?'

'Especially about naiads.' Dad's voice was tense. 'She's scared for you, Dan, and I can't say I blame her. She says that naiads used to go looking for dryads' sons, to drag them into their scheming. Because they – you – can handle iron and steel, you can be used against other...' He struggled for the right words. 'Other wildwood folk and creatures. She says that naiads don't care if a dryad's son gets killed, because he doesn't share their blood. She says they've even been known to turn a son against his mother.'

Now he sounded embarrassed, and I guessed that Mum had explained how readily a naiad can tap into a man's wet dreams.

'I'm being careful, honestly I am.' There was no way I was discussing my experiences with Kalei with my dad.

'I'm sure.' He still sounded stressed. 'But she's scared for you, Dan, and honestly, after some of the stories she's told me, so am I. Has this naiad told you what's stirred up this wose yet?'

'How do you mean?' Uneasy, I remembered my suspicions that Kalei wasn't telling me everything.'

'Your mum says there has to be some reason this wose has started killing again.'

'Does she have any idea what might be behind it?'

'She says not.' Now Dad was frustrated.

'I will take care, I promise.' I wondered if there was any way I could find the naiad sooner than we'd planned, to ask her a few pointed questions.

'You know I trust you.' Dad sounded as if he were going to

say something else. Instead he changed the subject. 'How's everything else?'

'Not so bad.' I felt better now I knew my parents were okay. 'The reporters are leaving me alone while they're chasing after the—' I broke off, realising I was standing in the middle of a shop where anyone could overhear me saying scary words like 'rapist' and realise they'd seen me on the news. 'That other bloke.'

'Right.' Dad understood.

'Look, I'm in town at the moment. Can I call you back later? Maybe tomorrow?'

'Fine,' he said with a sigh. 'Take care.'

'And you. Give Mum my love. I'll talk to you soon.' I hung up with a guilty qualm.

Knowing he was already so anxious, there was no way I could tell Dad what I had planned. He'd be frantic with worry and I could hardly blame him. I was pretty nervous about it myself, and that was without wondering what secrets Kalei was keeping from me.

I also realised that I had absolutely no way to tell if Mum was listening to phone calls between me and Dad. If she overheard me telling him what Kalei and I intended to do tonight, she would be absolutely furious. Firstly because I was working with the naiad, secondly because I was going to tackle the wose, and most of all, she'd learn that I was deliberately setting out to murder those black poplar trees.

An angry dryad is not someone you want to cross. I had no idea how far her wrath could reach, or if she'd go easy on me because I was her son, but I had no desire to find out. This time, I decided, it would definitely be better to ask for my parents' forgiveness afterwards than hope for their blessing first.

I did the rest of my shopping and went home. By the time I got back to Kympton Grange Farm, driving with the windows open had cleared the last lingering petrol fumes out of the Land Rover.

That was a relief, since Chrissie Monkswell was in the

yard. Though as soon as she saw me, she blushed guiltily and hurried away towards the farmhouse. That didn't bother me as much as I expected. What was done was done. Now I was much more concerned with doing what was needed to rid these woods of the wose. If I survived the night without being maimed or arrested, I'd find somewhere new to live and lie low for a month while I worked out what to do next. I'd have just about enough money to do that.

Once I was back in the flat, I spread my wood carving tools out on the dining table. I had to do something between now and this evening, and this was as good a way as any to occupy my hands and my mind. Having some new work to show DS Tunstead would also bolster my alibi if I needed one. Not even another woodworker could say for definite how long it had taken to carve any particular piece.

Besides, I had tables at craft shows booked for the next few months and I didn't have nearly enough things ready to sell. That was as true as it had been ten days ago, before stopping on my way through Tila's wood had thrown my life into such utter, unexpected chaos. I began to work. Maybe if I could convince myself that everything would soon be back to normal, somehow that would happen.

I let my hands shape a girl's face from the curve in a piece of oak. Halfway through, I realised it was a likeness of Tila. I stopped working. A few moments later, I started again. That was okay. It was good to remember why I'd be risking my neck tonight.

Once I'd finished that, I carved a second Green Man's mask and then another one. It would be interesting to see how well they sold, if I got to those craft fairs. Meantime, they might draw his attention my way. If he'd brought me to the Peak District to rid these woods of that fucking wose, his help tonight wouldn't go amiss.

At the bottom of my box of oddments, I found a piece of ash laced with fine dark lines where mould had penetrated the pale wood. It reminded me of the rot consuming the black poplars in the water meadow. That was some comfort. It wasn't as if those were healthy trees I'd be destroying,

For a moment I was tempted to try carving the wose's face. Only for a moment. That would be far too much like tempting fate. I didn't want anything prompting its interest in me tonight.

I kept an eye on the clock. Around seven I made myself eat some beans on toast. I didn't have much of an appetite. Then I forced myself to concentrate on some decorative wooden spoons. Around nine I left the dining table covered with tools, carvings and wood shavings, and changed into my decent jeans and a new red T-shirt.

I drove to Lambton and parked in the market square close to the phone box. There were TV vans parked over by the police station again. I wondered if there had been some further development. Perhaps Raynott did indeed have ties to this area. I didn't bother switching on the radio to try and catch some news though. Nothing the reporters could say would change my plans.

There was no sign of any journalists or camera crews. I guessed they would be enjoying The George's hospitality. For the moment anyway. If everything went to plan, that would soon change.

The Griffin was packed. People spilled out through the front door onto the pavement and I could see a crowd in the car park as well as in the playground beyond. The night was already growing raucous with everyone trying to be heard over all the other raised voices.

Inside, the sleazy pub was even noisier. Shouted conversations competed with some talent show reject's latest single pumped through cheap speakers. I had to force my way through to the bar, offering half-hearted excuses. Good. People should remember me coming through.

'Bottle of Becks?' I waved a tenner at the barman.

'Be with you in a minute, mate.'

To my surprise, he actually was, swapping a beer for the note and coming back with some change before I'd taken a swallow. He slapped the coins down into a puddle, the classic trick to stop someone checking the total.

I didn't care if he'd short-changed me. Turning around, I leaned against the bar, gazing apparently idly around. Where was she? How long would it take me to catch the turquoise flash of her eyes in this crowd?

'Evening.' A wiry man slipped past a girl who'd just been served, to claim the vacant spot beside me.

'All right?' I barely glanced at him as I kept a close eye on the pool table. The would-be bikers were already there, though I couldn't see any sign of the smudge-eyed blonde who'd been so keen on my company.

'Busy, isn't it?' The man leaned one elbow on the bar, scanning the crowd. He had sharp cheekbones and a pointed jaw, and wore jeans and a grey-and-white checked shirt. His head barely came up to my shoulder. 'Haven't seen you in here before.'

I shrugged. 'Thought I'd see what the place has to offer.'

'Anything particular you're interested in?' He still didn't look my way.

I realised I'd attracted the attention of one of the local drug dealers. He must be searching the place for undercover cops, as well as making sure it didn't look like we were having a conversation.

'Just thought I might find some company, maybe.' That was even sort of true.

'Something to make a girl loosen up for a bit of fun?' He was persistent, I had to give him that.

'No, thanks.' I took another swallow of beer. My throat was dry with tension.

'Watch yourself with some of the girls in here. You don't know where they've been. Nor do they, come to that.' He laughed at his own joke.

I managed a smile. 'You don't say.' This shit probably supplied the date-rape drugs to wipe their memories.

'Mind you...' He gestured towards the pool table with his beer bottle. 'I wouldn't care who she came in with, if she was interested in leaving with me.'

A long-legged girl took a cue from the rack. She wore a white mini-skirt and a loose silver-sparkly top hanging off one shoulder to leave the other bare. Wavy black hair cascaded down her back.

As she leaned over to line up her shot, the bikers couldn't decide whether to stand behind her in hopes of seeing up her skirt or take a stool on the other side of the table to learn whether or not she was wearing a strapless bra.

As she sank the first ball and straightened up to laugh at the man beside her, I caught a tell-tale glint in her heavily mascaraed eyes. Kalei was here and playing the temptress, just as we'd agreed.

Apprehension still tempered my relief. If she couldn't set the first part of our plan in motion, there'd be no point attempting the rest.

I watched her offer her cue to a long-haired and bearded bloke in dirty jeans and a leather jacket with the sleeves torn off. The man she'd been talking to first didn't seem too pleased about that. Not until Kalei pressed herself close to his shoulder, whispering into his ear. Now he grinned, squaring his shoulders and sucking in his beer gut.

'She'd better watch her back if she needs a piss,' the drug dealer observed. 'Hair spray in those pretty eyes could ruin her whole evening.'

'If you say so.' I followed his gesture to a trio of sour-faced women who were watching their men gather around this newcomer like wasps around an alcopop.

For a second I wondered if Kalei had provoked more than she could handle. Then I caught the intent flash of her glance towards the three women. No, she knew precisely what she was doing.

'Time to see a man about a dog.' The dealer finished his beer, left the bottle on the bar and headed straight for a handful of youths who'd just come in. They looked so self-conscious they might as well have worn T-shirts saying 'Under Age'.

I glanced at the barman. He was making very sure that he

didn't catch the pimply newcomers' eyes.

I waved another tenner and got another bottle of beer. I barely touched it to my lips while I watched Kalei at work. Once she'd done her part, I'd need all my wits about me.

She shifted from one man to the next, laying a hand on a forearm here, pressing against a shoulder there. I didn't see who she won the first notes from, but she was soon playing for money against a succession of eager volunteers. The crowd around the pool table grew thicker, with men and women jostling to see each match.

Kalei wasn't winning every game. She had more sense than that. Of course, that meant plenty of men competing to buy her a consolatory drink, hoping to offer her a shoulder to cry on, somewhere more private, later on.

I didn't see how she provoked one of the women she'd displaced into making the first move. The woman hurled her drink into the naiad's face. At least, she tried to. Kalei's fluid sidestep meant the glass's contents went all over one of the bikers instead.

A frisson of ferocious delight surged through the bar. I was braced for the sensation. Even so, I still shivered as I was momentarily consumed with an urge to join the spreading fight. To get stuck in, to relieve all my tensions and frustrations. To let loose all the anger I couldn't express in my tedious, day-to-day life. To revel in unrestrained violence.

Kalei had warned me this would happen, so I fought it, reminding myself I had more important things to do. I forced myself to picture Tila's mutilated body as I shouldered my way to the front door. Men threw unthinking punches at me regardless. Some didn't even see me clearly, their eyes glazed as though they were drunk.

I dodged one erratic fist and shoved another man backwards, hard, as he tried to grab my arm, ready to smack me in the face. He tripped over a chair where a girl sat, huddled and cowering. Her bolder friend sprang forward to rake long fingernails down the hapless bastard's cheek. As he called her a cunt and retaliated with a stinging slap she wasn't expecting, both girls' screams joined the growing cacophony.

By the time I made it out of the door, the madness was reaching men and women outside. Kalei had promised me chaos reaching far beyond The Griffin, and she hadn't been kidding. The pavement crowd was breaking into knots of sharp-tongued disagreements. Men were squaring up to each other, chins jutting, while women faced off with vicious insults and belligerent hands on hips.

A skinny lad reeled across my path, blood dripping from his nose. He clutched a broken bottle and for one appalling moment I thought he was going to try glassing me. Our eyes met. Some instinct for self-preservation overrode the naiad-madness and he staggered away.

I ran across the market square, feeling as guilty as hell. There'd be plenty of injuries before the night was done, and that blood was on my hands. I gritted my teeth. I'd better make sure all this was worth it, by making absolutely certain the wose wouldn't be murdering any more runaway girls.

The phone box was empty. I pressed my back against the glass and metal, looking back towards The Griffin to be sure I couldn't be taken unawares as I dialled 999.

The operator got straight to the point.

'What service do you require?'

'Police, and you'd better send ambulances. A fight in The Griffin in Lambton is getting completely out of hand.'

I didn't need to fake my alarm. The bloke on the other end of the call picked that up at once, quick to assure me that help would arrive soon.

'Can I take your name and address, please?'

'Daniel Mackmain, Kympton Grange Farm.' I spelled my surname for him. This was all going to be on the record, along with the number and location of the solidly hardwired landline I was calling from.

'Okay, I can hear sirens. Thanks.' I hung up before the operator could give me any inconvenient instructions to stay where I was. I had to get away so this chaos would give us the cover we needed for the next stage of our plan.

As I drove out of the market square, I caught a glimpse of

blue flashing lights in my mirrors. I didn't stop, all my attention focused on the road ahead, driving well below the speed limit and definitely with all due care and attention. I took the lane through the valley.

Blue lights and headlamps came racing towards me well before I reached Kalei's hump-backed bridge. I pulled onto the verge to let the police pass by, mob-handed in two patrol cars and a mini-bus with a wire visor over the windscreen. All going to reinforce their colleagues in Lambton.

Kalei had assured me she could provoke enough trouble to have half the county force called out. That was looking like no idle boast. But I still needed the riot to pull all the coppers out of Tila's wood.

Driving past the lay-by, the signs looked hopeful. There were no lights on in the mobile incident room and no cars parked up. I slowed, searching the trees for any hint of police still patrolling the woods. I couldn't see any glimmer of torches or a light glowing inside a scene-of-crime tent.

I didn't stop, accelerating until I reached the rutted lane where the wose had been lurking for his pawn to bring him their next victim. Once again, I looked for any sign of the police still searching for evidence. Like before, there was nothing to see.

I was breathing deeply by the time I reached the junction with the main road. So far, so good, but the night wasn't half-way over. There was still no telling what I might find when I came back.

# Chapter Nineteen

Arriving back at the farm, I parked the Land Rover in the end bay so it was clearly visible from the farmhouse windows.

Up in the flat, I switched off the living room lights and went into the bedroom to turn on the bedside lamp. The glow through the window in the roof should help convince anyone who came knocking that I was in bed.

I changed into my darkest trousers and my most faded black T-shirt. As I got a drink of water from the kitchen tap, I opened the window a crack. Mist surged through.

'Are you ready?' Kalei appeared beside me, still in her guise of seductress. This close I could feel how devastatingly effective it must have been.

'Are you staying like that?' I looked down at her feet, silver-painted toenails peeping out of teetering strappy sandals.

She laughed, bright-eyed and flushed with pleasure. 'Hardly.'

She shimmered into an ethereal form. Not the naked temptress I'd seen before but an opaque blue figure as lithe and purposeful as a wet-suited diver.

I drank the glass of water to ease my dry throat. 'How does this work?'

'Follow me.' She walked towards the door and continued straight on through it as though the solid oak wasn't even there.

I followed in more usual fashion and locked the door behind me. I weighed my keys in my hand, wishing there was some way to leave them in the lock inside. That would convince anyone who came looking that I was safely at home and stop the Monkswells coming in uninvited. But even if Kalei could pass through the door unhindered, she couldn't handle the cold metal keys.

'Hurry up.' She was heading down the outside steps.

190

I followed, my heart thumping in my chest. Kalei glided swiftly and silently across the yard. I had to take slow, painstaking steps to move quietly on the gravelled surface.

Pausing by the Land Rover, I tucked my keys and phone on top of the front tyre, hidden inside the wheel arch. I couldn't risk losing anything in the woods tonight.

Kalei had already reached the lane, heading away from the holiday cottages. I glanced apprehensively at the hill as I reached the gate. To my relief, there was no hint that the darkness in the trees framing the packhorse trail was anything more than the usual shadows. Though I couldn't help wondering where the boggarts were and what they might be doing tonight.

As soon as we were far enough from the farm that heavy boots thumping on tarmac wouldn't disturb any holiday-makers, I broke into a run. I soon drew level with Kalei. 'How much further?'

I was more breathless with apprehension than exertion. The longer I was on the lane, the greater the chances of some passing car. Any driver with half a brain would wonder what I was up to, out here on foot in the middle of nowhere, in the middle of the night.

Even if I managed to persuade any Good Samaritan who stopped that everything was fine and no, I didn't need a lift, that would only get me off the hook for tonight. Any driver who was such a good citizen would immediately reach for his phone when DS Tunstead was on telly tomorrow appealing for anyone who'd seen something suspicious this evening to get in touch.

'There.' Kalei pointed at a dark crag thrusting forward from the wooded hill. It forced the road into an awkward dogleg.

'Really?' I was dubious. I hadn't seen so much as a crevice whenever I'd driven past here, still less a cave big enough for someone my size.

'Do you still think I'm trying to deceive you?' Kalei demanded. 'This was your bright idea.'

That wasn't true, strictly speaking. I'd told Kalei I needed to get to the valley unseen, while my Land Rover stayed parked at Kympton Grange Farm to convince everyone I'd been asleep in my own bed all night. I'd imagined that a naiad shared a dryad's ability to carry a mortal through the air unseen.

Kalei told me that shifting herself from place to place by means of a mist was easy enough, but naiads can only overwhelm the physical limitations of a mortal's body when they're touching running water. She could only carry me along a watercourse.

So that was that, as far as I was concerned. My plan to kill the wose was too risky. I wasn't going to leave the Land Rover parked somewhere and come back to find the police waiting, handcuffs at the ready.

The fury on Kalei's face had been chilling. I'd gauged the distance to the kitchen knife block, in case I had to defend myself. Then she shot me a glance of lightning-bright triumph. She'd remembered an underground route we could use between Kympton and Tila's valley.

'In here.' She skirted the rock and climbed the slope beside it, unhindered by the soft leaf mould.

I clambered awkwardly after her, my heavy boots slipping on the crumbling surface.

'This will be a tight fit, but it opens up on the other side.' Kalei walked through a dense cluster of hart's-tongue ferns rooted in a gully where the limestone met the hillside.

As she disappeared, I swept the ferns aside. There was indeed a gap, but calling it a tight fit for someone my size was bloody optimistic. I had to turn sideways and edge inwards, feeling my way with one blind hand while the unyielding rock pressed into my back and my chest.

I could barely force myself through. The pain of tape tugging chest hair out by the roots made me gasp. I hastily pressed my free hand to the gauze dressing beneath my T-shirt. Jagged stone edges scraped the skin off my knuckles instead. But I could feel a void opening inside the hill as my leading hand flailed in the darkness. I forced my body through the narrow cleft until I very nearly fell headlong into the hidden cave.

'Kalei?' My voice echoed back from some unseen rock face.

She laughed, and I saw her outlined with silvery phosphorescence. 'I'm here.'

The radiance grew, or my eyes adjusted, until I could see more of the cave. What I couldn't see was any way through the treacherous maze of stalactites clawing at my head and the stalagmites surging up from the uneven floor to trip me.

'Wait!' Kalei was walking away through the hanging shadows, and the light was going with her. I hurried to follow. As something brushed my scalp, I stooped lower and lower, unable to distinguish limestone tendrils from empty gloom above me. Gashing my head open or knocking myself out wouldn't just put an end to tonight's plans. I could die in here. No, I would die. There was no sign of flowing water, so Kalei couldn't carry me out. I wasn't even convinced she would try. We were allies as long as I was useful to her. My mother had been right about that.

Now I realised something else, proving I was my mother's son. Before that night, if anyone had asked me if I suffered from claustrophobia I'd have said no, of course not. Now I was in that hidden cave with oppressive stillness surrounding me, breathing damp, stone-scented air. My longing for open sky above my head, sunlit or night-time, was a physical pain beneath my breastbone. My need to feel a breeze on my face and hear shifting leaves became desperation bordering on panic.

But I had to go on. My only other option was fighting my way back through the darkness, hoping against hope that I hadn't lost my way. I'd have no way of knowing if I was still scrambling towards that narrow cave entrance. All the while I'd be at Kalei's mercy. I didn't imagine for one second that she would show me the least compassion. Worse, I wouldn't put it past her to punish me for such cowardice. I'd have broken our agreement, after all.

I should have listened to my mum. It was all too easy to imagine what a vengeful naiad could do to me. She could leave me lost beneath these hills, bringing down rocks to block my exit. No one would ever even find my bones.

I clenched my fists and told myself to get a grip. I wasn't doing this for Kalei. I was doing it for Tila. If I didn't see this through, the wose would strengthen his stranglehold on the valley and more evil things would come to join him.

Then there were all the people caught up in the uproar spreading from The Griffin. It didn't matter if they were low-lifes or innocent tourists. If I turned tail, all tonight's blood-shed in Lambton would be for nothing.

I was doing this for myself. If I succeeded, then Kalei was honour bound to tell me where to find that dryad's grove where Tila had been born. Fuck it, I had every chance of success against the wose, I told myself sternly. It had been a good plan to start with and Kalei had improved it.

All I had to do was get through this sodding cave. People did this kind of thing for fun. Of course, pot-holers had to be fucking insane. Gritting my teeth so hard that my jaw ached, I forced myself onwards.

The ground sloped away and I had to watch my step as the rock became slippery with moisture. At least the roof was rising, stalactites disappearing into the darkness overhead. I could be less concerned about splitting my skull open.

On the other hand, the cave walls were drawing in, soon confining me to a narrow, winding path. After what felt like an eternity, the stone on either side retreated into the dark-ness once again. Now I had to follow Kalei's ethereal light cutting across the trackless expanse of a massive cavern.

She was leading me deeper and deeper underground. The rocky floor grew steadily steeper, though it remained treach-erously smooth. The slickness underfoot became a sheet of water splashing around my boots. I moved more cautiously with every step. Breaking a leg down here didn't bear think-ing about.

Kalei laughed with unkind amusement. 'Don't tell me you

can't swim, woodsman?'

'I can,' I said shortly.

Only because lessons had been compulsory at prima-ry school. One year, we'd been bussed once a week to the nearest public swimming pool and ordered to strip off our warm, comfortable clothes in a chilly changing room reeking of chlorine. If the other kids were to be believed, the whole place was rife with lurking verrucas ready to infest our bare feet.

I'd hated it, and as soon as I'd proved I could swim a length unaided, I did everything possible to get out of those lessons. I hadn't set foot in a public pool since. I'd joined the rest of a forestry working party taking a dip in a Scottish loch at the end of long, hot days, but only so I wasn't the odd one out.

I wondered uneasily where all this water was coming from. If it was raining up on the surface, how long before enough filtered down through soil and rock to flood these subterranean passages and drown me? Even experienced cavers died that way. I'd seen the stories on the news.

I shuddered, though not from cold. The cavern was cool, but not unpleasantly so. I was cursing myself for a fool. I should have told Mum and Dad what I was planning, even if I didn't tell them the details. If I died down here, they'd be waiting for the phone to ring, but that call would never come. They'd never know what had become of me. Like Am-ber Fenham's parents.

That thought was like a slap in the face, halting my grow-ing panic. Amber Fenham and Shevaun Thomson. I was do-ing this for those raped and murdered girls. I had to see the wose destroyed once and for all, to make sure no one else's family suffered the same grief.

Come to that, I had to get out of here in one piece, other-wise everyone who'd seen my face on the news, who thought I was somehow involved in those murders, would tell them-selves my sudden disappearance surely proved my guilt. I sure as hell wasn't going to leave that as my legacy.

'We're here.' Kalei strode up to a flowstone curtain seemingly blocking the way ahead. The creamy ripples glistened as tiny crystals sparkled in the naiad's cold light. 'I can reach the river now.'

She knelt on the bare rock, one dusky blue hand pointing towards a narrow gap where the undulating mantle of limestone met the water-smoothed bedrock. She reached towards me with her other hand. I shuddered. I couldn't help it.

Kalei chuckled. 'You are your mother's son.'

As our fingertips touched, she exploded into a cloud of vapour. The last thing I saw was her silver radiance swirling through the crevice. Then I was swept along in the naiad's wake.

When Tila had carried me through her woodland on the breeze, to show me Amber Fenham's bones, I'd been caught unawares but that hadn't been too unpleasant. At least I'd already had the experience of being taken from place to place by my mother a few times. Being caught up in a dryad's ethereal power is like missing a step in the dark or hitting a rise in a road too fast. There's a surge of weightlessness in the pit of your stomach. When your feet hit solid ground, your heart races until your senses catch up, to reassure you that you haven't fallen into some unforeseen void.

This was utterly different. Sensation like cascading water ran down my skin from head to toe. It was like standing in a downpour or under a relentless shower, when you have to keep your eyes closed and suck in breath through your open mouth. Except there was no way to get out of it. No way to stop myself gasping faster and faster, however hard my chest heaved. If I stopped, the unceasing water would fill my nose and mouth, choking me. My hard-won composure dissolved. If I could have, I'd have screamed.

Then the drowning feeling was gone so suddenly that I went limp with shock. If there hadn't been a stone wall behind me, I'd have collapsed to the ground. Struggling to calm my ragged breathing, I forced myself to unclench my fists. As I did so, I was surprised to realise my hands were dry. So were my clothes, even though I'd been convinced I was completely sodden only seconds ago.

I opened my eyes. The impenetrable blackness definitely wasn't just my imagination. Without any light, I had no idea which way to go. Nothing to warn me of chasms opening up underfoot, just waiting for me to fall down them and break my neck. Then I saw faint radiance outline a corner where the tunnel turned.

'These are old lead workings, but no one's been down here for years.' Kalei's voice struck eerie echoes from the rock. 'Mind your head.'

As my eyes grew accustomed to the dimness, and with the help of her phosphorescent outline ten paces away, I appreciated the warning. Whoever had dug this mine had been nowhere near my height. One time when my hard hat would actually have been some use, and I didn't have the bloody thing with me.

Never mind that. Kalei's radiance was heading away. Ducking into a crouch, I hurried after her, the darkness lapping at my heels.

'How do I get to the surface?' I heard the harshness of fear in my voice.

'This tunnel leads out onto the hillside.' Kalei was amused. 'The old miners traced veins of ore straight back from the surface.'

Some other time I might have been interested in that local history. At the moment, all I wanted to see was some moonlight. I still felt stifled, dry-mouthed and panicky.

Catching up with Kalei as we rounded another curve in the tunnel, I felt a breeze on my face. For one marvellous moment, I caught the scent of the greenwood, full of life and promise. In the next instant, the dry, dusty air I was breathing redoubled my claustrophobia.

I was still trapped in this breathless labyrinth of tunnels writhing beneath uncounted tons of stone. There were tons and tons of rock and soil hanging above my head with nothing but a few rotten pit props to support them, just waiting to come crashing down around me. I had to force myself not to run headlong towards that hope of escape.

I swallowed hard. 'How much further until we're outside? Where do we go then?'

'We'll be some way down the valley.' As Kalei spoke, her ethereal light faded. 'I'll go and see what the police are doing.'

Before I could protest, she dissolved into a shimmering mist, leaving me in total darkness. I froze, unable to move. Choking on pure fear left me breathless. I may have whimpered, but if I did, I couldn't hear it over the pounding of blood in my ears. Then I realised I could see something ahead. I blinked and strained my eyes, peering through the darkness. Was my imagination playing tricks on me?

No, that pale smudge was really there. I edged forward, still hunched down, with one hand groping for the unseen tunnel wall. Slowly I could make out the edges of a roughly hewn door shape. A way out of this hellish blackness. Once again, it took all my strength of will not to break into a run. I felt my way step by careful step, testing the floor with a wary boot before trusting my full weight to it.

By the time I reached the open air, my legs were trembling. I stumbled out onto a narrow path winding along a hillside thick with saplings and brambles. I sank to my hands and knees, drawing in deep breaths of cool night air. As my racing heart slowed, I sat back on my heels and gazed up at the creamy moon. I began tracing the familiar arcs of the constellations my dad had taught me.

Kalei returned in a gust of chill mist. She coalesced beside me, a midnight-blue shadow with glittering turquoise eyes. 'All the police have left the woods. Are you ready to do this?'

I stretched my arms up and rocked my head from side to side to ease the stiffness in my neck. 'Come on then.'

# Chapter Twenty

The narrow path took me down the steep hillside and out onto the road through the valley. We crossed the tarmac and Kalei led me through the scrubby trees and undergrowth to the rising ground on the far side. I recognised the rocky outcrop and headed for the hollow behind the fallen tree.

I tossed the cut brambles aside and dragged out the toolboxes I'd stashed there earlier. A second too late I remembered the wooden mask I'd left on top of everything, in hope the Green Man would help keep it all hidden. Fuck. I couldn't leave a clue like that here. DS Tunstead would be knocking on my door five minutes after he found it.

But I couldn't see the carving anywhere, and I didn't have a torch to search for it. Planning this escapade, I'd decided a flashlight was one thing I could do without. I had my mother's night vision, and a torch beam would be far too visible from the road. I didn't want to draw any attention to the poplar trees until it was absolutely unavoidable.

'What are you doing?' Kalei demanded.

'That carving of the Green Man.' I looked around again. 'Can you find it while I get started?'

'All right. Get moving,' she said, exasperated.

I heaved the box of jars onto one shoulder, not about to trust that much weight to the plastic handle. At least the other toolbox wasn't so heavy. I picked it up and headed for the river while Kalei began searching for the bloody carving.

The corner of the box of jars was soon digging painfully into the side of my neck. I ignored it, more concerned with finding a safe path up the slope to the crest overlooking the water meadow. Taking the road would have been quicker, but I wasn't going to risk being seen.

When I reached the ridge line though, I realised I already knew the best way through these boulders and hazel thickets. I remembered all this from my dream, when the Green Man had tried to tell me Tila was in direst trouble.

Guilt knotted my guts as I walked cautiously down the slope to the meadow. If only I'd realised what the Green Man had meant. If I'd come straight here that night, maybe I could have saved her.

Or perhaps not. Cold night air cut through my T-shirt and the gauze dressing beneath it to make the gash on my chest ache. If I'd come here that night, I'd have had no idea what a vicious fighter the wose could be. If I'd met him unprepared, DS Tunstead would surely be investigating my death along with the two murdered girls right now.

Feeling guilty was pointless. Tila was dead and I couldn't change that. But I could make sure the bastard creature wouldn't kill anyone else, mortal or ethereal. Or at least, I could try.

Now that I'd reached the water meadow, heading for the river through the tussocky grass, I was grateful for my work boots, laced tight and bracing my ankles to save me from a sprain. By the time I reached the poplar trees lining the river bank, sweat was stinging my cuts and grazes. It took conscious effort to lower the jellied fuel to the ground without a thump that might crack the jars.

Breathing hard, I dragged both toolboxes into the shadows, to be sure I wasn't seen from the road. I couldn't resist a shiver of unease as I looked and listened for any hint of movement among the split and gnarled trees. Nothing. Nothing yet, anyway. That wouldn't last.

I left the jellied petrol unopened and took out work gloves, a rubber mallet and a broad-bladed chisel from the other toolbox. Everything was cheap and disposable. The edge on such a crappy tool wouldn't outlast a weekend DIYer's enthusiasm, but that didn't matter for tonight's job.

Kneeling beside the closest poplar, I worked the end of the blade deep into the furrowed trunk. Using the rubber mallet meant only a dull thud when I hammered on the handle, but the cracking was brutally loud as I worked the blade up and down to lever up a slab of bark. I pulled the chisel free then stabbed it down hard to cut through the bark, and tossed the length away. Exposed sapwood shone moist and pale in the gloom.

I shoved the chisel in again hard, driving it sideways with the mallet to rip another strip of bark free. It wasn't easy. These were hardy trees with thick, ridged bark. Rare survivors of an endangered species. Vandalizing them made me feel sick. It was hardly the poplars' fault that their sodding wose had turned murderer.

The next thrust of my chisel exposed white wood threaded through with black lines. Not evil, not the wose's malice, just ordinary, natural rot. These were old, untended trees, I reminded myself, abandoned decades ago. They would be dying naturally soon enough, even without me doing this. Without the wose to sustain them, they might already be dead. I was just restoring the natural balance.

Who was I kidding? This was my revenge on the wose for Tila's murder. I hoped he'd feel every second of these trees' deaths. That would be some payback for the agonies he'd inflicted on all his victims. I drove the chisel deep with savage anger. A few more blows with the hammer and I had the first poplar trunk completely ringed by naked sapwood. I moved on to the neighbouring tree. And the next, and the one after that. I was doing more damage to these trees than a whole deer herd browsing on saplings.

After I'd mutilated the fifth poplar, I had to stand up and take a break. My fingers were starting to cramp. I remembered the first month of my apprenticeship, when Vince had insisted I learn a carpenter's skills properly without using power tools. Since then I'd got too used to electric screwdrivers and drills.

Flexing my hand, I stared into the night, trying to get some idea of just how many more poplars I needed to ring-bark. I was tempted to skip every other one, to save time. I still had to fill these gouges in the wood with jellied petrol.

No, I had to do all the trees. I had to make sure they would die. I couldn't rely on the fire spreading among them. Once the fuel was lit, the first person to drive down the valley would see the flames. They'd surely stop and call 999, and the fire brigade would be on the scene within minutes, bringing foam extinguishers and everything else they used to stop people burning to death in crashed cars.

So I had to set all the trees alight. With luck, there'd be enough damage done to kill them before the flames were snuffed out. I'd better just get on with it. I dropped to my knees and attacked the next tree harder and faster, ignoring the ache in my hand. A shallower score through the bark would hold enough fuel to start a fire. As soon as a blaze really got hold of those first trees, flames would leap from branch to branch.

'How enterprising of you.'

The voice was so close behind me that I felt cold breath on my neck. It reeked of mould and decay. The wose was here, and the bastard had caught me on my knees with my back to it.

Lurching forward, I grabbed the poplar's trunk to haul myself to my feet. I spun around, my skin crawling as I expected to feel the wose's thorny hands ripping into me.

It didn't happen. The bastard thing was laughing, a wholly human laugh. This wasn't the eerie creature who'd attacked that poor girl in the woods, that monstrous effigy woven from ivy and branches. He was the sharp-faced, wiry man who'd chatted to me in The Griffin. The one I'd assumed was a drug dealer.

I felt sick as I realised my mistake. All this time, I'd been thinking the wose was akin to the Green Man, a spirit who remained an ethereal presence, whatever his dealings with humans.

Of course he wasn't. The wose was like the dryads and naiads, able to take on a human guise. He was well used to going out into the world to mingle with men and women who'd never suspect his true nature. Well able to learn all he needed to take advantage of mortal ignorance for his own ends.

I'd made a very bad mistake. I tensed. It remained to be seen if it would prove fatal.

'You're trying to kill my trees?' He shoved his hands in his pockets and cocked his head. 'Whose idea was this? Yours or the water-bitch's?'

He didn't sound too concerned. He didn't need to be. Even if his ethereal vigour couldn't repair the damage I'd already done, plenty of the poplars remained unharmed.

'It's my plan.' I took a moment to work out how far I was from the toolboxes.

'What are you?' As the wose took a pace towards me, a faint red light glowed in his eyes.

A swift sidestep kept me out of his reach. 'A friend of Tila's.'

'Ah.' He laughed as realisation dawned. 'You're a dryad's brat. Tell me, was your mother as much of a whore as she was?' He jerked his head in the vague direction of Tila's grave.

'Why did you kill her?' I took another step away. If he thought he was going to provoke me into attacking him, he had another think coming.

'She was interfering.' He moved to block my path. 'Just like you.'

'Why did you kill those girls?' I genuinely wanted to know.

He shrugged again. 'Why not? They have no place here.'

'You brought them here,' I objected. 'You and that man—'

'Humankind has no place here,' the wose snarled. 'Your father's people should have stuck to their shorelines and hill-tops and left our vales alone. Well, the time has come to re-claim what was once ours, from the mountains through the forests to the lakes. Once enough of your father's kind die, they'll soon shun the dark woods and the wild waters again.'

'You're doing this to scare people away?' I shook my head, contemptuous. 'That's bollocks. No one would even know about these murders if someone hadn't stumbled over the poor girl you two bastards murdered last week. The first one lay dead for ten years and more, until Tila showed me where you dumped her.'

He laughed. 'You think this is all I'm talking about? This is only the start of your people's troubles, my friend. Though you won't be alive to see it.'

I took a firm grip on the chisel and raised it to show him the moonlight glinting off the steel. 'You won't find me easy prey.'

'You think that toothpick will stop me finishing what I've started? I can smell your torn flesh from here.' The wose bared his teeth in a vicious grin. 'But I don't think I'll bother just yet. You'll be more use as a distraction for the police while I find someone else to help hunt down my prey.'

He raised a hand, but not to attack me. He held it at the side of his head, thumb and little finger extended. I watched blankly until, incredulous, I recognised the universal gesture for making a phone call. So it wasn't only my mum who'd learned that particular trick.

'I need the police. Please help me.'

He was using a different voice. A frightened, feminine whisper.

'I don't know where I am. I was in Lambton and there were fights starting everywhere. A man said he'd give me a lift home in his Land Rover. He seemed really nice but he went the wrong way, driving into some woods. I jumped out when he had to slow down for a bridge...'

I wondered which of his victims the wose was mimicking as he gabbled lies in answer to the dispatcher's unheard questions.

'Tall, he was really tall, with really short hair, and strong—'

The wose choked as Kalei appeared beside him and shoved her hand into his face. I don't mean she hit him. Her open palm dissolved into a wash of iridescent water, filling his nose and mouth.

His eyes blazed with scarlet rage. In the blink of an eye, he transformed into the nightmare creature I'd fought a few nights before. He lashed out at the naiad with a many-taloned hand, hissing venomously.

At first I thought he'd missed her. Then I saw the pale

gash spreading across her midnight-blue arm. Moonlight glistened on oozing golden ichor. I expected the naiad to vanish in a cloud of mist. Instead she darted away, only to stop and taunt him.

'You think we don't know what you're up to? You don't think we can frustrate your plans? It's a shame you won't be here to see it.'

He sprang after her. She dodged and ran a short distance before halting again. 'Not even the shadow creatures that live here believe you.'

I realised she was luring him away. I ran the other way to the toolboxes, dropping the mallet though keeping hold of the chisel. Throwing back the lid of the first box I'd opened, I grabbed my nail gun. I'd plugged the battery pack into the mains to charge it all day, and it had a brand-new gas cartridge and a full strip of nails already loaded.

I turned to see the wose intent on killing Kalei. He had her trapped against a trio of poplar trees. Either that, or she'd allowed him to corner her, risking Tila's fate to distract him from what I was doing. He clawed at her, those crooked hands swiping to and fro. This time she was ready. His talons passed through her as easily as water, and doing as little damage. Ripples shivered up her arm and across her body.

He snarled. She shimmered sideways. But now he was expecting that move. His free hand seized her forearm and she couldn't flow out of his grasp. The rootlets that cloaked him like a pelt writhed towards her, lengthening in their eagerness to leech on her moisture.

I heard the pain in Kalei's gasp as she tried to pull his hand away. That only gave him the chance to seize her other arm. Now the wose was laughing with the harsh, inhuman glee which had paralysed me with fear that first night.

Forewarned was forearmed. I wasn't rooted to the spot this time. Yes, I still wanted to run away. If Kalei hadn't been there, I probably would have. But I couldn't leave her to be murdered like Tila. I charged at the wose's back, nail gun in hand.

He heard me coming. Dragging Kalei around with him, he spun to face me. Throwing her bodily at me was a mistake though. In the instant before she crashed into me, she collapsed, as shapeless as water, and vanished into the ground.

I was on the wose in one long stride, stabbing the chisel deep into the angle of his neck and shoulder. He hissed and spat at me. Slime hit my face, stinking like the dregs from a dustbin. He clawed at my shoulders, tearing through my T-shirt and ripping deep into the skin and flesh beneath. His touch burned like acid. He snarled, his foetid breath choking. Grabbing him around the neck with my empty hand, I tried to force his head backwards, to get his splintered gash of a mouth as far away from my face as possible.

I stamped on his feet. I kicked him, driving my solid work boots into his shins. He flinched. I could feel the shudders running through him, all the way to my grip on his neck. Even covered with leather, steel toecaps gave my kicks added impact.

I rammed the nail gun against his chest. I'd already set it to maximum penetration and for rapid fire. I pressed the trigger and the tool rammed four inches of stainless steel deep into the monster, one, twice, three times. Now his spiny-twigged head was thrashing from side to side, burning red eyes flickering madly.

I fired again, but this time the power tool clicked without delivering more nails. Forget what you see in the movies. Nail guns have safety mechanisms insisting that they're pressed hard against something solid to fire. The wose was more like a bundle of sticks than a tree trunk. Plenty of gaps for me to hit, for the nails to miss.

Even so, those three nails were doing him no good at all. His grip on my shoulders had slackened and he was screaming like a fox caught in a snare. Planting my feet as solidly as I could, I brought all my weight to bear. He toppled backwards and I landed on top of him. I raised myself up on one hand and fired the nail gun again and again into his torso.

He fought back with all his strength, trying to roll away, out from under me. I forced my free hand into the tangled darkness of his throat and clamped my feet around one of his legs. Unable to shake me off, he could only keep rolling over and over.

I was on top of him, and then he was on top of me, sticks and stones on the ground digging into my back. I held tight regardless. I kept on pulling the trigger, every time I felt the tool press anything solid enough to take a nail. Finally he went limp beneath me.

'Enough!' Kalei grabbed my shoulder. 'I can hear a car—'

'Okay.' I scrambled to my feet, finally letting go of the wose.

He was still struggling feebly, but the fire in his eyes had faded to a dying ember.

I was tempted to empty the nail gun into him regardless, but the naiad was right. That sodding fake phone call would surely mean police cars were already on their way. I hurried back to the toolboxes and swapped the nail gun for a jar of jellied petrol and the wallpaper paste brush.

'Keep a look out,' I called to Kalei. 'Tell me as soon as you see blue lights.'

But she was gone. I had no idea where, and no time to wonder. I smeared fuel around the scarred trees, dragging the clinking toolbox with me so as not to waste time swapping an empty jar for a full one. The poplars I'd attacked first took the most, but the jellied petrol clung to the shallower scores well enough.

I was halfway down the line of poplars when Kalei erupted from the water. As she stepped up onto the bank in one lithe motion, I saw that her wounds were still oozing ichor.

'Police. They kept on driving though.'

I took a cautious step towards the water to get a better view of the road. A police van went past at speed, without sirens or lights.

The wose had pretended to be an abducted girl. She was lost in some woods. That didn't give the coppers much to go on. I hoped they were starting their search in the clearing where the rapist had parked the other night, or at one of the

207

other sites where they'd found a body.

I gripped the brush. If whoever had taken that phone call thought they recognised me from the wose's description, DS Tunstead could already be knocking on my door at Kympton Grange Farm. I hated to think what he would suspect if he roused the Monkswells for a key when he got no answer and they found I wasn't there.

There was nothing I could do about that. I needed to see this job through. There was no reason for the police to suspect I was here, not as long as I stayed in the shadows, not until I set the trees alight.

'Keep watching. Tell me if they stop anywhere close.' I looked across the water towards Tila's grave. 'Or if they come back this way through the woods.'

'Hurry up.' Kalei stepped back into the river and disappeared.

# Chapter Twenty-One

Now I was painting the fuel onto untouched trees. I was grateful for the deep natural grooves in black poplar bark; they held the jellied petrol nearly as well as the gouges I'd made. I could only hope the flames would reach deep enough into the thick, weathered surface to kill these trees as well.

By the time I reached the last few, I'd emptied all the jars. Glass clanked in the cheap plastic toolbox as I dragged it to the final poplar. Now it was time to light the fires that would kill the wose once and for all. The thought of killing these innocent trees still made me feel sick though, or perhaps that was the petrol fumes.

There was still no sign of activity across the meadow in Tila's wood. No more vehicles had come rushing along the road to cross over Kalei's bridge. That didn't mean I could hang around. I had to light the fuel and get the hell out of there before the police searching the woods from the top of the valley got this far.

Setting fires is something else which isn't nearly as easy as it looks in the movies. Throw a lit match into a puddle of fuel and the chances are the flame will go out before it even lands. Even if it keeps on burning, the odds are good that the petrol itself will quench the match instead of going up in flames.

So I'd bought a disposable lighter. I got my penknife out of my pocket and stripped off the cheap work gloves I was wearing, ripping them apart with the blade. The rough cotton and leather was well coated with the jellied fuel. I was going to burn as much evidence as possible so I'd only have a few things to carry away, like the nail gun which would lead DS Tunstead straight to my door if he found it.

I knelt down and flicked the lighter wheel, once, twice. Finally I got a flame. Even though it was barely bigger than the tip of my finger, I shielded it with my hand, unable to stop myself glancing towards the road. There was still no sign of police vehicles. I held the flame to the petrol-soaked cotton until I was sure it was well alight. Then I wondered how best to wedge the rag into the ravaged bark.

I could always just nail it there. I had the tool for the job to hand. Of course, if I'd thought of that a few moments ago, I wouldn't be the idiot going back to the toolbox with flames already burning, to catch the eye of anyone driving past.

'Kalei?' I called out as loudly as I dared. She'd said her touch could quench flame. I was relying on that to stop this escapade turning the whole valley into an inferno. I hadn't had a chance to remind her though. 'Kalei!'

The naiad didn't appear. I didn't call her again, and I didn't bother trying to put out the first fire. The whole point of using jellied petrol is the stuff is so damned hard to snuff out once you actually get it burning.

I hurried back to the toolbox. The wose was lying motionless on the ground. From this angle, it was hard to see it as anything that looked even vaguely man-shaped. If I hadn't known better, I could have walked right past it, not sparing a glance for a bundle of sticks tangled with ivy and brambles.

The toe of my boot caught something and a glint of metal bounced across the ground. A nail. I wondered where it had come from. If the nail gun didn't fire, it didn't drop the fixings.

The wose sprang onto my back. He wrapped one strangling arm around my throat and dug his other clawed hand into my scalp, wrenching my head backwards. His legs twined around my thighs. I stumbled and fell to my knees.

After an instant of pure panic, I realised he wasn't as strong as he'd been before. However he'd got rid of the nail I'd kicked, the rest were still poisoning him. His breath in my ear smelled weirdly metallic, and for an ethereal creature with no apparent lungs, he was wheezing like a lifelong smoker. There was no hint of the crushing grip that had left those bruises on my thighs before.

His stranglehold was still strong enough to leave me

light-headed though. It doesn't take much to make someone black out from insufficient air or a lack of blood to the brain. As I raised my hands to try and pull him off, I realised I was still holding my penknife. I dragged the blade along the arm he was tightening around my throat. The wose's shriek nearly deafened me, but his hold loosened.

Sucking in air, I hooked my hand onto his forearm. I used all my strength to drag him bodily up and forward. It cost me deep cuts through my scalp as his talons dug into my head. That was worth suffering to throw him sprawling onto the ground in front of me.

I was on him before he could move, pinning him with a knee driven deep into his torso. There was a snapping noise like old dry sticks. I seized his throat to hold his head still and stabbed my penknife into his burning red eye. I held it there, embedded, using all my weight to force it in as hard and as deep as I could. The wose's hands flailed and he went rigid from head to toe. The scarlet glare in his other eye flickered and faded to a smouldering pinpoint.

Leaving the blade embedded in the monster's face, I got to my feet, wiping blood out of my eyes with my forearm. 'Kalei?'

She was nowhere to be seen. I looked down the river bank. The first poplar I'd set alight was burning fiercely. Flames circled the trunk just as I'd planned, licking upwards into the branches. But the blaze wasn't spreading nearly as fast as I'd hoped. I wondered if that was the wose's doing. Well, he wasn't doing much now. I had to work out the best way to get the rest of the trees alight, as quickly as possible while he lay there helpless.

I snapped a trailing branch from the closest rot-ravaged tree. I tore off the ruins of my shirt and wound the cloth as tight as I could round the wood. It wouldn't pass muster with living history re-enactors, but it would make a good enough flaming torch for me.

Hurrying along the river bank, I found the toolbox of pickle jars and forced the torch's head into each of them to soak up any smear of fuel left inside. I kept looking towards the road. There was still no sign of anyone yet, but it couldn't be long. I listened hard for fire engine sirens.

I thrust the crude torch into the flames of the burning poplar. As soon as the rags caught alight, I hurried from one as yet unburnt tree to the next. Holding the torch to the fuel until it ignited seemed to take ages, every sodding time. All the while, I kept a close watch on the wose. There was no sign of him moving, and his stillness seemed to have a different quality now. I allowed myself to hope he really was finally dead, not just lying in wait.

Leaves crackled as the doomed trees flared. I picked up the box of empty jars and wedged it between two branches to make sure everything would burn into an unrecognisable, unfingerprintable glob of melted plastic. The heat from the flames was getting fierce. My boots and trousers protected my legs, but I could feel the hairs on my bare chest and forearms singeing.

I'd set maybe two thirds of the poplars alight when I saw blue roof lights on the valley road. I halted and drew deeper into the shadows of the untouched trees. I willed the lights to keep on going, but no such luck. The cop car slowed and stopped by the hump-backed bridge.

A door opened, triggering the light inside. I saw the silhouette of a uniformed copper getting out. His mate stayed in his seat, doubtless busy on the radio to the fire brigade. No more than a black outline, the first copper was crossing the road. He swept the meadow with a powerful torch's white beam.

As soon as I stepped out from the shelter of the trees, he would see me. I couldn't see how the hell I was going to escape without Kalei to help me disappear. I wondered if the naiad had been seriously injured by the wose. Perhaps she was just leaving me to my fate now I'd done what she wanted. I shook my head. Never mind that. I had to get away. My efforts at arson were proving all too successful. The fire was spreading through the poplar trees towards me.

I'd be a fool to try to sneak back to the road, and I didn't think much of my chances of finding a route through the woods in the darkness. If I tried to cross the river, I'd be spotted at once. Perhaps I could follow the bank upstream without being collared. If I could make my way to the viewpoint where the road overlooked the river, where I'd thrown the Green Man carving into the water, I could find my way back to Kympton Grange from there. As long as no patrol car stopped and arrested me for so obviously fleeing the scene of a fire.

Flames snapped and hissed all around me. I could feel the heat on my bare shoulders. It was definitely time to go. I tossed the make-shift torch into the last of the fuel-soaked poplars, which were now catching alight, and headed upstream along the river bank, doing my best to keep the trees between me and the cops on the road.

I don't think I'd gone ten paces when an outraged shout echoed across the meadow. That copper with the torch had spotted me. Worse, blue lights and fire engine sirens were charging up the road from Lambton, shattering the peaceful night.

I could only hope there'd be no saving these trees. Not unless the wose survived. I couldn't risk that, not after everything Kalei and I had done, after all that we'd risked. I dashed across the open ground and scooped up the creature's body. Caught unawares, I stumbled and nearly overbalanced. After the last time, I'd been expecting the creature to be as heavy as it had been strong. Now it was as light as a bundle of scavenged firewood. Did that mean it was really dead? I fucking hoped so.

The copper shouted at me. He was running across the meadow, torchlight jerking up and down. His colleague was out of the car, waving down the fire engines. The first one halted, slewed across the road. Firefighters spilled out of the cab, wrenching metal hatches along the sides open, dragging out their gear.

Running back along the blazing line of trees, I kept the flames between me and any pursuit. If they couldn't see me, they couldn't chase me. Unfortunately this also meant I couldn't see them coming. The flames were painfully bright and the roar of the burning poplars was deafening. My bare skin felt sunburnt.

I tightened my grip on the wose and felt dead, rotten wood crumble to splinters and dust. I thrust the motionless creature into the fiery embrace of the closest tree. As I wedged the ungainly effigy into the crook between branch and trunk, the wose exploded. A shower of searing sparks engulfed me. I stumbled backwards, clutching at red-hot agony piercing my chest. I couldn't see what had stabbed me. My eyes were streaming, everything was a blur. Fuck. Had the heat done lasting damage to my vision?

My fingers brushed something hard sticking out of my chest. I yelled with shock and pain, but some calmer fragment of my mind recognised it as a nail head. I seized it with thumb and forefinger and wrenched it out. A second later I remembered all those films where someone pulling out whatever's stabbed them turns out to be rapidly fatal.

Cold mist wrapped itself around me. Not soothing, but as painful as a cold shower on a hung-over morning, as brutal as jumping into an icy loch. Shivering uncontrollably, I gasped and then struggled vainly to take another breath.

Now I couldn't see anything at all. The densest fog I'd ever encountered enveloped me in featureless grey. I could still hear voices though. Muffled shouting getting closer. Angry voices repeated curt warnings not to run away, to stay where I was.

If I couldn't see them, they couldn't see me. I lurched away, quickly growing dizzy for lack of oxygen. I still couldn't breathe properly, my lungs locked in an agonising spasm triggered by the icy air. I could only pant like a desperate dog. My hands and feet were already numb, as if I'd been working outside in a Scottish midwinter. But there was no warm bothy with a wood-fed stove waiting to restore me with a cup of hot soup thick enough to stand a spoon in.

I hadn't a hope of seeing where I was going as I stumbled over the uneven ground. All I could tell was that the light was changing. The fog was definitely brighter behind me, with the greyness ahead thickening to shadowy dusk. So my only chance was to keep on going, heading away from the fire.

The ground fell away beneath my feet. I had barely a second to realise I'd fallen into Kalei's river before I hit the water. Swirling foam filled my ears as I was swept along. I screwed my stinging eyes tight shut and tried desperately to hold on to my last inadequate breath.

The stream rolled me over and over, buffeting me against its stony bed. Every time I brushed against the undercut banks, I thrust out a hand or a foot, trying to slow myself, to right myself, to get my head above water and take a frantic gulp of air. I didn't care that the current must be taking me back towards the police and the firefighters. I'd rather be arrested than dead.

It was no good. I couldn't get my footing. I couldn't make my way to dry land. Shallow as this river was, I was going to drown in it. I'd done what Kalei wanted, so now she had no more use for me. As soon as I was dead, her valley's secrets would be safe again.

# Chapter Twenty-Two

It took me a long, long while to realise that I was, in fact, still alive. Gradually, I pieced together the most crucial facts. I was alive and I was cold and I was wet. More than wet. I was sprawled face down on a stretch of pebbles with my legs lying in a few inches of water. My trousers and boots were sodden. Though I wasn't shivering, which struck me as faintly strange.

It was dark. More than dark. I rolled over onto my back. Above me, a line of impenetrable blackness cut across the starlit night sky. I stared at that for a bit, wondering what it was. It finally occurred to me to try and find out. Reaching up with considerable effort, my fingertips brushed rough stone. After some more thought, I decided it was a big slab of barely smoothed rock, raised up on shallow supports. For some reason, I was lying underneath it.

It was a bridge. I don't know how long it took me to work that out, but once I had, I finally realised where I must be. Somehow, I'd washed up under the clapper bridge that carried the packhorse trail across the meadow opposite the Goose. So all I had to do was follow the path past the long-lost medieval village and head over the hill to Kympton Grange Farm. Then I could fall into my own bed. That would be nice.

Or I could just stay here and sleep. That would be okay. The shingle was oddly comfortable, and it wasn't as though I was cold, even though I'd lost my shirt. I couldn't remember how that had happened, lying there with the night and the stream flowing past me.

The dawn would wake me and then I could take care of... of whatever it was I was supposed to be doing. Because there was something important I needed to do. I could remember that much. I just couldn't quite bring it to mind. Never mind. It could wait until morning. Everything could wait till the morning. I could take a nap. I closed my eyes.

In the darkness on the far side of the river, I heard water surge over the stones. Something rasped against the shingle. Then something else, something on the bank behind me, growled. I didn't hear the noise so much as feel it. Dark vibrations ran through my bones and sluggish concern penetrated my hazy thoughts. Something out here was dangerous.

Whatever was in the water hissed, softly menacing. The growling answered it, louder. Somewhere more distant than either sound, I heard a familiar chittering. Boggarts. My legs might be numb, but the burning bites stirred in my memory. The sight of those vermin ripping into Tila's dead body floated through my thoughts.

Reluctantly I concluded I'd be a fool to stay here. If I fell asleep where no one would pass by until tomorrow morning, those little bastards would eat me alive. There was no way I could fight them off just at the moment. So I had to get away, I decided laboriously. I must get back to the flat and lock the door behind me.

Taking a deep breath, I rolled over onto my belly and braced my hands beneath me. Getting to my knees took more effort than I could have thought possible. All the strength in my shoulders had deserted me, and my boots kept slipping as I tried to dig their blunt toes into the wet stones.

My feet lost hold completely and I landed hard on my chest. Gasping with pain, I rolled onto my side and explored the deep gash on my breastbone with water-wizened fingertips. That was scabbing over, I realised vaguely, so that was good. There were newer sore places though, several deep puncture wounds that were tender to the touch. What had happened there?

The wose. Recollection hit me like a two-by-four. I'd killed the wose, and it had damn near killed me. The nails I'd used to disable it had exploded from its burning body to bury themselves in my chest.

The thing in the darkness hissed again, louder and more menacing. Now the noise set my pulse racing. Fear or adrenaline or both cut through the cold fog in my mind. I was still breathing and I wasn't bleeding, so those nails couldn't have hit anything vital. Right here, right now, whatever was out there skulking in the water, that was the real threat. I had to get away. I couldn't fight off a kitten in this state.

Making a massive effort, I got to my hands and knees. Crawling out from under the packhorse bridge, I grabbed hold of an ancient masonry pillar. I hauled myself to my feet, rough mortar biting into my water-softened palms. I didn't care. The pain helped me focus as I stumbled out of the shallows onto the sloping grassy bank.

I stood there for a moment, swaying, trying to get the measure of my situation. My first thought was that this was so sodding unfair. Killing the wose should have been the end of it. I discarded that pathetic notion. Self-pity is never any use, and life isn't fair. I'd learned that long ago.

The unseen menace hissed again, longer and louder. I backed further away from the water as some resonance in the sound hinted at a creature a hell of a lot bigger than a boggart. What the fuck was out there? That noise sounded nothing like the wose's spiteful cackle, and besides, I'd seen that bastard thing burn.

I wished I could ask Kalei, but I had no idea where the naiad was or how to summon her. She must have brought me here while I was unconscious, though I had no clue how Kympton's little river and the stream through Tila's valley could be connected.

I rubbed my hands up and down my arms, trying to warm myself. Shocked, I realised how deathly cold and clammy my skin was. I needed to get home, get a hot drink inside me and change into some dry clothes before I collapsed with hypothermia. Looking around to get my bearings, I forced myself to concentrate.

I was standing upstream of the clapper bridge. The long-abandoned church was over there, between me and the road. I could see the half-circle of its broken west window framed by jagged stonework clawing at the heavens.

Something rushed over the raised stone slabs, crossing

over the river from the bank behind me. Whatever had been growling in the darkness was now snarling with vicious intent. I barely glimpsed a four-legged shadow with a thrusting head and hunched shoulders before it vanished into the night. Whatever was on the far side of the bridge thrashed in the water. I heard the boggarts' chittering rise to a frenzied squeal.

I retreated as fast as I could, stumbling backwards, desperate not to turn away from whatever might be out there and let it sneak up behind me unseen.

Sudden silence fell beyond the bridge. That was almost worse than the noises. I tried to see what was over there, amid the shadows and shimmers of moonlight. It was no good. Exhaustion or the cold or the lingering effects of the fire seemed to be playing havoc with my night vision.

I remembered I needed to get home. I staggered away, trying not to stray from the path passing by the deserted village. Falling into one of those nettle clumps with no shirt on was the last thing I needed. I'd nearly reached the hawthorns that bordered the wood when I heard faint panting in the darkness behind me. Claws clicked on stone. Something was following me. A faint growl sounded suspiciously like a snicker. It was that shadow from the bank by the bridge.

Horribly stiff, I was too exhausted to even try running. The best I could do was stagger onwards as fast as I could. My wet trousers dragged at my thighs and my numb feet sent me weaving from side to side.

The trees at the top of the hill. I just had to reach the trees. That's where I'd be safe. The Green Man had seen me through these woods before. As soon as I reached the old oaks, I could call for his help. He sodding well owed me for avenging Tila by killing the fucking wose.

The thing following me through the darkness growled. It was getting scarily close. I stumbled on, gritting my teeth against all my aches and pains. The agonising effort was worth it. As I left the hedgerow behind me, I began to feel some warmth return to my fingers and toes. Painfully so, as bad as anything I remembered as a kid, after playing snowballs until my fingernails were blue, but still welcome.

Reaching the oaks that crowned the hill, I had to stop, struggling for breath. I looked warily around, searching the undergrowth for any hint of slithering darkness. Nothing. That was a relief. I glanced up into the leafy branches, hoping for some sign of the Green Man's presence. I tasted sour disappointment. Not a twig stirred.

As I looked back down the path, panic threatened. That black shadow was creeping up the hill. I looked desperately for a fallen branch, for something, anything I could use as a weapon.

Close at hand, something rustled in the undergrowth. The shadow raced up the hill, its growls erupting into ferocious snarls. With a flash of vivid red eyes, the four-footed black shape tore past me and crashed into the brambles. I heard the fleeing boggart squeal in terror. Its shrieks were cut short with horrifying abruptness. The savage growling was muffled now that the black beast had its mouth full. I heard satisfied slurping amid the sounds of cracking bone.

I found myself running through the wood. I raced down the winding track on the steeper side of the hill overlooking the farm cottages. This time I did lose my footing. I rolled over and over all the way down to the bottom of the field, only stopping when I slammed into the stone wall by the roadside.

I lay there until the world stopped spinning. I couldn't tell how many new bruises and scrapes I'd added to the ones I already had. Cautiously moving my arms and legs, I established that at least I'd escaped broken bones. Though I'd lost most of the skin on my elbows, which I discovered when I leaned on one. Gritting my teeth to avoid swearing out loud, I struggled to my feet and looked warily around. There were no slinking shadows to be seen, nor the black beast or any skulking boggarts.

So far, so good. I looked cautiously both ways along the lane. There were no lights on in the holiday cottages. I guessed everyone must be asleep. Then I realised I had no idea of the time. How late was it, or should I be asking, how early? If Sam Monkswell was already up and about for the cows' morning milking, I wouldn't give much for my chances of sneaking back into my flat unseen.

I searched the eastern sky for some hint of dawn. Nothing. That was a comfort, but my relief was short-lived. I was assuming this was still the same night when I'd burned the wose. It could be days, weeks, even months later, if I'd been swept up in a naiad's wake.

I pulled a leaf off a scrubby elder, self-seeded by the wall. It was full of summer sap. So this was the same time of year. Just as long as it was still the same year. I might be able to explain away a couple of days' absence, but if I'd been away any longer than a week, the Monkswells could have got rid of my stuff, my Land Rover...

Enough. I got a grip on my racing fears. I needed to get over the road and up the stairs to the flat. There was still no sign of life in the farmyard. I walked along the wall to the stile, carefully climbed over and crossed the road as quietly as I could, socks squelching inside my boots.

Fervently grateful to Sam for keeping the farm gate's bolt and hinges free of rust, I slipped silently into the yard and crouched low. No lights snapped on in the farmhouse. I looked towards the barn and relief seized me so hard I forgot to breathe. The Land Rover was there in its parking bay.

I hurried over, still hunched low, and found my keys and phone on the front tyre. Switching on my phone, I established it was still the same night and not long after 3 a.m. So far, so good.

Though it didn't seem that killing the wose had put an end to anything much. I looked back at the shadowy hill and those ancient trees silhouetted against the stars, wondering if the black beast that had followed me was still out there, watching me with those smouldering eyes. Let me guess: what Kalei had told me was the truth. She just hadn't told me all the truth about what was going on.

All I could do for the moment was put thick oak planks and solid stone walls between me and whatever horrors lurked in the night. I hurried up the steps, quickly and quietly. I locked the door and drew the curtains over the sink to block out the view of the hillside. Turning all the lights on banished every shadow, and I breathed a little easier as I sat down to take off my boots.

Between the fire and the water, they were wrecked. I gave up trying to unknot the laces with my broken fingernails and reached into my pocket for my penknife. Of course, it wasn't there. I had to find scissors from the kitchen drawer. I dumped boots and socks into a black bin bag. My trousers were beyond hope as well, torn and full of holes from flying sparks.

That gave me pause for thought. I considered my arms, turning my hands this way and that. Most of the hair had been singed away, but I should have been covered in burns. I must have Kalei to thank for saving me from the worst of the fire. Then I wondered what recompense she'd demand for doing me such a notable favour.

I found three puncture wounds in my chest and one in my right arm. At least the holes had been washed pretty clean, and the gash on my breastbone didn't look any worse than it had before. All in all, I reckoned I'd got off lightly.

There was a jar of instant hot chocolate in the back of a cupboard. I didn't like it, but Victoria did. I forced myself to put the kettle on and drank a big mugful regardless. With that warming me from the inside, I showered away the river's cold clamminess until the hot water turned tepid. I dressed the worst of my wounds with my supplies from the chemist's, then fell into bed, exhausted.

My last weary thought was that I only had Sunday to recover. I had to be at work on Monday morning if I wanted to keep my job at the barn conversions. Then I had to find somewhere new to live.

The temptation to just head for Warwickshire and home was immense. Kalei could find some other fool to do her dirty work hereabouts.

# Chapter Twenty-Three

It was bright and sunny when I finally woke up. I lay in bed, enjoying the warmth and comfort, wondering what the hell I'd been thinking last night, considering going to sleep by the packhorse bridge. I would have died of exposure.

Getting up, I assessed how stiff and bruised I was. Not too bad, all things considered. Better yet, once I'd had something to eat and drink. Though once I'd done that, I couldn't put off the challenge I'd been dodging ever since I woke up. I had to decide what I was going to do next.

I had to work out what I was going to say to Kalei. Come to that, I had to decide if I was even going to talk to her at all. The wose was gone, so that was the end of its killing spree. I'd done what the Green Man had brought me here for.

Though I wondered if the naiad had any way to track me to Warwickshire. Mind you, if she did, I didn't reckon much to her chances if she turned up and tried to take on my mum.

On the other hand, Kalei owed me. She'd promised to tell me where Tila had come from, where I could find some other dryads. Unless she was going to renege on our deal, proving my mother right about never trusting a naiad.

Then there were the niggling questions that had occurred to me as I lay in bed, thinking over the night before. Thinking about what the wose had said to me. All that stuff about reclaiming the wildwood, the mountains and the lakes. *We'll* be doing that, he'd said. Who did he mean?

I hadn't asked Kalei if the wose had any allies apart from the human he'd beguiled. I hadn't had any reason to. Now, perhaps I should. Perhaps I hadn't finished whatever the Green Man had brought me here to do. That wasn't a particularly cheery thought.

All right, I decided, I'd go and talk to the naiad. I was pretty sure Kalei would turn up if I went to the water meadow. Then I could decide what to do. While I was at it, I'd take a look at those black poplars, to make quite certain they were dead. I reckoned the fire had been fierce enough to do fatal damage to the mature trees, but there was always the possibility of an offshoot, overlooked and sheltered in some crevice of the river bank. Hopefully Kalei could tell me if she sensed any surviving seedling.

I got dressed in comfortable old jeans and a rugby shirt which covered the scrapes and bruises on my arms. As I dragged the shirt over my head, a cold shiver ran down my spine. I remembered the cheap black toolbox I'd left in Tila's valley. The one with my nail gun in it. The nail gun with its serial number easily linked to the warranty's registration. If the fire brigade picked that up, it wouldn't be long before DC Redmire traced it back to me.

I racked my brains, trying to recall exactly where I'd left it. As far as I could remember, the box had ended up close by the first poplar trees. Everything should have gone up in flames, nail gun included. That would be a costly loss for me, but I'd rather have to find the money for a new one than explain what it had been doing there.

I wondered how fierce the fire had been, how far the flames had spread. I still felt sickened by what I'd done to those trees. Worse, if Kalei had been badly hurt by the wose, there would have been nothing to stop it spreading.

The whole valley might have gone up in flames. Everywhere was dry as tinder after these weeks without rain. Embers could have easily blown across the river to set the grass on the far side alight. The scrubby undergrowth fringing Tila's wood would soon have been ablaze. Firefighters would be hard put to stop the fire taking hold of those broad-leaved limes, those centuries-old oaks.

That prospect made me nauseous. I went to open the kitchen window, taking in deep breaths of clean, fresh air until the sensation faded. Then I stood there for a while longer, waiting for Kalei to appear. There was no sign of her. I wondered if the fire had injured her somehow. I had no idea how vulnerable she might be as a cloud of mist, with those flames roaring all around her.

I searched for the scarf she'd given me, moving DVDs and dog-eared paperbacks and junk mail waiting for the recycling bin. I got on my hands and knees to look under the furniture in case it had ended up on the floor. Finally I was forced to admit it wasn't anywhere in the flat. Somehow, Kalei had reclaimed it.

I looked at my phone. If I called home to ask for advice on how to contact a naiad who didn't want to be found, I wouldn't bet on Mum telling me. I'd also have to admit what I'd done last night. Maybe Mum would forgive me for burning the poplars, when I explained it was the only way to be rid of the wose, but she'd want to know how far the fire had spread and ask how many innocent trees had died.

I turned my laptop on and clicked through to the Buxton Argus website. There was nothing about half the countryside between here and Lambton going up in smoke. That was good to know. On the other hand, the top story was the riot breaking out in The Griffin last night. Apparently the mayhem had spread all around Lambton's Market Square. I winced as I read about shop windows being smashed and arrests for looting and assault. Seven people ended up in hospital with what the paper called minor injuries.

I remembered Dave Fulbrook giving my primary school a talk on road safety when I was a kid. He explained that 'minor injuries' wasn't cuts and bruises but things like a broken arm or leg. 'Major injuries' was losing a leg. Everyone had ridden their bikes more carefully that summer holiday.

I closed the laptop. If I wanted to know what had happened in Tila's valley, I'd have to go there myself. I only needed to drive down the road; I wouldn't have to stop to get some idea how far the fire had spread. If I saw the blaze had reached far enough to destroy any evidence that I might have left, then I could hope I was in the clear.

That was definitely a better plan than sitting here waiting for Tunstead's knock on the door, wondering if I'd be spending another night in the cells. I grabbed keys, phone and wallet and headed for the door.

Then I stopped and went back for the black bin bag holding my ruined work boots and trousers. Downstairs, I slung it into the Land Rover's passenger footwell. Thankfully there was no one around to see me. Not that carrying out a bag of rubbish should look suspicious, but I was getting paranoid. I needed to get rid of it where there was no chance anyone would find it, to make sure CSI Buxton couldn't link me to last night's fire.

I turned right out of the gate and drove as far as the outcrop forcing the road into a bend. Checking to make sure no vehicles were approaching, and keeping my fingers firmly crossed that none would appear, I scrambled up to the cleft hidden by those leathery green ferns. I shoved the black plastic bag deep inside the rock. Once I'd taken a step back, even I couldn't tell anything had been disturbed.

Now to find out what had happened in Tila's valley. At least the trees flanking the lane at the junction with the main road looked perfectly fine. I was steadily more reassured the further I drove along. There was no sign of damage to the ancient woodland. Though it could still have burned out of control on the side of the river where the poplars grew, I reminded myself. I wondered what I'd see when I got closer to the water meadow.

I passed a gaggle of coppers in the lay-by, clustered around the mobile incident room. A sizeable Mitsubishi four-by-four was parked there too, red with yellow reflective stripes and fire and rescue service badges on the doors. Arson investigators.

I kept driving. As I approached the hump-backed bridge, I was relieved to see the fire hadn't crossed the river. The rough grassy stretch between the water and the trees looked untouched. Though I had no way of knowing if that was Kalei's work or just dumb luck.

A single TV van was parked on the verge, though the people sitting in the front seats weren't doing much. I guessed the rest of the media scrum must be in Lambton, filming reporters standing in front of smashed-up shop fronts. A few trees being set alight couldn't be very interesting compared to that.

I slowed as I crossed the bridge. Ordinary cars lined both sides of the road again, full of people come to gawp at this latest local drama. Not as many as last time. Presumably arson wasn't as big a draw as murder. I wondered what they would do next weekend, without some catastrophe to entertain them.

Spotting a space, I pulled up on the verge and looked across the meadow to the river bank. A handful of firefighters were walking around the charred poplars, presumably making sure the fire was really and truly out. About half of the trees had been reduced to blackened stumps. The rest were wizened skeletons that were just as dead. I didn't need to go any closer to be certain, thanks to my mother's blood.

Somehow, at the very limit of senses I'd never known I had, I could feel the lifeless void in the middle of the flourishing grass. The contrast with the leafy trees away beyond the river was striking. It was an unnerving sensation, not like anything I'd experienced before and quite unexpected.

Even though I kept telling myself that I'd had no choice, the charcoal stink of burning coming through the air vents sickened me. I was responsible for all that destruction, for the irreparable loss of those living, breathing trees. Some had been rotten, granted, but others could have been saved. Now they were all gone and black poplars were that little bit more endangered.

I wondered if the remains of my nail gun were buried beneath that blackened tangle of branches, over where the trees I'd first set alight had collapsed into flaming ruins. I had no idea whether the fire brigade would clear that away to uncover whatever evidence might condemn me. Perhaps the burnt wood would be left to slowly decay into the bare, scorched soil.

One thing was certain. There was no chance of me searching through the dead trees myself, to take away whatever I might find. Not now, not until the fire brigade were done here. I wondered how long that would be, and how soon after that some randomly curious dog walker or bored teenager would go poking around, stumbling across something that could still make trouble for me.

I needed to talk to Kalei. Where the hell was she? I looked down the lines of cars and the knots of people standing between them. No onlookers ventured into the meadow today. I guessed the firefighters had told them to stay on the tarmac and there were enough police around to back them up.

'Mr Mackmain!' A woman broke off from a huddle of people further along the road and waved a hand. She walked towards me, down the middle of the road. It was DS Tunstead's sidekick, DC Redmire. She must have recognised the Land Rover.

I stayed where I was and wound down the window. I could hardly start the engine and run her down to escape.

'Mr Mackmain.' She gave me the same tight, professional smile used by her boss as she arrived at my wing mirror. 'You look like you've been in the wars.'

'Like half of Lambton last night.' I wasn't about to antagonise her, but I didn't want to prolong this conversation.

'Could you give DS Tunstead a call when you get a moment? You've still got his number?'

'What about?' I did my best to hide my concern. Though she was being so polite I couldn't imagine they'd linked me to the nail gun already.

'I understand you rang 999 when the trouble started in The Griffin last night?' She waited for me to nod agreement. 'We'd like to take a statement, when that's convenient. You went straight home, did you, after you'd made that call?' she asked, just a little too casually to sound convincingly natural.

'Straight back. You've seen my record. Like I told your boss, I do my best to stay clear of trouble.' I gestured ahead down the road. 'That's all, is it? I was just on my way to town.'

She looked at me curiously. 'Haven't you seen the news? I don't think many shops will be opening today.'

'No,' I agreed, thinking quickly, 'but there might well be work for a carpenter, mending windows and door frames.'

Doing something practical to help might soothe my conscience a little.

DC Redmire nodded. 'That's very public-spirited of you.'

I shrugged and she turned away.

'Detective,' I said quickly, 'could you do me a favour? I really don't want people knowing I made that 999 call. The last thing I need is reporters turning up on my doorstep again. You've seen last week's papers.' I shook my head, not bothering to hide my anger. 'I've been given notice to quit my flat, thanks to all that, and I've barely managed to keep my job. I really don't need any more grief.'

DC Redmire looked embarrassed. 'We really did make it clear that you had only been interviewed as a witness—'

'Officer! I say, officer!' A stout, grey-haired woman stepped out from between two cars. She was dressed for a country walk, in a thorn-proof coat and corduroy trousers despite the sunny day. A placid black Labrador followed obediently at her heel.

I reached for my keys, ready to drive off. Then the imperious lady glanced at me and I saw her eyes flash turquoise. I rested my hands on the steering wheel and waited to see what DC Redmire had to say for herself.

'Officer.' Kalei's impersonation of a well-to-do local woman was note perfect. A stalwart of the Women's Institute, I decided. An established county family with considerable resources to draw on, well connected with the sort of people who could make a young detective constable's life uncomfortable.

'Is this outrage thanks to those teenagers who were messing about here last night?' She gestured towards the ravaged trees. 'Have you caught them?'

'Teenagers?' DC Redmire pulled a notebook from her pocket.

'I was sure they were up to no good. I tried to ring the station in Lambton but I couldn't get through.' There was the faintest note of accusation in Kalei's voice, as though DC Redmire should have been answering the phones herself. 'I know we mustn't use 999 unless it's a real emergency.'

'What were they doing, exactly?' DC Redmire flipped to a clean page.

'Larking about on their phones to begin with. I think they were making prank calls. I heard one of the girls pretending she'd just escaped someone who was trying to abduct her, or some such nonsense.'

DC Redmire wrote quickly. 'You were close enough to hear this? Where exactly were they?'

'Down there, just by the bridge.' Kalei pointed. 'I suppose they thought it was a joke, after everything that's been in the news about these poor young girls who've been killed. I must say I don't see anything particularly amusing about rape and murder. Young people have some strange ideas these days.'

Her contempt was scathing. I could just imagine her writing a letter to the Buxton Argus. Disgusted of Matlock Bath. I wondered where she'd got the dog.

'As for setting fire to those trees, I don't know what possessed them. They're lucky they didn't kill themselves. They could have set the whole valley alight and burned themselves alive. I take it the firemen didn't find anyone caught in the flames?'

Her tone made it perfectly clear that she wouldn't lose much sleep if these mythical teenagers had been caught in a trap of their own making.

DC Redmire frowned. 'What sort of time was this?'

'Around ten, I suppose.' Kalei gestured towards her dog. 'I was giving Midnight a last walk before bed.'

The Labrador looked up and wagged its tail. DC Redmire reached down to pat its head. 'Good dog.'

I gripped the steering wheel so hard I'm surprised I didn't break it. As the dog glanced over at me, I saw a glint of red in its eyes. For a breath-taking second, I glimpsed its true form. A gigantic black shadow straight from a nightmare.

It was still a dog, or something close, even though it was more than twice as big as any dog I'd ever seen, and Dad knows a farmer back home who breeds prize-winning mastiffs. This wasn't a mastiff. This wasn't any sort of dog that a breeder would recognise. It wasn't just its eyes that smouldered like hot coals. Dull fire clung to its jowls like hellish drool.

It was a black shuck. The terrifying spectral black hound of countless folktales found the length and breadth of the British Isles, inspiring chilling stories all the way down to *The Hound of the Baskervilles*. If Sir Arthur Conan Doyle hadn't seen one himself, I was now certain that he'd talked to someone who had.

Then I blinked and all I could see was an amiable, elderly Labrador, slowly wagging its tail as the policewoman scratched behind its ears. Kalei was still expressing the grey-haired countrywoman's disgust, though I'd been too distracted by the sight of a real-life, no-shit black shuck to register what she was saying.

DC Redmire gave the dog a final pat and readied her pen. 'If I could just take your name and address—'

Shouts from the crowd interrupted her. People surged forward, crossing the road to get as close to the meadow as possible. Yelling echoed across the river, urgent, as startled firefighters warned each other about some new danger. I opened the Land Rover door, hauling myself up to stand on the sill so I could see over the heads of the crowd.

A lengthy section of the river bank was slowly giving way. As the ground crumbled beneath them, skeletal trees toppled into the water. As each one splashed into the stream, the crowd around me cried out, unexpectedly sorrowful. The firefighters retreated as clouds of black-flecked ash surged up around the remaining stumps.

'Sorry about that, madam. Now, if I—' DC Redmire looked up and down the road, her expression turning from surprise to shock. 'Where did she go? The old lady with the dog!'

'Sorry, I didn't see.' I lowered myself back into the Landy's driving seat and raised my voice over the engine as I turned the ignition key. 'Actually, I think I'll give Lambton a miss. Get lunch at the Goose in Kympton.'

DC Redmire wasn't listening, anxiously searching for her supposed witness in the crowd. I heard her mutter something heartfelt under her breath; I'm pretty sure it was 'bollocks'.

Well, that was her problem. I could only hope that Kalei could hear me, and that she'd take the hint about where to meet. I really needed to talk to her.

As the exasperated policewoman began walking back down the road, I edged the Land Rover along after her. The people milling around on the tarmac soon got the message and stepped back to let me through.

Once I was safely clear, I put my foot down and took the long way round back to Kympton.

# Chapter Twenty-Four

There were no TV vans in The Grey Goose's car park. That was good. Unfortunately there was no sign of Kalei either. Locking up the Land Rover, I wondered where to look for her. Would she have gone into the bar to wait for me?

If she had, Donna would want to know who my new friend was, the next time I was in there on my own. We'd better come up with some convincing lie between us. On the other hand, if she wasn't, it would look pretty odd for me to walk in and walk straight out again without at least saying hello to Jim.

Teddy barked from the brewery yard. A single, alert bark, not furiously warning off boggarts. I looked over, wondering what he'd noticed. The dog was standing still, quivering, all his attention on the footpath across the road.

A massive four-footed shadow raced across the grass to vanish into the ruined church. With a shiver, I recognised the black shuck which had followed so meekly at Kalei's heel beside the water meadow. I also realised it was the apparition which had pursued me the night before. The monster which had killed and eaten the boggart. On the other hand, it had chased off whatever other unseen menace had been out there in the night.

That wasn't overly reassuring. I couldn't help thinking the beast might just have been going after anything it saw as prey. I licked dry lips and wondered if it had been tempted to kill me, or if it had somehow known me for a dryad's son. If it had, I wondered if that would put me off the menu. I couldn't see any particular reason why it should.

At least Kalei had the creature under control, if it had been pretending to be a Labrador. Though that was an even more unnerving thought. I'd never imagined such a fearsome beast could mingle with ordinary people as easily as naiads and dryads. But the wose had. Perhaps I should pay more attention to what was going on around me, using my ability to see the supernatural.

I forced myself to concentrate on the here and now. The shuck came out of the ruined church, a shifting mirage of shadow and threat in the bright sunlight. It trotted back down the path and paused, incongruously dog-like for all the fire in its eyes. Standing there for a moment, it stared straight at me. Then it turned around and loped off again. A few moments later, it halted and looked back over its shoulder, ears pricked, expectant.

I reluctantly concluded that it wanted me to follow. I could only hope Kalei had sent it to show me where to find her. So I crossed the road and followed the track towards the long-abandoned village.

She was sitting on the flat slabs of the clapper bridge on the packhorse trail, beside the curve of shingle bank where she'd dumped me last night. Swinging bare feet over the water, she wore the same form as she had the first time I'd seen her: a tall woman around my own age with long brown hair and a swimmer's build flattered by dark blue jeans and a green T-shirt.

I sat down beside her. 'I'm glad to see you're okay.'

She looked at me, amused. 'Why shouldn't I be?'

I raised my eyebrows. 'The fire?'

The naiad smiled. 'Fire can never destroy water. It can only change its form. Though,' she allowed, 'being turned into vapour against my will does sting. Imagine being caught up in an angry swarm of bees.'

'No thanks.' I checked that my trainers weren't going to dip into the rippling stream. 'Tell me we're done with all this. Tell me the wose is destroyed and every last one of those poplar trees is dead.'

'Why are you asking me?' Kalei looked quizzically at me. 'Yes, the wose is gone, never to return. Your greenwood blood must have told you that, when you looked at his trees. You have proved you are your mother's son, and more besides.'

'You said—' I cut myself short. First things first. 'If the police find the tools I left behind, they'll know I started those fires.'

'I brought the toolbox here. It's in the church and the shuck's been guarding it.' She nodded towards St Werburgh's ruins.

I was surprised. 'You could cope with getting so close to the metal?'

'I won't pretend that it was pleasant.' She grimaced and held up her hands.

I winced at the ragged blisters searing her palms.

Kalei tucked her hands under her thighs. 'Once I'd got everything into the box, it wasn't so bad. I can handle plastic easily enough.' She smiled. 'It makes our dealings with humanity much easier, compared to the centuries when there was metal everywhere.'

I realised she was contemplating the grassy lumps and bumps, all that remained of the long-lost medieval village.

'Do you remember the Kympton that was here centuries ago?' I was curious.

'Why do you ask?' She looked sideways at me with a flash of turquoise.

'No reason.' I shrugged. 'Just making conversation.'

'Just make sure no one sees you carrying the toolbox out of the church and you'll have nothing to worry about.'

'What about the shuck?'

'He won't hurt you,' she said impatiently. 'I sent him to shepherd you safely home last night.'

Safely home and scared out of my wits. I decided not to say so in case I sounded ungrateful. Given the state I'd been in, that gang of boggarts could have made a hell of a mess of me.

'Is this where it lives?' Now I wondered if the shuck had been the unnerving presence I'd sensed up on the hilltop that first night when I'd walked back from the Goose and felt unexpectedly pursued.

'Of course not.' Kalei seemed to think that should be obvious. 'He lives in my valley. What else do you think keeps the

235

deer from nibbling all the saplings? Though I imagine he'll be hunting hereabouts until all the boggarts are eaten or fled.'

'Is a shuck...' I tried to recall how she'd described herself and Tila. 'Of the wood or of the water?'

'Neither. He's of the shadow.' The naiad shuffled backwards to sit more securely on the bridge and looked thoughtfully at me. 'You may have proved you're your mother's son, but you have a great deal to learn of your true nature and of her world.'

She was right, and I was curious. I wanted to ask what the shuck had been doing when the wose murdered Tila. I wanted to know why it hadn't come to her rescue or chased off the boggarts gnawing her corpse. But I wasn't sure how much longer the naiad would stay sitting here. I had more immediately important questions.

'You promised me you'd tell me where to find more dryads,' I reminded her. 'The grove where Tila used to live, before she came to the valley. You said there are still dryads there.'

'Quite so,' Kalei agreed with a satisfied smile. 'You can repay me for my help last night by telling her mother and sisters what became of her. You can assure them that you avenged her.'

'One of them is her mother?' Hell, I'd never had to tell anyone their child had died before. So much for assuming Kalei was doing me a favour.

I squared my shoulders. 'Where do I find her?'

The naiad stared into the distance for a long moment, considering her reply. 'If you follow my river downstream, it leaves these hills and joins another river. The mingled waters flow towards what was once a hunting ground for your people's kings. Another river joins the flood as the waters turn towards the rising sun and drain towards the sea.

'If you trace that river back, you'll find a place where your father's people built channels and sluices to drain a marsh long ago. Upstream, not very far, you'll find the place where the family who did that have lived since the last invaders crossed the salt sea to seize this island. They've built and rebuilt their home over the generations. That family have dryad's blood, and the women of the grove have helped them safeguard their lands for generations.'

'Okay.' I did my best to commit these details to memory. Once Kalei's stream left the White Peak, it became a tributary of another river which met a second lesser river somewhere to the south. That shouldn't be too hard to find. I'd see what maps I could find online.

'Is there anything else you can tell me? Anything I should look for, to help me find it?'

Kalei laughed. 'It's called Blithehurst House. Look it up online.'

She braced her hands on the edge of the limestone slab, pointing her bare feet at the river below, as if she were about to slip into the water.

'Wait a minute. I haven't finished.' I put a hand on her arm. 'What did the wose mean last night, when it was talking about humans dying, to scare people away from the woods and mountains? What's going on?'

'I don't know.' Kalei hesitated. 'There is... something amiss. Something deeper, something darker, that made the wose so bold all of a sudden. But I don't know what it is,' she insisted.

I thought quickly about what she was saying and what she wasn't. 'Okay, you don't know for certain. What do you suspect?'

'See what you can learn at Blithehurst. Remember, you've proved yourself against the wose.'

Before I could ask her what she meant by that, the naiad pushed herself off the bridge. Dropping into the sparkling water, she disappeared as completely as if she'd dissolved.

I sat there, wondering why she played these games with me. I wondered who had won. Kalei had rid her valley of the wose, so that must be a good few points for her. On my side of the score sheet, now I knew where to find some dryads and they weren't too far away, from the sound of it. On the other hand, I had to take them grievous news, even if I could assure them that Tila's killer had paid for his crimes. Overall, I concluded reluctantly, the naiad had come out ahead.

Though I couldn't help feeling elated at the prospect of meeting these dryads. Maybe they would tell me where to find some of their male descendants. Perhaps I could finally find someone else who'd had dealings with the Green Man.

Still, I decided, I'd keep Kalei's name out of the story, as much as I could. She hadn't said anything about her own dealings with Tila's family, and they might be as hostile to naiads as my mum.

I wondered what she'd make of this news, and Dad, come to that. Perhaps they would want to meet these unknown dryads too. Though that would mean Mum leaving her own woods. I realised I had absolutely no idea how far she'd ever gone from the house where we lived. How far could dryads travel now that so much of this country was barren of trees?

First things first. I got up and headed for the ruined church. There was no sign of the black shuck lurking any-where as I walked into the cool shade of the broken walls. That was a relief.

The black plastic toolbox was tucked into the far corner beyond the stone slab commemorating the long-lost altar. Glancing over my shoulder to be sure there was no one around, I crouched down and opened the lid. Great. My nail gun was in there, along with the spare nails, gas cartridges and batteries. That was going to save me all sorts of grief as well as a fair amount of money.

That wasn't all. The carved mask of the Green Man's face lay on top of the tools. I reached for it, only to snatch my hand back, startled. Warm green light glowed in the empty eye sockets and the fresh scent of spring filled the air. I'll swear till my dying day that those wooden lips momentarily curved in a satisfied smile. Then the wildwood perfume was gone and the mask was a simple carving once again.

My hands shook as I clipped the lid securely shut. Was the Green Man telling me he was pleased with my work last night? Or was he warning me that I wasn't finished yet? Kalei might have ducked my questions, but she'd made it pretty damn clear there was more to worry about than just the sodding wose.

I tucked the toolbox under my arm and began walking back towards The Grey Goose. When I got back to Kympton Grange, I could see what the Internet could tell me about this Blithehurst House. I wondered who lived there. I'd need some excuse to go knocking on their door. Unless I just sneaked into the grounds one night to see what I could find on a stroll through the local woods. Tila had recognised me as a dryad's son. It had to be a safe bet that anyone from her family would do the same.

As I reached the Land Rover and stowed the toolbox in the back, my phone buzzed in my pocket. I had a text message from Phil Caister.

*Hope you kept clear of trouble in town last nite. OK 4 work tomoro?*

I sent a quick reply.

*Mostly & yes. C U 7am*

Then I saw another message had come for me earlier.

*Pls call to confirm yr booking w Living Crafts. Email follows.*

That was from Lynda Stansley. She took it very personally when people who'd booked tables at the craft fairs she ran failed to turn up. Once she'd realised I didn't check my email every day, she'd taken to texting me as well.

I decided that encounters with ethereal creatures and discovering I had unexpected supernatural senses were all very well, but I'd had enough of it all for the moment. These messages were a forceful reminder that I had a real life to get back to, and I wanted to get back to it.

I needed to keep my head down and keep busy until the barn conversions were finished. Those wages would have to see me through however many weeks it would take me to find another job. I needed to make all the money I could from the summer season's craft fairs as well, if I wanted any spare cash over the winter. Not forgetting, I needed to find somewhere to live that was close enough to Lambton for me to get to work without spending half my pay packet on diesel.

I sighed. That wasn't all. I still owed DS Tunstead a statement about Saturday night. At least that should be straightforward enough. I'd go to work bright and early tomorrow morning and call in at the police station at lunchtime. I could give them back that sweatshirt at the same time. That should convince someone I was an honest citizen.

Whether I saw DS Tunstead or someone else, I'd just say I made that 999 call and went straight home to bed. If anyone asked about the scratches and bruises on my hands, I'd say I'd got them fighting my way out of The Griffin. Good luck to anyone who thought they could prove differently.

Once I had my life straight again, I could visit this Blithehurst House. Apart from anything else, I should let myself heal a bit before I turned up there. I wouldn't get very far if everyone there recognised me as that possible murderer who'd had his face all over the telly and the papers. Like my dad says, you never get a second chance to make a first impression.

I'd do a bit of research and work out a sensible strategy. I'd talk it over with Mum and see what advice she could offer a complete stranger approaching a family of unknown dryads. Maybe I'd go home for a weekend and we could discuss it, all three of us.

I didn't think there needed to be any great hurry. If these dryads had lived there for centuries, they were hardly going to up sticks and disappear in the next few weeks. If there was some more urgent reason for me to talk to them, well, Kalei or the Green Man could be a little less bloody cryptic about it.

I put my keys in my pocket and went into The Grey Goose. Since it was Sunday, Donna offered a selection of roasts in the restaurant. I opted for local pork and crackling with apple sauce and vegetables. Sticky toffee pudding and coffee rounded the meal off nicely. Better yet, though the pub was busy, no one seemed inclined to give me a second glance. With any luck I'd had my fifteen minutes of unwanted notoriety.

On my way out, I checked the pub's pin board. There were several notices offering vacant rooms in shared houses in Lambton. I took a few photos with my phone, so I could make some calls. I prefer living by myself, but I'll take a house share over sleeping in the Landy.

All this normality lasted until I got back to the flat at Kympton Grange and opened up my carving box. I'd been thinking I'd spend the evening knocking off a few trinkets for tourists. The first thing I saw was the Green Man carving, which should have still been in the back of the Land Rover. As I picked it up, I realised he was frowning. I caught a momentary glint of russet anger beneath those leafy brows.

Startled, I dropped the damn thing. The mask hit the floor with a clatter and lay there, a lifeless piece of wood once again. I still didn't want to pick it up. Turning my back on it, I sat at the table and resolutely sorted through my tools and carvings.

It was no good. I couldn't concentrate. Worse, my hand was shaking. I sat there, chisel in one hand and the dog fox in the other, and I knew beyond a shadow of a doubt that as soon as steel touched wood, I'd wreck the damn thing beyond saving.

The skin between my shoulder blades prickled. The carved mask on the floor was looking at me, I was sure of it. The only question was, were those eye holes still empty or were they bright with supernatural light? I didn't want to look around to find out.

'All right.' I put everything away and got out my laptop.

It turned out that Blithehurst House would be easy enough to find, because it was a privately run stately home open to the public from Wednesdays to Sundays and on Bank Holiday Mondays. It was less than an hour's drive away, just over the county border into Staffordshire.

The website was clear and informative, giving the opening hours and promising plenty of parking, along with a locally sourced menu in the cafe and country crafts in the shop to make ideal gifts all year round. The photos showed a Tudor manor house built on a rise in the land as well as the substantial ruins of an older building surrounded by a moat down in the bottom of the valley below it. All very pictur-esque.

According to the History of the House page, the manor had been granted to Sir Graelent de Beauchene in 1086. He'd come over from Normandy with William the Conqueror; at least, that was the story according to family tradition. As the website made scrupulously clear, the records of who actually fought at the Battle of Hastings are incomplete and disputed. So I'd learned something new today.

Well, whoever Sir Graelent might have been, he didn't enjoy his new estates for long, dying in 1092. Luckily, he'd had the forethought to father a daughter. The dead knight's squire, Robert, promptly married the girl, taking on the Beauchene name as well as the estate. His descendants apparently still owned the manor, which had been open to the public since 2005. I wondered what the resident dryads made of that.

Still, if the house and the grounds were open to visitors, I'd have no problem getting in to see if I could find them. If I did, I'd give them the news about Tila and see what they had to tell me about meeting someone who shared my human and ethereal heritage.

'Yes, I'll ask them about whatever it is the wose was hint-ing at, whatever's got Kalei so concerned.' I twisted around to look at the carved mask lying on the floor. 'I'll go and visit the place next weekend. Satisfied?'

I didn't get any answer, but when I picked up my chisel again, there was no sign of that aggravating tremor in my hand. So I put the finishing touches to the fox and worked on a few other pieces until the daylight faded. Then I went to bed early, with a few more painkillers to stave off the linger-ing after-effects of Saturday night.

I slept well enough, though I woke with a fading memory of dreams full of water flowing beneath the shifting shadows of leaves.

# Chapter Twenty–Five

The Blithehurst House car park was a gravelled expanse beside a square of old stable buildings between the main road and the Tudor manor house. Following the path indicated by discreet arrows on stubby posts gave me and the other recent arrivals a good view of the shallow valley below.

'All the parkland that you can see from the house will have been laid out in the 1700s,' a middle-aged man said confidently to his dutifully meek wife, 'by Capability Brown or one of his pupils.'

People do talk a lot of crap. The view ahead was nothing of the kind, though I didn't bother correcting him. That sort of conversation never goes well. I'd already made a very different assessment of the broad expanse of wooded pasture that swept up the far side of the valley, beyond the ruins of the moated manor house down by the river.

This was a medieval landscape as old as those crumbling stone towers. Grazed by pale cattle which I could see here and there, the grassland was dotted with ancient pollarded oaks. Those trees must be centuries old, their trunks so thick that five or six people would have to link hands to circle them. The oaks all looked to be flourishing and my spirits rose. If this place had stayed unchanged for a thousand years, I'd put money on dryads being involved.

'Are you just here to visit the park or do you want a ticket for the house as well?' An amiable middle-aged lady was in charge of the gate opening into the formal gardens. 'There are guided tours at eleven, one o'clock and three p.m. If you want to walk round on your own though, that's fine.'

A younger, sharp-eyed man sat behind a desk in an open-sided hut on the other side of the gate, looking after an electronic till and a stack of guidebooks. He was busy processing the Capability Brown fan's credit card.

'Both, please, house and park.' I smiled as inoffensively as I could as I reached for my wallet.

Thankfully, there wasn't a hint of recognition in the woman's face as she smiled back. Well, I'd healed quickly over the past week, and the media had already moved on to fresh outrages. Shevaun Thomson, Amber Fenham and their grieving families were old news, which was as depressing as it was a relief to me personally.

There wasn't any flicker of anything else in the nice lady's faded hazel eyes. Whoever she was, she wasn't a dryad. Well, that would have been too easy.

'Would you like a guidebook?' She offered me the one in her hand.

'Yes, thanks.' I handed over a twenty and flicked through the book as she went over to the till. Good. There was a map of the park inside the front cover, with designated routes for walking clearly marked with dotted green lines. I mentally apologised, just a little, to the Capability Brown fan. One path led up to a distant Temple of Venus, built in 1731.

'The red one's for the house, and the green one's for the park.' The lady in the pale blue polo shirt came back with my tickets and change. 'Do be careful not to approach the cattle. They have this year's calves with them and they're very protective.'

I nodded. 'I understand.'

She moved on to her next customers, and I studied the Tudor manor house as the gravelled path led me through a meticulously maintained knot garden. Craft fairs have taken me to any number of stately homes which have been built, rebuilt and mucked around with over the centuries in ways that would never get planning permission today. I've got pretty good at spotting alterations and additions. This house looked to have been pretty much left alone since it was built, as far as I could tell.

As we approached, symmetrical wings on either side flanked a substantial entrance porch and a carriage drive cut across the gardens to bring guests right to the front door. Rooms on the other side of the house would overlook more gardens and down to those ruins. The house was two storeys tall, built from weathered limestone, with typically Tudor windows and chimneys and a steeply pitched, russet-tiled roof. There was battlemented stonework around the roof, but that was purely for show. This place hadn't been built to be defended against any serious assault.

It was a sunny day and the scent of herbs planted in ornate patterns filled the warm air. Bees hummed among the flowers and birds flitted overhead. I checked my watch. Ten to eleven. I might as well take the guided tour and learn a bit about this place before I searched the parkland for any sign of the supernatural.

A handful of people loitered around the entrance porch, sharing polite smiles by way of acknowledgement without inviting conversation. That was fine with me. A few moments later, a woman in grey cotton trousers and the blue polo shirt that was evidently the staff uniform here came out through the open front door. The carved oak was silvered with age and older than the stonework around it, if I was any judge. The woman was a few years younger than me, as far as I could tell.

'Good morning. Are you all here for the tour?' She smiled as everyone dutifully held up their red tickets. 'This way, please.'

The entrance lobby was gloomy, facing north and with only one window overshadowed by the house. Dark wooden panelling didn't help, and the Victorian parson glowering from a portrait looked unimpressed. When our guide opened the inner door though, sunlight flooded through tall, mullioned windows looking southwards over the valley. Chestnut panelling reached halfway up the walls, warm and welcoming. Above that, creamy painted plaster gave the lofty room an airy feel.

There was a massive fireplace to our right-hand side, with comfortable chairs and a sofa arranged in front of it. In case anyone felt inclined to sit down, the furniture was discreetly guarded by a low velvet rope which also protected the table under the north-facing window where some bronzes statuettes and enamelled vases were displayed.

The flagstone floor was mostly covered with a faded

carpet with tassels at each end. Side tables along the far wall offered a selection of old photos of the room with its long-dead inhabitants in Victorian and Edwardian dress. I wandered over to take a look as our guide outlined the early history of the manor which I'd already read on the website. Though it turned out they had kept back a few interesting stories for their paying customers.

'Local legend has it that Sir Graelent was killed fighting a dragon that had been ravaging the countryside and eating the peasants' cattle. Of course, the dragon was a common symbol used by Saxon lords, and local records show that the eorl who held this manor before the Norman invasion was particularly brutal, so it's easy enough to see where that story came from. There's good evidence that locally, the change from Saxon to Norman rule was more welcomed than resisted.'

I went to look out of the windows at the valley as our guide covered the Black Death; that hadn't been nearly as bad hereabouts as in a lot of places. Through the Wars of the Roses, the family had been Yorkists but mostly kept their heads down and stayed out of trouble. They'd done that successfully enough to profit when Henry VIII dissolved the monasteries, when they'd added a local priory and its lands to their estate.

'That brought in enough money to build this new house, with all the modern comforts and conveniences like chimneys and fireplaces that the original medieval manor lacked. Being built higher up on the valley side also means this house has none of the perpetual problems with damp that come from having a moat.' Our guide gestured towards the windows and the valley beyond as the tour group smiled.

'Though the family did have to move back into the old manor during the English Civil War. As Royalists, they were in a minority, as most people locally supported the Parliamentarians. This whole area was a battleground between the Roundheads and the Cavaliers, with towns like Lichfield and Burton changing hands several times. In fact, a Roundhead force was sent to capture Blithehurst. They were ordered to destroy the old manor's remaining fortifications in early

1643. Fortunately the soldiers got thoroughly lost in thick fog and never found their way here. Then Queen Henrietta Maria landed in Yorkshire with a cargo of weapons from France for Charles the First, and the Roundheads had better things to do than spare men for another attack.'

She gestured to a substantial wooden partition to the left of the entrance, pierced by two open arches.

'The great hall was the heart of any Tudor house, and this was originally all one room. As you see, though, when the house was modified in the early eighteen hundreds, it was divided to give the family this reception room and a separate dining room through there.'

She walked over to stand beneath the painting dominating the partition wall. That had caught my eye as soon as I walked in. Now I was very interested in whatever she might have to say.

'This is Edmund Beauchene and his family –' she pronounced the name 'Beechen' '– and he nearly saw the manor pass out of the direct line of descent from Sir Graelent. As you can see, he had five daughters, and just like a Jane Austen story, if he didn't have a son, the estate would have passed to a cousin living in Hampshire. Luckily, his wife did give birth to a baby boy, Francis, though tragically she died shortly afterwards. That's her portrait.' She gestured to a small painting of a dark-haired, sallow woman in a blue dress, hung over the northerly archway.

I was still studying the big painting of Edmund and his children. They were standing out in the gardens with the wooded valley and the medieval ruins as a backdrop. Neither Edmund nor his daughters were overly tall, and the girls were as dark-haired as their mother. The son was a different matter. His father's sandy head barely reached his broad shoulders, and Francis was fairer still. Though he was clearly Edmund's son; the family resemblance between them was strong enough to have countered any gossip that he was some cuckoo in the nest. People only needed to look at the line of his jaw and the set of his eyes.

Who his mother might have been though, that was a very

different question. I stood there, contemplating the younger man's physique as the rest of the tour group went on through to the inner half of the hall. There was no question in my mind. He was a dryad's son. So Kalei hadn't sent me on a wild goose chase. Though of course, I still had to find the dryads themselves.

Someone coughed politely behind me. I turned to discover another mild-faced middle-aged lady, this one in a blue sweatshirt. Each room had a volunteer to keep an eye on the visitors.

She smiled. 'If you're staying with the tour, you'll need to move on.'

'Of course.' I went through the archway to find the dining room, vast by modern standards. The elegant mahogany table could have seated twenty and it still looked insignificant in that high-ceilinged space. Several glass-fronted cabinets offered displays of decorative china, and while various visitors exclaimed over those I wondered about ditching the rest of the history lesson. I'd seen all the proof I needed that this trip hadn't been a waste of time. Now I wanted to get out into those wooded pastures.

On the other hand, I didn't want to draw any attention to myself, and the house wasn't exactly huge. I checked my watch. It wasn't even noon. I decided I might as well stay as our guide took us through the inner hall to the comfortably furnished Great Parlour, which took up the ground floor of the easterly wing flanking the porch. Then we retraced our steps to visit a huge, antiquated kitchen in the westerly wing.

Various closed doors hid smaller, presumably uninteresting rooms, though I saw a couple of visitors purse their lips as they realised their curiosity wouldn't be satisfied. Then our guide led us across the passage leading to a side entrance and into another room big enough to hold the whole flat I'd rented at Kympton Grange Farm with plenty of space left over.

'This is the library. When the house was originally built, it was intended as the chapel. Even though Henry the Eighth had broken England's ties with Rome, it wasn't until later that being Catholic became a real problem for families like the Beauchenes. By the reign of Elizabeth the First, though, things were very different.'

As the guide went on to explain about recusants and Midlands plots to free Mary Queen of Scots, I walked slowly around the room. Tall windows set in two deep bays ringed with seats looked southwards over the gardens. Each bay had an imposing writing desk claiming the best of the daylight. The other walls all had shelves reaching high enough that I'd need a stool to get to the topmost books. Above that, a line of carved heraldic shields ran around the top of the bookcases. Then the coffered ceiling was divided into squares by false beams that framed panels with more ornate carving. Those weren't 1800s workmanship, or even 1600s. I guessed the panels had come out of the medieval manor's chapel.

More than that, it wasn't just religious zeal that had inspired those long-dead craftsmen. A Green Man's face gazed down from each corner of the room where the coffer beams crossed. I spotted several sprites among the wreaths of fruit and flowers, and a boggart was gurning behind a spray of leaves. What might have been a wolf's head could easily have been a shuck, though without a stepladder to get a closer look, I couldn't be certain. I had no doubt that whoever had carved these vivid creatures had seen the real thing. Thankfully nothing was looking back at me with any eerie glint in its eyes.

The rest of the group had circled the armchairs and sofas surrounding a low table in the middle of the room and were moving on again. I followed dutifully, through the dining hall and into a south-facing sitting room that balanced the library on the floor plan, with a magnificent carved-oak staircase leading to the upper floor. There were plenty of places to go to get away from the rest of your family in a house like this.

Fortunately the upstairs had far fewer rooms on show. At the top of the stairs, there was a morning room where the ladies of the house could sit and sew or gossip, directly above the dining hall. I looked out of the windows again while everyone else admired elegant eighteenth-century furniture and china shepherdesses.

The successive owners of the house apparently slept in an elegant bedroom, dressing room and sitting room suite, above the Great Parlour in the north-east corner. The furniture was a mixture of everything from Jacobean to Edwardian, and the faded embroidered hangings on the four-poster bed in the so-called King Charles bedroom were apparently original. I wondered about possible reasons for the oak leaf motif so prominent on the bed curtains and in the carved frieze that circled the top of the walls.

Then our guide led us the length of the house past more resolutely closed doors and into a long gallery that must straddle the passage between the kitchen and the library below.

'These are the family portraits, all the way down to Gerald Beauchene. This was painted in 1962, just after he got married.'

'Does he still live here?' one keen visitor enquired.

The guide shook her head with a smile. 'He retired from running the estate seven years ago. He lives in a farmhouse which the family owns a few miles away.'

'Does the house still have to pass to a male heir?' someone else asked.

'Not these days,' the guide assured her. 'Blithehurst is set up as a family trust now.'

As the tour group spread out to look at the various pictures, I studied the painting of an unremarkable young man in the sort of suit and haircut familiar from early James Bond movies. I couldn't see any hint of wildwood blood in his face. Well, he was the sixth generation to come after Francis, so that was hardly surprising.

I checked my watch as I made a slow circuit of the long room, trying not to look too impatient as I waited for us all to be ushered back downstairs. Our guide was listening to some convoluted tale of one visitor's forefather's service in Normandy in World War Two, by way of asking about the Beauchenes' wartime experiences. The guide explained that Gerald's father had defied the family tradition of keeping their heads down in time of trouble and parachuted into the D-Day landings.

As soon as the man finished his story, our guide clapped her hands with a politely apologetic expression. 'The gallery concludes our tour, ladies and gentlemen, so thank you very much for your interest, and please, enjoy the rest of your day. Do visit our restaurant and garden centre, and there's a cafe in the old manor ruins, if you want a drink and a sit down after visiting the park.'

'Thank you.' I smiled briefly to our guide as I headed back downstairs. Outside, I circled the house and followed the path to the valley bottom, skirting a securely fenced drop into an unexpected hollow. A sign informed me that was where the stone to build the new house had been quarried and that the current rock garden had been planted between the World Wars.

Further on, beyond a kissing gate in the iron fence, the path branched. The right-hand fork led to the ruins inside the moat while the left headed for a second gate and then over a rustic wooden bridge crossing the shallow river and into the wooded pasture beyond.

The metal fence gave me pause for thought. I would have thought that any local dryads would have objections to something they couldn't pass without pain.

If I could find them, I'd ask. I crossed the bridge, glancing down and wondering if Kalei had visited these crystal-clear waters recently. Keeping my eyes open for any white cows wandering towards the path, I headed up the valley side.

# Chapter Twenty-Six

These ancient oaks were most definitely thriving. Each one must have been home to a multitude of birds and animals and insects. If I spent the afternoon here, there was no telling what I might see. What I couldn't see was any hint of a dryad.

I wondered if they could see me, or rather, if they would know that I wasn't just another tourist. Tila hadn't recognised me for a dryad's son until she'd been standing right in front of me. At first, the only thing she had realised was that I could see her ethereal form. That's what had made her sufficiently curious to speak to me.

No matter how hard I looked, I couldn't see any hint of a green-clad figure walking between these trees. Maybe I should have asked Kalei's advice about making contact with dryads, I thought belatedly. I couldn't see any trace of the Green Man's presence either. Perhaps I should have brought that carved mask with me.

I went on, regardless, and by the time I reached the top of the path curving up the valley side, I was ready to take a breather. That long, gradual slope was deceptive, so I was glad to see curved stone benches framing the Temple of Venus, doubtless installed for that very reason. Though at the moment nobody else was enjoying a sit down. I couldn't see anyone walking through the park at all. They must all be in the cafe buying lunch.

I studied the temple. A circle of pillars on a round plinth with three steps was topped by a neat dome. The goddess in the centre was a marble statue in the classical style. She wasn't one of those coy ones with hands fluttering over her tits and pubes, like some actress on a beach caught out by paparazzi. She stood proudly naked except for a twist of cloth around her hips, challenging onlookers with her serene gaze.

I wondered if she'd been brought here from an Italian grotto by some Beauchene doing the grand tour, or if the statue had been carved by a local artist. Either way, I was convinced the sculptor had seen a dryad for himself. I felt my pulse quicken.

'I'm glad you like it,' an amused voice whispered in my ear.

I spun around so quickly that I nearly fell over.

The dryad's smile widened. There was no question that's what she was, even if she was pretending to be a tourist in sensible shoes, casually smart trousers and a striped shirt with a cashmere cardigan draped around her shoulders. Apart from anything else, she'd clearly been the model for that statue.

She assessed me with pupil-less emerald-green eyes. 'What brings you to our home?'

I cleared my throat. 'Kalei—'

The dryad crossed her arms, her expression hardening. 'What does the naiad want with us? What is she to you?'

'Perhaps she's sent him to settle her debts,' another voice suggested.

A second dryad had appeared out of nowhere to sit on the closest stone bench. She was also masquerading as a human, a white-haired old woman in a raincoat. A woman who had once been as gorgeous as any Hollywood screen goddess. One of those who scorned any notion of trying to disguise her advancing years. Her withered hands rested on a carved wooden cane, and as she studied me I realised her opaque eyes weren't green but the rich colour of a copper beech.

'Or to serve some other purpose.' The third dryad had a distinctly suggestive smile, her shrug tossing long red hair back over one shoulder. She sat with her feet up on the other bench, hugging her knees. The youngest of the trio, she could have been a student in her black leggings and baggy yellow T-shirt. She might be the youngest-looking, I reminded myself, but there was no telling how old she actually was.

Though I felt sure I was seeing their true relationships to each other. Maiden, mother and crone. The archetypal trio. I just wished that I could guess what the hell that might mean here and now. Kalei hadn't told me there would be three dryads. Then again, she hadn't told me anything different. Obviously, I hadn't asked the right questions. That was something else I'd better remember.

I took a deep breath to settle the butterflies in my stomach. 'Kalei told me you were here. She asked me to tell you what has happened to Tila.'

The dryad standing in front of me stiffened. For an instant, I glimpsed her in her ethereal form, gowned like an ancient queen and crowned with summer flowers.

'What has happened?'

'I'm so sorry.' My heart was pounding now. 'She was killed by a wose.'

'The naiad has always been a deceiver,' the old woman hissed.

'No, forgive me, it's true.' I swallowed bitter regret, still addressing the queenly dryad. 'I saw her body for myself.'

'Speak.' Her single word was as sharp as splintering wood.

More than that, her voice seized me, supernaturally compelling. I couldn't have stopped talking if I'd wanted to. By the time I'd told the whole sorry story, including every detail up to my last conversation with Kalei, my throat was agonisingly dry and I was struggling to catch my breath.

I'd had no idea dryads could do that. My stomach hollowed as I realised how little I knew about the powers they might call on. After all, my mother had never had any reason to see me as a threat. Clasping my hands painfully tight together behind my back, I tried to look as harmless as possible.

'Thank you.' The queenly dryad disappeared before I could open my mouth.

I looked from left to right. The other two remained, both still studying me, unblinking. I felt like a mouse between two cats.

'You're not of local stock.' The young one put her feet down on the grass. Her eyes were the pale green of spring leaves. 'Where have you come from, cousin? Before today, I mean.'

Her voice didn't carry the same terrifying compulsion, but I told her all the same. For one thing, that was much easier than asking who Tila had been to them. Though I could see a family resemblance that I thought went beyond the dryads' shared nature. The youngest one in particular reminded me uncomfortably of Tila.

Whether she was her sister or not, she looked thoughtful, sensuous lips pursed. 'I wonder if we've ever had dealings with your foremothers.' She leaned forward to look past me. 'What do you think, Grandmother?'

The old woman didn't answer, staring at me instead. 'You've delivered your message, boy, yet you're waiting.' Her copper eyes were as piercing and merciless as a hawk's. 'What more do you want with us?'

'Be nice,' the younger one reproved. 'Perhaps he's looking for companionship among his own kind.' She smiled sweetly.

I had no reason not to tell them the truth. 'I've never known another dryad's son. I'd like to know if there's one anywhere around here. I'd like to meet someone else who understands my life.'

'You won't find such a man here.' The old dryad vanished in the blink of an eye.

I turned back to the other bench, but the youngest had gone as well.

'Hello?' I walked around the temple, but there was no sign that they'd ever been here. Straining my eyes, I searched every leaf and branch of the closest oak trees for any suggestions of an ethereal presence. I wasn't only looking for the dryads. Some glimpse of the Green Man would have reassured me this conversation wasn't all I was going to get.

All I could see was twigs and leaves shifting in the breeze. I dropped down onto a bench. I didn't know whether to be more disappointed or annoyed. The dryads had come, they'd gone, and I'd learned nothing at all. At least, none of the things that I really wanted to know.

Though I supposed that discovering a dryad who wasn't your mum could be scarily intimidating was potentially useful. But if being born to a rich family who owned a stately home was an answer to the challenges a dryad's son faced, I could have worked that one out for myself.

I looked around again. There was still nothing to see in the trees. I turned back to the statue, but the marble goddess just stood there, mute and motionless.

I reviewed our conversation, if you could call it that. I'd done pretty much all of the talking. The queenly dryad had asked me maybe a handful of questions and the others had said even less.

Perhaps they had told me a couple of things, whether or not they'd meant to. Firstly, the grandmother had said Kalei was a deceiver. I had a feeling she meant something more specific than my mother's general distrust of naiads. Secondly, when I'd said I was looking for someone who understood my life, she'd said I wouldn't find such a man here. That could either mean there wasn't a dryad's son here at all, or that there was, but he and I wouldn't have much in common. I wondered which was the right answer.

That was something I could ask Kalei, if I could find her to ask her. I wondered what she'd demand in return for more answers. After all, she'd got what she wanted from me: someone who could handle metal and kill the wose. Then she'd fulfilled her end of our bargain by sending me here.

Fuck it. I rolled up the guide book and relieved my frustration by smacking it against the stone bench. I stood up. I was still viciously thirsty, and hungry as well now. At least I could do something about that. The tour guide up at the house had said there was a cafe in the ruined manor.

# Chapter Twenty-Seven

Walking back downhill was easier going. There were more people out and about and I nodded as they acknowledged me on the path. Reaching the kissing gate, I realised I'd completely forgotten to ask the dryads about that iron fence. Pausing to trace its route as it enclosed the gardens around the ruins, it struck me again as an odd thing to find where dryads lived. It ran along the edge of the river as well. Maybe I'd ask Kalei what she thought about that, if I ever got to speak to her again.

For the moment, I followed the path towards the footbridge that crossed the moat. I could see it was kept supplied by a channel dug to enclose the medieval buildings in a loop of water drawn from the river. Solid towers flanked a flat-roofed, battlemented gatehouse guarding this approach. It was apparent that Blithehurst's ancient manor house had originally been a hollow square with a great hall on the furthest side. Whatever the other rooms had been, they'd been demolished to make the ruins look more romantic, according to the information board by the footbridge. Apparently, enthusiasm for Keats and Wordsworth had succeeded where Cromwell's men had failed.

Still, the ground-floor rooms of the ivy-draped gatehouse were intact. One was selling drinks and sandwiches while the other offered tables and chairs, mostly taken up by cheerfully chattering families. I bought a ham salad baguette and two cans of lemonade, sticking one in a side pocket of my combats as I drank the other. Wandering through to the cobbled courtyard, I saw a couple of blue-shirted staff on folding chairs on either side. They were presumably there to deter small children from climbing up the waist-high ruined walls and falling into the moat.

The Great Hall was raised above the cobbled courtyard by a lower storey of storage rooms set half above, half below ground level, and lit by shallow windows now blocked with bars and thick glass. The hall itself had lost its roof and the inner wall, but the stone tracery of the tall windows at either end was still impressive. I climbed the steps to the entrance to get a better look as I unwrapped my lunch.

'Who the hell are you, and what did the dryads want with you?' a low voice demanded.

I'd just taken a big bite of baguette. Trying not to choke, I turned to see one of the staff had come up the steps behind me. As she glowered at me, I recognised the tour guide who'd shown us around the house.

I took my time swallowing my mouthful and matched her challenge with my own. 'Who the hell are you?'

'Eleanor Beauchene.' Her raised eyebrows demanded an answer to her first question.

'Daniel Mackmain.' With both my hands full, I didn't offer to shake.

She glanced around to make sure there was no one within earshot. 'You can see the dryads. How? What did they say to you?' Her tone was somewhere between incredulous and exasperated.

'My mother—' I'd never said this out loud to another human being. That realisation hit me like a smack in the face. I barely managed to continue. 'She is one.'

'What?' The girl gaped at me. If she'd had any fillings in her teeth, I could have counted them all. She looked in the direction of the hillside path leading up to the temple, her eyes wide.

'No,' I said hastily as I realised her mistake, or my mistake. 'Not one of yours. She's—' I broke off as I also realised I wasn't at all sure how much I wanted to tell this complete stranger. 'So you can see them too?'

'Yes.' She narrowed impatient eyes. 'Where have you come from? Where are these other dryads? How did you get away?'

She had hazel eyes. Wholly human eyes, I was relieved to see. Now that I took a proper look at her, I could also see a family likeness with the five Beauchene daughters in that big portrait of Edmund and his children. She had the same long dark hair, held back in a thick plait. She was taller though, at least five foot ten, and had an athlete's build. It seemed I'd been too hasty when I'd assumed that the family's greenwood blood had run thin by this generation.

'What else can you see?' I asked her. 'Sprites? Boggarts? What else lives around here?'

'This is mad.' She was talking to herself, not to me. Shaking her head, she turned to go back down the steps.

'Wait, please.' I tried not to raise my voice.

She stopped and looked back. 'Why?'

'Please, I've never known anyone else...' I spread despairing hands. 'Can we get a coffee? Swap notes?' As soon as I said it, I realised how ridiculous that sounded.

Being ridiculous got me somewhere. The corner of her mouth twitched with the suggestion of a wry smile. 'Wait a moment.'

'Okay.' While she went back across the courtyard and into the gatehouse, I finished eating my baguette. Seeing one of the seated custodians looking at me with ill-concealed curiosity, I tried to look as though I was studying the architecture.

Eleanor Beauchene reappeared with a tray holding two mugs, milk, sugar and a plate of the cafe's homemade biscuits. She jerked her head to the right, and I went to join her in the remains of a room where the ruined walls made a convenient seat.

She set the tray down between us. 'So?'

I kept my explanation short. I told her about my parents, mentioning in general terms where they lived. I explained what I did for a living, both the building site work and the craft fairs. I told her what my mother had said about dryads' sons' lives in the past. I explained that I'd always been keen to meet someone else with greenwood blood.

'I like to visit places with old woodlands and historic landscapes, especially if they have famous trees.' I gestured towards the park and then nodded towards the manor house. 'When I saw that picture of Francis Beauchene, I was sure he was a dryad's son, so I thought I'd see if I could see any sign. Three of them appeared when I reached that little temple.'

I smiled, trying to look open and honest, before hiding my qualms by drinking some coffee. Kalei would have been proud of me, I thought sourly. I hadn't told any lies, but I hadn't told anywhere near the whole truth.

'There are just the three of them here.' Eleanor looked at me over the rim of her own mug, clearly assessing me. After a long moment, she put her coffee back on the tray. 'You're right, about Francis. Asca, his mother, that's a statue of her in the temple.'

'And the other two?' Maybe if I knew their names, it would be easier to get them to talk to me.

'Frai's been here since before the Normans arrived, as far as I can tell.' Eleanor grimaced, which surprised me. 'Sineya was my playmate when I was little, but I've no idea how old she actually is. I know she remembers the First World War like it was yesterday.'

'And Tila?' I still reckoned she was Sineya, the youngest one's, sister, but I didn't want to make trouble for myself by getting that wrong.

Eleanor looked at me blankly. 'Who's Tila?'

Shit. I had no reason to assume these dryads would have mentioned her, especially if they'd had some falling out. I grabbed a moment to think by eating a biscuit.

What the hell. I could hardly expect Eleanor Beauchene to share this place's secrets if it was obvious I was holding back my own.

'Tila is—was...' I told her tragic story for the second time that day, but this time I did it very differently. Even so, stripped to its bare essentials, it sounded insane when I was talking to another ordinary person.

Eleanor took a biscuit, studied it and put it back on the plate before looking at me, her eyes cold. 'So you did come here on purpose. You didn't just happen to visit and see that picture and think, ooh, I bet there are dryads in those woods.' Her sarcasm verged on anger.

'No, I mean, yes, that is what I was thinking about that picture, and I do visit places like this on the off chance. Why I came here specifically—' I wondered how to salvage the situation. 'It's complicated.'

'Complicated.' She pushed the mugs into the centre of the tray and picked it up. 'When it was just you, your mum and your dad, growing up, and all three of you knew who was who and what was going on. I've got Grandma, Grandpa, Nana and Grandad, two parents, two brothers, one sister, four uncles, three aunts and a whole load of cousins. I'm the only one who can see the dryads. That's complicated.'

She got to her feet and looked steadily at me. 'When you're six and you chatter about your friend who lives in the trees, they pat you on the head and laugh at your lively imagination. When you're still insisting she's real when you're nine, they start talking about child development specialists and psychological assessments.'

Breaking off, she shook her head. 'Never mind. It was... interesting to meet you.'

She walked away without a backwards glance. I wanted to follow her, to try to talk some more. Unfortunately I couldn't think what to say that wouldn't risk making things worse. I could also see the other custodian looking intently at me from the other side of the courtyard. She'd be asking who I was and what I'd wanted, I had no doubt of that. I was also convinced that stirring up gossip among the staff by pursuing Eleanor would get me no thanks at all.

But I wanted to continue this conversation and I needed to let Eleanor Beauchene know. She needed to know how to get in touch with me. She knew my name, but I wasn't easy to find, not like Victoria with all her social media profiles.

Walking back to the car park, I noticed the gift shop and garden centre were busier than ever. Some people wandering round a display of woven hazel trellis archways gave me an idea. I looked up the Blithehurst website on my mobile and found the main contact phone number. I pressed the link.

'Good afternoon, Blithehurst House. How may I help you?'

The woman answering wasn't Eleanor. That was a relief.

'Good afternoon. I just wanted to leave a message for Miss Beauchene. Eleanor Beauchene,' I clarified quickly, remembering she'd mentioned a sister. 'My name's Daniel Mackmain and I've just been visiting Blithehurst. I'm a craftsman – I work with wood – and I was wondering if she'd be interested in seeing what I could offer for your shop? Maybe she could call me?' I gave my number, twice, to make sure she wrote it down right.

'Thank you, I'll pass that on,' the woman said smoothly. 'Thanks for your call and I'm glad you enjoyed your visit.'

I hoped Eleanor wouldn't just decide to throw the note in the bin. Well, there was nothing I could do about that. I spared a moment to hope the dryads might prompt her to find out more about me. With any luck, they'd still be curious about Kalei's motives for sending me here. Unless they decided they wanted nothing more to do with a conniving naiad.

I drove back to Lambton and circled the streets around the house where I was renting a room until I found a parking space. The prick in the room below mine was playing his godawful music loudly again, so I found my headphones and watched a film on my laptop until it was time to go out and get some dinner from the nearest chip shop. The shared kitchen was so cluttered and grubby that I used it as little as possible.

As I ate, I glanced at the carving of the Green Man, propped on a stack of boxes holding my stuff. It sat there, a lifeless lump of wood, and that night I slept soundly without dreams.

The next day, I drove to Tila's valley and walked along the stream through the water meadow. The stink of burning from the devastated black poplars was fading, but I still felt guilty about killing those trees, however certain I was that the wose had to die.

There were plenty of Sunday dog walkers, but none were Kalei and the shuck. There was no sign of them around the ruins of St Werburgh's. Though I did spot Chrissie

Monkswell's nosy cleaner walking over the packhorse bridge, presumably heading for the Goose. I changed my mind about eating there and got a Chinese takeaway in Lambton.

On Monday morning I went to work. Phil told us all there'd be another fortnight for us on the barn conversions, give or take. I asked him, and Mick and Geoff and Nigel, if they knew of anyone looking for a carpenter. They all said they would let me know if they did, though they couldn't think of anything at the moment. I had to take them at their word, but I still felt they were looking at me differently after the past few weeks.

# Chapter Twenty-Eight

Eleanor Beauchene sent me a text on Wednesday. If I was free, could I come over next Monday when the house was closed to the public? I wondered what that was all about. I thought about ringing to ask but decided not to push my luck.

I texted back to explain that I'd be working on Monday, but I could come over in the evening if that was okay. She replied with a single word. Fine.

Fair enough. It wasn't as though I'd seen any sign of the Green Man or Kalei to give me a hint about what I should do next, even though I'd visited the valley and St Werburgh's ruins several more times.

I spent the weekend at a craft fair in Lincolnshire and sold enough pieces to earn some useful cash. That was a relief, because I hadn't got any leads on a new job yet and eating at the Goose after I'd failed to find Kalei was getting to be an expensive habit. Though I told Phil Caister I had to see someone about some possible work, to explain why I kept going through lunch on Monday and was heading back to Lambton by four-thirty.

I grabbed a quick shower, and with everyone else still out of the house, there was enough hot water for a change. I texted Eleanor Beauchene as I walked out of the door, to let her know I was on my way. She was waiting by the car park entrance when I arrived around a quarter past six. As I parked, she pushed the wide gate closed and bolted it to stop anyone else driving in.

I got out of the Land Rover and locked it. This time I did offer a handshake as she walked up. 'Hello.'

She shook. 'Hello.' She was wearing jeans and a loose cream cardigan over a black T-shirt. Her long hair was in a ponytail today.

There was an awkward silence.

'So,' I said slowly, 'do you want to talk about garden benches?'

She managed a strained smile. 'No, well, maybe later, who knows. But—' She broke off with a shake of her head and an expression I couldn't read. 'Just come with me, please. Then it'll be easier to explain.'

I was willing to let her set the pace. 'Okay.'

The whole place had a different atmosphere with no one else around. The restaurant and the garden centre were all locked up and the hut by the gate to the gardens was shuttered. The only sound was the chatter of birds settling down to roost in the trees, though there was still plenty of the long summer evening left.

Eleanor had the key to a padlock securing the gate. She relocked it behind us. 'This way.'

She didn't take the path towards the house but headed off to the right where a slender chain with a 'No Access' sign blocked off a narrow route into a tangle of shrubs. She unhooked it. 'Watch your step.'

I soon saw why the Blithehurst people wouldn't want the general public risking this path. It zigzagged tightly down the steep slope to the valley bottom, all slippery earth and tree roots underfoot. Leafy branches reached out to brush against each other overhead and the first hints of dusk were gathering in the undergrowth. I looked warily around as I followed Eleanor, but nothing beyond ordinary shadows caught my eye.

Reaching the valley floor, we walked through an impressive collection of carefully chosen trees. These were all mature specimens, planted in previous centuries and flourishing tall and straight in the valley's shelter. Each one had a neat plaque on a little post giving the tree's names in English and Latin and its country of origin. Unsurprisingly, non-native varieties of oak were well represented. I detected a dryad's hand in that.

Eleanor left the trees to cut across the neatly mown grass towards the medieval manor. She climbed over the fence rather than detour to the gate, so I did the same, after testing the horizontal iron strut to make sure it was up to my weight.

Another chain hung across the footbridge and the gate-house was locked up tight. Inquisitive ducks on the moat came paddling up to see if we had any food for them, before drifting off, disappointed.

Eleanor unlocked a small wicket gate set in the iron-studded wood of the main entrance. I barely managed to get through it without banging my head or scraping my shoulders. She was already halfway across the cobbled courtyard, sorting through the heavy bunch of keys in her hand.

A flight of steps headed downwards, to the right hand of the ones leading up to the Great Hall. This lower staircase ended at an uncompromisingly locked wooden door with another 'No Access' sign. Eleanor unlocked it and looked back to make sure I was following. Her face still gave nothing away.

'I want you to tell me what you can hear.' She led the way into the undercroft.

Given the lie of the land, this long storage space didn't offer much headroom. I could only just stand upright in the middle of the shallow, curved stone vault. I looked around. Green stains spread along the window sills where dim light filtered through the thick glass and bars. The floor was beaten earth and the whole place smelled damp and musty. That was hardly a surprise with the river so close.

Eleanor closed the door behind us, shutting out what little noise came from outside. The hush was absolute. Only she'd said she wanted to know what I could hear. That told me there must be something to listen for. Otherwise she'd have asked *if* I could hear anything. I closed my eyes to concentrate and did my best to ignore the sound of my own breathing.

There was something, though it was so faint I thought I was imagining it at first. As I focused my attention, the noise became a little louder, a little clearer. Not a noise, a voice. Keening, wailing, mewling. All of those words sprang to mind, but none of them conveyed the eerie torment thread-

266

ed through the sound. That wasn't all. There was something darker, resentful, menacing in it. I couldn't tell where the noise was coming from though. It seemed both impossibly far away and yet somehow so close at hand that apprehension raised the hairs on the back of my neck.

I opened my eyes and looked at Eleanor. 'Something's in pain or distress. Something or someone.' Though if it was a someone, it would be a person to add to my new tally of those who weren't remotely human.

She nodded and opened the door. I shivered, and not from the draft that came in with the daylight. Now I'd heard it I found I simply couldn't stop listening to that misery. It was making my skin crawl, but I could hardly move my feet.

'Come on.' Eleanor jerked her head towards the daylight. 'It'll be okay once we're out of here.'

She clearly found the noise as unnerving as I did. Edging past her through the doorway, I saw her hands shaking as she locked up the undercroft.

'What the hell is that?' I took a deep, cleansing breath of summer-scented evening air.

'I have no idea,' she said frankly. 'But at least, if you can hear it too, then I know I'm not going mad like Great Uncle Harold. Would you like some coffee?'

'Yes, please. Thanks.' That seemed like the safest answer.

We walked back across the courtyard. By the time we were halfway across, it was hard to believe I'd felt so uneasy in that earth-scented undercroft. Starlings chattered and bickered on the gatehouse roof without a care in the world as Eleanor gestured for me to go ahead through the wicket door.

I looked around as she locked it behind us. 'So, it's just you here when the house isn't open to the public?'

'On Mondays.' She shoved the keys in her pocket. 'Some staff will be in tomorrow, to tidy up and restock. There's a rota.'

We crossed the footbridge and headed for the main path leading up the slope past the rock garden in the hollow.

I wondered where the horde of relatives she'd mentioned might be. 'Your family, they don't live here these days?'

'We did, until Grandpa retired. Then Dad decided the only way to keep the place going was to open up the house. There are enough other places to live on the estate now that we run all the farms as a single business. Dad and Mum managed everything between them until a few years ago, then Robert, my older brother, took over the farming side. I've ended up running the house and visitor stuff.' She didn't seem overly thrilled about that.

'And your other brother and sister?' If I kept her talking, maybe she'd tell me something I wanted to know.

She glanced at me, considering, and I didn't think she was going to answer, but as we reached the terrace overlooked by the south face of the house, she continued.

'Ben lives in London, he's an architect. Sophie's a solicitor in Manchester. They have shares in the family trust that keeps everything together. We all do, but Blithehurst's only ever really been able to support the heir and his immediate family. Everyone else goes off to make their own way.' She scowled. 'That's the theory, at least.'

'And you—' I hesitated. 'You're the only one who can see the dryads?'

'That's right, and they were thrilled about that,' she said grimly.

I decided to stop asking questions. We skirted the library, and I realised we were heading for the side door that opened into the far end of the corridor leading from the Great Hall to the kitchen. We went in and I looked around for a kettle, but the place still looked like a cookery museum.

'In here.' Eleanor opened a side door to reveal modern kitchen units and appliances fitted into what must have been a scullery or something similar in days gone by. She opened a cupboard and took out a jar of coffee. 'Instant okay?'

'Fine with me.' I leaned against the counter as she filled the kettle at the sink on the other side of the small room.

'Have you eaten?' She looked at me with belated concern.

'If you've come straight from work...'

I waved that away. 'I can grab something later.'

The sound of the kettle heating up filled another awkward silence.

Eleanor got mismatched mugs out of a cupboard and a spoon out of a drawer. 'Sugar?'

'Please.' I moved to let her get to the fridge and take out a pint of milk.

The kettle boiled and she made two coffees. She was chewing a stray wisp of her hair.

'So,' I prompted. 'Have you any idea what that weird noise could be?'

'Let's go into the library.' She picked up both mugs. 'Can you get the doors?'

'Okay.' Leading the way, I found the book-lined room warm with the evening sunlight falling through the uncurtained windows. There were papers, a laptop and a packet of chocolate digestives on the low table as well as dents in the sofa cushions. One of the armchairs had been pushed aside. It was surprising how these small changes turned last week's showpiece into a room where you could believe people actually lived.

Eleanor put the mugs on a mat on the table and sat on the sofa, kicking off her shoes. As I took a chair, she pushed the biscuits towards me. 'Help yourself.'

I took a couple, glancing around the carved ceiling. I couldn't see anything unnerving, but I had the distinct sensation of being watched.

'So,' Eleanor began with a glint in her eye. 'Let me tell you about Great Uncle Harold.' She picked up her mug and settled back into her cushions, stockinged feet up on the sofa seat.

'To be accurate, he was my grandfather's great uncle, and he was born in 1894. So he was twenty when the First World War broke out, and like all honourable young men of his class and generation, he enlisted to fight. He spent three years on the Western Front until he was invalided out, after being buried alive when his regiment's trenches were shelled.' She twisted around to gesture towards the desk in the closest bay window, where a couple of old-fashioned notebooks lay open. 'We have his journals. Even before that, he'd had a hell of a time.'

She took a mouthful of coffee, her eyes distant. 'Unsurprisingly, he came home with what they used to call shell shock. The family tried to look after him themselves, but he took to wandering the gardens, and especially the old ruins, at all hours of the night. They locked his bedroom door, but somehow he always found a way out. He insisted that he could hear cries for help from the men who'd been buried with him, the ones who were never found. More than once, they found him with a spade, ripping up the cobbles in the old manor courtyard, or down in the undercroft, digging into the floor.'

She grimaced. 'They tried whatever passed for therapy in those days. Drugs, long walks and cold baths, sending him to the seaside for a rest cure. Nothing seemed to help. Then early one morning in June 1918, he was found drowned in the moat. The coroner's verdict was an accident, even though his journals make desperate reading by then. Everyone agreed it was a tragedy, and as far as anyone was concerned, that was that.'

'Until you heard those noises in the undercroft.' In this warm, sunny room, a shiver at the recollection surprised me. 'When did that start?'

'March. At least, that's when I first realised there was something down there. We do a full inspection of everything before we open to the public each spring, and I was checking the state of the ruins against the previous year's survey. When I went into the undercroft, and since I've read Harold's journals...' She shrugged. 'But if you can hear it too, at least that should mean I'm not going mad.'

She finished her coffee and put her mug on the table. Leaning back, she looked at me, expectant.

I wish I knew exactly what she wanted. I played for time.

'Could Harold see the dryads?'

Eleanor looked thoughtful. 'I'm not sure. There are a few hints in his journals, but it's hardly something he'd write down, don't you think? I've asked Asca, but she won't give me a straight answer. Frai won't discuss him at all, and Sineya just says I must ask her mother.' Now she was scowling.

'I think I might know why she doesn't want to discuss that,' I said slowly. 'She's never mentioned Tila to you? Neither of the others have?'

As she shook her head, I drank the last of my coffee. 'As far as I can make out, she left here around a hundred years ago, to settle in that valley between Lambton and Kympton. She said it was because her family were fools. That would be around the time this Harold of yours was being tormented by those voices.'

Another thought struck me. 'Have you asked them about the noises in the undercroft?'

'Frai and Asca both say I need not concern myself.' Her face reflected her annoyance. 'Sineya won't tell me what's going on either, but she did ask me to let her know if the voices get any louder, or if they stop.'

'She said "voices" specifically?'

Eleanor nodded. 'What does that mean?'

'I don't know,' I admitted, frustrated, 'but a voice implies someone, not some creature like a boggart, don't you think?'

'Disgusting things.' Eleanor shuddered. 'They're everywhere this summer.'

'They seem to be.' I glanced at the ceiling again.

'Why do you keep doing that?' she demanded.

It wasn't as if I had anything to lose by answering. 'I've started seeing something strange in a piece that I've carved.' I explained about the Green Man's mask.

'Goodness,' Eleanor said faintly as she gazed around the carvings. 'I've never seen anything like that here.'

'It's new to me as well,' I assured here. 'The thing is though, I was convinced he wanted me to come to the Peak

District. When I met Tila, I thought that was why. He knows I want to find more of my mother's people. Then, when she was murdered, I thought he wanted me to avenge her death by killing the wose. Afterwards, Kalei told me about this place, and so I thought finally, that's what I've been looking for. That's why he set me on this path. Only I get here and your dryads want nothing to do with me. Now there are these eerie voices, and whatever they might be, I don't think they can be anything good.'

'Me neither.' Eleanor seemed relieved that I shared her apprehension. 'I've never seen a naiad, not that I know of anyway. I suppose this Kalei could have come up our river and mingled with the tourists. I'd never have known, not unless I was close enough to see her eyes.'

'She's very good at going unnoticed.' I explained what little I knew about her, and about naiads more generally.

Eleanor looked thoughtful. 'There's an old Breton legend about a Sir Graelent who falls in love with a mysterious woman who he finds bathing in a forest stream. He ends up drowning till she brings him back to life and carries him off, never to be seen again.'

I found I could imagine a naiad doing something like that all too easily. 'Is there any connection with your Sir Graelent?'

She shrugged. 'I've no idea, but our Sir Graelent, he could certainly see the dryads. So could his squire, Robert. Frai once told me that.'

'There's greenwood blood on both sides of your family?' I hadn't expected that.

'Once upon a time,' she said wryly. 'There's not been much sign of it in recent generations. The last person who could see the dryads before me was Great Uncle Charles, and he was killed in Sicily in World War Two. That's why—' Eleanor broke off and looked at me with that unreadable expression again. 'That's why they give me such a hard time, especially Frai. As far as they're concerned, if I'm the only one left, and there's no sign of the next generation being born any time soon, then I have a duty to stay here and make sure their trees and the pastures are protected. Never mind what else I might want to do with my life.'

'What might that be?' I asked cautiously.

She sighed. 'I managed to get them to agree that I could go away to university, as long as I promised to come back here for every vacation. I read medieval history at Durham. The thing is, I'd like to go back and do a doctorate, but they're not having that. I don't suppose you've ever pissed off a dryad?'

'Not personally, not beyond just being an annoying kid, but I know it's not a good idea.'

'It's not that I don't like running this house and the garden centre,' she said, frustrated. 'It's interesting work and the challenges are always changing. I know I'm helping to keep Blithehurst and its history in the family, so my mum and dad are really grateful. It's just... I'd like to have some choices. Does that make sense?'

'It does.' Though I found it hard to think that having a job for life that came with rent-free housing was any real hardship. Better to change the subject.

'I don't know if Kalei's visited your river. I can't imagine any naiad would like that iron fence you have running the bank. What do the dryads have to say about that?'

'They say that it doesn't concern them as they have no interest in visiting the ruins.'

'Another answer that's no answer.' I decided we needed to ask elsewhere. 'I reckon Kalei knows more than she's letting on. I wonder, if you came to Tila's valley, maybe we could persuade her to tell us what she knows about these voices.'

Eleanor sat up straight. 'That's a thought.'

I checked my watch and the twilight sky outside. 'It's too late tonight. It's an hour's drive and we've both got work tomorrow. Is there any chance you could come to Lambton tomorrow evening?'

'I can try.' Eleanor's expression made me pretty sure she would manage it.

# Chapter Twenty-Nine

She texted me at four-thirty to say she was on her way, so I left work promptly at five-thirty. We'd found a map in the Blithehurst library and I'd shown Eleanor where to find the bridge in Tila's valley, so when I got there she'd already arrived. Leaning against a neat silver hatchback, she was contemplating the skeletons of the burnt black poplars.

'That's where you fought the wose?' She turned her head as I got out of the Land Rover.

I nodded, walking over. 'Not something I'm keen to do again.'

'Is that...' Eleanor looked at the wooden carving in my hand.

'The Green Man.' I handed it over. 'If we need to, we can throw it in the river to get Kalei's attention. Though I don't know how long—'

'That won't be necessary.' The naiad was standing on the bridge parapet. She was in her blue ethereal form rather than masquerading as any sort of human.

'That was easy,' Eleanor murmured, wide-eyed.

Easy enough to unnerve me, and I wondered what Kalei's choice of appearance might signify.

'I see you share Tila's blood.' Calm and composed, Kalei jumped down to the road, landing without a sound.

'I do,' Eleanor confirmed cautiously.

'So what brings you here?' A faint smile curved Kalei's mouth, as if she already knew the answer.

I braced myself for more manipulation. 'Did you know Harold Beauchene? The man who drowned in the moat at Blithehurst? Was that something to do with Tila's quarrel with her family?'

'I knew him.' Kalei was still looking at Eleanor, studying

her.

Eleanor handed my carving back as she took a pace towards the naiad, intent on getting answers. 'What can you tell us about the voices that drove him mad?'

'Tila did her best to soothe him, to save him.' Kalei gestured towards the oak trees up on the ridge where I'd found the dryad's body. 'But her mother and grandmother said if he didn't have the strength to resist within him, then he was no loss to the bloodline.'

'Were they lovers?' Perhaps I'd been wrong about Tila's ties to humanity. After meeting the Blithehurst dryads I was forced to conclude that what my mother had told me wasn't a guide to them all.

'No.' Now Kalei did look my way. 'Though they might have shared such pleasures, given time.'

Before I could decide how incestuous that would have been, Eleanor snapped her fingers to reclaim Kalei's attention. 'You still haven't answered my question. What are these underground voices at Blithehurst? We can both hear them.'

'Wormsong.' Kalei's gaze challenged us to understand.

I was at a loss. 'Worms?'

Eleanor was quicker on the uptake. 'Do you mean wyrms, spelled with a "y"? A serpent dragon? Not one with wings, but something akin to a giant snake?'

I realised what she meant. 'Your Sir Graelent killed a dragon, supposedly. Was that a wyrm?'

'According to the oldest records we have.' Eleanor nodded. 'It lived in the marsh that was there before Blithehurst. Sir Graelent drained the swamp to build his castle.'

I stared at the naiad. 'You mean they're not all dead?'

One thing you learn reading books of old British folklore is just how many counties and castles have a dragon story. An awful lot of those are wyrms, venomous, destructive creatures a world away from the dragons in high, heroic fantasies. I'd never been able to kid myself that they couldn't possibly be real, but I'd always been reassured to think they were long gone. It wasn't as though something like that could stay hidden in the modern world.

Kalei pursed her lips. 'The wyrms in these islands were all slaughtered, after the Norman king crossed the sea and when so many of his warriors made alliances with the dryads here. Your foremothers were determined to rid these islands of the serpent worshippers who came here after the Romans, crossing the northern seas in their dragon-headed boats.'

'You mean the Vikings?' Eleanor looked disbelieving.

'How else do you imagine they won so many victories?' Kalei shook her head, mildly exasperated.

'Even so, some of those beasts had already spawned before they were killed. As long as the places where their eggs were hidden stayed cold and dry, the wyrmlings would not hatch, even though they couldn't die. Now though, the earth grows warm and wet for the first time in long centuries. Here and there, hatchlings are stirring. As they stir, they sing, to call their parents to come and defend them. Any wyrm that comes across hatchlings that aren't its own spawn will kill them. That's why they hide their eggs away.'

I remembered reading that baby crocodiles called out to their parents while they were still in their eggs. That wasn't what I found hard to believe. 'These hatchlings have been calling out for help for over a hundred years?'

'Such creatures don't measure time by your people's meagre lifespans.' Kalei looked amused, and more inhuman than ever. 'All species of dragon are extremely long-lived, even more so than dryads and my own kind.'

'All species?' I wanted to know what else we had to worry about.

Kalei waved an airy hand. 'Drakes, wyverns, wyrms.'

'Wait a moment,' Eleanor interrupted. 'Are you telling me there are dragons hatching underneath Blithehurst?'

'Wyrms,' Kalei corrected her.

'Is there a cave down there?' The thought of being dragged underground again by the naiad's power made me shiver.

To my relief, Kalei shook her head. 'When they first hatch, such beasts are wholly ethereal, living deep in the earth and the darkness. They cannot take corporeal form until they encounter open air and the light of sun, stars or moon.' This time her gesture was impatient. 'But tell me, Tila said Harold spoke of voices, which means there was more than one. How many have you heard singing?'

'It's not that easy to tell.' I looked at Eleanor. 'I'd say there was only one.'

She nodded. 'Definitely just one. Does that mean the others have already died?'

'That means there's merely one of them left.' Kalei's smile was chilling. 'Once a wyrm clutch hatches, the strongest eat the smaller ones before turning on each other, to sustain themselves until a parent digs the survivors out. Sometimes only one wyrmling remains.'

'Is that what Harold was trying to do? Rescue whatever was down there?' I didn't understand. I'd found the noise in the undercroft repellent.

'No, he was trying to kill whatever he might unearth,' Kalei said, matter-of-fact. 'Tila had convinced him that any such hatchlings must die.'

'Frai and Asca didn't agree.' Eleanor barely asked a question. 'That was their quarrel with Tila?'

Kalei shrugged.

I waited, but she didn't seem inclined to say anything further. 'Why are you telling us all this?'

The naiad shrugged again. 'You asked.'

'But you were ready and waiting here to tell us.' I shook my head. 'There has to be more.'

'How did Harold and Tila plan to kill whatever he dug up?' Eleanor demanded.

I had a different question. 'That iron fence that runs along the river—'

But Kalei was dissolving into a skein of mist. Vapour poured over the side of the bridge and flowed downstream

277

on the shallow river's surface.

I watched the last wisps shimmer in the sunlight. 'We need to talk to your dryads.'

'I wonder what their version will be.' Eleanor vented her frustration with a wordless growl. 'If we can even get them to talk.'

I knew what she meant. If we asked the wrong question, we might lose our chance of learning more entirely. 'Shall I come over to Blithehurst when I finish work tomorrow? We should plan a strategy.'

She shook her head. 'It's peak season. We keep the gardens, and the garden centre and cafe, open till six, and then there's clearing up and restocking. I won't be finished till late.'

'I suppose there's no great urgency,' I said reluctantly. 'If whatever's down there has been stirring for a century, there's no reason to suppose something disastrous will happen in the next few days.'

'Let's hope not.' Eleanor looked around the valley. 'Surely that naiad or the dryads would know if everything was about to turn into a low-budget horror movie?'

'I think they'd be a bit less mysterious if they needed us to do something in a hurry.' I fervently hoped so. I scrubbed my free hand over my hair. It needed a trim. 'My job finishes this week and I've got a craft fair in Cheshire booked on Saturday and Sunday. I could come over next Monday morning. We could see if the dryads will talk to the two of us.'

'Please.' Eleanor dug her car keys out of her pocket. She stood there, indecisive. 'Doesn't this all seem insane to you? I thought hearing those voices was bad enough, but now... dragons?'

'Wyrms.' I looked at the ravaged poplar trees. 'It would have freaked me out a month ago, but an awful lot's happened since then.'

'And there's no denying that something's making that bloody noise down there.' Eleanor didn't sound much happier.

'Dryads and naiads might be selective with the truth, but

they don't lie outright. Even if they could, I can't imagine they would deceive us about something like this.' I looked around and hoped the Green Man was listening, even if Kalei had deserted us. 'I wonder what we're supposed to use to kill a... What did she call it? A wyrmling?'

Eleanor cracked her knuckles absently. 'Well, we've still got Sir Graelent's sword back at home.'

'The one that killed the original wyrm?' I looked at her, astonished.

'No, a Victorian fake, made for Sir Richard when Ivanhoe was all the fashion.' She managed a faint smile. 'But it's still nearly two metres long and over three kilos of double-edged, razor-sharp steel. That should do most things a whole lot of no good, and you look tall enough to use it. Don't worry,' she added. 'I'm joking.'

My face must have given me away. My first thought was I'd most likely take my own foot off. A moment later, I decided an axe might be worth considering. That was a tool I knew how to use.

I was still trying to make sense of all this. 'Do you want to go for a drink, maybe have a chat about what to do next? Get something to eat before you head back?'

She shook her head. 'I just want to get home. I've still got things to do before we open up for visitors tomorrow.'

'Doesn't it get lonely there, living on your own?' All by herself in that big, empty house, especially now with that insidious voice wailing under the valley floor.

Eleanor surprised me with a grin. 'After spending the week surrounded by people, most of them strangers, I love it. I get my home back to myself. I told you we lived there when I was a kid. Besides, you'd be amazed how much having someone actually living in the house brings down the insurance premiums.'

There wasn't much I could say to that. 'Okay then.'

'See you Monday.' With a wave, she headed for her car.

I stood by the Land Rover and watched her drive away. Then I studied the carving, which I was still holding. The

Green Man had always been insistent in my dreams, whenever he'd wanted me to do something. I remembered the bruises he'd left when he'd shaken me awake so violently that night I'd found Tila's body.

Though I'd been at Kympton Grange when that happened, out in the countryside and surrounded by trees. I'd been just a stone's throw from the ancient woods cloaking the hill between the farm and St Werburgh's ruins. Now I was living in Lambton's backstreets and I couldn't even think where the nearest greenery might be. Nothing bigger than shrubs in someone's back garden anyway, and I couldn't even see those. My room was at the front of the house, overlooking the road. I wondered if the Green Man would be able to reach me in my sleep there.

Though he should know I was here in Tila's valley. I'd seen his face in the trees here before. I looked down at the mask again. 'If there's some way I can convince those dryads to tell us what we need to know, you need to give me a clue.'

The wooden carving lay still and lifeless in my hands. The evening breeze idled through the trees and birdsong mingled with the ripples of the river in its stony bed. Wherever I looked, there was no sign of anything out of the ordinary stirring.

As I tossed the carving onto the passenger seat through the Land Rover's open window, my phone rang. It was my dad. For one awful moment, I hesitated before answering the call.

Swearing at myself, I swiped the screen so hard I nearly knocked the phone out of my hand. 'Dad, hi!'

'Hello.' He sounded relieved to hear my voice. 'Just thought I'd give you a call to ask how things are going. Any news about a new job?'

'Nothing at the moment.' I wondered what to say next. 'Still, I've got plenty of craft fairs booked.'

Now it was his turn to hesitate. 'There's been no... come back? Nothing more from the police?'

I'd had to tell him about killing the wose, giving him the

barest bones of my adventures. While I'd still been debating with myself about confessing, he'd gone online and read the Buxton Argus's breathless accounts of the riot at The Griffin. Suspected arson in nearby woodland on the same night wasn't as big a story, but Dad had seen that as well. Given everything he already knew, I could hardly pretend I wasn't somehow involved. Mind you, I hadn't admitted to nearly succumbing to hypothermia.

'Nothing, not a word,' I assured him, thankful that was true.

'Why don't you come home for a few weeks?' he suggested. 'Have a change of scene for a bit.'

'That would be nice –' at least that wasn't a lie either '– but I'd have so much further to travel at the weekends. All my bookings are north of here.'

'I could—'

I interrupted before he could offer to pay for my extra fuel. 'Besides, there's a good chance one of the blokes I've been working with can put me onto some local work here.'

Okay, it was a faint chance, but still not an outright lie.

I forced myself to ask. 'How's Mum?'

Now I heard Dad's voice tighten. 'She's fine.'

'Good to know.' As long as I didn't ask what he meant by that, he wouldn't have to tell me how furious she still was with me. 'Give her my love. All my love.'

'I will,' he promised.

I wondered if she was listening in to this call. I had no way to tell. All I did know was she'd been so incensed when I'd admitted what I'd done that Dad's phone had been cut off for three days. When she'd relented and let him call, she'd refused to speak to me.

'Anything new with you?' I prompted.

'No, just the same old routine.' His voice sounded easier. 'You?'

'Nothing worth talking about. Just pain-in-the-arse housemates,' I explained, before he could ask what I meant. 'As soon as I get some regular work, I'll be looking for a place of my own again.'

'Oh dear.' He sounded much more concerned than I'd expected.

'It's no big deal.' I tried to reassure him, explaining about the downstairs tosser's lousy taste in music and the apparent inability of anyone to do their washing-up before the sink filled with dirty plates stacked in scummy water.

'So what's going on with you? How's the badger sett doing?'

As Dad brought me up to date with the nature reserve's news, I kept an eye on the trees for any hint of the Green Man. Still no joy.

Barely a month ago, I'd have made some joke to my dad about my slovenly housemates waiting for brownies or pixies to turn up and do the housework. Now I didn't want to start any conversation that involved supernatural creatures.

I could only hope Dad felt the same. He certainly hadn't asked if Kalei had fulfilled her promise to tell me where to find some other dryads. So I hadn't told him about visiting Blithehurst House, and after today's revelations, I wasn't going to. Not and worry him sick with the notion that I might be going up against an actual, no-kidding dragon, even if it was only a baby one. Not when I had absolutely no clue how big the bastard creature might be. Baby whales might only be babies, but they're still bloody enormous.

Not and risk having my mother never speak to me again. I was desperate to ask her advice, but I knew she would demand I walk away. She would insist this was more naiad trickery, to get me risking my own neck for Kalei's benefit, whatever the naiad's scheme might be. She would say that I barely knew Eleanor and that I certainly didn't owe her anything. It was up to Blithehurst's own dryads to protect their own.

I'd thought all those things myself. I remembered the satisfaction in Kalei's voice when she'd said I'd proved myself against the wose. I suspected she'd been intending to pit me against this wyrmling all along, assuming I survived.

But Mum hadn't heard that eerie, insidious wyrmsong. It didn't matter that I'd only just met Eleanor or that we had so little in common. I wasn't going to leave anyone to handle a threat like this on their own. Facing the wose alone had been bad enough for me.

Dad came to the end of telling me about Dave Holbrook's latest triumph in the pub quiz team. He sounded a lot happier, so I seized my chance.

'Look, I'm on my way home from work, and I'm starving. Can I call you later in the week? Earlier if I get any news about a job?'

'Oh, right, yes, that's fine,' he said.

'Okay then. Take care, Dad, speak soon.'

'Look after yourself, Dan.' He rang off.

I stood there for a moment, looking at the silent phone and wondering if I'd imagined a plea in those last words.

Well, I could hardly ring back and ask. I drove back to my cramped and noisy room. I didn't bother with fish and chips or a takeaway. Beans on toast would do, given I'd pretty much lost my appetite.

I'd never had to keep secrets from my dad. Of course there were things about my life I didn't tell him, about girlfriends mostly. This was different though, and I hated it.

I also understood Eleanor Beauchene's anger, when we'd first met. She was right. Not being able to tell your family these things did complicate life horribly.

# Chapter Thirty

The rest of that week saw the Lambton Farm barn conversions finished, so on Friday night we all went to The Osprey to celebrate. I reminded Phil, Nigel and the others that there'd be a drink in it if they passed my name and number on to someone who needed a carpenter, even just for a few days. They all promised to keep me in mind.

I got up bright and early on Saturday to drive to Cheshire, where the craft fair was a wash-out. Rain pissed down all day and more than halved attendance. The people who did come into the dealers' marquees were more interested in finding somewhere dry to stand and chat than buying irresistible artisan work. I barely sold enough to cover my costs and slept badly in a cheap bed and breakfast that smelled like an old dog's basket. By Sunday lunchtime, so many people were calling it quits that I did the same and headed off. At least that gave me something to chat to my dad about in the evening.

Monday morning and I had no work to go to. Opting for a lie-in till after what passed for rush hour in Lambton, I reached Blithehurst by mid-morning. The day was overcast and blustery, with a chill breeze for the time of year.

Eleanor met me in the car park again, wearing a waterproof coat and walking boots. 'Shall we go straight up to the temple?'

'If that's the best place to find the dryads.' I grabbed a fleece out of the back of the Landy and followed her through the gardens and down the path that skirted the stony hollow of the rock garden. As she went through the iron kissing gate, she stopped, her eyes distant.

'What is it?'

'Nothing.' She shook off her distraction. 'I'm just tired. I've had a few bad nights, and then lousy dreams when I do manage to get to sleep.'

'Hang on.' I put my hand on the gate. 'Do you dream

much, as a rule?'

'Almost never, but I've never had a wyrmling to worry about before.' Eleanor looked at me, curious. 'Why do you ask?'

'I'm the same, not dreaming much,' I explained, 'but when I do, it's often about the Green Man, and he's usually telling me something important.'

'The Green Man?' Eleanor raised her eyebrows.

I realised how much I still had to tell her. That would have to wait. 'What were you dreaming about?'

'All this falling down. The business going bankrupt and everything being my fault.' She shivered as she looked around at the ruins. 'But I didn't see any Green Man, the dryads, a naiad or anything like that. It's not as if this place doesn't run on tight margins. I worry about those things when I'm awake.'

I wondered if I was making something out of nothing. Then again, Great Uncle Harold had been driven mad by dreams woven from his real-life anxieties. 'Did you hear the wyrmsong in the night?'

She frowned. 'Of course. I can hear it all the time now. Can't you?'

'Out here?' I took a moment to listen. 'Only if I really concentrate.' Now it was my turn to shiver. The eerie noise made my skin crawl.

'I can only get away from it when I'm in the house.' Eleanor's coat rustled as she hunched her shoulders. 'In the library for preference.'

The library where those carvings of the Green Man oversaw everything below. I wondered if I should suggest she slept in there. 'Let's ask the dryads what they think about that.'

'That's a good idea.' Eleanor nodded.

I was glad of my own boots on the muddy slope. By the time we reached the top of the valley path, the clouds were spitting. The statue of Venus in the round temple stared at us, icy cold, as the rain began to come down more heavily.

'Where do—'

'Good morning.' Asca waved a hand, prompting an obedient breeze to carry the raindrops away.

All three dryads had appeared. They were in their ethereal forms, decorously draped in shades of green and dauntingly beautiful, even the ancient Frai.

'What do you want with us, stranger's son?' The crone fixed me with her burnished copper gaze.

Eleanor spoke to Asca instead. 'Why didn't you tell me there were wyrmlings hatching under the manor?'

'You had no need to know,' the queenly dryad assured her, serene. 'The last of them will die soon enough.'

'Soon enough for you, maybe,' Eleanor retorted. 'How long do I have to listen to their torment?'

The youngest, Sineya, looked more self-conscious about all this secrecy. 'Even if a wyrmling could somehow reach the open air and take corporeal form, it could never pass the fence around the ruins. It would soon retreat to the depths again.'

'Why else do you think we permitted your forefathers to build that iron cage?' Frai challenged, waspish.

Eleanor wasn't about to be intimidated by the ancient dryad. 'Why didn't you ever explain that to me? I've asked you about it more than once.'

I interrupted, afraid that an argument would see the three of them disappear on us. 'What's prompted the wyrmsong now? Eleanor only heard it for the first time this spring.'

Sineya defied quelling glances from her mother and grandmother. 'The wyrmlings only stir when the ground grows sufficiently warm and wet—'

Frai spoke over her. 'And then the years turn and cold winters return and they fall silent again.'

Asca nodded her agreement. 'Before long, even this last hatchling that's so determined to linger will never reawaken.'

'You really think so?' I looked at all three dryads. 'When

we've had all but one of the hottest years on record in this past decade?'

I knew the latest statistics said something like that. If I'd known I'd be debating climate change with near-immortal tree spirits I'd have checked.

Again, Sineya's expression suggested she didn't necessarily agree with her elders. 'No matter how long the wyrmling might endure, it can only sing—'

'And no parent can possibly hear its cries, to come and dig it out.' Frai was relentless in her certainty. 'Graelent slew the wyrm that hid its spawn here, and Robert drained the marsh which would have sustained the hatchlings. This lone survivor will never grow strong enough to take corporeal form.'

'Then why is Kalei so insistent that whatever's down there must be dug up and killed?' I demanded. 'She convinced Tila, didn't she?'

For the first time, some reaction flickered across Asca's face. Unfortunately I couldn't tell if it was grief at the mention of her lost daughter, guilt at being somehow caught out or simply annoyance that we'd been talking to the naiad.

'When the last wyrmling dies, there will be no ethereal creature to consume its remains. Boggarts cannot venture so deep,' she explained in measured tones. 'As the hatchling decays, its essence will leach into these waters. That's all that concerns the naiad.' The queenly dryad waved a dismissive hand.

'What exactly does that mean?' Eleanor persisted. 'What will that essence in the river do?'

'Plants will wither, and beasts and men alike who drink such tainted water will not thrive.' Asca was irritated, unable to avoid a straight answer.

'In time, all such corruption drains away.' Frai looked from Eleanor to glare at me, accusing. 'Naiads have suffered far worse from the filth your kind have poured into their waters over the years.'

'How long before that blight passes?' Eleanor wasn't about to accept Asca's assurances. 'Years? Decades? Centuries?'

Sineya spoke up once more. 'It will be tens of years before the streams here run clean. Even a hatchling wyrm is a fearsomely venomous beast.'

I tried to picture the maps of the area, and wondered where Blithehurst's little river featured in the local water authority's catchment plans. I hated to imagine what traces of wyrm poison in the tap water might do to babies or the sick or the elderly.

'What happens to the body if we do dig it up and kill it?' Eleanor persisted. 'Kalei wouldn't suggest we did that if the outcome would just be the same.'

'The most likely outcome would be the death of you both,' Frai said swiftly. 'Not that the naiad would care.'

'You are born of greenwood blood, and precious to us,' insisted Asca. 'We will not see you risk yourselves when the creature is doomed regardless.'

'Even if the price of letting it die in the depths is such a blight on our home. We will gladly pay it.' Sineya looked unhappy, but clearly agreed with her mother and grandmother.

I still wasn't convinced. 'When did any of you last leave this valley? Have you any idea how many thousands of human beings live within fifty miles of here?'

'You didn't answer my question.' Eleanor wasn't letting Asca get away with distracting her. 'What happens if we dig the creature up and kill it?'

The dryad answered reluctantly. 'If such a creature is slain in its corporeal form, then its venom remains contained within that flesh.'

Eleanor glanced at me. 'So we'd have toxic waste to deal with, compared to a radiation leak.'

All three dryads looked understandably confused. I tried to think of ways to dispose of a sizeable and noxious corpse.

'Oil drums? An old shipping container? It depends how big it is.' Another potential problem occurred to me. 'How long before it rots down into something unrecognisable?'

Wherever we dumped it, Sod's Law meant we risked

someone stumbling over it. We didn't want council workers hunting down fly-tippers selling dragon photos to every tabloid.

'You don't understand how hard such a beast is to kill,' Sineya protested.

'You said Sir Graelent killed a full-grown wyrm,' I reminded Frai. 'Did he do that with a sword or an axe? How did he corner it?'

'He prevailed at the cost of hazarding all and losing his life to his wounds,' she shot back, 'and he was a warrior proven in battle, a swordsman since his earliest youth. You are no such thing.'

'The creature is already as good as dead,' Asca said firmly. 'There is no need for you to risk your lives, and we will not allow such folly.'

'This isn't your decision to make.' Eleanor shoved her hands into her waterproof's pockets. 'I'm Sir Graelent's heir. You've told me that often enough.'

She turned her back on all three dryads and started walking back down the hill. I was left standing there, dumbfounded. In the instant before they vanished, I saw the dryads were equally astonished. Frai's disbelief was coloured with outrage. Asca and Sineya both looked distressed. As soon as they disappeared, the rain came down as hard as it possibly could.

I hurried after Eleanor. 'Hold up!'

As I drew level, she glanced at me from under her hood. 'What do we do now?'

'I don't know,' I admitted.

'We can't just leave it down there to poison the groundwater. Nearly all of Blithehurst's farmland is downstream and our profit margins are tight enough as it is. Any drop in crop yields would be a disaster. Then there's the herd.' She slowed and looked at the creamy cattle placidly grazing without a care in the world. 'There's nowhere else for them to drink except the river, and even if there was, how would I explain to anyone else why I wanted them to use it? I don't suppose wyrm-ooze shows up in the standard water purity tests.'

It wasn't much of a joke, but I acknowledged it with a momentary grin. Then I sighed. 'I don't think there's much use going back to Kalei. It's clear enough what she wants us to do. What we need to know is how.'

Eleanor surprised me. 'Let me show you what I've found out about that.'

We went into the Tudor house through the side door again. She shed her boots and waterproof and I dumped my wet fleece on the floor.

'Coffee?' she suggested.

'Definitely.'

Mugs in hand, we didn't go through to the library. Instead Eleanor opened an unobtrusive door in the hallway's panelling to reveal a servants' stair.

'I've got a sitting room upstairs.'

In fact, she lived in a set of three rooms over the library, which must have originally been laid out like the King Charles suite that I'd seen on the visitors' tour. However, the fixtures and furniture in here were all comfortable, modern and unremarkable, and as Eleanor closed the connecting doors, I saw that the original dressing room was now a compact bathroom.

There was a gateleg table in the bay window, counterpart to the left-hand window in the library below. It was piled high with books, a notepad and a laptop. Loose sheets of paper were stacked neatly to one side, covered in writing.

'If there's one thing I can do, it's research.' Eleanor put her coffee on the windowsill and took a chair at the table. 'Mind you, I had no idea there were so many local legends to read.'

A two-seater sofa by the fireplace faced the window. I sat down and drank some coffee. 'So how did knights of old kill wyrms?'

She wrinkled her nose. 'As a rule, by hacking them into pieces. It seems serpent dragons were hard to kill, not least because any wounds would heal as soon as they could get back into water. A river or a lake ideally, but even a well would do. Even one that had been cut into pieces could join itself back together again. So they had to be kept on dry land for a knight to have any chance of winning. The bigger the wyrm, the tougher the hide, so stabbing them through the eye or the mouth comes up quite often as a tactic. It was definitely best to attack the head.' She shuffled a few sheets of paper and looked up at me. 'Shooting them with arrows from a distance was popular, unsurprisingly. Are you any good with a bow?'

I shook my head. 'Never tried archery. You?'

'Sadly, no. I'm a fair shot when it comes to clay pigeons though.' She started leafing through a book.

'I don't suppose skeet cartridges would be much good against dragon hide, but can you buy loads with a bit more punch?' I've never been interested in game shooting so didn't have much of an idea.

'Three-shot for geese is about the most a dealer would sell us without asking questions. I can't see that doing the trick.' She hesitated. 'My dad has a rifle which he uses for taking down deer. That's properly licensed and everything, but I've never used it, and anyway, there's no way he'd just let me borrow it without saying why I wanted it.'

'And we wouldn't want to be explaining ourselves to the police.' I finished my coffee. 'This would be so much easier in a movie. One of those where some monster says "no weapon forged by man can kill me", so the good guys just blow him away with a grenade launcher.'

Eleanor grinned. 'Or one of those zombie series on TV where there just happens to be an endless supply of machine guns and ammo.'

'Do you watch those?' I was surprised.

'No,' she scoffed. Then she sighed, serious again. 'It does seem to come down to brute butchery.'

If so, I had a lot more questions before I'd be prepared to try it. 'Are there any clues how big it's likely to be?'

She found another page of notes. 'When Sir John first came across the Lambton Worm, some accounts say it was about the size of an eel.'

She didn't sound convinced. Neither was I.

'Why would the dryads be so adamant that we leave well alone, if a wyrmling was something we could kill with a kitchen knife?'

Eleanor looked up from her papers. 'Most of the legends say they're very venomous and some of them spit poison as well.'

'Snakes don't have to be big to be deadly,' I acknowledged.

'We've no idea how fast it might grow. Most of the stories where someone's fighting them say they're a good deal bigger. I'd say somewhere between nine and twelve feet long and about as thick as a man's thigh.'

'Okay.' I wondered about using a chainsaw. I'd felled bigger trees with one of those, though of course, trees weren't a moving target, and couldn't bite back. 'What else do these legends say?'

'They seem to be constrictors, like a python or an anaconda. Quite a few of the stories say the knight who killed one wore special armour covered in blades.' She held up an open book so I could see a medieval picture.

'I don't suppose your Victorian fakers made any of it?' I waved that away. More seriously, that ruled out a chainsaw. I wasn't taking any chances of having one of those crushed against me while it was still running.

'Last but not least, hunting hounds get plenty of mentions.' She closed the book and put it down. 'I'm guessing they were something like mastiffs, but they must have been very well trained to face down prey like that.'

Maybe not mastiffs. 'I wonder if Kalei would lend us the shuck.'

'The what?'

'You must have heard of black shucks?'

Before Eleanor could reply, we both heard a door opening and closing below.

'Who's that?'

'I have no idea.' She was already on her feet.

I followed her out into the hallway between the morning room and the long gallery and immediately heard footsteps on the main staircase.

'Hello?' Eleanor called out, more puzzled than concerned.

'Hi, Ellie.' A man with a definite resemblance to that portrait of Edmund Beauchene rounded the turn in the stairs. He had a heavy black bag slung over one shoulder and was dragging a wheelie suitcase.

'Rob?' Eleanor looked bemused.

'Okay to use my old room? Have you got anything in for dinner or shall I treat you to a takeaway?'

He concentrated on lining his suitcase up for the final steps. I couldn't help noticing that meant he didn't have to look at his sister.

'What are you doing here?' Now she was irritated.

He looked up at me. 'Who's this? New boyfriend?' He offered me a welcoming smile. 'Hi, I'm Robert Beauchene.'

'Good to meet you,' I said politely. 'I'm Daniel Mackmain, and no, I'm here on business. I'm a woodworker.'

'My mistake.' Reaching the top of the stairs, he let the heavy bag slip off his shoulder and held up both hands in mock surrender. 'Don't let me interrupt whatever you were doing.'

'Rob,' Eleanor snapped. 'What are you doing here?'

'Since you ask so nicely,' he retorted with some indignation, 'Nicole and I have decided we need a break—'

'Oh, Rob!' Eleanor protested. Though I noted she no longer seemed surprised by his arrival.

'Shall we discuss it later?' His glance at me made his meaning clear. This was a family matter.

I took the hint. 'We've done all we can today,' I said to Eleanor. 'You can always give me a ring later, or maybe a text?'

'Send me your email address.' She knew as well as I did that there'd be no more discussing how best to kill wyrmlings with her brother wandering around.

'I'll see you out.' She headed down the stairs while Robert dragged his case towards one of the doors leading off the morning room.

A few paces later, he stopped, looked back and called out. 'Excuse me, Daniel, is it?'

I turned on the stairs. 'That's right.'

'Eleanor manages this side of the business, the house and the garden centre, but I'm in charge of all the land management. I don't know what she's promised you, but I've got all the contracts I need for forestry work set up.' He smiled, charming, but his eyes were cold. 'Just so there's no misunderstanding.'

'Okay.' Taken aback, I went on my way downstairs.

Eleanor was waiting by the open front door, holding my damp fleece. 'I'll walk you up to the car park,' she muttered as she handed it over. 'It's going to be non-stop bloody phone calls here this evening once word gets round the family. Everyone likes Nicole.'

'You don't need to explain to me.'

She went on as if I hadn't spoken, as we walked through the knot garden. 'Rob can be a real sod with women. He finds a nice girl and everything's fine for a year or so and then his eye starts wandering and he ends up in bed with someone else. He usually doesn't have the guts to break up with his current girlfriend though. He starts telling lies and tries to keep everything going until he gets found out. Then he's all, "But I didn't want to hurt her feelings, it was only a fling, it meant nothing, I just hoped she'd never need to know," which is utter bollocks because if he cared about anyone else's feelings but his own, he'd keep his bloody trousers on!'

Her irritation was turning to anger. 'Oh, he says it's never his fault, that these women always make the first move, but he could say no, couldn't he?' She swiftly answered her own question. 'Apparently not. He's always been the same. According to Ben he shagged his way through every hall of residence in Leeds. It was hardly a secret, but girls still threw themselves at him.'

We walked on in silence to the garden gate. Eleanor fumbled with the keys, still furious.

I found myself wondering if this family's greenwood blood was running quite so thin in their sons after all. I'd gone from willing bed to willing bed pretty rapidly in Glasgow, until I'd realised my fellow students were drawn more by my mother's blood than my charming personality. At least I knew enough of my heritage to understand that. Robert had no reason to think his success with girls was down to anything but his winning ways.

'He's the oldest of you all, isn't he?' I guessed he was maybe five years older than me. 'You're absolutely sure he can't see the dryads?'

'Certain,' Eleanor said curtly. 'It would make my life so much easier if he could. But they tried everything they could think of to open his eyes. Sineya spent most of a summer in her corporeal form, turning up day after day. He flirted with her every chance he got, but she could still walk past him stark naked in her ethereal form and not get a flicker of any response. All he was interested in was getting into her knickers, when he thought she was a real girl.'

I wondered if he'd succeeded. I didn't ask. 'How long do you think he'll be here?'

'Who knows?' Eleanor sighed as we walked across the car park. 'If Nicole packs her bags, because they live in a Blithehurst Trust property... But where will she go? She works in Buxton. Come to that, why should she be the one to move out? They've been together for nearly three years. We all hoped they were going to get married.' She shook her head, distracted. 'I wonder if she threw him out or he decided to leave? That might make a difference.'

'Well, it's not as if that wyrm's going anywhere soon,' I reminded her. 'Not according to the dryads, and we still need to come up with a plan before we can do anything about it.'

'I suppose we can wait until he sorts himself out.' She was still in a thoroughly bad mood. 'But if he thinks he can hide out here and think everything's just going to go away, he's got another think coming.'

295

Until then, I'd hoped I could keep my distance. I hate getting dragged into other people's arguments, and in any case, there wasn't anything I could do to help.

'I'll get the gate.' Eleanor walked off before I could work out what to say for the best.

As I slowed the Land Rover, waiting to turn onto the main road, I wound down the window to say goodbye. 'I'll let you know if I come up with any bright ideas.'

Thinking about everything she'd told me kept me busy most of the way home. I pondered various ways to deal with wyrms of different sizes, factoring in the added potential hazards of venom and strangling coils. It made for quite some risk assessment.

It wasn't till I got back to Lambton that something Robert had said struck me as strange. He'd specifically told me Blithehurst didn't need anyone to manage their forestry. But why would he think I was interested in that? All I'd said was that I was a woodworker.

I couldn't imagine Eleanor had said something. I didn't suppose she'd said anything about me at all. She had no need to, and every reason to avoid awkward conversations about my interest in Blithehurst.

I tried to ring her but she didn't pick up. I sent a text asking her to give me a call, but got no reply. I told myself that meant nothing. All the same, I went to bed uneasy.

# Chapter Thirty-One

I slept restlessly and woke up early. It was another grey day, but at least it wasn't raining. Heading out before Lambton's traffic stirred meant I was at Blithehurst in time to see the car park gates open to let the first deliveries in. As several more vans and cars arrived, I recalled what Eleanor had said about spending Tuesdays restocking and preparing for the working week ahead.

I followed the vehicles in and parked. Texting Eleanor got me a swift response.

*Stay put. I'll come over.*

She wasn't long, and in any case, I forgave the delay when I saw she was carrying two takeaway cups of coffee. I met her halfway to take one. 'Thanks.'

Whatever she might have said to me was lost in a yawn. 'Sorry,' she said.

'Another bad night?' I noted the shadows under her eyes.

'A late one.' Eleanor glanced around to see who might be close enough to overhear us. 'Rob won't give anyone a straight answer about anything. Nicole's in pieces. She says she had no idea anything was wrong between them. They were talking about starting a family, for God's sake. Apparently there is someone else, but Rob won't say anything about who she might be or how they met. He's just insisting that he and Nicole are over and he's ready to move on. Of course, Mum insists there must be some explanation, something that means Rob's not just being an utter bastard. He's always been her golden boy, so it can't possibly be his fault.'

To my relief, she broke off to drink some coffee.

'How did you sleep?' I asked. 'Did you have any dreams last night?'

'Badly, and yes, I did.' She looked at me, curious. 'Why do you ask?'

'What did you dream about?' I wanted her to tell me first.

'The iron fence,' Eleanor said slowly. 'It was rusting and twisted, all broken down.'

'I had pretty much the same dream.' I hadn't seen the Green Man in my sleep, but I didn't imagine a warning like that had come out of nowhere. 'It's why I came over. There's something else odd as well. Yesterday, when you were already going down the stairs, Robert told me specifically that there was no woodland management work for me here.'

She stared at me, bemused. 'Why on earth would he say that?'

'Assuming you've said nothing to him?' As Eleanor shook her head, I nodded, glad to have that clarified. 'I've no idea, but I think we should find out. Do you want to ask him, or shall I?'

'Let me.' She scrubbed her face with her empty hand. 'Whenever he turns up. We had a blazing row over breakfast and he stormed out when he realised he couldn't win. He hasn't gone home though. His car's still here.' She nodded towards a red BMW parked in the corner closest to the garden centre.

A young man in a blue sweatshirt was hovering in the entrance. When he saw her looking that way, he waved a hand to attract her attention, calling out, 'Miss Beauchene?'

'I do need to get on,' she said, exasperated, 'regardless of Robert's dramas.'

I glanced at the waiting lad. 'How about you see what he wants while I go and check the fence?'

'Would you? Thanks.' She was relieved. 'I was going to walk around it in my lunch hour, but I don't always get a break, so...' She shrugged. 'If anyone asks, tell them you have my permission.'

'Okay, I'll see you later.'

As she headed for the garden centre, I grabbed my pocket binoculars out of the Land Rover. When I reached the entrance to the house and the grounds, the man who'd been manning the till when I visited before was counting stacks of guidebooks in his shed. He made a quick phone call to check with Eleanor before unlocking the gate.

'Hang on a minute.' He fished in the desk drawer, finding me a laminated 'CONTRACTOR' badge on a blue Blithe-hurst lanyard. 'Keep that with you, please.'

'Of course.' I looped the lanyard round my belt and tucked the card into my pocket, ready to show it if needs be. I dislike wearing anything that could strangle me if it gets caught on something when I'm working in woodland.

A couple of people were busy in the knot garden with rakes and secateurs, and I could see a few others down by the medieval manor's gatehouse. They were unloading catering packs for the cafe from a fat-wheeled trolley. No one took much notice of me.

I walked to the edge of the drop down into the stony hollow of the rock garden and studied the black painted fence that saved incautious visitors from a nasty fall. My dream had been unpleasantly vivid. This whole quarry face had crumbled away, ripping the iron posts out of the grass as the ground collapsed beneath them.

In broad daylight, it looked as sturdy as the first time I'd been here. I took a firm hold of the closest post and gave it an experimental shake. Nothing shifted, and that was a relief, but what about the rest? One break, however small, could allow a wyrm to get through. I was convinced of that.

Using my binoculars, I traced the three lines of horizontal iron struts and regularly spaced posts down the slope on the far side of the rock garden and all along the river bank. Everything was clearly intact, but then again, any break out in the open would have been so immediately obvious that some staff member would have told Eleanor about it.

Looking past the old manor ruins, I couldn't see where the fence went after it disappeared into a tangle of shrubbery on the far side of the moat. I lowered the binoculars, thoughtful. The fence circled the ruins on the outside of the moat, with a grille cutting across the channel that linked it to the river. Those wide-set bars were no great obstacle to the ducks or presumably to any fish in the water flowing through them.

Why wasn't the fence on the inside of the moat, if it was there to contain any wyrmling that survived to reach the open air, especially if they were so dependent on water to thrive? I couldn't see any reason for not putting the fence right up against the ruined walls, or even along the top of the crumbling masonry. It wasn't as if there'd been planning permission rules to stop the Beauchenes doing whatever they wanted between the wars. Even if someone had queried it, they could have said the fence was going up to stop anyone falling into the moat.

Though of course, if it had been put up for genuine safety reasons, to stop someone like tragic Uncle Harold sleepwalking into the water, putting it around the outside of the moat did make sense. Though it wasn't much of a barrier to anything mortal that could pass through iron. It wouldn't stop anyone determined to drown themselves.

Before I could pursue that thought, I heard a sharp noise over to my right. Seeing movement where the shrubbery that cloaked the slope gave way to those splendid specimen trees, I quickly raised my binoculars. A boggart's arse vanished into the undergrowth. Then I glimpsed another of the stinking vermin, and a third, all scurrying away.

As I wondered what they were doing here, I remembered what Kalei had said about them being drawn to the wose. To his dark miasma, she'd said. The wyrmsong must be a similar lure. That made checking the fence all the more urgent. No wonder the Green Man had warned both me and Eleanor.

If boggarts could get through it, presumably the little bastards would try digging down to the wyrmling. That locked door might stop them getting to the undercroft's earthen floor, but ripping up the cobbles in the manor house courtyard shouldn't be beyond them, assuming they could swim the moat.

I really needed to go and make sure the fence was intact. Doing that right now would be best. I should get on with it at once. I stood, twisting the binoculars' strap round my hands. My leg throbbed with the memory of those bites from the boggarts in Kympton. The deepest punctures had only just properly healed.

I had my penknife in my pocket as always, but maybe I should go back to the Land Rover and find something more substantial by way of iron or steel. A sledgehammer for preference, since walking around with an axe would be a bit hard to explain to the Blithehurst staff.

Or I could just keep the fence between us, I realised, feeling stupid. The boggarts wouldn't be able to reach me through that. I headed down the path and through the kissing gate, making very sure it was closed behind me. Keeping close to the fence line, with the moat on my left, I began to circle the ruins. Faintly, as though coming from some great distance, I could hear the eerie keening of the wyrmling. I shivered, and not just because of the cool breeze.

Beyond the neatly mown lawn, the iron fence headed into what the guidebook map called the wilderness garden. That was a fancy name for a stretch of largely untended grass where the space between a spread of mature trees was cluttered with self-seeded saplings. I guessed there would be a blaze of wildflowers in the spring, but few were blooming beneath the dense summer foliage.

The air was pungent with wild garlic until a shift in the breeze momentarily offered me honeysuckle's fragrance. Most importantly, I couldn't smell any trace of a boggart's stench. Still, I advanced cautiously, fishing in my pocket for my penknife. If there was any break in the fence around here, I really didn't want to stumble across one or more of them on this side of the barrier.

The ground rose towards a shallow rise bounded by the fence. As I reached the modest crest, I saw a meadow fall away on the far side. The knee-height grasses were spangled with the bright colours of corncockles, cranesbill and more. To my left, the grassland sloped unbroken to the river. To my right, and curving around to the far side of the meadow, a ridge of limestone broke through the turf. It was dotted with tangles of bramble and gorse.

Movement in a sheltered hollow opposite caught my eye, and I lifted my binoculars. If I knew where the boggarts laired, maybe the Blithehurst dryads had some way to chase them off.

It wasn't boggarts. Rob Beauchene was screwing some woman. I could see him clearly enough, facing me with his arms braced and his shirt unbuttoned. His eyes were closed tight and his mouth gaped open as he thrust frantically into whoever lay beneath him. All I could see of her was her knees spread high and wide, with a vivid yellow skirt rucked up to flutter in the breeze.

I lowered the binoculars, unwilling to be a Peeping Tom. I wondered how best to tell Eleanor that her brother definitely had a new lover. She deserved to know that much, but I really didn't want to get dragged into the Beauchene family's mess.

A hand grasped my shoulder. Startled, I turned my head. The Green Man was right beside me. We'd never been so close, not since that night when he'd shaken me awake, and when that had happened, I'd barely seen him in the darkness. Now he stood there, in the broad light of day.

He was half a head taller than me with a tunic seemingly woven of leaves hanging loosely from his broad shoulders. His bare arms and legs were as smooth and golden brown as rowan bark, his physique human in form and formidably solid. Oak leaves still masked his face, merging seamlessly into his mossy hair and beard. Beneath his brows, his eyes glowed emerald, bright enough to defy the daylight.

As I realised that I'd stopped breathing, he reached forward and raised the binoculars to my eyes. As firm as he was gentle, there was no gainsaying his wishes. Reluctantly, I looked across the meadow to see that Robert was still fucking his mystery woman. That's not all I saw though.

Boggarts were creeping along the ridge line, ten or more of them. They were peering down to leer at the screwing couple, and I felt sick as I saw them lasciviously licking their stained, pointed teeth. It got worse. One thrust a hand between its legs and began wanking enthusiastically.

Robert Beauchene was oblivious, his head ducked down, his slack mouth greedy for his lover's tits. A moment later she rolled him over. Now I got a clear view of her as she straddled him, naked to the waist and throwing her head back as she clasped his hands to her breasts.

'What the fuck?' It was that nosy woman who cleaned the Kympton Grange holiday cottages for Chrissie Monkswell. It took me a moment to remember her name. Liz? Lindsey? No, Lin, that was it.

When she rolled her head from side to side, apparently in ecstasy, the boggarts recoiled from her gaze. One was slower than the others, but she bared her teeth and the dirty little beast scrambled frantically away. She could see them as clearly as they could see her. My heart pounding, I had absolutely no doubt of that. More than that, they were scared.

Then she looked straight towards me. Through the binoculars I could see her eyes clearly. They were completely blank, without iris or pupil. They weren't green though, like a dryad's leafy gaze, or the glossy blue of sunlit water like a naiad's. Whoever she was, whatever she was, her stare was as bleak and pale as a winter moon.

My throat was dry with a terror that I didn't understand. The Green Man's grip on my shoulder tightened, reassuring. I realised she might be looking in this direction, but there was no reason to think she'd seen me standing here hidden among the trees. Not with the Green Man at my side.

Fighting to stop my hands shaking, I swallowed and forced myself to stay focused on the far side of the meadow. The woman was still riding Robert mercilessly hard. His hands fell away. As she looked down, I saw her lips curve with calculated satisfaction rather than with any true passion. Then she stretched forward to embrace him, disappearing from view. Now all I could see was the boggarts, still avidly enjoying the show.

The Green Man drew his hand back to turn me to face him.

*GO.*

I didn't see him speak. His voice simply echoed inside my head with all the force of a thunderclap. I didn't need telling twice. Retreating as fast as I could without tripping and falling, I went backwards through the wilderness garden. The Green Man stayed at the edge of the trees. I kept my eyes fixed on him until I reached the neatly mown grass encircling the ruins. My pulse was still racing, though that unreasoning panic had faded away. Now I could think what to do next.

First and foremost, we needed to know what exactly had seduced Rob Beauchene. He might well be a lifelong bed-hopper, but I didn't think he'd done the chasing this time. I remembered how scarily easily Kalei had triggered unthinking lust in me, and I'd had some forewarning. That poor bastard could have no idea he was dealing with someone who wasn't human. No wonder he was so utterly cunt-struck.

I'd start by asking the dryads here. Continuing towards the river, I circled the medieval manor and followed the fence line until I reached the second kissing gate that led to the bridge across the river.

About to head for the wooded pasture, I hesitated. As long as I stayed inside this fence, I could tell myself I was safe. Outside, there were boggarts and who knows what else. I looked back towards the wilderness and wondered if the Green Man was still keeping an eye on Robert and his unearthly lover. Was he still keeping a separate watch over me?

Rubbing sweating hands on my thighs, I went through the gate. I made very certain to pull it up hard against the curved metal behind me. I crossed the water, looking up as I passed through the oak trees on the far bank. 'I'm trusting you to warn me if that creature or anything else comes after me,' I said quietly.

I followed the path up the far side of the valley. By the time I reached the temple, I was out of breath and sweating. The marble statue didn't care, staring at me blankly.

'Where—' I gasped, dry-mouthed.

'What's the matter?' Sineya was there in the blink of an eye, in her student guise. 'I could hear your heart racing when you were all the way down the valley.'

'What sort of...' I coughed to cover my hesitation. I didn't want to call that unknown woman a 'thing' in case that insulted her, but dryads and naiads and whatever Rob's lover was weren't exactly people. I tried again.

'Robert, Eleanor's brother, he's been seduced into leaving his girlfriend and coming to stay here. We don't know why but it can't be good. The Green Man just showed me his lover, and she isn't human. I can see it in her eyes. They're pale, cold and flinty. Have you any idea what she could be?'

'None.' Sineya was mystified.

I believed her. It was a straightforward question and she hadn't tried to evade it. 'Can you ask your mother? Your grandmother? Tell Eleanor if you can't find me. Be careful. Whatever she is, there are boggarts in thrall to her.'

'They don't usually cross the river.' Sineya looked uneasy all the same.

'I saw them on the other side of the meadow, over beyond those trees.' I pointed. 'Where the limestone breaks through the grass.'

Sineya nodded. 'We seldom pass that way.'

'Steer well clear until we know what we're dealing with.' I grimaced at an unwelcome memory of Tila's murdered body. 'I'd better warn Eleanor too.'

'Do so.' With that, Sineya vanished.

I stood there, still catching my breath. A few moments later, I decided there was no point in waiting for an answer from the older dryads. As I headed back down the hill, I got out my phone.

Calling Eleanor only got me her voicemail. I decided against leaving a message. If she played it when someone else was around, whatever I said would sound utterly mad. More than that, I remembered how easily the wose had been able to tap into mobile phone signals. It was safest to assume the blank-eyed woman could do that too.

She obviously knew I was here. That solved the puzzle of Rob Beauchene telling me there was no work for me. Sam Monkswell must have told Chrissie about our conversations about coppicing and setting up a workshop, and Chrissie must have told this woman who she thought was just an everyday friend.

That was an unnerving thought. It meant whatever the blank-eyed woman might be, she'd been keeping watch on me around Kympton for quite a while. I had no idea why, and I didn't like that. It explained why she'd kept her distance though, when she'd been around Kympton Grange Farm. Presumably she'd known me for a dryad's son and didn't want me to see she wasn't human.

She hadn't reacted when I'd seen her though the binoculars. So she wouldn't know I'd seen her here at Blithehurst. She had no reason to think I had any idea that she wasn't the human she was pretending to be. I wasn't sure how that might give us an advantage, but as long as it might, I would keep things that way.

I cut quickly through the gardens and went around to the front door of the house. Two women were dusting the entrance hall and I recognised one of them from the tour.

'Excuse me, do you know where I might find Eleanor Beauchene?'

'Up at the restaurant, I think.' The woman looked at me, mildly curious.

'Thanks.' I left before she could ask any questions.

# Chapter Thirty-Two

Before I went into the restaurant, I stopped at the Land Rover. When Eleanor saw me coming through the door, she headed over to see what I wanted. I handed her the first Green Man's mask I'd carved, the one made out of lime wood.

'What's this for?'

'Just in case.' It was the best way I could think of to tell him that I wanted him watching over her. 'With any luck it'll ward off any more bad dreams.'

She made an 'I'll be right back' gesture to the two chefs she'd been talking to. 'What about the fence?'

'That's fine, but there's something else.' I told her what I'd just seen. 'Look, I've felt just how powerful this sort of lure can be. I could barely resist it, and I knew what I was dealing with. Your brother hasn't got a clue.'

'Then Rob's...' She looked at me, stricken.

'As long as he's useful to her, let's hope she'll just string him along. When we can work out what she wants, we can see how to untangle him. There's no point in guessing though, not until we know exactly what we're dealing with. If Sineya learns anything useful from Frai or Asca, she'll come and tell you. I hope so, anyway. Meantime, I should go and see what Kalei knows.'

'Okay.' Eleanor still looked apprehensive.

'Keep out of this woman's way,' I stressed. 'If she realises you can see she's not human, she'll know that means you could be in touch with the dryads here. Who knows what she'll do then.' I remembered how slavishly the boggarts had been behaving.

Eleanor's face hardened. She took out her mobile phone and made a call.

'Rob? No, you listen. I've been thinking about what you said, so now you can listen to me. You're right, your private life is your own affair, but you can damn well show me some consideration too. I don't want you bringing your new girl-friend here.'

'No. No. NO.' She cut off his attempts at protests. 'Nicole's my friend and I know you're ducking her calls. Until you get things straightened out with her, I'm damned if I'm going to make small talk with whoever you're screwing. You're certainly not taking her to bed just on the other side of the hall from my room.'

He called her a bitch so loudly I could hear him. Eleanor went red, visibly hurt. 'We'll see what Mum thinks then, shall we?'

Robert told her to fuck off and ended the call. Eleanor took a deep breath and put her phone away. 'Well, that should keep whoever she is out of the house itself.' She still looked upset despite her resolute words. 'He's not normally like this. We really need to get him away from her.'

'I'll let you know as soon as I find anything out,' I promised. 'Better be on a landline though. What's the best number to call?'

'Why?' She shook her head, astonished, as I explained what dryads could do with phone calls. 'We need to find time for a good long chat about this stuff. Hang on a minute.'

I waited while she fetched a customer comments card from the shelf holding baskets of cutlery and condiments. She scribbled a number on it. 'That's my direct line, straight through to me upstairs in the house.'

'Great.' I put it in my pocket. 'I'll be in touch soon.'

I left her to her day job and headed back to Lambton. As I stopped for fuel on the way, I wished I had some dry-ad-blood talent to carry me between places as quickly as they could travel. That would be a damn sight cheaper, particularly since I wasn't working at the moment. I couldn't afford to keep racking up the miles like this for long.

Before I got to Lambton, I saw the road signs for Kympton. On an impulse, I took the next turn and followed the familiar route to Kympton Grange Farm. Sam Monkswell was working on a hay rake hitched to his tractor in the yard. I'm not sure what I'd have done if he hadn't been there. Since he was, I pulled up onto the verge.

'Dan?' He stood up, surprised, as I got out of the Land Rover.

I held up placating hands. 'I just want a quick word.'

'That's fine, no problem.'

As he approached the gate, wiping his hands on a rag, he looked oddly embarrassed. That was unexpected, but I had more immediate concerns.

'You know that woman, Lin, the one who cleans for Chrissie? Do you happen to know where she lives? What her last name might be?'

'Oh, her.' Sam scowled, and not at me. 'She doesn't work here anymore.'

'Was there some trouble?' Now I was curious.

'No, she just never turned up, the next day she was supposed to work.' Sam hesitated. 'It was the day after you left. We thought—' He shook his head and didn't finish.

'What?' I wasn't about to let that go.

Sam looked even more embarrassed. 'Well, she'd been on at Chrissie, asking questions about you, ever since she took the job. But I didn't think she could be interested. I mean, not like that. She'd been saying all sorts, about how we didn't really know anything about you, when there was all that stuff in the papers...'

So whoever this stranger was, whatever she was, she didn't want the Monkswells trusting me. I'd think some more about that later. For the moment, it gave me an idea. 'Well, I'd like to find her if I can. I think she's been telling more lies about me, to stop me getting a new job.'

'Shit.' Sam looked genuinely distressed. 'Why?'

'I have absolutely no idea,' I said fervently. 'There must be some misunderstanding. If I can find her, maybe I can straighten things out.'

'Sorry, mate, I can't help. I wish I could.' Now he was irritated again. 'When she didn't turn up, we still owed her a few quid – you know how it is, paying cash in hand. But when Chrissie went round to the address she'd given us, turns out they'd never heard of her.'

'How did she get here, when she came to work?'

'Got a lift, I think she told Chrissie,' Sam said vaguely.

'How did she hear about the job?'

He was more certain about that. 'Someone in the Goose told her about it.'

I shrugged. 'Sounds like you're well rid of her.'

'I'll say. Look, I can spread the word, if you like, that she's not to be trusted. Tell people to talk to me or Phil, if they want a reference from someone who knows you.'

I was tempted to say yes, but we still didn't know what we were dealing with. 'Just leave it for now. If she's one of those nutters who get fixated on hating people, the last thing you need is her spreading lies about you and your business.' I gestured towards the holiday cottages.

He twisted his torque wrench in his hands. 'I am glad to see you. We've been thinking we overreacted, asking you to leave. We've got a few bookings for the barn flat until the end of the school holidays, but if you wanted to take it on again after that...?' He looked at me, hopeful as well as self-conscious.

'I'll see how things stand. I'd be happy to come back, but if I can't get a job locally...'

'Right.' Sam nodded. 'If I hear of anything going, I'll be in touch, okay?'

He offered me his hand and I shook it. 'Appreciate it.'

Sam was still standing at the gate as I turned the Land Rover around and drove back towards Lambton. I gave him a friendly wave and he did the same. I was tempted to start counting down the days till the autumn school term started. I'd move back into the barn flat in a heartbeat, as long as I could find the rent. But who knew what might happen before then?

310

As I passed the jutting rock where Kalei had taken me into her hidden caverns, I glanced at the woods cloaking Kympton Hill. Even on a grey day like this, the trees looked invitingly picturesque. I started wondering about the unease I'd felt walking back from the Goose. If this unknown creature had been hanging around up there, for whatever reason, then maybe her presence was the darkness that I'd felt on the path. I thought about those unhappy holidaymakers in the farm cottages. Maybe they'd been feeling some threatening miasma spread by whatever was masquerading as the woman Lin, rather than being unsettled by news coverage of those poor dead girls. Maybe that shadowy pall had drawn the boggarts to the pub car park. Though none of that explained why the creature was here, or why she'd turned her attention to Blithehurst.

I should have been watching the road. As I rounded the next bend, I had to stand on the brakes to avoid rear-ending a blue Ford. It was parked in the middle of the road with its hazard lights flashing. The Land Rover came to a halt barely three inches from its rear bumper.

I took a moment to catch my breath, switched on my own hazards, and got out. 'What's the problem? Can I help?'

A retired-type couple were at the front of the car. The bonnet wasn't raised to show they'd broken down, and I couldn't see any flat tyres.

The woman hurried towards me, beckoning. 'Oh, do you live around here? Do you know the closest vet?'

As I went closer, I realised her husband was looking warily at something on the ground. A sizeable brindled dog lay sprawled on the road. It looked like a cross between a Great Dane and one of those really big German Shepherds. As I took another step, the beast raised its head a few inches and growled a ferocious warning. I didn't blame the Ford bloke for keeping his distance.

'I don't see any blood, but it can't get up. I wonder if its back is broken.' Visibly distressed, he gripped car keys in one hand, a mobile phone in the other.

'Have you rung the police?'

'We came round the bend and it was there in the road. We didn't hit it, honestly,' the agitated lady assured me. From her Welsh accent it was a fair guess they were tourists.

'I can see that from your car.' The front fender, grille and lights were intact.

Her husband answered my question with a wave of his phone. 'No signal.'

I wondered what to do, because I could see something this nice couple never would. Every time I blinked, I caught a glimpse of the beast's true form. This wasn't some stray, or a farm dog that had got loose. It was the shuck lying there, incapacitated.

Straining to turn its head, it looked at me and whined. One paw scrabbled on the tarmac, pathetic. When I blinked, I saw that the fire in its eyes had sunk to a dull ember.

'Does it know you?' the Ford bloke asked hopefully. 'Do you know who owns it?'

'Yes. I think so, anyway.' I wasn't sure if the shuck or Kalei would agree with that definition of their relationship.

I took another step. The shuck looked at me, panting desperately. The Ford driver followed me, and the beast showed its teeth, snarling deep in its throat.

'I would try to help, but...' He spread helpless hands.

I rubbed a hand over my head, thinking fast. I couldn't leave the shuck in the middle of the road, even to fetch Kalei as quickly as I could. Someone would be sure to try to take this poor injured dog to a vet. There was every chance some Good Samaritan would get savaged. Even the best trained dogs are unpredictable when they're hurt, and the shuck was the very essence of a wild animal. Someone getting bitten would mean the police getting involved, looking to enforce the Dangerous Dogs Act and all sorts of other complications.

A motorbike roared past, the rider anonymous in leathers and a black helmet. I heard an engine behind the Landy as some other vehicle pulled up. So far, no one had come from the other direction, but sooner rather than later, somebody surely would. If they braked hard with another car too close behind them, a pile-up could block this narrow road completely. That's always assuming they didn't run over the shuck in the first place.

'We need to get him somewhere safe.' I walked cautiously forward.

The shuck watched me, unblinking.

I crouched down and extended a hand, as if I were trying to befriend any other dog. The shuck didn't respond with a lick or a whimper like an ordinary dog, but at least it didn't snarl.

'Should you be moving him?' the nice lady asked, anguished. 'If he's badly hurt—'

'He'll be hurt a damn sight worse if another car hits him.' The man's voice was rough with his own distress.

I tried to work out how best to pick the shuck up. I had to shut my eyes to block out glimpses of the beast's spectral shape, because that really wasn't helping. I slid one hand under its current manifestation's haunches and the other under its shoulders. That wasn't easy. Gravel on the road gouged the backs of my hands and my forearms. This shape might be an illusion, but I'd be lifting all of the shuck's true bulk.

'Can you open my passenger door, please?' I called out.

Shuffling my feet as close to the shuck as I could, I squatted and tried to remember everything I'd been told about weight-lifting, on the couple of occasions I'd joined a gym. The beast growled softly, though thankfully it didn't struggle. I couldn't tell if it had realised I was there to help, or it simply couldn't move. I had no idea if anything could be done, if the nice lady was right and the shadowy beast's back was broken. All I could do was get it to Kalei.

'Ready when you are,' the Ford driver called.

Someone getting annoyed at the holdup leaned hard on their car horn somewhere back down the road. I took a deep breath and hoisted the shuck up to my chest. I'd never tried to lift anything so heavy. The shuck whined, heart-rending. For one appalling instant I thought I was going to drop it. I held on tighter and focused all my efforts on standing up.

I've no idea how I managed that. As I staggered around the Ford, I could only hope no cars were coming up behind me. There was no chance I could get out of anyone's way.

My lungs and biceps were burning by the time I reached the Land Rover. As the helpful Ford driver opened the passenger door, my thighs were trembling and my knees felt about ready to give way. Putting the shuck on the seat came closer to dropping it than laying it down. The beast whimpered. I'd rather it had growled. The flame in its eyes was definitely fading.

'I'm really not sure we should have moved him.' The Welsh lady stood beside me, wringing her hands.

'I'll go straight to a vet,' I assured her. 'As soon as you move your car.'

That sent her hurrying off. Her husband was already waiting to start the engine as soon as she closed her door. I stayed close behind the Ford until we reached the junction where I turned off to head for Tila's valley.

The shuck seemed to be flickering between the dark shadow of its ethereal shape and its manifestation as the dog those tourists had found on the road. I had no idea what would happen if its true form became solid reality inside the Land Rover. There was barely enough room for us both as it was.

I put my foot down. The lay-by was empty now, scarred by countless tyre tracks. I slowed but decided stopping there would be too far from the water. I needed to alert Kalei as quickly as possible, though I still had no idea how to do that.

As I reached the bridge, the shuck howled. Terror hit me so hard that I braked, throwing the Land Rover into a skid. As the front wheels hit the verge and the engine stalled, I threw open my door. Gasping, I fell out of my seat to land on the grass on my hands and knees. I scrambled to my feet, fighting an urge to run, somewhere, anywhere, to just get away.

The shuck howled again, its ferocious agony making my ears ring. Adrenaline surged through me, leaving my mouth dry and my stomach churning. I couldn't think straight. Every instinct was screaming at me to panic. I was in mortal danger and I had to run.

'What's happened?' Kalei was beside me, in her jeans and T-shirt guise.

'I don't know,' I barely managed to say, my voice shaking. 'Can you help?'

'Not here.' She looked up at the sky. 'He needs shadow.'

'Okay.' Even overcast, the daylight was far brighter here than it had been on the Kympton road. 'Where?'

She took a moment to think. 'Where we hid the tools to fight the wose.'

I nodded. 'Okay, but—'

She'd already vanished. I took a deep breath. Biting my lip so hard I drew blood meant I could focus on that pain instead of the fear that threatened to overwhelm me. Even so, my hand was trembling as I reached for the door handle. Getting back into the driving seat was one of the hardest things I'd ever done. By the time I reached that single-lane track turning off the road, my T-shirt was sodden with rank, fearful sweat.

I stopped by the jagged grey crag. As soon as I turned off the engine, Kalei appeared at the passenger door. She opened it and lifted the shuck out. All pretence at being an ordinary dog vanished, revealing its true, daunting form. Kalei was unconcerned, settling its head and forepaws on her shoulder as easily as someone cuddling a lapdog, with her hands interlaced beneath its haunches. As she carried the beast towards the rock, I realised she was heading for a cleft that was dark with moisture. She showed no sign of slowing as she shimmered into her blue naiad form.

'Wait!' I ran to catch up. If she disappeared underground, she could go anywhere. 'I have to talk to you!'

She narrowed her eyes at me, stormy blue. 'He needs deep darkness.'

I reached for her arm, desperate to hold her back from the cave. 'There's something threatening Blithehurst.'

The shuck cracked open its smouldering eyes and growled feebly. I held my ground and tightened my grip.

'There's a woman. She's not human, and she was making trouble for me in Kympton before I ever heard of Blithehurst. Now she's there and we don't know why. She has glassy white eyes, for those of us who can see your kind.'

The shuck growled again. Kalei stopped dead and looked at the creature, aghast. If something was passing between them, I had no idea what that might be, but the naiad laid the beast down in the faint shadow cast by the crag. The shuck lay on its side, panting, as she knelt and ran her hands over it, from nose to tail and from shoulder and haunches down to all four massive paws.

She sat back on her heels. 'Tell me.'

I felt something of the same compulsion that Asca had used on me and scowled. 'You don't need to do that.'

Then I told her everything as quickly as I could. 'Well?' I demanded. 'What is she? What does she want, and why was she fucking with my life before she decided to wreck Robert Beauchene's?'

'Tell me about her eyes.' Kalei looked at me, her turquoise gaze impenetrable. 'Did they remind you of moonstones?'

'What?' I tried to think if I'd ever seen moonstones. A moment later, I remembered a jewellery maker at a craft fair. Not as talented as Victoria, but he'd favoured semi-precious stones. 'I suppose so, yes.'

Kalei reached out to stroke the shuck. I saw her hand tremble and felt a shiver of apprehension.

'What is it?'

'It shouldn't be possible.' She seemed to be talking more to the shuck than to me.

'Tell me!'

'You describe a wyrm,' she said simply.

'It's already broken free?' I was horrified. 'How the fuck do we catch it?' Then my brain caught up with my mouth. This creature masquerading as a human woman had started cleaning the Monkswells' cottages weeks ago. 'What's still singing under the ruins? Did this one get out and leave another one behind?'

The naiad shook her head. 'She's not a wyrmling. There is only one of the ancient clutch still surviving beneath Blithehurst. That creature is far too weak to escape the darkness without help. What you describe is a mature wyrm, and an old one, if she can disguise herself as a human so convincingly.'

I was about to protest that all the old tales said full-grown wyrms were big enough to eat cattle whole. Then I looked at the shuck and thought how many different shapes and sizes I'd seen it take. 'You said they were all dead,' I objected instead.

'So we thought.' Kalei reached for the shuck's heaving flank. 'But this explains what has poisoned him.'

'He's been bitten? Will he survive?' I didn't hold out much hope, seeing the beast lying so limp and helpless.

'He may, if you allow me to take him into the darkness.' She glanced at me, her eyes glinting. 'What puzzles me more, is why did the monster let him live? She could easily have crushed him and killed him outright.'

I'd already worked that out. 'To keep you occupied. To keep you away from Blithehurst.'

'While she helps the wyrmling break free,' Kalei agreed, grim-faced.

'Which must be why she seduced Robert. He can pass through the iron fence, even if she can't. What's she going to do next?' I wondered.

'Once there are two wyrms in these isles again?' Kalei looked at me as though I were stupid. 'Spawn more wyrms!'

I wanted to ask how soon. If these creatures measured their lives in centuries, there was every chance that Eleanor and I would be long gone. The return of serpent dragons would be someone else's problem. But that was a coward's way out. Besides, that wasn't what I was asking the naiad.

'What is she going to do, to get to the wyrmling? How do

we stop her letting it loose?' How the fuck we were supposed to kill a full-grown wyrm wasn't a question I even wanted to contemplate, still less ask aloud.

'Talk to the dryads.' Kalei scooped up the shuck and headed for the flat face of the crag.

Before I could say anything, she and her burden shimmered into translucency. She stepped through the crack no wider than my hand as easily as I'd go through an open door.

Thanks for nothing. There was no use me sitting here fuming though. I found my phone to check the time and was surprised to find it was already mid-afternoon. I also realised I was hungry.

I headed for Lambton and parked in the market square. I got some chips, and once I'd thrown the empty paper in the bin, I used the payphone to call Eleanor. I got an answerphone. Sod it. Asking her to call me back was too risky, since I didn't have a landline. I hung up.

A moment later, I hit the payphone buttons again. I still had to warn her. I let the message play out and waited for the beep. 'Hi, it's Daniel. Listen, you know Junior, who we're so concerned about? It looks like one of his relatives—'

'Hello?' The line crackled as Eleanor picked the phone up. 'Yes, this mystery woman is a wyrm. Frai just told me.'

I could hear her instinctive disbelief at war with growing apprehension. I knew exactly how she felt. She'd heard the wyrmsong. She knew dryads didn't lie. She couldn't kid herself that this wasn't real, any more than I could.

'What does she suggest?' If anyone had any answers, surely the oldest dryad would.

'I've no clue,' Eleanor said curtly. 'She and Asca started having a row and all three of them vanished.'

'Do you want me to come over?' I should tell her about the shuck and Kalei.

'Tomorrow. I've got to spend the rest of today on the phone.' Eleanor vented wordless exasperation. 'Rob's arranged for a team of archaeologists to dig up the undercroft.'

'They'll find a hell of a lot more than they're expecting.' And I guessed the wyrmling would find an all-it-could-eat buffet.

Eleanor agreed. 'I'm looking for some way to stop them.'

'Is there anything I can do?' I had to at least try.

'Go online and find out everything you can about wyrms,' she said grimly. 'Bye.'

So I went back to my rented room and spent the rest of the day on research. I turned my phone off, in case I got a call from Dad. I couldn't think how to tell him about all this, and I couldn't bear the thought of lying.

# Chapter Thirty-Three

I slept soundly and didn't dream. I hoped that meant the wyrm woman was still far away at Blithehurst with the Green Man keeping watch on her. Still, I drove over early, arriving with the first few staff. Thankfully, I still had that contractor badge so I slung the lanyard round my neck and got nodded through the gate.

Eleanor was in the house's entrance hall, talking to one of the custodians. She handed over a bunch of keys as soon as she saw me, jerking her head towards the back stairs. 'Come on up.'

I followed her past the kitchen door. 'How was your night?'

'Fine. You?'

'Good.' I waited till we reached her sitting room before saying anything more. Today the table in the bay window was covered with serious-looking books and paperwork.

'I've had no luck stopping these archaeologists.' Exasperated, Eleanor dropped into a chair. 'I've been on to their university, rung English Heritage and everyone else I can think of who needs to sign off on this. Every time, Rob's been there first and talked them all into agreeing. Up to and including Mum and Dad, who can't understand why I'm not delighted.'

She shook her head. 'It's not as if I've got any convincing reason to object. As long as they're working in the undercroft, they won't be disrupting the usual flow of visitors. They can use the old dairy as a base of operations, and that's well away from the house and the gardens. If anything, this sort of project could boost our footfall, especially if I agree to a "Meet the Public" tent. They're suggesting they could talk to people about what archaeologists really do, showing off some of their equipment and displaying whatever they've found.'

I walked over to look out of the window towards the ruins. 'What are they expecting to find?'

She shrugged. 'They reckon there could be artefacts from the first Norman manor all the way through to the English Civil War. It's entirely possible. The undercroft was in use all that time.'

I could see the problem. 'When will they arrive?'

'Next week, to make a start with ground-penetrating radar and test pits.' She looked at me. 'So we need to kill the wyrmling before then.'

It was incredible how something could sound so completely insane on the one hand, and absolutely unarguable on the other. 'When?'

'Sunday night.' Eleanor had clearly been thinking this through. 'As soon as the last of the staff have left. That gives us all Monday to clear up –' she gestured vaguely '– whatever there is to clear up.'

I had no idea how much mess we were going to make. 'What about Rob and his girlfriend?'

She hesitated. 'I honestly don't know. He hasn't spoken to me since I told him not to bring her here. He hasn't been back. I don't imagine she's let slip any particular interest in Blithehurst. He's always dropped girlfriends who fancy playing lady of the manor hard and fast.'

'He may not be thinking straight,' I warned. 'In fact, I'd put money on that. He'll do whatever she wants, when it comes down to it. I thought of something else on the drive over. As soon as that wyrmling realises it's in trouble, it's going to start screaming for help, and I'm betting she'll be able to hear it, however far away she might be. Then she's bound to try something to rescue it. I only wish we had some idea about what she might do.'

Eleanor nodded, frowning. 'I can see what the dryads think, and you can ask Kalei?'

I grimaced. 'She may be a bit busy at the moment.'

I went to sit in one of the chairs by the fireplace and explained what had happened to the shuck. Obviously that involved explaining all about the shuck. That led on to me telling Eleanor about the boggarts in The Grey Goose's car park. By the time I'd finished running through my unnerving experiences in the Kympton Hill woods, and my recent conversation with Sam Monkswell, we could hear the first tourists of the day walking along the hall from the morning room to the gallery.

'Just a minute. There's always someone who tries the door handles up here.' Eleanor got up to lock the sitting room door. 'So you think the boggarts might attack us?'

'We have to consider the possibility, though they shouldn't be able to cross the iron fence, so we'll be safe inside the ruins. Meantime, I'd say there's every chance they're spying for the wyrm woman.'

Eleanor returned to her chair, leaning forward with her elbows on the table. 'So we need to get everything we'll need to tackle the wyrmling inside the fence without any nosy boggarts working out what we're planning.'

'I've been thinking about what we could use to kill it, and I keep coming back to an axe as the best idea.' I swallowed my distaste. I'm not particularly squeamish, but the idea of hacking a living creature to bits was revolting.

To my surprise, Eleanor grinned. 'I've been thinking about that too. Come on.'

She took yet another bunch of keys from a basket on the table. I wondered how many doors this place had.

We went into the hallway and she locked the sitting room behind us. We went down the main staircase this time, getting mildly curious glances from the morning's visitors. Eleanor simply smiled at them, unremarkable in her blue uniform polo shirt. I did my best to look as if I belonged here, and once they noticed my badge and Blithehurst lanyard, people seemed to lose interest.

When we reached the ground floor, Eleanor turned right and opened a door that I hadn't even noticed before. It was cunningly concealed in the wooden panels beside the fireplace. A narrow staircase led downwards on the right-hand side. Ahead, there was just a dead end.

'What's this?' I tried to calculate the length of this odd

space, compared to the Great Parlour on the other side of the wall to my left.

'There's a secret chapel above here,' Eleanor explained, matter-of-fact, as she headed down the stairs. 'There's a priest hole behind that wall, and these stairs lead to the cellars and an escape route.'

I wondered what it must have been like to grow up in a house full of these secrets. Though the cellars weren't particularly exciting nowadays. Brick-walled rooms on either side of a central corridor were mostly full of shabby furniture and boxes of whatever wasn't wanted upstairs.

Mostly, but not all. I followed Eleanor through the end door and looked around as she switched on an unshaded light bulb hanging from the curved ceiling. 'You have an armoury?'

'Hardly. It's just where we keep the pieces that aren't good enough to display.'

I could see what she meant. A stack of Roundhead helmets and breastplates were so dented and rusty, I hated to think how long it would take to restore them. On the other hand, I only needed something proof against boggarts, not broadswords. I picked up a helmet and wondered if it would fit me.

Eleanor laughed. 'I was thinking more along these lines.'

She pulled a halberd from the shadows at the far end. 'The handle's Victorian, and it's badly notched but it's heavy enough to do some real damage. And it's a lot longer than an axe.'

'Let me see.' I took it, checking the long handle for any sign of woodworm. The last thing I needed was a weapon breaking on me.

As it turned out, the wood was sound and Eleanor was right. This six-foot shaft would give me a lot more reach than an axe handle. Better yet, the halberd would give me far more options than a wood axe with a single cutting edge. The halberd was tipped with a spear head as long as my hand, and below that, a sizeable axe blade on one side was paired with a vicious downward-curved spike on the other. That was the good news. The bad news was that every edge of the weapon was so blunt, I'd be better off trying to kill the wyrmling with a spoon.

I considered the dull steel from several angles. 'I don't suppose you've got an old grindstone sitting around somewhere?'

Eleanor shook her head. 'Not that I know of, sorry.'

I shrugged. 'I'd better get to work with a whetstone. I've got one in the Landy if you can find me somewhere out of the way with decent light to work.'

She nodded. 'The old dairy.'

I followed her out, careful not to smack the halberd against any doors or brickwork. Once we were back upstairs, I carried it with the shaft leaning against my shoulder, trying not to feel too conspicuous. There wasn't much chance of that, with the tourists gaping at this unexpected sight. A few of them even took photographs.

'Have you got re-enactors coming?' one excited little boy asked Eleanor.

'Keep an eye on our website,' she said with a smile.

As we went out of the front door, I remembered to lower the halberd just in time to avoid wrecking the panelling above the lintel. We got more intrigued stares in the knot garden, but thankfully Eleanor turned right to take a path running past the Great Parlour windows. At the end of the house it forked. One branch circled back around the house while the other was blocked by a chain with a 'No Access' sign stretched between two sturdy posts. Eleanor unhooked one side to let me through. Once she'd re-secured it, she led the way through an expanse of well-tended ornamental shrubs and trees. Passing through a gap in a yew hedge, we arrived at some dilapidated outbuildings loosely grouped around an expanse of cobbles.

Eleanor pointed to a path on the far side before detaching a key from the bunch she was carrying. 'That will take you back to the restaurant and the garden centre.'

She used the key to open the door to the closest, largest building. 'How's this?'

'Fine.' Ancient limewash was flaking off the brick walls and the tiled floor was badly cracked, but that didn't matter. It was light and airy and there was a grooved wooden work-bench running all along one wall. It was just what I needed to fix up a vice. There was even a battered old stool.

'Can I leave you to it?' Eleanor handed me the key. 'I have to get back to work.'

'Of course.'

She headed back to the house and I fetched the tools I needed. Once I had my vice solidly fixed to the workbench, I locked the halberd's head tight. My first task was getting to work with a coarse file, to establish fresh edges on all the cutting blades. Once I'd done that, I took a break and wandered up to the restaurant to buy a sandwich and a drink. The place was packed, which must be good news for Blithehurst. I only hoped we could kill the wyrmling quickly and cleanly enough to avoid any problems for the business.

Before heading back to the dairy, I made a quick circuit of the grounds, looking all around me for boggarts. There was no sign of the little bastards, so I thought about asking the dryads what they knew about the wyrm woman. When I crossed the river though, I could see the wooded pasture was full of visitors coming and going from the dryads' temple. So I headed back to the dairy and worked on the halberd with successively finer files until it was ready for honing oil and my whetstone.

By the time the daylight was yellowing, I was satisfied. Stroking the back of my forearm carefully along any edge shaved the hairs off easily. That was sharp enough.

I looked at my filthy, oily hands and wondered if the taps on that sink in the corner still worked. I'd brought a tub of heavy-duty hand-cleanser from the Land Rover, and a bundle of rags, but I'd still prefer to wash the residue off before I tried a few practice swings with the halberd.

My phone rang while I was halfway through cleaning my

hands. Answering it with slippery fingers wasn't easy. I laid it on the bench, in speaker mode.

'Dan?' Eleanor's voice echoed back from the brickwork.

'What's wrong?' I could hear the strain in her words.

'The water level's rising in the moat.'

'What?' That was a stupid thing to say. 'I'll be there as quick as I can.'

I left the halberd and locked the door, scrubbing my hands on a rag as I went back past the house. I kept my eyes open for boggarts, but just like earlier, there was no sign of them.

The only thing wrong was the moat. When I'd been pretending to be a tourist here, there had been five or six courses of brickwork visible between the waterline and the grassy slope of the bank. Now there were barely three lines of bricks, and I didn't think there'd been enough recent rain to explain that much of a rise.

I could see Eleanor standing on the footbridge. As she waved to me, I pointed towards the river and the inlet into the moat. Several ducks were fussing around the grille where the iron fence passed through the water. There wasn't enough room for them to pass under the bars now.

'When did this start?' I asked as Eleanor joined me.

'No one's really sure,' she said, exasperated. 'What are you thinking?'

'How useful a naiad could be about now.' I took another look at the river. The recent rain might not have brought the level up much, but the water was definitely flowing faster. If something blocked its path, the stream would back up pretty quickly. I looked past the medieval ruins. 'What's downstream?'

'An old watermill.' Eleanor followed my gaze. 'We haven't found the money to restore it for visitors yet. What do you suppose she wants to achieve by doing this?'

So she was as convinced as me that the wyrm woman was behind this.

'If the ground below the ruins gets saturated, maybe that will strengthen the wyrmling. Water's supposed to heal them.' That was my best guess.

'We'd better take a look.' With the iron fence running along the bank, Eleanor had to double back.

'Hang on. Where do your gardeners keep their tools?' I had no idea what we might find downstream, but regardless, I wanted something heavy and made of steel in my hand.

Once again, Eleanor didn't need an explanation. 'This way.'

There was a discreet shed tucked away where the selection of specimen trees met the shrubbery. One of Eleanor's ubiquitous keys opened the door and she quickly found herself a billhook. I helped myself to a pair of long-handled shears. Hopefully the visitors thought we were just on our way to some gardening emergency as we hurried past the ruins.

Cutting through the wilderness garden, we soon reached the rough pasture beneath the limestone ridge. There was still no sign of boggarts as we headed for the water's edge. The tussocky grass was already sodden, but the slope of the land wouldn't give the rising water much room to spread. As the river cut through the rocky ground, both banks were steeper than they were upstream at Blithehurst. That inlet into the moat would be any flood's first chance to escape.

Eleanor took a narrow path that had been scraped through the coarse grass, leading up and over the ridge. Pausing on the crest, I saw that the valley beyond was cluttered with the untended remnants of coppiced hazel trees. Barely visible through the leafy branches, I glimpsed red brick walls and angled, tiled roofs.

'That's the mill? Are the waterwheels and sluices still working?'

Eleanor was already hurrying onwards. 'Not to grind corn, but someone could still shut off the flow to the mill pond and the mill race.'

That would bring the river level up, but I wasn't

convinced it could account for such a rapid rise.

'Keep your eyes open,' I warned. 'We don't know if she's here, or what might be with her.'

'You too.' Eleanor picked up the pace.

We reached a narrow channel dug centuries ago to draw water off the river and hold it in a millpond until it was needed to drive the mill. A narrow, rickety bridge carried the path across this manmade gully, with wooden sluice gates built underneath.

Those gates weren't just closed. Eleanor clearly knew how the ancient mechanism was supposed to work, but she couldn't get the levers to shift, no matter how hard she shoved them. 'Something's broken.'

'Do you want me to try?' Though I'd have to be careful. These green-slimed timbers didn't look too sturdy. Wrecking the sluice might solve part of our problem, but if this foot-bridge went down with it, we'd have no safe way to cross the channel.

I looked down to see if we could wade through it. The water was still and so clouded that I couldn't see the bottom. That meant I couldn't see if there might be something lurk-ing down there. I still didn't know if boggarts could swim, and a faint, rank smell from somewhere was making me very uneasy.

Eleanor still couldn't open the sluice.

'Shall I have a go?' I offered again.

Before she could answer, a loud splash came from some-where down by the mill.

'Come on.' She began hacking a path with the billhook.

The hazel thickets gave way to tangles of brambles and nettles doing their best to reclaim the cobbled expanse around the L-shaped mill. It had been built into the steep valley side so that it looked like a single-storey building as we approached, with wide double doors where corn and any other supplies could be unloaded from carts.

Viewed from the waterside though, the building had two

floors. Those sacks of corn would have been carried inside up top, ready to be emptied into the hoppers and chutes feeding the millstones on the floor below. Those were driven by two great water wheels, still hanging, battered and broken on their axles. One would be fed by the millrace leading from the pond filled by the channel we'd crossed. The other drew water straight from the river along a narrow trough, or at least it would have done, if those wooden sluices hadn't been closed as well.

There was no one to be seen as we drew closer, both of us careful on the slippery, mossy cobbles. We heard another splash from the far side of the building. Eleanor headed for the river. I followed to see her run along the narrow embankment between the river and the waterwheel.

'Rob!' she shouted, furious. 'What the hell are you doing?'

As I followed, as fast as I dared, I saw that I was right. Shutting the mill sluices wasn't nearly enough to force the river to flood. Somehow Robert Beauchene had brought down several young willow trees on the far bank. Now their leafy branches were choking the stream. He was shoving and hauling on another bushy sapling. As he wrenched the trunk back and forth, the earthen bank crumbled around its roots and the river snatched the soil away.

'Robbie!' Eleanor yelled.

'He can't hear you.' I could see his unfocused eyes from here, and I recognised that slackness in his face. 'He's in thrall to the wyrm.'

Eleanor looked at me, desperate. 'We have to get him away from there. Maybe we can bring him to his senses.'

I didn't imagine he'd come willingly, but I nodded all the same. I was at least four inches taller and considerably more muscular, if it came to a fight. 'Then we can get those trees out of the water.' The pruning shears I'd brought would come in handy.

'We can cross over there.' Eleanor gestured towards a narrow footbridge a short distance downstream.

I looked at the willows that had already fallen in the river.

It wouldn't be long before the fast-flowing water washed them downstream to wedge against the bridge and make an even more effective dam.

A figure stepped out from the trees on the far bank, a woman in a pale yellow dress. Unhurried, she walked forward. She stood in the middle of the bridge, her hands on the rails on either side.

Eleanor recoiled. 'Is that her?'

'Yes.' I recognised her at once: Lin, the cleaning woman. At the same time, she seemed like a total stranger. It was as though I'd never seen her before. More than that, I couldn't understand why I hadn't felt her unnatural presence. As she looked straight at us now, we both shivered. Menace came off the wyrm woman like a chilling wind.

I looked at the river. The water wasn't as ominously opaque as the mill race had been, but it was flowing fast, dark and menacing. I wouldn't give much for my chances of swimming across to the far bank before I was swept away. That would take me well past the point where Robert was still fighting to bring down that sapling. Then I'd be carried straight to the footbridge where the wyrm woman was waiting.

Eleanor was already heading for the bridge, billhook raised. 'Get out of my fucking way!' she yelled at the motionless figure.

I followed, gripping the long-handled shears. I could use them to threaten the wyrm woman without getting too close, but there was no room on the narrow path for me to get past Eleanor. No way to stop her walking into such danger. Her billhook was a fearsome tool, but she'd have to be within arm's reach before she could use it.

Eleanor reached the bridge. As she set foot on the weathered planks, the wyrm woman let go of the rails, her hands falling to hang loosely. No, that wasn't right. An instant later, I realised her hands and arms were pressed tight to her sides. Not just pressed tight, but disappearing into her body. Her feet seemed to be flowing together and her yellow dress was lengthening and darkening. Her hair disappeared as her nose flattened and vanished to leave a broad, blunt head with wide, bone-white eyes, lit with cold radiance defying the daylight.

The wyrm hissed, its wide mouth gaping to show us fearsome teeth. The creature was all snake now, and covered in glossy scales like evergreen leaves. It reared up like a cobra, one thick coil resting on the bridge with its tail disappearing into the water. I couldn't guess how long it was, but its body was as thick as my waist.

Eleanor hesitated. I tried to judge if I could get close enough to grab her, to drag her away before the giant serpent struck. I had no idea what to do after that.

The wyrm moved, but not to attack us. Boneless, it looped down its own length to dive into the water.

'Where did it go?' Frantic, Eleanor searched the stream.

'There!' I pointed at a dark green coil breaking the surface.

It was swimming upriver. Within moments, it reached Robert Beauchene.

'Robbie!' Eleanor yelled. 'Get back!'

He didn't hear her. He didn't even move as the wyrm reared up out of the water in front of him. He stood there, expressionless, as its head darted forward. Inside a minute it had looped itself around his body, once, twice, three times, pinning his arms to his sides. He didn't even struggle.

Eleanor's scream was lost in the splash as the wyrm fell back into the water, dragging Robert with it. Limp in its coils, he disappeared under the surface. Mud boiled up from the river bottom, fouling the water so we couldn't see a thing.

Eleanor ran across the bridge. She began fighting her way through the willows clustered thickly along the bank. She was trying to reach the place where Rob had been standing.

I saw willow branches thrashing. Earth at the water's edge was beginning to crumble. The flow convulsed, sending great swells up the banks. One wrong step and Eleanor would find that her footing had been washed away. That's if a falling willow tree didn't crush her first.

I headed after her. 'Stand still!'

I don't know if she heard me. We both froze as the water surged upwards like a boiling pot. Robert Beauchene's body floated to the surface. There was no sign of the wyrm. He drifted in the water, face down, his arms and legs slack.

'Robbie!'

For one heart-stopping moment, I thought Eleanor was going to jump into the river. Maybe she thought about it but sanity prevailed, and she began making her way back to the bridge. Robert's body floated closer. Lying flat on the planks, I reached down, ready to grab him as he reached the bridge.

Fuck. I couldn't get close enough to the water. I forced my shoulders between the wooden struts holding up the hand-rail. Something splintered. I ignored it, hanging on with one hand as I shifted forward until my belt buckle scraped on the edge of the planks. My whole upper body was hanging over the river now, but that meant I could reach down and grab a handful of Robert's shirt before he disappeared under the bridge.

Getting him out of the water was going to be a whole other challenge. I was seriously worried that I'd overbalance if I tried to move, and join him in the river. I really, really didn't want to fall in. Quite apart from the risk of drowning, I had no idea where that fucking wyrm had got to.

'What can I do?' The bridge shook as Eleanor arrived.

'Sit on my legs. Hold me down.' Relieved, I felt her weight on my thighs. Now I was firmly pinned I could let go of the strut. I used both hands to haul Robert up and out of the water. I still couldn't get him onto the bridge though. He hung limp in my grip, a sodden, dead weight. My chest heaved with the effort of trying to lift him.

Eleanor shifted to sit with her knees straddling my waist, all her weight on my backside. Leaning forward, she reached over my shoulder to grab for her brother. Somehow, between us, twisting and turning, we managed to drag him up onto the planks. He lay there, pale and glassy eyed, with his arms and legs bent in unnatural angles.

As I scrambled backwards, I realised my shoulder was wet, but not with splashes from the river. Eleanor had been crying all the time we were wrestling to save him, silently, endlessly. Now she looked down on her brother's body, her face twisted with anguish.

CPR. Kiss of life. I knew the theory. I laced my fingers together and tried to start chest compressions. Robert's ribcage squelched beneath my hands. It felt as if every bone in his chest was broken. I felt like throwing up.

Eleanor screamed, but this time with ear-splitting fury. She scrambled to her feet, ready to rush back to the mill-side bank.

The wyrm had reappeared. Great green coils broached the river's surface close by the embankment running alongside the waterwheel.

'No!' I grabbed Eleanor's arm. I wasn't carrying two dead Beauchenes back to Blithehurst.

The wyrm reared up out of the water and threw a great coil of its scaly body against the embankment. As the earth cracked, the monster surged up and over the path to wrap itself around the broken waterwheel. Wood splintered and brickwork disintegrated. The wyrm thrashed back and forth, churning the river into filthy foam. A screech of stressed metal told me it had got a hold of the waterwheel's axle.

Tiles started sliding down from the roof to splash into the river. A great slab of masonry broke free from the side of the mill. The shattered waterwheel came crashing down after it, and the wyrm darted into the building through the cavernous gap it had made. The din of destruction grew louder. Moments later, the roof began to cave in.

'Move!' I shoved Eleanor so hard towards the far bank that I nearly pushed her over. As she got off the bridge, I hauled Robert's corpse up onto my shoulders in a fireman's lift and staggered after her.

I reached the safety of solid ground just as wreckage from the mill began thudding into the bridge supports. The bits that could float, anyway, rafters and beams and the remains of the waterwheel's buckets. The collapsing walls simply slumped into the river, dragging twisted black ironwork with them.

I lowered Robert's body onto the grass as gently as I could. Eleanor gathered him in a hug, sobbing hopelessly. I looked upstream and down. There was barely a path worth the name on this side of the river, even before the wyrm had set Rob to work uprooting those willow trees.

Crossing back over the footbridge didn't look like a good idea. It grew shakier every time something hit it, and now that wreckage was damming the flow so thoroughly, water was seeping up between the planks.

I also had no idea where that fucking wyrm had gone. I really didn't want to be trying to carry a dead man over the river if the bastard thing came back to finish the job by killing me and Eleanor.

For lack of other options, I dug my phone out of my pocket. After everything I'd just been through, I was surprised to find the screen wasn't broken. I was fucking astonished to find I had a signal.

I dialled 999. The nice lady asked which emergency service I required.

Exhausted, I couldn't decide. 'All of them.'

# Chapter Thirty-Four

By the time the local fire and rescue team found the old track leading to the mill, we had our story straight. We had no choice. Telling the truth wasn't any kind of option. Not that anyone asked what had happened when they first arrived. We were led back across the bridge by firemen secure on safety lines, using aluminium ladders to reinforce the shaky planks. Then, with both of us still shivering from shock, and Eleanor choking on tears, we told our lies to the men who turned up to take charge of all the different uniforms.

We'd come down here to see why the river was backing up. Why was I at Blithehurst? Miss Beauchene and I were discussing the possibilities of bringing the manor's neglected hazel coppices back into cultivation. When we'd reached the mill, we'd realised Robert Beauchene was inside.

No, he hadn't told anyone that he was going to inspect the place. No, Eleanor had no idea what he was thinking. She'd had no reason to believe the structure had become so dangerous. Regardless, she'd have warned Rob to be careful, if she'd only known what he was doing. No, the watermill wasn't open to the public. Hardly anyone knew it existed and all the doors were always kept locked.

No, we had no idea why the building had suddenly collapsed. We'd seen Rob's body floating in the river and hauled him out, only to find he'd been crushed to death.

We'd got as far as that part of the story when the firemen arrived with Rob's corpse strapped to a stretcher. He was handed over to the paramedics, who immediately went to work. A few moments later, they could only step back and shake their heads with professional detachment.

It was as much as Eleanor could stand. Her inconsolable grief put an end to any more questions. We were both wrapped up in blankets and ushered to seats in a Fire Service four-by-four. When Eleanor finally stopped crying, for the time being at least, the sombre fire-fighter set off and we bounced along the track until we reached a back road leading to the manor.

I wasn't much better able to cope. I couldn't shake the appalling memory of feeling Rob Beauchene's shattered body beneath my hands. It wasn't like finding Tila's corpse ravaged by the boggarts. I might be a dryad's son, but there was still some ill-defined, indefinite distance between my humanity and those creatures like the dryads and naiads who lived in the paranormal world.

This was horribly different. Rob Beauchene was just an ordinary bloke. Okay, we'd barely met, but we'd spoken, if only briefly. I don't imagine we'd have ever been friends, but we could have passed the time of day easily enough over a beer in a pub. More than that, he'd had a family who loved him, whatever his flaws. Now though, he was dead.

Not dead in some freak accident, whatever the rest of his family would have to be told. The wyrm woman had used him and killed him and tossed him aside like a broken tool. He hadn't deserved that. No one did.

I wondered if she'd meant to kill him all along. Probably, but I guessed she'd have wanted to keep on using him until the wyrmling had been freed. As the four-by-four sped along the narrow tarmac, I couldn't help thinking that Rob might still be alive if only we hadn't turned up at the mill. That must have been when the wyrm woman realised that we knew what she was. Maybe she'd thought we knew what she was up to. I couldn't help thinking she'd decided to kill him then and there, just to distract us.

A further thought chilled me as we arrived in the old dairy yard. Now the vile creature would be out to take every possible advantage she could, not just of Eleanor's grief but of all the chaos that would follow Rob's death.

Blithehurst was in turmoil. The whole place was being closed, according to the police officer waiting to escort us back to the manor house. She said there were safety concerns about the river's high level. I wanted to argue that point. I could see why rising water would mean closing the medieval ruins, but if they seriously thought the knot gardens might flood, they'd better start building an ark. I kept my mouth shut though.

Besides, when we reached the front door, I realised my mistake. The blue-shirted staff were in no fit state to deal with the usual visitors. The ones who weren't in tears were blank-faced with disbelief at the awful news. I reminded myself that this was a family business, with long-standing ties between the Beauchenes and the people who worked for them.

The Family Liaison Officer seemed to assume I had the same sort of history here. As we walked into the entrance hall, I decided not to tell her differently.

'Go on upstairs. I'll put the kettle on.' Knowing where the real kitchen was tucked away should make me look as if I belonged.

'No.' Eleanor spoke for the first time since we'd left the mill. 'I'll wait down here.'

I was about to ask why when we all heard a vehicle draw up on the gravel outside. It was closely followed by another. Car doors opened and closed, and moments later, voices loud with distress echoed in the porch.

'Mum!' Eleanor had stopped crying sometime on the drive back. Now she started again.

A whole load of distraught people came in. Family resemblance was enough to tell me this was the rest of the Beauchenes and their husbands and wives. Seeing the police-woman looking around for seats, I tapped her on the arm. 'The library's probably the best place to take them.' Then I hoped the Green Man could see what was going on.

As she went to gently suggest this, I withdrew down the corridor to the kitchen. By the time the FLO had ushered everyone into the library, I'd put all the mugs I could find out on the worktop and was opening the cupboards to search for teabags, instant coffee and sugar.

The policewoman appeared as the kettle was boiling. 'Good thinking,' she said with relief. 'How's the milk situation?'

I checked the fridge. 'Not good. Can someone bring some more down from the restaurant?'

She nodded and reached for the radio fixed to her shoulder as she went back out. I filled a cereal bowl with sugar and found some teaspoons. I was loading a tray with a mix of black coffees, white coffees and teas when a young woman came into the kitchen. She didn't look like a Beauchene, but her eyes were red with crying.

'Who wants what?' I stood ready to change the mugs on the tray.

She shook her head, distracted. 'That'll be fine, whatever.'

'Hang on.' I managed to add a packet of chocolate bourbon biscuits before she took the tray away.

The daylight faded and I stayed in the kitchen. A harassed-looking young constable appeared with two four-pint plastic bottles of milk, handing them over without a word before hurrying off again. As more people came and went, some in official uniforms, some not, I made more tea and coffee. Whenever the FLO brought the tray back to the kitchen, I washed up all the mugs and got everything ready for the next time.

While I was left to my own devices, I used my phone to check the local news on various websites. They were all reporting variations on the 'tragic accident' version of events, and saying that Blithehurst Manor would be closed until further notice. That was straightforward enough.

The local paper had a paragraph about the possibility of legal action over Health and Safety breaches, but when I read it a second time, I decided that was just speculation to fill some reporter's word count.

Though I had no doubt that there would be all sorts of inspections and investigations that could be a real headache for Eleanor. What I couldn't decide was what this would mean for our plan to kill the wyrmling. Though it occurred to me that this should put an end to the archaeologists digging up the undercroft. Not that I'd be saying so. There are no silver linings when someone has died.

I was looking out at the last fading twilight through the high windows in the old kitchen when Eleanor appeared in the doorway, startling me. She looked utterly exhausted and wretched with misery.

'I'm going over to Mum and Dad's for the night.' She offered me a bunch of keys. 'Can you stay here? We keep the guest rooms ready upstairs, so just pick one. The alarm code's one-three-four-one, and you only need to lock up behind us. Everything else has been taken care of.'

'Right.' I took the keys. Nothing more needed saying.

I kept out of everyone's way as Eleanor and her family left. The FLO looked in on me one last time as I heard the first car engine start up outside.

'You'll be okay here?'

I nodded. 'Fine.'

She looked around the kitchen with impersonal sympathy. 'Right then. See you tomorrow.'

As soon as everyone was gone, I locked the front door and went to check on every outer door that I could find. When I was convinced everything was secure, I raided the fridge and made a bacon sandwich and fried a couple of eggs. I was starving.

Once I'd eaten, I went upstairs and hesitated outside Eleanor's sitting room door. I didn't want to intrude, but I sure as hell wanted some chance at a warning if the wyrm woman tried anything tonight. So I took a deep breath, went in, and took the Green Man's carved mask off the mantel shelf.

Finding a spare bedroom where the bed was made up was straightforward. There were towels and shower gel waiting, just like a hotel. It took me a few tries to find a bathroom, but once I did, a long shower made me feel a lot better. There wasn't much I could do about my dirty clothes and I didn't fancy putting them back on until I absolutely had to, so I went downstairs wearing just a towel to get one last drink and set the alarm before going to sleep.

I was absolutely knackered, and the bed was comfortable

with crisp, clean bedding and a fluffy duvet. I put the Green Man's mask on the side table and hoped he'd get the message. Even so, I was still lying awake, stiff with tension, as I heard clocks all through the house strike midnight. I couldn't help wondering if there was still some way that the wyrm woman could slip into the house. I'd spotted the blinking red lights of motion sensors all through the downstairs when I'd set the alarm, but I had no idea if something in an ethereal form would trip that modern technology.

Maybe the monstrous creature was busy doing something awful down in the ruins, hoping to set the wyrmling free. There would be no one to stop her. Had anyone checked on the iron fence since the disaster at the watermill?

A series of piercing beeps woke me up. I'd just registered it must be the alarm when the noise stopped. I'd got as far as working out that I'd somehow fallen asleep and it was now the morning, and early morning at that, when Eleanor called out from downstairs.

'Daniel? Are you awake?'

'I am now,' I muttered, reaching for my phone to check the time. Twenty-five past five? Very early morning.

'I'll be right with you,' I shouted, dragging on my clothes.

By the time I got downstairs, Eleanor was scrambling some eggs while the last of the bacon sizzled in a pan. She wore hiking boots and jeans, an old sweatshirt and one of those green cotton waistcoats with umpteen pockets that the hunting, shooting, fishing types favour.

'Make some toast, please.' She waved the wooden spoon at a sliced loaf beside the toaster.

After one look at her pale, set face, I did as I was told. 'What's the plan?'

'We kill the wyrmling.' She began scooping eggs onto the plates laid ready.

That was simple enough. Of course, simple didn't necessarily mean easy. In fact, in my experience, it very rarely did.

When I didn't answer, Eleanor looked up, concerned. 'We can't wait. There's no knowing when we'll get another chance. By mid-morning, there'll be people all over the place. They'll be here for days, weeks maybe, trying to find out—' Her voice cracked.

'I know. I agree. The wyrm won't wait, whatever it's planning.'

That wasn't all. In Eleanor's shoes, I'd want my revenge on the bastard creature. I had a feeling that was pretty much all that was keeping her on her feet at the moment.

'Let's eat.' She carried two full plates out into the big old kitchen so we could sit at the table.

I'd barely finished when Eleanor shoved back her chair. 'Come on.'

She headed down the corridor towards the house's side door and opened one of those anonymous doors into what had once been the servants' quarters. There wasn't much in there besides a battered table and some mismatched chairs, along with a bookcase holding tattered paperbacks. 'I got a few things done yesterday, before...'

'While I was sharpening the halberd.' I searched my pockets and was relieved to find I still had the old dairy key. Meantime, Eleanor was dragging a weighty bag out from behind a chair. 'What's that?'

'Chain mail,' she said succinctly.

I stared at her. 'You're kidding.'

'It's abattoir work-wear. Safety gear.' She managed a faint, humourless smile. 'You don't think we keep those cattle on the pasture just because they look pretty, do you? Organic, rare-breed beef earns us a decent income, so I called in a couple of favours from the guys who do our slaughtering.'

'Right.' I opened the bag to find a knee-length tunic made from gleaming steel rings and two gloves that would reach all the way up to my shoulders if I could work out how the hell their dangling straps worked. Any notion that I'd look a right idiot didn't stand a chance against the memory of the wyrm's teeth.

'Safety glasses.' Eleanor put a couple of pairs of industrial goggles on the table.

341

I was well used to wearing those whenever I used an angle grinder or similar power tools. The next bag she dumped on the table surprised me, though.

'I thought we didn't reckon a shotgun would be much use.' I watched as she broke open a double-barrelled twelve-bore and peered down the barrel.

'Not with lead shot.' She took a box out of the bag and began filling her waistcoat's pockets with cartridges. 'I made up some loads myself using ball-bearings from those magnetic toys we sell in the gift shop.'

'Right.' I had no idea if that was legal, still less if the cartridges would be safe, but seeing Eleanor's expression, I wasn't about to argue. 'I'll get the halberd.'

'The front door's open.' She didn't look up, still intent on her own preparations.

I went out in the clean, cool morning air. After the last few grey days, the sky was cloudless, pale blue. I took a deep breath and looked around. The gardens were flourishing, birds were singing. Everything looked so normal. Yet here we were, the two of us, when we'd known each other barely a fortnight, about to do something that sounded utterly insane. But it was what we had to do. There was no question of that.

I headed for the Land Rover before I went to the dairy. Chainsaw safety boots should give me some protection against a wyrm bite below the chainmail, so I put them on. I fetched a spade and an entrenching tool as well, for digging up the wyrmling.

When I got back with the halberd and the tools, Eleanor was waiting by the front door. She had the black bag with the chainmail by her feet.

As I drew on the long gloves, she buckled the straps that went round my chest to hold the metal fabric in place. Trying to get into the tunic as if it were some sort of sweater turned out to be a painful mistake, and I had to fight to get myself free. I ended up threading my hands through both armholes, holding the chainmail all bunched up before

342

ducking my head through the neck. Holding that burden on my arms was brutal, but thankfully, as the tunic slid down my body, I realised the overall weight was pretty evenly distributed.

I picked up the halberd. 'Let's do this.'

Eleanor snapped the shotgun closed and led the way.

# Chapter Thirty-Five

As soon as we reached the fence above the rock garden, I saw movement down the slope to our right. Boggarts were scurrying through the tall trees between the shrubbery and the open grass, trying to stay out of sight. A lot of boggarts. More than I remembered ever seeing before, bigger and bolder.

'Eleanor,' I warned.

She nodded. 'I see them.'

I was carrying the halberd propped over my shoulder, with the digging tools in my other hand. I decided I'd drop the polearm if the boggarts attacked us. Swinging the spade with one hand and the entrenching tool in the other should give the little bastards something to think about.

Eleanor halted. 'Can you hear it? The wyrmsong?'

There was an eerie, desperate note in the plaintive keening. I looked at the moat. The water level was still much higher than it should have been. I didn't know if the river was still blocked downstream or if this was something the wyrm woman had done, but if moisture was seeping through the earth beneath the ruins, to revive the fading wyrmling, Eleanor was right. We couldn't delay any longer.

We started walking down the sloping path. The boggarts grew bolder. A couple of the largest scampered forward to hide behind the closest trees.

'Do you want to get behind me?' I suggested. 'Remember what I said about them biting.'

Before Eleanor could answer, we heard falling stones behind us. We spun around. The quarry face behind the rock garden was crumbling, slabs of stone and rough boulders crashing down to smash the plants and trees. The strip of turf running between the path and the fence was torn apart like cloth.

Metalwork screeched as the ground fell away, leaving the

iron posts with no footing. The struts between them were holding for now, but I couldn't guess for how much longer. Between the rising dust and the cascade of soil, I caught a glimpse of a dark green coil. The wyrm thought it had found a way to get through Blithehurst's age-old defences.

I turned to Eleanor. 'Get to the gatehouse!'

But now the boggarts were attacking. They bounded over the open grass on clawed hands and feet. I changed my mind and dropped the tools, grasping the halberd in both hands. A good, swinging stroke should cut these vermin in half.

'No!' the youngest dryad, Sineya, shouted at us. 'Get to the wyrmling!' She was on the far side of the bridge over the river, barely visible in her ethereal state. 'Move!' she yelled.

The fastest boggarts were barely ten paces away. They stopped in their tracks, hissing and snarling. It wasn't the dryad's words that halted them. As they started clawing at their own feet, I saw that the grass was growing impossibly fast, twining around their ankles.

That didn't mean they couldn't rip themselves free. One had already done so, at the cost of torn and bleeding skin.

'Come on.' I scooped up the digging tools and ran for the kissing gate in the iron fence. As I did so, I realised how much the chain mail's weight was sapping my strength. There was going to be a price to pay for its protection.

More boggarts erupted from the shrubbery. Dozens of them swarmed towards us. Even if only half reached us, we would be overwhelmed. There was no way we could reach safety in time. My blood ran cold.

Seconds later, tendrils of honeysuckle and climbing roses darted out from the dense greenery behind the boggarts. Leafy sprays coiled around their hands, their feet, their necks. Boggarts died choking, mouths gaping, eyes bulging, spitting and sputtering on strangled gasps. Worse, where different plants seized a foot and a hand, the thrashing veg-etation ripped the boggarts to pieces. Dark blood and scarlet guts spilled across the lawn as arms and legs were tossed in all directions. I nearly stopped to throw up.

Some were still coming though, fleeing the vengeful plants as much as attacking us. There were a handful between us and the fence. I was encumbered with too many weapons because I didn't want to drop anything. I could still hear the rock garden being demolished behind us. That meant we had to get inside the ruins before the wyrm broke through the iron fence. The moat and the ancient walls would still offer us some protection.

A black shadow sped over the grass, appearing from behind the ruins. It was the shuck, or a different shuck. I couldn't tell. That didn't matter. It pounced on the closest boggart, pinning it to the ground. The shuck's massive jaws closed on the vile creature's head, crushing its skull with an audible crack. Springing for the next one, it knocked the boggart off its feet and buried its teeth in its belly with a ferocious snarl. The other boggarts' hisses and spitting took on a panicked tone. They began running for safety in the wilderness garden instead of attacking us.

I threw the halberd and the tools over the fence before dodging through the kissing gate. Shotgun in one hand, Eleanor vaulted the fence like an athlete. I risked a quick glance back at the rock garden.

The iron fence had given way as the posts were pulled apart by the stone crumbling beneath them. Broken metal struts pointed in all directions. The wyrm was writhing through the narrow gap, pale eyes gleaming with lethal intent.

A moment later the monster recoiled and roared. The ravaged trees and plants in the rock garden were tearing themselves apart to reach for the broken fence. Branches and fronds wrapped round twisted metal to bend it into hooks. As the greenery convulsed to claw at the wyrm, dark lines were scored along its scales.

'Asca!' Eleanor pointed. The dryad was standing on the precipice above the wyrm. It thrashed from side to side, still determined to get through the fence.

'Keys?'

Eleanor thrust a hand in her jeans pocket as we ran over

the footbridge to the gatehouse door. I stood with my back to the ancient stonework while she unlocked the wicket gate. The wyrm was heading for us now. Asca had slowed it, but with the fence broken she couldn't stop it completely. Frighteningly fast, it writhed across the grass, crushing the remnants of dead boggarts. There was no sign of the shuck and I couldn't blame the shadow beast. Now I got a good look at the wyrm's full length, I realised it was easily ten metres long.

Ancient iron hinges creaked. 'Come on!'

I followed Eleanor through the gate, barely managing to avoid sticking her with the halberd. I slammed the gate shut and drove the heavy bolts home to secure it.

'Here.' She handed me another key, this one tagged with 'Undercroft'. 'Kill it. I'll see if that fucking thing likes being shot in the face.'

Before I could argue, she opened a door to reveal a spiral staircase. As she disappeared up it, I ran through the archway and across the cobbled courtyard. The most important thing was killing the wyrmling. Then I could help Eleanor fight the wyrm. Meantime, I could only hope the Blithehurst dryads were doing all they possibly could to save the last of their bloodline who could see them.

As I jumped down the steps, I could hear the frantic wyrmling howling. I unlocked the undercroft door and stepped inside, halberd in one hand, entrenching tool in the other. The reek of river water was overwhelming and the ground squelched, sodden beneath my boots.

Suddenly leaving the sunlight for those shadows, I was as good as blind. I closed my eyes for a moment, to help my sight adapt to the gloom. When I looked again, the earthen floor was rucked up like a carpet. The ridges and furrows shifted. Something was moving just below the surface. The wyrmling was fighting to break free.

Swallowing hard, I closed the door behind me. I really didn't want to be shut in here with it, but the last thing I wanted was to be trying to kill the wyrmling with that full-grown monster forcing itself through the open doorway behind me.

Heads or tails? Propping the halberd against the wall, I wondered where to attack first, to do the most damage. Until the wyrmling emerged though, I couldn't tell which end was which. Never mind. I swung the entrenching tool as high as I could beneath the low arch of the ceiling and dug into the middle of the churned earth.

The iron bit deep into something. The wyrmling's contortions tore the entrenching tool out of my hand, its cry deafening, and I staggered backwards. The beast fought free of the clinging soil. It was about three metres long, its body as thick as my thigh. Its scales were pale yellow, as sickly as a plant that has sprouted trapped beneath a fallen fence. Its eyes shone in the dimness, but with a sallow light, not the white intensity of the adult's gaze.

I'd wounded the creature about a third of the way down its length, leaving a wide gash that spouted dark blood every time it moved. That didn't seem to be slowing it down much. It might be smaller than the adult, but it was a damn sight faster. The wyrmling reared up to strike at me like a snake, once, twice. Each time it missed, it screeched in frustration.

My head ringing from the ear-splitting sound, I grabbed the halberd. Not quickly enough. The wyrmling bit my forearm with teeth as long as my fingers. The chain mail saved me from losing a hand, but the crushing bite left my fingers numb. The wyrmling's weight nearly dragged me to my knees.

Nearly but not quite. It recoiled from the sting of the steel, wailing even more loudly. Recovering my balance, I used all the strength in my other hand to drive the halberd's spear point at the wyrmling's neck. I hit it just under its pointed jaw. The tip skidded across tough hide, ripping several scales loose but not penetrating the flesh.

Never mind. As the wyrmling reared up, ready to strike at me again, I rolled the halberd around in my hands and used the curved hook on the side to catch the creature behind its head. Digging my boots into the soft ground, I hauled on the shaft with all my strength. Now the wyrmling was caught between the steel weapon digging into its neck and its fear of the chainmail I wore.

I yanked again and felt the halberd's hook bite deeper. The creature thrashed and coiled in a frenzy to free itself. Its tail swept forward to slam against my shins. As I stumbled, the wyrmling seized its chance to twist free of the halberd's hook. It fell to the floor, writhing in pain. Gouts of black blood from its wounds smoked as the gore soaked into the earth. I smashed the halberd down as hard as I could, using the axe edge now.

My first strike skidded off its yellow scales. I aimed for the wound the entrenching tool had made, while the wyrm-ling was still vulnerable in its ethereal form. The blade bit deep. I felt the cutting edge slice through flesh to meet the resistance of bone. The wyrmling shrieked, but it fought on, twisting and thrashing. However badly it was hurt, it was still nowhere near dead.

Now I had it pinned, but I had a problem. As long as I leaned all my weight on the halberd, the wyrmling was going nowhere. Getting a killing blow in, though, meant lifting the weapon up and risking the creature getting free.

Before I could decide, its head shot up towards mine, and even though it couldn't reach me, pure instinct sent me scrambling backwards. A moment later, I realised that instinct was right. The wyrmling spat venom that stung my face like acid. Without the safety glasses, it could have blind-ed me.

I tried to rub my stinging cheeks on the cool metal of my shoulders as I swore at the bastard thing. It made to dart between my feet. I don't know if it was trying to trip me up or just hoping to escape through the door, but I smashed the butt of the halberd down. Whatever Victorian faker had made the weapon had added a fancy steel ball on the end. I felt the creature's scales crack beneath it.

A few steps back gave me room to flip the weapon over. I attacked with the blade again. The wyrmling was trying to rear up, but this time it was noticeably slower. I swung the axe edge in a horizontal stroke that opened up the wound in the back of its head. The creature reeled away.

Now it was bleeding so badly it looked as if it were covered in tar. I discovered wyrm blood stinks worse than hot asphalt. Every breath was burning in my chest and the toll the chainmail's weight was taking on my strength was becoming apparent.

I needed to kill the wyrmling quickly, and not just before my arms gave out. It was trying to dig itself into the earth, to escape where I couldn't follow. I drove the halberd's spear point into the wound on its side and twisted the weapon before wrenching it free to use the cutting edge instead.

I hacked and hacked, again and again. The wyrmling's lashing tail hammered my feet and my knees, bruising me badly. It spat venom, and though it couldn't reach me, the acid reek added to the choking airlessness. The creature's ceaseless screams were making my ears ring, and my head was aching.

Gritting my teeth, I kept hitting as hard as I possibly could. The wyrmling's struggles grew weaker and its wailing began to fade. The end caught me unawares, when I got in a blow that cut it clean in half.

I took a moment to lean on the halberd, my chest heaving. Drawing deep breaths didn't do much to help. If anything, sucking in the noxious fumes made the pounding in my head even worse, even in the blessed silence. I summoned up one last effort and used the halberd to cut off the wyrmling's head. I remembered Eleanor saying that was vital.

A fresh surge of adrenaline shot through me. Eleanor was holding off the adult wyrm. At least, I assumed she was, since it hadn't come crashing into the undercroft to kill me before I could kill the spawn.

Dragging the halberd, I hauled open the door. The sunlight outside dazzled me and I tripped on the bottom step. I landed on my knees, pain shooting through my right ankle where the wyrmling had landed a hard blow. I couldn't see for the tears filling my eyes.

Pulling off the safety glasses, I wiped my face as best I could. That wasn't a good idea. My cheeks were as sore and tender as they'd been when I'd had flash burns from an un-expected aerosol can exploding in a site rubbish fire. At least I had fresh, clean air to breathe though. I sucked in deep lungfuls. The first sent me into spasms of coughing, but that didn't last. My head cleared.

With the wyrmling's cries no longer deafening me, I could hear Eleanor's shotgun. She fired, once, twice. I scrambled up the steps to the courtyard. Shading my eyes with a hand, I squinted at the gatehouse. Eleanor stood silhouetted on the flat roof between the two towers. As she retreated, I saw her break open the gun, swift to reload it. The wyrm was roaring outside the ruins.

Grabbing the halberd, I ran. Getting the long weapon up the tower's narrow spiral stair took some doing and I left nasty gouges in the white-washed plaster. At the top, a door opened onto the leaded roof. It stood ajar and I could see the wyrm's head swaying, level with the battlements.

As I stepped out onto the roof, Eleanor gave the monster both barrels in swift succession. Whatever she'd loaded into those cartridges bit deep into the wyrm's head. Its scales and its gaping mouth were already peppered with black, bleeding holes. The creature fell away backwards, to land in the moat with a splash that sent filthy water surging up and over the grass.

'It's no good.' Eleanor was haggard with despair. 'It just ducks into the river and comes back good as new. I'm nearly out of cartridges.'

'You kept it busy long enough for me to kill the wyrmling.' I gripped the halberd and wondered where I could stab the adult to kill it.

A bone-shivering hiss told us it was coming back. Eleanor stepped forward, raising her gun to her shoulder. I ducked down to hide behind the parapet as best I could. The wyrm's head appeared. I realised it was straining at full stretch, balanced on the smallest possible coil of its tail.

I could only be thankful the monster wasn't longer or that the gatehouse didn't stand any lower. A metre either way and the wyrm could have lunged across the battlements to snap at Eleanor. Its teeth were as long as my hand and pointed like daggers.

Eleanor fired, making my head thump again. I sprang up regardless and swung the halberd, aiming the hooked blade for the wyrm's great pale eye. A shudder rang through the creature from murderous head to pointed tail, and I missed the fucking thing by an arm's length. Its forked tongue flickered, tasting the air like a snake's. Darting forward, impossibly swift, it licked the halberd. Now its roar made the roof beneath our feet shake.

Those cold, gleaming eyes fixed on me. I realised the blood on the halberd had told it I'd killed the wyrm spawn. Now it was going to kill me, for sheer revenge, for the sake of all the time and effort it had invested here in vain. I scrambled backwards as it spat noxious slime, turning my shoulder to shield my face. That gave it a chance to snap at the halberd. Those great teeth closed on the shaft, smashing the wood into splinters. The black-stained blade fell into the moat.

Eleanor shot the monster again. 'That's it,' she said, grim-faced, as the wyrm twisted away out of sight. 'I'm out of cartridges.'

'Run.' I pulled the door to the stair wider open. 'You first.'

I could only hope the adult wyrm would realise I was wearing mild steel before it tried biting me. Unless it decided the pain would be worth it for the sake of crushing me to death. After feeling the wyrmling's bite, I had no illusions. The full-grown monster could easily kill me.

The whole gatehouse shook, but this time I felt a reverberation somewhere low in the stone walls. Instead of heading for the stairs, Eleanor cautiously approached the battlements, lifting her shotgun to use it as a club. I was ready to grab her around the waist and drag her back, but there was no sign of the wyrm returning to the attack.

I heard something cracking and falling into the water, and we both looked down. The wyrm had smashed the footbridge crossing to the ruins. Now it was hurling itself against the ancient oak doors. The wood creaked ominously.

'What the hell do we do now?' Eleanor looked at me, wide-eyed.

I had no idea. 'Will it try getting up the stairs?'

If it did, we'd be trapped, and I didn't fancy trying to jump into the moat. Eleanor might survive that, but the chain mail's weight would drown me. I thought about trying to get out of the tunic. Then I realised I might still be able to keep the beast occupied while Eleanor escaped.

'Can Asca get you out of here, or Sineya? If the fence is broken, they can reach the ruins.'

Eleanor wasn't listening, still leaning out over the battlements. 'Look!'

I went to see. 'What the fuck?'

All the water was draining out of the moat. Hell, the river itself was running back up the hill. The wyrm was left thrashing in a sludgy morass. It roared with fury as it struggled to get up out of the moat and onto the grass.

'Kalei.' I pointed. The naiad was standing amid the gory slaughter of the boggarts. Shining blue, she raised her hands as the irate wyrm twisted towards her. The sticky mud coating it dried in an instant, hard as concrete. The wyrm writhed, its scales dulled and cracking. The monster didn't stop coming though, despite the pain the naiad was inflicting. As its coils undulated ever closer, Kalei was forced backwards towards those lovingly tended trees planted between the shrubbery and the lawn.

'Can we get out of here before it reaches her?' I tried to work out how fast I could retrieve the spade. Maybe digging into the bastard thing's tail would give Kalei a moment to escape. Then I remembered we had no way to cross the moat. Fuck!

Wood cracked. Not the medieval ruins' ancient timbers. The canopy of the tallest tree in the plantation swayed. I heard Sineya's scream echoed by Asca's cry of anguish. The Green Man stepped out from behind the majestic Douglas fir. He must have been ten feet tall, his eyes blazing with emerald fire. Laying a hand on the tree's rough bark, he stroked it like a beloved animal.

The wyrm lunged at Kalei. The naiad vanished in a cloud of vapour. The great fir tree crashed down to pin the monster like an earthworm under a gardener's trowel. It all happened in the blink of an eye, and then the Green Man vanished.

Beneath Eleanor's gasp and my next indrawn breath, the ancient dryad Frai appeared beside the wyrm's frantically thrashing head. She raised a hand and the wyrm recoiled. Tearing up the turf, it desperately burrowed down, disappearing deep into the earth. The neatly mown grass looked like a battlefield.

'How the fuck do we explain this away?' Eleanor looked on, numb with shock.

'Let's go.' I had more immediate concerns as I ushered her towards the spiral stair. We still had no way to cross the muddy trench of the moat. Wading wasn't an option. The water had been at least five metres deep, and there was no telling how far we'd sink into the silt that remained.

But by the time we'd got down there and unbolted the gates, the water was returning. An instant later, Sineya appeared beside us in the ancient archway.

'Get out of that.' She gestured at the chainmail. 'I cannot carry you still wearing it.'

Getting the tunic off nearly defeated me, until I remembered seeing a fantasy warrior on TV bending double to shed a hauberk. I leaned forward to brace my hands on the cobbles and shook like a wet dog until the whole thing slithered down over my head. Eleanor grinned wearily as she helped me undo the straps to get the long metal gloves off.

'Hold on.' Sineya offered a hand to us both.

A dizzying swirl of sunlight dazzled me. When my vision cleared, we were on the path at the top of the slope. Asca was waiting.

'Go and get yourselves cleaned up.' Her wry grimace made her look almost human. 'We'll do what we can to put things right.'

Eleanor and I exchanged a helpless glance.

'Go,' Asca urged.

As we looked towards the ruins, I saw a frothing surge send the river up and over its banks to flood the torn and bloodstained lawn. White foam poured into the ruins through the open gatehouse, as the moat lapped halfway up the ruined walls.

We turned our backs in unspoken agreement. There was nothing more we could do.

# Chapter Thirty-Six

We walked back to the house in silence. When we got back to that seldom-used room, I was astonished to see from the clock that it wasn't even seven in the morning yet. Eleanor collapsed onto a chair, her face drawn with exhaustion. I did the same, rubbing my forearms.

The pinching steel rings had ripped off pretty much all the hairs. I hadn't even felt that. The wyrmling's bite was a different matter. Each individual tooth mark was plain to see. I would need to wear long-sleeved shirts until that vicious bruise faded. I wondered what my seared face looked like, testing tender skin with cautious fingertips.

'I should get out of here,' I realised reluctantly. 'At least to get some clean clothes, before anyone official turns up.'

What I was wearing had been rank enough before this morning's battles. Now I was drenched in sweat and spattered with stinking black blood. One look at me and anyone would start asking questions.

Eleanor nodded. 'I should shower before anyone asks what I've been out shooting.'

'Will you be okay?'

She nodded again. 'I think the dryads will see to that.'

That made me feel a little bit less of a shit for abandoning her, even if I couldn't see how to stay without making things worse.

'I'll ring you.'

She nodded a third time on her way to the door. 'Later. Sometime this afternoon.'

I followed, and watched her walk down the corridor to the back stairs. She didn't spare me a backwards glance.

So that was that. I headed for the car park. Leaving the front door unlocked gave me a momentary qualm, till I decided Eleanor was right. Any opportunistic burglar would be in for a hell of a shock just at the moment, whether that was the dryads surrounding him or Kalei setting the shuck loose.

It's a good thing there wasn't much traffic on the roads. I was so knackered that I really shouldn't have been driving. Getting back to Lambton without being stopped by a traffic cop was a huge relief.

I opened the front door and went straight up to my room, ignoring my startled housemates as they were getting ready for work. I collapsed fully dressed onto my bed and was asleep within minutes.

When I woke up the house was empty and quiet. I stripped off, bundled all my clothes into a bin bag and took a long bath. Now I could look in a mirror, I was relieved to see that my face could be explained away as a bad sunburn. Though shaving would be no fun for a while. Maybe it was time to try a beard.

I got dressed, made myself a sandwich and rang Dad, to tell him everything that had happened since I'd first gone to Blithehurst.

When I finally finished, silence hung in the air between us. I left it as long as I could stand it, waiting for him to speak, wondering if Mum was listening. 'Well?'

'What's that old saying? It's easier to ask for forgiveness than permission?'

His chuckle made my eyes sting with relief.

'Do you think Mum will ever forgive me?'

He took a long moment to think about that. 'I think you'd best come home for a visit, so she can see you're okay for herself.'

'Soon,' I promised. 'There'll have to be an inquest for Robert Beauchene.'

'Of course,' Dad agreed sombrely. 'Let us know when to expect you.'

'As soon as I can get away,' I assured him.

Then I cleaned my boots and wondered vaguely what the hell had happened to my spade and the entrenching tool.

Sod it, those could be replaced. I reached for my phone to ring Eleanor two or three times, only to change my mind and hold off. I had no idea who she might be talking to, among her family or maybe from the police.

Halfway through the afternoon, my phone pinged with a message. Eleanor had sent me some photos of Blithehurst. I scrolled through, astonished. Between them, Kalei and the dryads had washed the lawn clean of dead boggarts, and somehow they'd persuaded the grass to smooth itself out again. No one would guess what had happened there, as the river flowed peacefully past, restored to its usual flow.

Though they hadn't been able to do anything about the quarry face collapsing into the rock garden, or restore the fallen tree that had pinned the wyrm. I was just wondering about that when another message came through.

*They're saying there's been some sort of subsidence. Probably brought down the mill as well.*

I didn't envy whatever expert was trying to establish that, one way or the other. But I reckoned it must be good news, if the authorities were looking for that sort of explanation. I sent Eleanor a reply.

*Anything I need to come over for? Cops want a statement about yesterday?*

My hand shook as I pressed send. It was incredible to think that Robert Beauchene was barely twenty-four hours dead.

*No, thanks, we're fine. Police say they'll contact you.*

So that was that. The Staffordshire coppers did send someone round a few days later. I stuck to the story I'd agreed with Eleanor and they wrote it all down. I signed my statement, and off they went.

As soon as they left, I went to find that solicitor Andrew Willersley's card and spent the rest of the day expecting another visit from the local police. I felt sure DS Tunstead would feel I deserved a closer look when he learned I'd been mixed up in another unexpected death. But nothing happened.

Mick from the barn conversions job rang me at the weekend. A farm shop over towards Castleton wanted some new counters and cupboards fitting, so that was a useful bit of work. Then I went home for a few days, to find that my mum seemed to have decided we weren't going to mention naiads or shucks or wyrms at all. We took long walks around the nature reserve and she showed me how the badger sett was thriving.

I found Blithehurst's local paper online and followed their reports about the dramatic series of accidents that had closed the manor. To my relief, they covered Rob Beauchene's funeral with tact and sympathy. A brief paragraph explained that the inquest into his tragic death had been opened and adjourned while enquires were made.

A while later, I got a letter from the Beauchene family solicitor thanking me and explaining that I wouldn't be called to give evidence, as there was no need for a hearing in court. Apparently all the written reports and statements were sufficient to explain what had happened to Robert. That was a relief. I didn't like the idea of lying on oath, even if no one would believe the truth.

Blithehurst was closed for a month, until everyone was finally satisfied that the ground beneath the ruins or the house wasn't about to give way again. Eleanor texted me an invitation to the grand reopening. By then I was working on a small development of five new houses in Lambton, where an old District Council depot had been demolished.

The first breath of approaching autumn scented the air as I drove past newly harvested and ploughed fields. Sheep and cows were in prime condition after the summer's good grazing.

The Blithehurst car park was packed. That must be good news after the business had lost so much money at the peak of the tourist season. Though I wondered how many people had turned up today just to look for signs of the recent disasters. Well, as long as they paid for the privilege, I didn't imagine the Beauchenes could quibble.

I still had that contractor badge but I'd left it at home.

Getting out my wallet to pay my way wasn't doing much, but it was something to help. I didn't recognise the blue-shirted staff on the gate today, and they didn't seem to know who I was. That was a relief. I was happy to stay anonymous among the crowds.

The manor house and the knot garden looked just the same as before. From this distance the medieval ruins looked unaffected, apart from the new wooden footbridge. Its timbers were still freshly golden but they would soon weather down to a softer grey. Then I realised the iron fence had been completely removed. New galvanised safety barriers had been installed along the tops of the broken walls, to keep the adventurous kids I could see climbing the masonry from falling into the moat.

A new path skirted the upper edge of the rock garden, with a solid post-and-rail fence and warning signs keeping visitors at least three metres back from the quarry face. As I headed down the slope past a cluster of slower walkers, I saw how busy the gardeners had been, replacing and replanting around the new landscape created by the falling rocks.

The toppled Douglas fir was gone, leaving a circle of earth surrounded by newly laid turf. A sapling had been planted in the centre and it looked to be thriving when I walked over for a closer look. I guessed Blithehurst had the dryads to thank for that.

'Good morning.' Frai appeared from behind a tree. In flat shoes, a plain skirt and a weatherproof jacket, she would have fitted into any of the groups of retirees ambling around.

'Hello,' I said cautiously.

'Why have you stayed away?' Her tone accused me.

I wasn't having that. 'Eleanor knew how to reach me, if she wanted to.'

Frai's autumnal eyes darkened as she scowled. 'What she might want isn't necessarily what she might need.'

'What's that?' I challenged her. 'You think she needed my shoulder to cry on?'

'Why not?' Frai squared up to me. 'You think she wouldn't

welcome comfort from someone who knew exactly what she'd been through?'

'She has her family.' I'd seen the newspaper photos of them all at the funeral.

The old dryad persisted. 'She needs someone who can see what she sees, who understands.'

'That's it, isn't it?' I'd been thinking about this ever since the day I'd first met the three dryads. 'You'd like me to sweep Eleanor off her feet and into bed, to get her pregnant with a new generation of Beauchenes who can see you, to keep your woodlands safe.'

'Would that be such a hardship?' Frai was unrepentant.

'I don't fuck girls I hardly know,' I retorted. Okay, not these days, anyway. 'Why not think about her for a change, instead of your own interests? Let her have the life she wants, not what you think she needs.'

Frai looked at me for a long moment. Long enough to make me nervous. 'Do you think that we don't care for her? That my long life leaves me indifferent to those I see born here, since I know that I will see them die? That my only concern is how they can serve me? You couldn't be more wrong. Knowing my time with my mortal grandchildren is so limited makes every day, every moment all the more precious. It makes them infinitely precious to me. It makes their loss a wound that will scar me till the end of my days. There are so few of us that remain, and fewer still who carry our blood.'

She turned away. I grabbed her shoulder.

'Wait. What happened to the wyrm?'

'It fled.' Frai shook her head, regretful. 'I thought that I could kill it, even if doing so would cost me my life. That was a price I was ready to pay. But I was wrong.'

She vanished before I could speak. Before I could draw my next breath, Asca appeared, though only to me, translucent and draped in ethereal mist.

'The Green Man is searching for the beast. Kalei and her kind are searching for other mortals with greenwood and wildwater blood. We will not see humanity become prey to the likes of the wyrm and the wose.'

Before I could ask what the hell she meant by that, Asca disappeared as well. I barely managed to swallow a torrent of frustrated swearing, as a cheerful young family eating ice creams came towards me through the trees.

I headed back to the knot garden. When I reached the path that cut across the front of the house, I saw Eleanor surrounded by people outside the front door. She was nodding and smiling and shaking hands, but I could see the strain in her face.

She caught sight of me and waved. There are some uses to standing out in a crowd. A moment later, she made a drinking gesture with a cupped hand. Her expression made it clear that was a question. I nodded my reply and she jerked her head towards the side door. I gave her a thumbs-up and rounded the corner of the house.

A few moments later, she unlocked the door to let me in. 'Quick.'

I followed her into the old kitchen, and on into the modern one behind the inner door. 'How's it going?'

'Exhausting.' She opened the fridge to take out a can of Coke. 'I may thump the next person who asks if I've had a good break. I've just buried my brother, for fuck's sake. Do you want something cold, or a coffee?'

'A cold drink is fine, whatever you've got.' I took the Coke she offered and popped the top. 'Everything looks pretty much back to normal.'

'Close enough, anyway.' She didn't look overly thrilled as she found another Coke and closed the fridge. 'Back to the usual routine.'

I took a deep breath and gripped the cold can. 'I've been thinking about that.'

Thinking about it. Dreaming. I wondered how well Eleanor had been sleeping this past month. Had she seen the same things as me?

She looked at me, curious. 'How so?'

362

'You still want to get away from here, don't you? Go back to university?'

'God, yes,' she said fervently.

'Could you run this place from there? Making the long-term, big-picture decisions, I mean. There must be people on the staff here who could take care of the day-to-day stuff.'

'I suppose so.' She looked torn. 'But the dryads—'

'The wyrmling is dead. That was the main reason they wanted to keep you here, don't you think?'

'I suppose so.' A hint of hope in her expression was quickly quenched. 'But the wyrm woman escaped.'

'True,' I allowed, 'but what's it got to come back for? There's no wyrmling for it to rescue, and now it knows it'll have a fight on its hands.'

Eleanor raised a hand. 'I meant to ask. Have you seen Kalei? I'd like to thank her.'

I shook my head. 'Sorry, no.'

At least now I knew what she was up to. I'd been quite worried when she hadn't come to meet me in Tila's valley, or by St Werburgh's ruins. Though I'd seen the shuck several times, or maybe two different shucks in each place. I still couldn't tell. I wasn't about to get close enough to see, however enthusiastically a nightmare hound wagged its tail at me.

'Have you talked to the dryads?'

Her face hardened. 'What about? About me leaving? They'll never agree to that.'

I shrugged. 'I was just wondering what they might have to say.'

Eleanor relented a little. 'I've seen Sineya a couple of times. She's grieving for Rob, like the rest of us.' Her voice shook.

'The dryads want someone they can talk to living here, don't they?' I spoke quickly, hoping she wouldn't start crying.

'I'm still the only one who can,' Eleanor said wearily.

'Does it have to be a family member?' I took a swallow of Coke to wet my dry mouth. 'It could be me. I could find somewhere closer to live, and work on those hazel coppices for you. Maybe use the old dairy as a workshop, making stuff for the garden centre.'

We could turn all those lies we'd told into some truth.

Eleanor put down her can and pressed her hands to her face, eyes tight shut. 'I've been dreaming. The Green Man—'

'Me too.' Night after night, he'd strolled through my sleeping thoughts. I'd seen myself working here at Blithehurst, while he looked on. He joined me as I tended the hazel woods and looked over my shoulder when I carved and turned treen for sale. I'd woken refreshed and keener than ever to use my skills for crafting art instead of fitting shelves. Though it had taken me a few weeks to realise that I never saw Eleanor in those dreams. It had taken me a bit longer to work out why.

I avoided her eyes by taking a long drink. 'Do you think your family would agree?'

'To you joining the staff here? Why not? Anyway, it would be my decision.' She drew a deep breath, like someone coming up for air. 'To me going back to Durham? I think so, if I could keep the business running smoothly. They've never wanted us to feel burdened by Blithehurst.'

'If anything came up, something that worried the dryads, I could always give you a ring.' I shrugged. 'Maybe you could come back at weekends, just to make sure everything's running smoothly?'

Eleanor managed a tentative smile. 'That might work.'

'Okay then.' I put my empty can on the draining board. 'Give it a think, and give me a call. I'll let you get on.'


So that was how I spent last summer. Now Eleanor's doing her thesis on the English Civil War and researching medieval monsters in her spare time. She comes back once a month or so, to check on the Blithehurst accounts and other business matters. We go out for a curry or a steak and she tells me what new fantastical creatures she's discovered.

No, we haven't fallen into bed together, no matter what Frai might be hoping for. We're friends. That's as far as it goes. Sineya and I though, we've become very good friends. Friends with benefits? Maybe, one day.

The shuck visits from time to time. He appears and flops down close by to watch me, when I'm working in the woods. I've just about got used to him. At least I know if he's peacefully snoozing with his nose on his paws, there can't be any boggarts or worse within sniffing distance.

I've got to know the other Beauchenes, as far as anyone gets to know their employers. They're nice enough, whenever we pass the time of day. I've done some handyman work for most of them, the ones who live locally anyway.

I still haven't seen Kalei again, nor the Green Man, not in my dreams or when I'm awake. I'm sure he's watching over us both though. Eleanor took that first mask I carved to Durham with her, and I made another to hang over the fireplace in the run-down estate cottage that I've been renovating in return for a nominal rent.

We haven't discussed it, but I know she's waiting to see a mossy glow in those eyes, the same as me. One day, we both know, the Green Man will warn us of a new threat. Maybe it'll be the wyrm reappearing. Maybe it'll be something else. Let's hope the naiad has found us some allies to fight it by then.

# Acknowledgements

This story is for all the fans, friends and family who encourage and inspire me to keep writing

I am tremendously grateful to Cheryl Morgan, for her personal and practical support with this project, and ever since we started working together. This book wouldn't be here without Wizard's Tower Press.

Toby Selwyn has done a stellar job as my editor; combining a merciless eye for inconsistencies and glitches with unfailing good humour. This story has been honed and polished by his professional skills which I very much appreciate.

Ben Baldwin has taken my words and created this book's stunning artwork. I don't know how he manages to see exactly what I want, when I can barely visualise it myself, but I'm so very thankful he can.

This novel has its origins in a short story I wrote for an anthology called *The Modern Fae's Guide to Surviving Humanity*, edited by Joshua Palmatier and Patricia Bray, published by DAW in 2012.

When they first invited me to contribute to the project, I told them honestly I had no idea what to write. They kept asking though, and encouraging me. A few days before the deadline, a local oak tree that's always out of sync with the others sparked my imagination and 'The Roots of Aston Quercus' was the result, where a group of dryads learn that a road is about to be built through their oak grove.

That story remarks, in passing, "The days were long gone when a dryad's son could walk for a turn of the moon, and then present himself in a village, looking for work, and offering a tale of seeking his fortune with the blessing of his family in some distant county which these locals had barely heard tell of."

Ever since then, I've been wondering just how a modern dryad's son might fare. Things I've read and things I've seen on visits to stately homes and museums have caught my eye and suggested answers as well as fresh challenges. This novel is the result.

So we can all thank  Joshua and Patricia for sowing that first acorn.